P9-DVB-214

KING IN HELL

WITHDRAWN
UTSA Libraries

WITHDRAWN
UTSA Libraries

KING
IN
HELL

by Beverly Balin

Coward-McCann, Inc.
New York

Copyright © 1971 by Beverly Balin

All rights reserved. This book, or parts thereof, may not be reproduced in any form without permission in writing from the publisher. Published on the same day in Canada by Longmans Canada Limited, Toronto.

Library of Congress Catalog Card Number: 71-136439
Printed in the United States of America

To Elizabeth, my light in the darkness . . .

PREFACE

Just what kind of man was Bothwell? Choose almost any historian dealing with his era in Scotland, and you will find Bothwell's name linked with the most odious crimes. A murderer, a thief, a tyrant and dictator, a ravisher of women, an ambitious adventurer, even a sorcerer. These crimes have been attributed to Bothwell with such authority, and by such highly respected writers, that one hesitates to dispute the charges. Yet, after an unbiased study of the facts, they must be disputed.

When the mist of prejudice and a disregard for the truth in exchange for false evidence deliberately given clears, Bothwell emerges as one of the few honest men in Scotland at that time. Reckless, somewhat overconfident in his own ability to overcome all the obstacles in his path, he nevertheless comes forth a very different man from the villain history has painted him these past four hundred years.

Naturally, questions arise when such time-honored traditions are challenged. Why did he have so few friends among the nobility? In an age when allies and enemies were determined by the faiths they followed, why could he claim no friendships even among his own co-religionists? Was he so unique in his creed, his contemporaries so corrupt? Incredibly, the answers must be in the affirmative.

There is a pension list of that period in the British Museum which lists the names of Scotsmen—nobles and commoners—who sold their "good-will and secret information" to England, a hereditary enemy for centuries. James Stuart's name heads that list; his allies follow—whereas Bothwell's name is conspicuously absent. Because he would not share in their dishonor, they labeled him an enemy.

Scotland in the sixteenth century was said to be one hundred years behind the times; civilized Europe regarded its people as somewhat barbaric, the nobility and their politics treacherous. Foreign contemporaries were often shocked by Scottish methods and conduct.

I wish to thank Colonel Robert Gore-Brown for having finally cleared away the debris of prejudice and false propaganda in his biography of Bothwell, and for his invaluable correspondence in which we had long, revealing discussions on the subject; Helen Marwick for helping me with all things Scottish that might otherwise have been so difficult for an American; Miss Jean Wilkes, without whom I might never have seen the Border country which was such an integral part of Bothwell's life. I would also like to thank the Laird of Pitgavney for allowing me to see the lovely ruins of Spynie Castle, and Mr. Robert Robson, whose special kindness made Hermitage Castle available to me.

My very special thanks to Mr. Christian Werbel of Faarevejle, who helped me with translations and routes for Bothwell's travels in Denmark, and who took me on an extended tour of the countryside surrounding Dragsholm, where Bothwell spent the last years of his life.

BEVERLY BALIN

I am Don Juan, curst from age to age
By priestly tract and sentimental stage;
Branded a villain or believed a fool,
Battered by hatred, seared by ridicule,
Noble on earth, all but a King in Hell,
I am Don Juan with a tale to tell.

JAMES ELROY FLECKER, *Don Juan*

PROLOGUE

Patrick Hepburn was dead. He had been ill for months, dying of consumption acquired in damp prison cells. He was finally sealed away in the family vault at Crichton Parish, and his son, James, breathed a sigh of relief.

There was no sorrow in James as he descended the grand staircase that day just two weeks after his father's funeral. Contempt, yes, even a little pity, but no sorrow or remorse for the man gone. He scowled darkly at the mourning cloths draped over the ornately carved banister and on the huge French windows in the Great Hall. He hated the spurious display of grief, for he knew that no one really mourned his father; not his mother, not his sister, and certainly not himself.

He glanced at the five men who had come to the foot of the stairway at the sound of his tread on it. Paris, his page, waited at the great nail-studded doors to hand him his gloves and plumed toque.

Striding ahead briskly, James called, "To horse, my billies."

They followed him out to the cobblestoned courtyard, bordered by lush green lawns and bright flower beds. Crichton gleamed white in the sunshine, the green-tinted windows glaring in the brilliant reflection. Mounting their waiting horses, they clattered over the rough stones onto the wooden moat.

James took the lead as the others followed in pairs. He turned to wave them on; they smiled at him with affectionate indulgence. They could look forward to some excitement now that Jamie Hepburn was back from France. His escapades in Paris had reached his cousins Willie and Thomas all the way to Gilmerton and Oldhamstocks. Gossip had it that Jamie had left a string of brokenhearted women behind when he sailed for Scotland—one had even threatened to take her life. Thomas and Willie had teased him about it, and Jamie, unashamedly delighted, had owned up to it.

There had been a remarkable transformation in Jamie since the day four years ago when he had left the Bishop of Moray's palace in Elgin. He had been a green lad of sixteen then, a dreamy-eyed, gangling youth who was a little frightened at the prospect of journeying to a foreign land with only a few servants for company.

The changes had come during his years at the University of Paris; the awkwardness had left him, his height had taken on breadth, his body had developed into hard, muscular lines. His eyes had lost the soft dreaminess of boyhood; they were dark and piercing now, with a hint of humor that turned cruel and brittle in anger.

Plainly, Jamie was no prick-me-dainty lad; he was a man whose face betrayed his strong, passionate nature, so evident in those heavy, dark brows, the long, well-shaped nose that flared at the nostrils, his sensual mouth. His hair, the color of red-brown autumn leaves, he wore cropped close to his lean face. He moved swiftly with the grace and litheness of a panther, totally unencumbered by his great height and powerful body.

He was not handsome, yet he possessed a certain magnetism that instantly drew women to him. Knowledge of this power gave him an air of self-assured arrogance, and he used it ruthlessly. He was possessed of a keen intellect and an inquisitive mind, and his education far exceeded most of his Scottish peers who could barely write a crude hand. However, his education at Spynie had not been limited to scholastic achievement alone, and he had taken quickly to the example set by his profligate great-uncle, the Bishop of Moray.

Certainly, the Bishop did not believe in a celibate life; his

wenches and numerous progeny disproved such lofty senti-
ments. Aside from his lack of virtue, the Bishop did little to
instill a deep sense of religion in his charge, for the ancient
foundations of Catholicism were rotting in the corrupt hands of
its clergy. Neither his uncle's rich churchly robes nor the
scriptures quoted from his pulpit at Elgin Cathedral could move
Jamie toward the old faith.

Although he had been born to the religion, Jamie had
developed serious doubts about it early in life. He was scarcely
nine when he heard George Wishart, a Reformed minister, speak
for the first time. Those dissolute years spent at his uncle's
diocese had merely served to confirm those doubts; the clergy
wallowed in debauchery and used their power to rob the
common folk.

Later, while on holiday from the university, Jamie had gone
to Geneva to hear Calvin preach. Here was a man who made
God accessible to the masses without having to diffuse Him in
pomp and ceremony. For a while he turned freethinker, but by
the time Jamie returned to Scotland he was a confirmed
Protestant.

Now his thoughts touched on religion during the twelve-mile
ride to Edinburgh. He had been summoned to Holyrood Palace
by the widowed Queen Regent, and she was Catholic. Scotland
was in the grip of a religious struggle; alliances and loyalty were
measured by the faith men followed. How would Mary of Guise
receive a professed member of the Reformed faith?

But his doubts went even deeper than religious difference—
he would also have to live down his father's memory. Patrick
Hepburn had been a traitor from his entrance into public life at
the age of seventeen. To curb his betrayals and double-dealing
with England, James V had inflicted upon Patrick a series of
prison terms and exiles. But Patrick never profited by his
experiences, continuing on his course of treason even after the
King's death in 1542.

James V had left his French wife, Mary of Guise, and an infant daughter of six days at the mercy of a greedy and irreverent nobility. Mary of Guise proved herself a match for these scoundrels, for she meant to protect her daughter's crown at all costs. Patrick officiated at the infant Queen's coronation, then left for an audience with Henry VIII—to Scotland's dishonor.

Scotland had been frustrating England for centuries, and Henry was determined to make an end to it with a betrothal between his twelve-year-old son, Edward, and Mary Stuart. Patrick obliged by signing a document that committed his infant Queen into Henry's care, his convenient conscience untroubled by the knowledge that once in England, Mary Stuart would likely never live to celebrate her first birthday.

Mary of Guise, and the few loyal nobles who supported her, thwarted the plot by removing the baby to the safety of the Highlands. There began the first five years of turmoil in Mary Stuart's life, the constant moves from fortress to fortress, out of the path of English invaders.

When it became apparent that Mary Stuart could no longer find safety in Scotland she was sent to the French Court, where she was to be educated and later wed to the Dauphin François. Mary of Guise had sought means, both fair and foul, to keep her nobles loyal, but she had failed with Patrick, until his own conceit betrayed him.

The Queen Mother was both shrewd and intelligent; she easily discerned the weaknesses of the men surrounding her. What if she dangled the prospect of a royal marriage before Patrick—using herself as bait? Patrick had once sued for the hand of one of Henry's daughters, the Princess Mary or Elizabeth—it was of small importance to him which one accepted.

Now Patrick competed with the Earl of Lennox for the widowed Queen. He exhausted himself in his attempt to win her, plying her with costly gifts that he could ill afford, courting her with all the ardor of a youthful lover. To prove his sincerity, he even divorced his wife on the grounds of consanguinity. If Mary of Guise had no intention of marrying him, she had at least kept him too busy to betray her.

Once Patrick realized that he had been duped, he resumed his treacherous pastimes by playing host to the English General Hertford who had crossed the border to lay waste to Edinburgh. This period marked the end of any security and family life that Jamie had; he saw his mother sent to Morham Castle, to be known from that day as the Lady of Morham. His younger sister, Janet, was sent to a convent, while he was pawned off on various unwilling relatives during Patrick's prison terms and exiles.

There had really never been any love between Patrick and his son. Jamie felt only contempt and shame for the father who had brought dishonor to the Hepburn name. In the past, Hepburns had given only loyal service to the Crown; their motto, "Keep Trust," had been a code by which they lived. One had risked his life for his King and had been rewarded with the title Lord Hailes. Jamie's great-grandfather had been created Earl of Bothwell and first minister to James IV. He had been plenipotentiary and a proxy groom for James IV in his marriage to Margaret Tudor of England. Patrick's father had died at Flodden with James IV and most of the Scots nobility. Some of Jamie's ancestors had been Princes of Orkney, but Patrick had defiled the past, had dragged its glory through filth and disgrace.

This was the heritage left by Patrick when he died in 1556. Jamie inherited an impoverished earldom with creditors both at home and in England, for Patrick's treacheries had not been bought cheaply. He would undoubtedly be judged by his father's deeds, but he meant to prove that the taint of one traitor need not spoil the rest.

He expected Mary of Guise to be mistrustful of him; experience would have taught her that much. But he was too proud to protest his loyalty; he wanted to be judged on his own merits. Not that he was interested in politics, to sit at Court and play at intrigue. The Border was Jamie's domain; his earldom encompassed a large part of it. Lawlessness and thievery ran high there; it would take a strong hand to govern it.

They were already at the Nor' Loch when Willie called to him. Edinburgh lay above them, and high on its craggy mountain perch the castle looked down on its charge in timeless watchfulness. They passed through the West Port Gate into the West Bow, lined with houses that seemed to lean one on the other, some ten and twelve stories high. Since the now crumbled town wall had been built in 1514, people strove to live within its protective confines. Lack of space had forced them to erect new houses above the old.

They approached the Lawnmarket, crowded with booths and stalls. This was Edinburgh's mainstream of life; women bargained with fleshers and fishmongers, children played and wallowed in animal entrails, fish guts, and rotted produce. A cloth merchant flapped a bolt of peacock-blue satin into the sunlight for a wealthy matron's approval, an armorer hammered on a steel breastplate to show its strength, beggars plied their trade, tinkers hawked their wares.

On the High Street, they drew rein for a shepherd leading his flock up Castle Hill. The High Street sloped downward on the Royal Mile toward Holyrood Palace. Two grisly heads swayed on pikestaffs atop the Tolbooth Prison, staring with empty, crow-picked eyes at the Nor' Loch.

They passed through the Netherbow Port to the quiet elegance of the Cannongate where the nobles had their houses, each with elaborately carved crests and armorial bearings to identify the owners. The Hepburn town house was here, too, built close to the palace by Jamie's great-grandfather. A three-storied structure with gabled roofs and the Hepburn crest and motto carved deeply on the portal, it bespoke the Hepburn fortune before Patrick had dwindled it away.

But Jamie Hepburn was not a young man to waste sympathy on himself, nor was he easily discouraged. He had a new French wardrobe, an earldom with all the honors and powers it entailed, and a lifetime ahead. Mary of Guise was only a woman, and he had never met one that he hadn't been able to conquer. Fortune was his; who could say to what heights he might rise?

CHAPTER I

1

"So, you are the new Earl of Bothwell," Mary of Guise said, extending her hand to him. "We had news of your father's death. My condolences."

Bothwell put her fingers to his lips and stepped back to appraise the woman who had nearly become his stepmother. She was lovely; he could not but admire Patrick's taste. But he saw more than a pretty face; those bright, almond-shaped eyes, the delicate nose, and her full, smiling lips bespoke intelligence. He sensed an unmistakable shrewdness and a quick wit. She held herself proudly, and despite her long, willowy figure, he detected a steel-like strength beneath the soft silken folds of her gown.

He knew that she was using these moments to appraise him, too. Was she comparing him to Patrick, wondering how the Fair Earl, so called because of his pale complexion and red-gold hair, had begot a son who bore him not the slightest resemblance? He hoped that his carefully chosen outfit was doing him justice. A last-minute inspection in the mirror had satisfied him: a hunter-green velvet doublet laced with gold, breeches and hose of a darker shade, brown kid boots, and a short, fur-trimmed Spanish cape, thrown back over one shoulder to reveal its gold satin lining.

She motioned him to a chair. "Frankly, you are not quite what I expected."

1

"Not all Hepburns are alike. But from the portrait that hangs at Crichton, I strongly resemble the first Earl of Bothwell in his youth."

She glanced quizzically at him. "Surely you are loyal to your father's memory?"

"Strange that Your Grace should speak of Patrick Hepburn and loyalty in the same breath."

"You must not be too harsh in judging him. Circumstance may make a man other than he would wish."

He shrugged. "Your Grace is well acquainted with his record—it speaks for itself."

She smiled. "The past is over. There is your future."

"The future will mind itself."

"Have you no plans?"

"There is my estate; it will take a mess of handling before it is settled."

She changed the subject abruptly. "You are just recently returned from France."

"Aye, scarce a month ago. I received my baccalaureate from the university July last."

"Where did you take your earlier instruction?"

"At Spynie Palace, under the supervision of my great-uncle, the Bishop of Moray."

"You were reared in the old faith."

He nodded. "Now I follow the Reformed religion."

"Then it must also follow that your sympathies lie with the new religionists. Do you also share their belief that a Catholic should not rule Scotland?"

"No, for I doubt their sincerity. The church merely serves to justify their anarchy. Nevertheless, Your Grace cannot deny the need for reform."

"Do you suggest that I convert?"

"Nothing so drastic. But there is room for improvement in the old, and much good sense in the new."

"You leave me in a quandary, my lord. On the one hand you speak of mistrusting your coreligionists, on the other you seem to favor those principles that threaten the Crown."

"A man's loyalty has naught to do with his faith."

"Can you be loyal to a Catholic queen, despite your chosen faith?"

His first impression of her had been accurate; how cleverly she had led him into this. She had called him here to test his loyalty, to evaluate his worth to her. Here was a woman who could match any man's wit, and he felt a growing admiration for her.

He stretched his legs and studied the tips of his boots. "Why must men be labeled one or the other? The name given a religion is unimportant; we all seek one thing in common—God. Each of us must find Him in our own way."

"Most men *are* one or the other. We cannot interpret God for ourselves."

"Then I am not like most men, for I do."

"Indeed you are not. I cannot but wonder the side you would take in a conflict between the Crown and those whose faith you follow."

"Your Grace does me an injustice. I've not been back long enough to study the situation, much less choose sides. My first two weeks back were spent at Crichton, where my father lay a-dying; these last two had me there in seclusion—a time of mourning is scarce the occasion to talk politics."

That should show her he was no brash young fool to be snared into taking sides on a moment's notice. But he hadn't missed her amused glance that traveled slowly over his bright attire.

"You keep your bereavement well hidden, my lord," she observed dryly.

"I wear it in my heart, Your Grace, rather than on my sleeve."

The solemnity melted and they broke into laughter.

"No," she said, "all Hepburns are not alike. You, my lord, are certainly no hypocrite."

He valued that compliment, for he knew that she had meant it as one. This brief interview with her had inspired his respect. She had turned serious again; he knew the sparring was over.

"I must ask you outright now, my lord; will you pledge yourself to serve the Crown?"

"Aye, Your Grace has only to command me."

He had come prepared to make that pledge. But he hadn't lied about not being fully acquainted with the dispute between her and the Protestant nobles. He only knew that he could never join with bigots who burned churches, tortured and killed priests, then stole their riches. God was not served by bloodshed and violence. In any case, he saw it more as a struggle for power, led by the Bastard, James Stuart. Believing as he did, and knowing that it was his obligation as a Scotsman, Bothwell could only choose in favor of the Crown.

Her soft voice broke in on his thoughts. "I am grateful, my lord, and I will hold you to that." She extended her hand then, to indicate the interview was over.

2

The few remaining months of that year were spent in bringing a semblance of order to Bothwell's estate. He engaged David Chalmers, a clever lawyer, to help him, and together they managed to salvage a fair portion of his inheritance. November 3, 1556, marked Bothwell's official succession to the earldom; he took up the inherited titles and duties of Sheriff of Berwick, Haddington, and Edinburgh, Bailie of Lauderdale, Lord of Hailes and Crichton, and Great Admiral of Scotland.

Bothwell's fierce love for his Border country had developed early in his childhood. His lands encompassed fertile valleys, swift-flowing waters, rolling hills, desolate moors, and always the strong tang of salt air, for the sea was never far away. But the Border was also the most lawless territory in Scotland. Here lay the Debatable Lands, drenched in English and Scots blood in the centuries-old struggle for possession. Berwick, too, lay in this district, shifted back and forth so often between the warring realms. Now the area lay divided, with a governor to rule each sector.

Reaving was an old established Border trade, and the inhabitants pursued it diligently. Nightly raids on English villages were a common occurrence; dawn brought the return of parties dragging their booty of livestock and movables behind. This seemed fair enough to Bothwell, for the English employed that trade with similar devotion. But he did object to these reavers using the same tactics on their fellow Scotsmen. It was too widespread a use for the Borderer to make up what he lacked from his neighbor's stock.

Winter and summer had flown by with Bothwell making only occasional trips to Edinburgh. Then in February of the following year the Court moved to Stirling, and a strange atmosphere fell on Edinburgh. There were wild rumors; men spoke in hushed tones; the wynds and closes echoed with the clatter of boots from scurrying shadows. Edinburgh lay still like a crouched beast ready to spring.

Then the muted voices became a roar; the cloud of lethargy lifted, and Edinburgh came violently to life. Scotland had been plunged into the midst of a religious struggle that had overrun almost all of Europe. Germany had Luther; Geneva, Calvin; France, the Hugenots; and England had abandoned Rome to establish its own church in Henry VIII's time.

The "Great Bastard," James Stuart, headed the Reformers in Scotland. They banded together to form a coalition called the Lords of the Congregation, swearing before the "Majesty of

God, to maintain His most blessed word and Congregation against Satan and all wicked powers that doth intend tyranny or trouble."

Bothwell remained on the sidelines, watching with growing uneasiness, for he knew that more than religion was at stake here. Their methods smacked of sedition, and he doubted that it would prove difficult for them to turn the people against Mary of Guise. She was Catholic and closely affiliated with Rome, which had become anathema to the people. But the Congregationists had first to establish their piety. They set about this with loud protestations of their faith, choosing ministers who could properly inflame the people to destroy the old churches and murder their priests.

Of the church treasure that escaped destruction, much of it found its way into James Stuart's hands, and what he didn't want he tossed to his closest associates. He was Mary Stuart's half brother, the eldest of her father's natural-born children. But for his unlucky chance of birth, he would have inherited Scotland's crown.

Unlike his coreligionists, Bothwell refused to prate his beliefs before others; he had chosen his faith quietly, with much thought, and his prayers were a private matter between him and God. Thus, he formed no alliances with Protestants or Catholics, adopting for himself the dangerous policy of isolation, which inspired mistrust for him in both camps.

3

Bothwell had a taste of this mistrust when he found himself suddenly confronted with the Earl of Huntly, a Catholic, and the Earl of Argyll, a Protestant. They, like himself, had been summoned to Stirling by the Regent. Seeing these two together, their heads bent in whispered conversation, made him suspicious, for they made a very strange duet, indeed. They were no less wary of him, for their talk ceased abruptly and each retired to chairs on the opposite sides of the room, leaving Bothwell to stand alone.

A small, turbaned blackamoor, dressed in gold lamé tunic and trousers, came out to announce that Mary of Guise would receive them.

She waited for them to pay their respects, and after they were seated, she began. "My lords, I have summoned you here because my daughter's throne is in grave danger. My authority as Regent has been placed under dire threat. It is not my wish to trouble the conscience of others, but the methods employed by the new religionists force me to act."

Bothwell had not seen her since the Twelfth Night revels in Edinburgh. He avoided the Court when he could, for he disliked the formalities observed there and many of the men who frequented it. Now his discerning eye took note of the subtle changes in her; her lustrous eyes had dulled a little, the stately slenderness he had admired was somewhat plumpish now, her shoulders slumped as though she carried a heavy burden.

Then his attention was drawn to Huntly and Argyll. Huntly sat red-faced, his fleshy fingers curling his graying beard, nodding vigorous assent to the Regent's words. He was called the Cock o' the North and fancied himself a king in his Catholic stronghold in the Highlands.

A sudden draft wafted across the chamber, flapping the wall tapestries. A log crackled and sputtered in the fireplace, causing Argyll to start. Bothwell wondered why Argyll was here, for he made no secret of his affiliation with the Regent's enemies; his name was second, just under James Stuart's, on the Congregationists' bond.

He chuckled inwardly, comparing Argyll's vacant, heavy-lidded eyes and long flattened nose to a sheep. The nobles had a common jest: that Argyll followed the Bastard like a sheep to the shearing. But he was married to another of James V's natural children, and for that the Regent likely thought to win his loyalty.

Huntly sneezed and drew his brocaded sleeve across his nose. He sniffled noisily. "Aye, Your Grace, the new faith breeds danger everywhere. Let my lord Argyll tell us why priests cannot perform the mass without fearing for their lives, why our churches are desecrated—"

"Perhaps so, my lord," Argyll said, "but we do not question the Crown's authority. Unfortunately, the people have chosen blood and destruction as their method of protest, but we remain loyal to the Queen."

"Is it an act of obeisance to abolish the mass?" Bothwell asked. "Our Queen is Catholic; if she were here would you forbid her the mass as you do her mother?"

Argyll's lids dropped, veiling his eyes. "You are of the new faith, my lord, yet you plead for the Papists."

"Aye, for I believe that it is a man's privilege to choose his faith for himself."

The Regent raised her hand to silence them. "I did not bring you here to quarrel among yourselves, my lords. I must ask for your pledges of support. In case of open rebellion, I will need all the forces you can muster."

"My Highlanders are at Your Grace's command," Huntly said.

Bothwell stood. "And my Borderers."

They glanced at Argyll, who seemed undecided. Finally he said, "I give my pledge, too."

They knelt before her; Huntly kissed her hand and turned to go, then Argyll. But as Bothwell took her hand, she said, "Please remain, my lord."

He stepped back and waited. She seemed to be studying him contemplatively.

When she spoke it was as though she were thinking aloud. "You are so young, my lord. Not quite twenty-two yet."

"Aye, Your Grace."

"I have great responsibilities in mind for you—I wonder if you are ready for them."

"Will Your Grace hold the lack of a gray beard against me?"

She smiled. "There is one thing in your favor: you have the daring and impetuosity of youth. Nevertheless, we will begin slowly. The Privy Council meets for the new year in two weeks; you will have a seat on it."

The Council held little appeal; he wanted action, not endless discussion in an airless room with men who couldn't even agree on the time of day.

"I am no politician," he said. "Of what use can I be there?"

"Let me be the judge of that."

"I can do more good on the Border. My ways are blunt—"

"Perhaps, but you appear to possess the virtue of honesty—a rare commodity among my ministers. You do not choose your friends by the church they attend, and you are too proud to court anyone for favors. But more, you are loyal to the Crown. These are attributes few of my nobles possess."

"It would seem Your Grace knows a good deal about me."

She nodded. "I have made it my business to know. I cannot risk my daughter's Realm on pledges given one day, then broken the next. For that reason I have kept a close watch on you since your succession."

"And did Your Grace find me to her satisfaction?"

"We would not be here now if I did not."

By God, he thought, *here is a woman!* And in that instant he became her devoted servant. In her woman's body there lived the brain and valor of a man. But there were two serious doubts against her Regency: she was French, therefore France had great influence over Scotland; and she was Catholic, which gave Rome a heavy hand in Scottish affairs. Bothwell was no courtier; the honesty she had spoken of made him speak his thoughts outright now.

"Doubtless Your Grace will expect me to vote in favor of her confirmation for the Regency."

"Have you any reservations on that, my lord?"

"Only that the lords object to the influence of France and Rome. Although I have always favored a French alliance, I must confess to agree with them, somewhat. Scotland should be governed by Scotsmen, not outsiders."

She showed no anger, but her tone implied a weariness that comes of answering a question too often asked. "We are an impoverished kingdom, my lord. These *outsiders* give us financial aid, and more, if ever the need arises, we can count on military strength from France. Are these not reasons enough to maintain their friendship?"

"Aye," he said, grudgingly.

She was right, of course; the treasury was scant enough, for the Crown's wealth lay not in money but in sheep. As for military strength, she had none, except for the men her nobles raised in her name, and those changelings were scarcely dependable.

"Then I can count on your support?" she asked.

"Aye."

She smiled, and some of the old luster returned to her eyes. "Except when you are in disagreement with me—then your honesty may become more a burden than a virtue."

4

Bothwell sat on Mary of Guise's Council and voted in favor of her Regency and for the necessary funds for Mary Stuart's wedding in France. Several weeks passed before he could return to the Border, and just in time to lead a successful raid against the English, who had put Langton to the torch. Old Huntly, the Regent's lieutenant of the Border, had given more thought to saving his own skin than to the protection of the town.

Mary of Guise sent for Bothwell and transferred the lieutenancy to him, feeling that post required the energy and daring of a younger man. More, Bothwell was a Borderer; the same hot blood coursed in his veins.

Being one of them, he could understand why they lived by their wits. He had shared in their bitter experience of seeing English invaders ravage their land, burn villages, murder their people. He knew why they placed so much importance on their weapons and the speed of a horse, whereas a house and possessions meant little, for such things could quickly disappear in overnight raids. He could even understand how they could scorn God in church yet accept Him as their Creator, for he shared these unorthodox views. He could look upon their lawlessness with a certain indulgence, for he knew that they held their honor more dear than life itself—a pledge given was held sacred, never to be broken.

With the lieutenancy went the cure and charge of Edinburgh, and the keep of Hermitage Castle with its lands and rents. This was the most powerful post in the Realm; now Bothwell could ride justice on all subjects, destroy their homes, confiscate their goods, and hang all offenders. Despite his youth, Mary of Guise deemed him capable of the position, and he was proud of the confidence she had shown in him.

Bothwell set up headquarters at Hermitage, a remote fortress that stood in the shadow of the Cheviot Hills, strong and impregnable, as it had for centuries past. It was the last outpost in Scotland, only three miles from the English border—the last sentinel of defense. He knew the area well, from the Cheviot's yellow whin-patched moors to the steep, hidden valley roads that ran between them. And across that range of hills lay England, where a Catholic Mary Tudor and her husband, Philip II of Spain, massacred Protestants. Refugees poured into Scotland for safety; now it was Bothwell's task to drive them back.

On the twenty-fourth of April, 1558, Mary Stuart and the Dauphin François were married at Notre Dame Cathedral. Edinburgh celebrated the event with free wine and largess for everyone, but Bothwell was miles away at Hermitage occupied with the duties of his new post. He gave immediate orders for refortifications, gun loops to replace the outmoded archers' slits, movable siege cannons for field use, and special earthworks to be dug in the ground surrounding the fortress for added defense. Throughout fall and winter he terrorized the English with swift, efficient raids, relying on a small force of men and the element of surprise. His patrols stalked remote hill roads, repelling the enemy, warding off the danger of invasion. Bothwell had brought a semblance of quiet to the Border, but elsewhere something ominous had begun to rear its head.

In the taverns of Hawick, Bothwell heard news of London and Edinburgh from passing ballad singers. Mary Tudor lay dying as her nobles worried the bone of succession. At Hatfield the Princess Elizabeth, the last of Henry VIII's children, prepared to mount the English throne.

John Knox had bade farewell to Geneva and returned to Scotland. A known fanatic in the Protestant cause, he was embraced by the Lords of the Congregation and established as head of their church. Bothwell remembered Knox from Geneva; he was a man who scorned the love taught by Christ, offering in its place hatred and revenge. Now, after years spent in exile, amid the gory struggle of religion in Europe, Knox spewed his bitter brew from the pulpit of St. Giles.

5

Having failed to win Bothwell to their cause since his succession, the Congregationists were courting him again the following October. A delegation called on him at Crichton, but

Bothwell suspected they were up to something and set Ormiston on their trail. It took a few weeks to discover their purpose, but it was worth the waiting.

The rebels were negotiating with England for financial aid; Elizabeth had promised them three thousand pounds, and John Cockburn, a known turncoat, was to transport the funds over the border to Scotland. But there were more weeks of waiting before Bothwell could act on this information.

He spent the time planning his strategy carefully. Should the money fall into rebel hands, Scotland would be theirs. The time to strike finally came, and with a small force of handpicked men, Bothwell waited to spring into action.

Friday, Saturday, and Sunday went by without incident. Then early Monday morning Ormiston came riding up.

Breathlessly, he rushed into Bothwell's study. "Johnnie Cockburn has left for Berwick," he said.

Minutes later Bothwell came out to the courtyard; his men were already mounted and waiting for him. Every man there had a Jedburgh ax hooked onto his saddle and a two-handed sword hanging from his belt. At a given signal from Bothwell they rode out, grim-faced and taut with anticipation.

It was past noon when they bypassed Haddington and took the road for East Linton. Bothwell chuckled as he heard their surprised whispers when they clattered over the moat at Hailes Castle.

The men camped in the courtyard for the night without knowing why they had been assembled or how they were to be deployed. They idled about the castle grounds all that day, and it wasn't until near midnight that Bothwell finally came out to order them into the saddle again.

Each man felt an odd hesitation to ride out on foray this particular night, but none dared voice an objection. It was All Hallow's Eve, the night for goblins and witches to ride the wild moors, and hardly a man dared venture out. But there were two who did, Bothwell and Cockburn, each traveling the same road toward each other.

Bothwell called his men to a halt in the woods just below Hailes, with a warning for silence. They waited in the dark, frosty woods, overshadowed by Traprain Law. Every tree seemed to be reaching out for them as winter-barren branches danced in the wild October wind. The moon played tag with the clouds, lighting the woods with its silvery glow, then shrouding everything in thick, impenetrable darkness.

The waiting would have gone easier had they been able to sing or jest, but a warning from Bothwell cautioned them against it. They waited for what seemed hours, then Bothwell motioned them to come closer; he was ready to tell them his plans.

Expectantly, they grouped around his horse, forming a semicircle.

He spoke so low they strained to hear. "We've a special job tonight, my billies. There's a bag of English gold headed our way, and before this night is done I mean to have it."

A voice spoke out. It was Tammy Lin, who had ridden on past raids with Bothwell. "We are at peace with the English. What will the Regent say if her own lord lieutenant breaks the—"

Bothwell cut in quickly. "If we carry this thing off, the Regent will have good cause to shake the hand of every man here."

Hobbie Grey, another veteran, asked, "Who is it that we relieve of this burden?"

"A distant kinsman of mine, Johnnie Cockburn of Ormiston. It's not a year since he pledged loyalty to the Crown; now he's back doing the rebels' dirty work. The gold is for them, to use against the Regent."

A muttering arose from the men. One said, "He'll not live to do more treachery when we've done with him."

"I don't want him killed," Bothwell warned. "A few well-aimed cuts will suffice, and I reserve that pleasure for myself. The rest of you can deal with his bodyguard."

They nodded and took up their positions again. Some men dismounted to stamp the numbness from their feet, then a signal from Bothwell had them back in their saddles. Everyone listened, watching him closely, waiting for his move. Hands crept to their saddles in stealthy silence, taking a firm hold on their axes.

The sound of oncoming horsemen grew louder, but still he waited. He had to be certain that it was Cockburn; the horses were not going at a gallop, they thudded along leisurely. Then he reasoned: Why should Cockburn hurry? This was home territory to him; it was only natural for him to assume safety here.

Suddenly the quiet was shattered by a clash of steel—then groans of pain. Someone—or something—crashed out of the shadows. For a fleeting instant a sword poised in midair, then, finding its mark, came crashing down, and Elizabeth's bag of treachery was torn from Cockburn's saddle. Another blow from the same sword cut Cockburn down from his horse, blood rushing from his head. A clatter of horses' hooves, and the assailants were out of sight in a swirl of dust, leaving Cockburn and his men to ponder on the supernatural.

With the bag of gold securely strapped to his saddle, Bothwell surprised his men for the second time that night by turning his horse for Crichton. In a short night's work he had deprived the rebels of their sorely needed funds and had laid the English open to ridicule by exposing their pretended neutrality.

No sooner had Bothwell arrived at Crichton, removed his boots, and made ready for bed when Captain Sommerville sounded the alarm. Lord James and Arran were but minutes away from the gates with four hundred horsemen and three hundred foot soldiers. Without waiting for boots, spurs, or saddle, Bothwell thrust himself on a horse and escaped with the gold. He told Sommerville to surrender the castle once he had made good his escape and rode away taking the satisfaction of knowing that Lord James and Arran needed so many men to catch one.

Farther along the road, Bothwell left his horse to graze and continued on foot until he came to the kitchen of another Cockburn, the Laird of Sandybed, one who was more inclined to friendship with his overlord. Bothwell stayed there three days, until the search for him was abandoned. Then he skirted the area back toward Crichton and took refuge with his old friend Lord Borthwick.

It was to Borthwick Castle that Captain Sommerville brought the rebels' ultimatum to Bothwell. They demanded that "he return the gold and undo the wrong he had done to John Cockburn." Should he refuse, they threatened to set Crichton to the torch and carry off his possessions.

"Well, let them," Bothwell said. "They'll not feed their rebellion with this gold."

"They'll not be deterred," Sommerville said gravely. "The house, its furnishings—everything will go up in smoke."

Bothwell paced the room savagely, his eyes blazing with reddish glints. "What in God's name do I care about a pile of stinking stones? It's worth all my gear, and more—I'd go to staves to put a clamp on the Bastard and Arran."

Sommerville shook his head sadly. "I've tried to talk sense to you, but as always when your mind is set there's no changing it." He sighed. "They've left fifty hackbuteers at the castle, and they'll be back to do their mischief."

The door banged shut on Sommerville, and Bothwell threw

his head back, laughing wildly. Even the loss of Crichton was worth frustrating the rebels' desperate need for that bag of gold.

Sommerville's warning was soon borne out. Bothwell's coup had inspired the French commander in town to lead an attack on the rebel troops. When Lord James and Arran returned to Edinburgh, they found their men had been driven to the city walls by the French. It had taken the French only two hours to disband the rebels and claim the artillery they had left behind. Now the rebels were destitute not only of money but troops and artillery as well. This, when added to their grievance against Bothwell, served only to acerbate their fury. On November 3, Arran and the Master of Maxwell rode to Crichton at the head of three hundred horses to carry out their threat.

Later in the day Bothwell stood on Borthwick Tower watching the flames rise from Crichton while his enemies sacked the richest of his estates. But he wasted no time on regrets.

Standing beside him, Lord Borthwick said, "You've risked everything for the Regent. This exploit of yours has made a breach with your enemies so wide it may never be bridged."

Bothwell looked at him as though he saw the grizzled old man for the first time. "It had to be done," he said, his voice strangely low.

He envisioned Patrick's great oak bed veiled in smoke, the green velvet hangings aflame, now nothing but black ash in the wreckage, the little gold clock he had brought from France—heat-twisted and silent. . . . He closed his eyes to shut out the sight of black smoke that rose in the sky.

Borthwick had said something, but Bothwell only heard ". . . don't underestimate your enemies."

"I don't," he said grimly. "I can foresee what a coalition of Lord James' ambition, Knox's vengeful preaching, and Lethington's scheming wit can do to Scotland."

Borthwick sighed. "And you," he said. "I pray that you don't live to rue the day you thought of this coup. You've chosen formidable enemies; it could be your ruin."

CHAPTER II

1

The tapers burned long into the night as Bothwell and the Regent sat in her audience chamber. He had brought her the English gold, and the rebels had been driven from Edinburgh, but he knew they would return—this time with English soldiers.

The Regent looked to the Border for support and depended upon Bothwell to bring it to her. But he wondered if they were enough to stanch a rebellion. What of arms, victuals—where would the money come from to pay for these necessities? God knows he had given all he could. He was already deeply in debt—ruined would be more accurate—his personal outlay had reached enormous proportions.

When he finally left her it was past two in the morning. Knowing he would not sleep, he walked for a while in the palace gardens. The night was clear and cold; stars twinkled from a black fathomless sky, and in the stillness he could hear the sounds of night creatures from Arthur's Seat.

He wondered at the outcome if he had kept the English gold for himself. His enemies called him a thief; why not wear the cloak they gave him? He had risked his life for that gold, had suffered the loss of Crichton, but he had not profited by one penny of it.

Behind him a twig snapped. He turned and tensed, his body taut and alert, his hand resting lightly on the hilt of his dirk, ready to repel a sudden attack. He saw the heavily cloaked figure of a man coming slowly toward him; then he relaxed.

Astonished to see anyone abroad at this hour, Bothwell called, "Father Black, are there not enough hours in the day to serve God—does He call upon you at night, too?"

The priest's good-natured laughter warmed him. Father Black was a Frenchman and the Regent's private confessor. His lights were always the last to be extinguished each night.

"And you, my son? What keeps you from your slumber?"

"Many things, Father."

"I have just come from the Regent; she is troubled tonight. I am on my way to the abbey to light a candle for her."

"Would that candles and prayers could help me, Father."

"They might. Have you tried prayer?"

Bothwell laughed. "You've been listening to my enemies. They say I am irreligious because I do not parade my faith as they do. I do my praying in private, where no one can hear me—except God."

"Come into the chapel, my lord. I can think more clearly when my brain is not numbed with cold."

They went into the Royal Abbey. Candles lighted the altar and threw their shadows on the golden images and huge stone pillars. Father Black knelt and made the sign of the cross. He approached the altar and knelt again, murmuring a short prayer before lighting a candle. Then he returned to Bothwell.

"Now the Regent may sleep easier," Father Black said.

"Candles will not ease her burden," Bothwell said. "It would take a miracle to do that."

"She tells me there will be an open struggle with her rebels soon."

"Aye, and without sufficient troops I doubt her chances for a victory."

"There are your Borders—"

"My Borders are not enough. We need more men, more

arms—so much more." Abruptly he turned to the priest and blurted, "Good God, why have I permitted myself to be dragged into this quarrel?"

"Because she is a woman alone and needs your help. She does not ask it for herself, but for her daughter—your Queen."

"Perhaps, but it does not explain why I continue to champion a cause that has won me the enmity of nearly every man in Scotland."

"For hope of reward?"

"*No!* My allegiance belongs to the Crown—I deserve no reward for that."

Father Black smiled. "There is your answer, my lord."

They started to walk back toward the palace.

Bothwell asked, "Father, is it useless to attempt to undo the evil of others?"

"Each of us is held accountable for his own deeds. No one can vanquish the evil of another."

Inwardly he had known that; if he spent his entire life in defense of the Crown it would not erase Patrick's infamy. He stood there awhile after Father Black had left him. The palace guards changed, the last star disappeared behind red-swelled clouds that came drifting in, and a light mist began to fall. Finally he left and turned homeward.

To the south, England gathered troops under the command of Lord Gray de Wilton, who joined forces with the Scottish rebels. An English army was rumored to be embarking soon to blockade the Firth of Forth to prevent the entry of the Regent's French reinforcements.

Frantically, Bothwell rode from one Border fief to another, enlisting support, signing bonds of friendship with those who would pledge themselves to the Regent's cause. He organized an army of French and Scots, hoping to immobilize the rebels at Stirling to prevent their joining forces with the English.

By the end of December Bothwell was ready to march, but he had a detour in mind. The burning of Crichton was still fresh before his eyes, and he decided to pay a call at Arran's Castle Keneil. This time Arran's riches went up in smoke, and Arran's movables became the booty of a ransacking army. And when there was nothing more to destroy, Bothwell gave orders to resume the march.

2

By mid-February of 1560, despite Queen Elizabeth's protestations of peace and good will, war with England seemed imminent. Edinburgh Castle became the official headquarters for the Royalists, and Bothwell called for a muster of forces from those who had signed pledges with him the previous December. The following month, the English delivered a formal declaration of war.

And in the midst of those difficult weeks, Bothwell began to notice a change in the Regent. Sadly, he watched the strain of the past years take their toll. Her face had become haggard; deep circles and finely etched lines marred the beauty of her eyes, and her complexion had taken on a peculiar pallor. In the chaos surrounding him, he paused to remember the heartbreak she had endured since her widowhood in 1542.

For eighteen years she had carried the never-ending weight of rebellion from within her realm, while staving off continual invasions from the English. And never once had she admitted defeat. Now he wondered how much longer she could bear the strain.

English troops occupied Leith Harbor, blocking all avenues of supply from the castle. Bothwell took raiding parties into the enemy camp nightly, inflicting heavy damage upon them, but he knew the castle could not hold out for long. Their food supply was giving out, water was becoming scarce, and their ammunition stores were dangerously low.

Then near dawn one morning, just after he had returned from another foray, Bothwell had an urgent summons from the Regent. He hurried down the narrow corridors to her apartments. The first light of morning filled her sitting room with dull gray streaks that fell across inky black shadows, producing the effect of a giant chess board. He thought her chambers deserted, then he saw her standing near the latticed iron-barred casement looking down at the Grassmarket. Her body was hidden in the darkness, except for the glow of light that illuminated her face.

She glanced up, but remained strangely silent. At last she spoke. Her voice came to him low and distant. "I regret having to disturb your rest, my lord; you've had so little of it these last weeks. But I had to know what chance there is if outside help does not come."

He hesitated; she was behaving oddly, and he hated to add to her grief. But it would be even more cruel to fill her with false hope. Her question seemed pointless, for doubtless she knew the truth—they could not hold out.

"There is no hope for victory without help, Your Grace. We are low on food, supplies—God only knows how much longer we can hold the castle."

She nodded. "I suspected as much. I merely wanted to hear you confirm it. There is still one remaining chance; you will have to leave me for a while, but there is no other way. As you know, arrangements were made some months ago with the King of Denmark to provide us with ships for the transport of five thousand German mercenaries. King Frederick has not embarked those ships yet, but he might release them now, if he knew of our dire need."

"Those ships would be heaven-sent. They would end the English blockade and supply us with additional manpower."

"Precisely, and that is where you can help. You are to impress upon King Frederick our desperate situation."

How could he leave her at such a time? If something were to happen to her and he were not here to help. . . . But he had sworn to serve her; if she thought this way best, then he must go.

Still he tried to dissuade her. "I am a soldier, Your Grace. A diplomat would be more suited to the task."

"No. You are the Admiral of Scotland—and I can trust you."

Resigned, he gave no further argument.

"Your mission does not end in Denmark," she told him. "From there you will go to France. You must urge my daughter and her husband for more help. Impress upon them the need for more substantial assistance." Her voice faltered and grew soft. "Tell my daughter that without help I cannot guarantee the outcome."

She went to her desk and took from it letters of travel that had been prepared for him. She went to him and put her hand on his arm. "You have been my rock these last four years—and for that it has cost you dearly. My only regret is that I cannot reward you sufficiently."

He wondered why she had fought so hard. She was no Scot. Why should she care what happened to this godforsaken land? Why give her life for a crown that even her daughter appeared not to want? Mary Stuart had the wealth and comfort of France; she seemed not to care what happened in this beggared kingdom of hers. He longed to shout, "Go back to France, to safety, where you can live—and die—in peace."

Aloud he said, "I have asked no rewards. This is my country."

"Yes, I know, and yet. . . ." Her voice trailed off.

He took her hand and put it to his lips, holding it there a moment. Then he turned quickly and left without looking back, for had he taken a backward glance, he would not have had the heart to go.

3

Bothwell's mission to Denmark would have been an immediate success had circumstances not rendered it useless. He had made a good impression on King Frederick; they were close in age and shared many things in common. But only a few weeks after his arrival news of the Regent's death reached him.

She had finally succumbed to dropsy. Her Protestant ministers would not even allow her the last solace of a priest as she lay on her deathbed, and immediately after her passing, the French, Scots, and English had signed a peace treaty.

Bothwell's enemies were in control of the government now, and the power he had had during Mary of Guise's rule vanished. It was still his intention to continue his mission to France; he had to convince the Queen that for Scotland's good, she had to unseat the rebels. But there was no urgency now; he could stay in Denmark awhile longer. There was a young woman he had seen at court who had drawn his interest, and he wanted to know her better.

She was unlike the fair, blue-eyed Scandinavian beauties; she was more like a Spanish senorita. Her hair was the color of black mahogany, and she had eyes to match. Even the way she dressed was different; the first time he saw her she was wearing a bright green silk gown, ornamented with long strings of multicolored beads that hung from her neck, and a wide gold chain encircled her hair and forehead.

Her name was Anna Throndsen, and she was the daughter of a retired Norwegian admiral, now in King Frederick's service.

According to gossip, her family was well-to-do, but there was little more Bothwell knew about her, except that she had flirted outrageously with him.

Bothwell used his page, Paris, to poke about and learn more about Mistress Anna Throndsen. The Throndsens were Norwegian, but they had adopted Denmark as their country. Anna was twenty and unmarried, and given much freedom by her family. She appeared to come and go as she pleased, and it was said that she was not at all niggardly with her affection, though none ventured a guess at her maidenhood.

Bothwell listened to Paris' information and told him, "Arrange a meeting with the lady for tomorrow night."

Paris gave him a sly grin. "A note in Your Lordship's hand would be all that is needed. She has spoken of you to a friend and appears interested."

"What did she say of me?"

"That she finds Your Lordship very attractive. She confessed to finding men of your height and proportions most appealing—and that you—" Paris broke into peals of laughter.

"That I what?"

"That Your Lordship impressed her with a sense of danger."

Bothwell laughed. "Bring pen and ink. I'll write the note."

The expense of Bothwell's tryst with Anna was something that he could ill afford, but an inn of lesser quality would have been less desirable. Doubtless Anna expected to be courted in proper style. Paris had told him that she was proud, though unrestrained.

Fortunately Bothwell was able to come to terms with the innkeeper for a small room on the top floor. It was a tastefully, though meagerly, furnished room, and what he had saved on rent could be used toward an extra fine dinner. He chose the menu carefully: smoked eel, lamb roasted with apples and pears on skewers, and plum tarts for the sweet.

He arrived at the Stag and Crow before Anna to see that everything was ready. The wines, Canary and Madeira, were mellow and heady, and the room seemed perfect. A pair of heavy oaken carved armchairs with comfortably rounded backs had been placed beside a round table set with fruit and wineglasses. The wall was decorated with a tapestry depicting a wood nymph succumbing to Pan. There was no couch, only a thick-piled bearskin pallet in front of the fireplace.

Bothwell heard the town crier call eight o'clock just as Paris ushered Anna in. She stood near the door demurely, waiting for Bothwell to come to her.

He put her hand to his lips. "I am honored, my lady."

She smiled shyly. "I pray Your Lordship does not think me overbold for accepting this invitation."

So, she wished to play the coquette. Amused, his glance swept over her slowly; she wore a pale-blue silk gown with sleeves that puffed at the shoulders and narrowed to the wrist. Frothy white lace covered the open bodice and buttoned to her throat. No jewelry adorned her gown, but she had been unable to resist a string of large pearls across her forehead. She had used little paint, wishing, he guessed, to appear *au naturel;* only a light dab of kohl on her lids accentuated her dark eyes, and a touch of pink on her lips. Her hair was bound in a blue satin ribbon and hung loosely over her shoulders. She obviously wished to appear a shy young maiden—and Bothwell was enchanted.

He led her to an armchair. "Bold? For accepting an invitation to supper?" he asked, innocently wide-eyed.

He watched her walk, admiring her carriage. The fluid motion of her gown swung from her hips; her full breasts strained against the lacy bodice.

"It would have been proper for you to call upon me at my father's house," she said, then quickly added, "but shyness may have prevented you from doing so."

He stifled the impulse to laugh. No one had ever accused him of being shy before. But if she enjoyed the deception. . . .

He poured the canary and handed a glass to Anna. The heavy scent of her perfume when he bent near teased his senses. Heaving a sigh, he said, "Would that all women were as considerate as you."

Her conscience was likely salved, for she leaned back and sipped her wine contentedly.

"Shall we have supper now?" Bothwell asked.

"If you wish, my lord," she said, her tone implying that anything so mundane was a wearisome necessity.

He went to the door and called the serving maid, who answered his summons with a tray of dishes.

After the maid left, Bothwell handed his dagger to Anna. "This should be eaten while hot," he said, uncovering a trencher of eel sizzling in melted butter.

Anna wiped the dagger daintily with a lace handkerchief and speared a piece for her plate. "My favorite dish," she said.

He chuckled. Such delicacy—even for an admiral's daughter. They waded through supper on a flow of small talk. Anna told him the latest court gossip, complimented the preparation of the lamb, and dropped a few casual hints of her family's prominence.

Bothwell said very little himself, encouraging her chatter with an occasional nod. He would let her talk herself out now; he'd give her little time for it later.

He drained the last of his Madeira and rose, unbuttoning the neck of his doublet. "It's uncommonly warm tonight—even for July," he complained.

"The wine, no doubt, but if it causes you discomfort, please feel free to remove your doublet, my lord."

He did so and tossed it carelessly over the back of his chair. Then, crossing to her, he pulled her to her feet. "How can you bear the heat of those petticoats?" he asked.

She blushed. "Without them you would see through my thin skirt—and it is fashionable to wear them."

He envisioned her legs, slender and shapely, leading to well-tapered thighs. "And for the sake of fashion you rob the gentlemen of their innocent pleasure."

She purred. "You forget, my lord, I spoke of modesty's sake first."

He stepped closer and drew her into his arms. She permitted herself to be led to a chair and sat down on his lap. Slowly, he undid the lace at her neck. He kissed her throat; a few more buttons and her bodice opened, revealing the cleavage of her breasts.

Her hands crept to his shoulders, then moved caressingly to his hair. His head lay nuzzled in the curve of her throat, while he unlaced the back of her gown. She pressed her soft bosom against his lips.

Weakly she protested, "You must not, my lord."

"Would you put me off now?" he asked on a wounded note.

"We scarcely know each other."

"Could you be so heartless as to deny me your loveliness because of our short acquaintance?"

The last fastening on her gown was undone, and it slipped down.

Anna buried her head in his neck. "You are the first, my lord," she whispered.

Slowly his hand left her waist. Good Christ—a virgin! The damned chore, the drudgery of molding her to his taste. And for what—a week, two, a month at best—then he would be off for France. He thought of the expense—the room, the meal, the wine—and all for nought.

She noticed the sudden change in him and asked, "How have I offended you, my lord? What have I done to cool your ardor?"

He eased her from his lap and got up. "Nothing can serve to

cool my ardor so soon as a virgin," he growled. "I've had my fill
of them."

Her voice was barely audible, muffled behind her hand. "I
lied—you would not be the first. My maidenhood has been
taken," then quickly, "but only twice before."

He turned, cursing himself for a fool. He should have known.
He had allowed her the other deceptions; why not this?
Contrite, he went to her, embracing her. He could still leave her
some pride.

Cuddling her, he said, "Forgive me, Anna. It was not my
intention to hurt you. A woman's virtue is precious—I could not
allow you to surrender it in the heat of passion."

He had chosen his words well, for she nuzzled close and
kissed him. "The candles," she murmured. "Put them out."

He snuffed them out and heard the rustle of her silk skirt
slip to the floor—the soft muted sound of her cotton
petticoats. . . .

He threw his own garments on a stool and waited for her on
the bearskin pallet. A moment later the soft warmth of her
body touched his.

4

After that night Anna made no secret of her feelings for him.
Her frank pleasure in his lovemaking delighted him. But there
was much he disliked in Anna. Given the chance, he knew she
would become possessive and cling to him with hawklike talons.
Despite her protestations of undying love for him, he knew she
would not hesitate to fight like a hellcat if he scorned that love.

Yet, though he knew her every fault, she still intrigued him.
He had never cared for the ordinary in women; he liked a touch
of the exotic, and Anna had far more than a touch. Though he
knew her for a vixen, he preferred that to a sainted nature

which would have driven him to wearied distraction. Besides, he could control her when there was need. He liked her aggressiveness and the lack of pretense between them. She wanted him to make love to her and encouraged him, and sometimes, to his vast amusement, she even demanded it.

He was invited to meet her bearlike father and her shrewish mother. Both the admiral and his wife seemed to like him on sight, although Bothwell surmised it was more his rank and the prospect of a good marriage for their daughter that prompted them. His suspicions were confirmed when Admiral Throndsen let drop a casual hint that Anna's future husband would be given a dowry of forty thousand crowns. A sum large enough to tempt men in lesser straits than Bothwell.

Admittedly, Anna lacked the qualities Bothwell might otherwise have favored in a wife; though she pretended to be a great lady, and a sophisticate, she was neither. She was full of guile and hot-tempered, and would likely develop into a shrew like her mother. He realized that he would tire of her quickly, for they had nothing in common that would endure life long association. But, he reasoned, men of his station married for practical reasons, not romantic notions.

And despite his doubts, Bothwell rushed headlong into the courtship. He disguised his lukewarm ardor in the glowing terms of French, with little love notes that alluded to their wedding. Both Anna and her family were delighted by his attention, but Bothwell hadn't yet made any formal offer of marriage to the Admiral—a delay he had good cause to be grateful for.

All talk of dowries had suddenly ceased, and now Bothwell heard more of the hard times that were upon the Throndsens. Anna's father spoke of his thankless position at court, bewailing the fact that King Frederick paid him so poorly for his services. Also, he never failed to remind Bothwell of his other two daughters who would soon begin to think of taking husbands.

"What of their dowries?" he would ask. And gradually it became apparent that the forty thousand crowns had been used as bait for the trap.

But they hadn't caught Bothwell yet—two could play the same game. If the Throndsens could renege, he thought, then he could withdraw his proposal. It was unheard of, especially for noblemen of his rank, to marry without the accustomed dowry. Even the poorest beggar knew that he had to provide his daughter with a suitable dowry.

By August Bothwell was seeing less and less of Anna, and he was certain that Anna knew the wedding was off. Her silent acceptance was somewhat surprising, but there was really nothing she could do about it. Besides, he was tired of Denmark, and thinking of France.

A week before he sailed, a very elaborately dressed woman called at Bothwell's lodgings.

"It's the Mistress Throndsen," Paris told him.

It was early morning, scarcely an hour for ladies to call. Bothwell had just finished breakfast, and he was still in his robe and slippers. But if Anna chose to toss convention aside so casually, then he would receive her dressed as he was.

He came into the sitting room and presented her with a flourishing bow. "I am honored," he said. Then, indicating his attire: "You must forgive my lack of formality, but I seldom receive ladies in my quarters—and at such an hour."

His words were courtly, but his tone left no doubt that he was furious with her. Looking at her now, he wondered that he had ever thought to wed her; she resembled a gypsy in her red tunic dress, adorned with a dozen strings of beads dangling from her neck.

"To what urgent matter of business do I owe this pleasure?" he asked.

She attempted coyness, but the determination in her voice betrayed her. "You have not been to see me. Why?"

"I have been occupied," he said indifferently.

Incredulous, she shrieked, "Occupied! Is that all you can say, after what I have been to you?"

He cocked an amused eye at her. "Just what is it you have imagined yourself to be?"

She was near hysteria. "You have taken me—made love to me—made me your mistress—now you would leave me. But I shan't let you," she screamed. "What am I to do now? No honest man will have me for a wife—you cannot leave me like this."

"I not only can, but I will. You were no maiden when I found you—why come complaining to me now? Since I was not the first, what made you think I'd be the last?"

"But you promised to wed me—you wrote—"

"And I had your father's promise of a fat dowry, which he has seen fit to withdraw since. Weigh that against what I may have said."

"What difference does the money make—if you love me?"

"All the difference. Besides, I've never spoken of love, and if I had, my love is not quite so abiding as to withstand so great a loss." His voice softened. "Come now, we've both had our pleasure; why weep over the past? I'm off to France in a week, so there's nothing more to be said. I'll send you a pretty trinket for your forehead from there—something to remember me by."

She dried her tears. Her eyes turned icy. "Nothing to say, is there?" she spat hatefully. "There is still a great deal to be said. You cannot toss me aside that easily."

Bothwell was nearly out the door; now he came back. His mouth turned hard and cruel; he went to her in tight-lipped fury. "Do I detect a note of threat in those words, my lady?"

His face was only inches from hers; she drew back in fright.

"I did not mean it as a threat," she said, faltering. "I am with child—your child."

He clamped his hand on her arm and pulled her to her feet.

"This is some new trick you've thought up to keep me here. If you are lying. . . ." He let his voice trail off ominously.

"No—I swear it, it is the truth," she cried, trying to pull free. "Now do you see why I came? If you go to France, you must take me with you."

"No! It's out of the question. Having you along would only hamper me."

"I cannot remain here now," she insisted. "In a few months everyone will know. Think of my shame."

He paced up and back furiously. Then, facing her again, he said, "Very well, you can come, but only as far as Flanders—no farther. I cannot have you on my neck at the French Court. And there is to be no more talk of a wedding. Is that clear?"

She ran to kiss him, but he pushed her aside and stalked out.

5

Bothwell didn't see Anna again until it was time to sail. Paris brought her to the ship and looked after her baggage. She came on board smiling gaily, as though she were about to take a pleasure cruise. Bothwell stood on the captain's bridge, shrouded in early morning fog, listening to the first mate call orders to the crew. Anna went to a lower deck and called farewells to a group of relatives who had come to see her off.

Bothwell watched her absentmindedly for a while, then something about Admiral Throndsen caught his attention. The Admiral kept glancing furtively at the ship's holding lines; he seemed anxious to have them leave—almost too anxious, Bothwell thought. There was in fact something strange about the entire situation.

Here he was taking the unwed daughter of a seemingly respectable family to a foreign country without marrying her, and no one seemed to object. Anna had sworn that she had told no one of her condition. Why were they letting her go like this? He mulled this over for a while, then dismissed it with a shrug.

Mindful of September's unpredictable storms, Bothwell thought August a good month to set sail, but the promise of good weather and calm seas was forgotten on their first night out. At twilight heavy rain clouds appeared; then toward midnight the watch in the crow's nest sighted sea swells and rolling whitecaps, and Bothwell knew they were in for a bad storm.

By morning they had drifted several points off course, and they were plunged into the midst of gale-force winds. Then later in the day a heavy downpour added to their troubles. The tiny vessel floundered about, tossed on mountainous waves, pelted by rain, battered mercilessly by winds.

Toward evening the storm lessened, but they were still drifting off course. A sudden gust of wind tore the topmast away and sent it crashing to the deck. Their doom seemed imminent, but when the storm had passed they were still afloat.

They had suffered tremendous damage, and in the bright early morning sun it looked even worse. The temperature had dropped, and a quick look at the compass told Bothwell that they had been blown past the coast of Norway. Their steering device was ruined, and with the mast gone there were only the oars to carry them to a port for repairs.

After eight days at sea, they sighted land and the crippled vessel made its laborious way into the Norwegian port of Bergen. Bothwell left Anna on board with most of the crew while he went ashore to arrange for repairs. He had no trouble finding workmen—but there was no money with which to pay for the things he needed.

He turned the problem over in his mind on the way back to the ship. He knew that Anna had brought money and jewels with her; she might be persuaded to loan some to him. Why should she refuse? Had he been obdurate, she would have had to stay in Copenhagen and face the consequences; the least she could do was help him now.

Of course, Anna was reluctant to part with one penny of her wealth.

"Sell your ring," she said petulantly. "The gold alone will bring you a vast sum."

She referred to the Hepburn crest ring. Indeed the heavy gold mounting and its thickly crusted emeralds would bring a handsome sum, but he would not part with it. It had been in the family for generations; father had passed it on to son for two centuries, or more. He might have a son one day. . . .

"Because I'll have none but a Hepburn wear it," he told her.

In the end she agreed to lend him the money.

Anna discovered that her cousin Erik Rosenkrantz was one of Bergen's high officials. She suggested that they pay a friendly visit to him, but Bothwell refused. "I've already met enough of your meddling kin to last me a lifetime," he told her. And Anna wisely let the matter drop there.

They left Bergen ten days later and reached Flanders by mid-September. Bothwell rented a small house for Anna and left two days later for France with only a few crowns jingling in his pockets.

CHAPTER III

1

Although shabby and penniless, Bothwell still had high
hopes for this mission, for he had served Mary Stuart well. Of
course, there was always the chance that she accepted his
service with royal indulgence, as her due. What then? What of
his outlay for men and arms, the sacking of Crichton, the
upkeep of this mission? He might never see a penny returned.

These dark thoughts persisted and lay heavily on his mind,
but as he neared Paris he felt the free spirit of his early youth
return, and his hopes soared. Whatever the outcome, he would
make the most of his meeting with the Queen.

He waited a day before sending Paris to St.-Germain-en-Laye
to request an audience. The Queen was quick to reply with an
invitation for him to visit her that same afternoon. He took
pride in her promptness. She might have put him off; this could
be a good omen, he thought.

As he dressed, he thought about Mary Stuart; she had been
only thirteen at their last meeting, tall for her age with a
childishly pretty face and long chestnut hair. Her figure had
been flat and undeveloped, and he had marveled that such a
child would be wed at fifteen. But she was nearly eighteen now
and two years wed; there was bound to be a difference. And
yet, he could not forget what folk said about her husband.

He had heard that the King of France was impotent—that

the Scottish Queen's husband was no husband at all. A few vows exchanged in church did not make a woman of a child. But he would know the moment he saw her; his experienced eye would soon discover the truth.

He chose a russet doublet with gold lacing and slashed sleeves to show his embroidered white lawn shirt, dark-brown breeches with hose to match, and highly polished boots which complimented his long, muscular legs. Then he added the final touches: a leather dagger belt that sheathed an emerald-hilted dirk and a dress sword fastened to his side.

At the palace, he presented his credentials and the gates swung open on a world of soft green lawns, long columns of huge shade trees, and fountains yielding delicate sprays of mist in gardens deep in fragrant blooms of autumn. He strode down the Turkey-carpeted corridors hung with mirrors and stopped for a last inspection of himself. Smiling back at his reflection, he tossed his short cape over one shoulder to reveal its gold lining and continued on to the Queen's audience chamber.

He heard himself announced and entered a room filled with crystal chandeliers, fragile gilt chairs covered in satin, thick Turkey carpets, and exquisite tapestries.

Mary Stuart was seated on a pink brocaded couch. Bothwell took her hand, put it to his lips, and knelt before her. As he rose, she motioned him to a chair.

They faced each other in frank appraisal. Then she said, "I have looked forward to this meeting, my lord. My mother mentioned you often in her letters. You did her commendable service."

"It was my duty, madam."

She smiled. "I think you are too modest—your record speaks for you."

"If modesty is among my faults, Your Majesty is the first to note it."

He leaned back in his chair and studied her. It had only been four months since the Regent's death, and she still wore the white robes of mourning. His glance traveled upward, from her white satin slippers to the lace veil that covered her hair. Taking note of her slenderness, he saw that she was still flat and immature, and she appeared even younger than her seventeen years.

He admired her lovely sloping shoulders, so much like her mother's, and the delicate, creamy skin of her throat. His gaze swept past her generous, rose-tinted lips and lingered on her eyes. Again he was reminded of her Stuart ancestors; she had their long, heavy-lidded brown eyes, flecked with gold. But he saw something more in her, and his suspicions were confirmed.

She was not yet a woman—at least not by his standards. Certainly she was not woman enough for him, and so he did not think of her as a woman at all. He was willing to swear that she had never given herself to a man—how incredible for her to have lived in the decadence of the French Court all these years without ever taking a lover. And with that special knowledge of his, Bothwell was also certain that her sickly husband had brought nothing to the marriage bed.

Her eyes twinkled with amusement. "I rather suspect that you are not loath to speak of your achievements, my lord." Then, sadly, she asked about her mother. "I knew she was ill, but there was never a hint it was fatal—she never complained in her letters."

His mouth turned hard and bitter. "They hounded her to death unmercifully," he blurted. "If it were not for her nobility, she might still be alive today. They could bring peace to Scotland only after her death—then celebrate it with a feast. I marvel they did not feed on her corpse, instead of English beef and bacon."

His vehemence shocked her. Doubtless no one had ever spoken this way to her before. She was likely convinced now that he was the crude barbarian folk said. *Then let her,* he thought, for she had lived too long in her soft pink satin world—time she faced the truth as her mother had been forced to do.

Her composure returned. "Those same men who rule Scotland now," she said.

"Aye, they are led by the Bast—the lord James. Your mother thought his blood ties would keep him loyal, madam."

"And you do not, my lord?"

"No. The past speaks for itself. He is too hungry for power." Then, forcing her to meet his gaze directly, he said, "You've had proof enough of that already, madam."

Abruptly she asked, "How were you received at the Danish Court?"

"With much good grace, madam. My mission was a success, but it came too late. It rankles to know that I had the means to destroy the rebels and could not use it."

"If peace prevails we may be able to look for harmony in the Realm."

Did she really believe this would be a lasting peace? Had her mother's fate taught her nothing?

"Surely you are not so optimistic, madam. Lord James and his party will never fully support you. Your brother may have finally reconciled himself to the fact that his birth forbids him your crown, but it's the regency he craves now. Do you fancy he will rest until he has it? He uses religion to excuse his anarchy; Your Majesty is Catholic, which provides him with the sound argument that you represent a threat to the new faith."

"What right have they to question my faith? I have never questioned theirs; I ask only that they band together for the good of Scotland."

"Even if your nobles did unite, Queen Elizabeth would never let you live in peace. She cannot forgive you for claiming her throne."

"In that I followed my uncle's advice—and yet I cannot but feel that I am England's rightful queen. Her father's parliament declared her illegitimate."

"And in 1554 they reinstated her."

"But my claim is recognized throughout Europe."

"By that you mean *Catholic* Europe, madam."

"You are not Catholic, my lord?" she asked sharply. "I had heard you are irreligious, yet you have shown yourself loyal to those whose faith you dislike."

He grinned. "I've no objection to the faith others follow, providing they do not attempt to convert me."

She smiled. *"Touché.* I had no right to probe your conscience. Now tell me more about the situation in Scotland."

By God, he liked that! He had given her a verbal rap on the knuckles, and she had admitted to her indiscretion. He began by giving her a fair evaluation of the men now in power. She listened without interrupting.

When he had finished she said, "And I must negotiate with them for Scotland's future. I have read almost everything Master Knox has written and I find him relentless. It is not his faith I question as much as his methods—yet he is revered as a saint."

Bothwell laughed. "Knox, a saint? Scarcely! He is no more a saint than are your priests. He preaches hatred and rebellion, filling his congregation with bitter intolerance. This is the love of God taught them by Knox."

"Then why did the people choose such a man to lead them in their faith?"

"Not the people, madam. The corruption and greed of the old church chose him. Catholicism spawned Knox and his like. While your priests and bishops grappled for more wealth their parishioners starved. Folk saw their children in rags and compared them to the clergy's gorgeous dress. They saw altars heavy with gold while they starved. Therefore, you cannot blame the people—or Knox, for that matter—Catholicism alone sentenced itself to death."

"But to kill—to desecrate? Is this the only way to abolish corruption?"

He cocked his head to one side innocently. "Have you forgotten the Cardinal's massacre at Amboise, madam?"

"That was a defensive measure. The Hugenots left my uncle no choice—they were in open rebellion against the Crown. And yet," she said, wistfully, "I would have preferred to see them put down bloodlessly. But to compare Amboise with Knox's methods is unfair."

He stood up to stretch his legs. "I make no comparisons, madam. I merely wish to point out the small difference between the two when they are faced with opposition. In France it is the Cardinal who strikes a victory for the old faith—in Scotland it is Knox for the new."

She was about to answer when the sound of tapping at the door distracted her. A young girl, close to the Queen's age, entered.

"Forgive the intrusion, madam," she said, glancing sideways at Bothwell. "The King asks for you."

Mary smiled and turned to Bothwell. "This is Mary Fleming, one of my ladies-in-waiting."

Taking Fleming's hand he bowed. "One of the renowned four Lady Marys that attend Your Majesty."

He addressed the Queen, but his eyes never left Fleming. She was more to his liking with her shining gold curls and laughing green eyes. And she had a figure to match her pretty face; she was tall and slender, well formed in bosom and hips, and Bothwell promised himself to explore her charms further.

"You will forgive me, my lord," Mary said. "The King has not been well of late. I will leave Fleming to entertain you. We will talk further—tomorrow perhaps."

He bowed to her, and she was gone in a whisper of silk.

Turning to Fleming, Bothwell asked, "Are all the Queen's Maries so pretty?"

Fleming lowered her eyes demurely. "You must judge that for yourself, my lord. But I can tell you a little about them; we are called by our last names to avoid confusion. Can you imagine someone calling the name of Mary and none of us knowing which was to answer?" she asked, dimpling. "There is Mary Seton; she is the quiet one and the mainstay of us all. And Mary Livingston, dreamy and mysterious but too fond of sweets with a figure that shows it. Mary Beaton is tiny and adorable and loved by all"—she paused—"but she has not so giving a nature as her aunt Janet, the Lady of Buccleugh."

His laughter came roaring out. Fleming had doubtless heard of his affair with Janet Beaton. Janet had been his mistress two years ago, when he had been appointed lieutenant of the Border. It had been a lovely, warm affair, a combination of intellect and passion, even though Janet was twenty years his senior. And when they parted, it had been as friends. She had sent him away, knowing he must eventually leave her, thereby sparing herself that hurt.

"I had no idea that news of my little flirtations had traveled so far," he said. "I marvel that you concern yourself with such dull gossip."

"It was not du—" She blushed. "I mean, since Beaton is Lady Janet's niece, it was natural for someone to write her about it."

"Quite natural. But that's past history now, and I would much rather talk of the present."

From the way her cheeks flamed, and her glance avoided his, he knew that she had not mistaken his meaning. Amused, he watched her assume a pose of displeasure.

"Surely I am not the first to remark on your loveliness," he said.

She smiled. Obviously she enjoyed his admiration and hoped

to hear more. But it had been a long afternoon, and he was anxious to leave. The pink and white satin room seemed suddenly stifling, and he felt the need for air. It was getting late; there were old friends he wanted to see. A carouse would come as a relief after the hours spent in polite haivering with the Queen.

He took a step toward the door and instinctively sensed Fleming's fear. He wondered just how far his reputation with women had preceded him.

"You will excuse me, my lady," he said. "It's late and I must go. I hope we shall see a good deal of each other before I leave France."

She went to the door with him. "I look forward to our next meeting, my lord," she said with a note of promise.

2

Mary again summoned Bothwell to the palace the next day. This time she kept him waiting more than an hour before seeing him.

She began, "Our talk came to an abrupt end yesterday, and there is still a great deal more I must know about affairs in Scotland."

Bothwell nodded. "You must decide on a group of men to govern in your absence, madam. Have you anyone in mind?"

"According to the terms, I am permitted to select six men to represent me in Parliament, and the Reformed party will name five of their choice."

"Aye, but it will not be easy to choose, madam. I doubt there are six noblemen you can really trust."

"There is one."

He glanced up quizzically. "Who, madam?"

"You, my lord. Before her death my mother had the

presence of mind to write out a list of men who could and could not be trusted."

Tears flooded her eyes. She said, "It was the last letter she wrote me. She placed great value on your loyalty; your name headed the list—a list that barely covered half a page. For the other—"

"It takes little imagination to know its length, madam."

He waited, for he knew she was thinking of her mother. But she couldn't know the Regent as he had. She hadn't seen her mother pitted against that pack of greedy, conniving scoundrels. She had been a mere child of eight when she had seen her mother last, scarcely able to appreciate her bravery. He could tell her of the woman who had steeled herself to bear treachery and heartbreak for her daughter's crown, of the woman who had won his respect and devotion . . .

She broke in on his thoughts. "Whom would you recommend?"

"You've a limited choice, madam. It's a matter of deciding on those who will do you the least harm." He leaned forward. "There is Huntly, called the Cock o' the North, and he fancies himself a king in his Highlands. He is old and quite useless in battle, but a Catholic, and he controls your last religious stronghold in Scotland. He'll likely support you, if only to save himself.

"The Earl of Argyll is married to one of your natural sisters, but he is also a Congregationist—his loyalty is dubious. Atholl has been known for change."

He waited while she poured some wine and handed him a glass, then he resumed. "You cannot ignore the Duke de Châtelherault, despite his faithlessness. He is a Hamilton; his son, Arran, is next in line to succeed you. Then of course, there is your base brother, Lord James. Past experience has proven him a traitor, and I doubt you can look for better from him in the future. There you have it, madam. Five men—all of questionable loyalty."

He watched the disappointment creep into her eyes, and briefly, she brought to mind a virgin in robes of white about to be offered in sacrifice to a pagan god. Thank God she had France, for he knew what her Scottish nobles would do with her if they could. Better for her to rule from afar, and yet, if she were there, he felt it would be best for Scotland.

"You do not embroider the truth, my lord," she said ruefully. "But I am grateful for your frankness."

There was something of her mother in her after all. He had presented her with a bleak picture of her kingdom, and she had not repaid his straightforwardness with a royal tantrum.

"Perhaps I should have filled you with false hope, madam."

The corners of her mouth turned up in a smile. "No, I have had my fill of lies. The truth is refreshing—you must promise to be honest with me always."

"My word on that. But the truth can be unpleasant—for all its sublimity, it destroys dreams and unmasks ugliness."

Wistfully, she said, "How I envy you your battlefields, my lord."

"Were the choice mine, I would never leave them."

"Then we have among us a unique man—one who does not seek power."

"Military power only, madam. I am a soldier. I lack the patience for a politician—my ways are too blunt."

"I cannot make war on my own Realm; therefore my only weapon is diplomacy."

"Scarcely an adequate weapon against such odds, madam. If only you could urge your husband's support. One of your mother's last acts was to commission me with the task of enlisting more French aid. Give me that aid now, and I can still bring the rebels to their knees."

Instantly he wished he could recall the words; what strange

fascination pulled him deeper and deeper into this abyss of intrigue and conflict?

"My husband and I wear the crowns here, but it is my uncle and my mother-in-law who rule. Both the King and I have made every effort to help, but we can do no more than we already have."

He nodded. "I suspected as much. But if Your Majesties knew the danger—you stand to lose all authority in Scotland."

"I am well aware of that, and because of it I have decided to commission you to convoke a parliament in our names. This is no small task, I know, since those now in power have professed themselves your enemies. Perhaps you should not return for a while."

"Scotland is my home, madam. I will live there despite all men."

She smiled. "I doubt you would hesitate to challenge the devil himself, if he stood in your way. The decision is yours—return when you wish."

Suddenly he was sick for the sight of home: the golden rolling carpet of the Cheviot Hills, unfurled and unbroken against the sky, the fog-drenched, bracken-tangled moors, the violent sea dashing itself against the rugged shores. He longed to turn his back on this girl and the problems she brought him. He had served her well; why didn't he refuse the commission and return to Scotland to live in peace?

Her voice pulled him back. "Now for more pleasant matters," she said. "According to my mother's will, you are to have the lands and rents of Melrose and Haddington abbeys. I shall confirm those grants, and add my own of six hundred crowns."

Her generosity was more than he had hoped for. She hadn't proved ungrateful after all.

"Your Majesty honors me more liberally than I deserve," he said.

"Nonsense. I wish it could be more. I know of the lands you've had to mortgage, the money you spent in espousing my mother's quarrels."

Even that had not escaped the Regent's notice.

Grinning, he said, "I bow to Your Majesty's will."

"I feared you might take offense."

"Offense, madam? I have great respect for money. Even if I were contemptuous of it, it is a luxury I cannot permit myself to enjoy. Unlike most of my coreligionists, I do not receive a bounty of English pounds."

She nodded ruefully. "Some of my nobility are not squeamish when it comes to accepting bribes."

"Some, madam! That may be said only of those who are *not* in England's pay. Queen Elizabeth's secretary keeps a long list—your brother's name heads it."

"To satisfy their greed they betray Scotland—and me."

He laughed harshly. "From the paltry sums paid them, it would seem that Scotsmen place small value on their services. In any case, Elizabeth's penuriousness would prevent Cecil's excessiveness."

Bothwell's reference to Elizabeth started her in another direction. "Have you ever seen her?" she asked.

"Aye, once, on your mother's business. She is not unattractive, but her features are too sharp for my taste. She is crafty and dangerous, no mean threat to you, madam. But I must admit that she has a genuine love for her kingdom and its people."

"And you think that I do not?"

"You cannot love what you do not know, madam. You left Scotland a child of six, whereas she grew up among her people. Her childhood was not easy—for the most of it she bore the stigma of bastardy. She had tasted the bitter with the sweet. And well you know that after her father's death she suffered many indignities at the hands of her stepmother's new husband."

"I have heard nothing to that effect."

He knew she must have, and her interest amused him. "The bridegroom merely took his fatherly duties too seriously."

"How so?"

"In his zealousness, he visited the Princess in the early morning, while she was still abed, treating her somewhat familiarly."

"How dreadful for her."

He shrugged. "His antics were the household scandal. He'd tickle her, smack her on the rump, kiss her on the mouth, and some such playfulness."

"Small wonder she is evasive when it comes to marriage."

"I doubt that's her real reason," he said, his eyes twinkling with amusement. "They call her the Virgin Queen—and God only knows how she has managed to retain the title. It's no secret that her Master of the Horse thinks himself her royal stud."

"Your jest is crude, my lord. Need I remind you that she is my royal cousin?"

But Mary's attempted severity was lost in a giggle that came bubbling out into laughter. Bothwell joined her, and they sat laughing at Queen Elizabeth's expense.

Everyone was laughing and gossiping about the Virgin Queen's love affair with her Master of the Horse. Just recently the English ambassador, Sir Nicholas Throckmorton, had been forced to make an embarrassed exit from the French Court because of the gossip involving Mistress Dudley's strange death.

Bothwell had heard that there were mysterious circumstances surrounding her untimely departure. Here was Dudley, Elizabeth's favorite, her Master of the Horse, with an inconvenient wife who had obligingly fallen down a flight of stairs and broken her neck. Now there was talk that Elizabeth intended to wed the bereaved widower. To Bothwell's thinking, it was the one thing for a queen to have a lover, and another for her to wed him.

3

In mid-October the Court moved to Orléans, and Bothwell accompanied them. The weather continued mild, and they hunted every day. Francis was often ill and unable to make the strenuous rides, but Mary seemed tireless. It appeared that she had a secret reserve of vitality that burst forth when she climbed into the saddle. Bothwell often found himself watching her with delight as she raced over fields, caught up in the excitement of the chase.

Then the weather turned to a gray autumn chill, and a biting cold east wind heralded the first frost of winter. Freezing temperatures forced the Court indoors, and Bothwell sought another kind of prey. He found it in the company of Mary's ladies, but Fleming remained his favorite.

But a restlessness was slowly creeping in on him; what had seemed good sport and ease at first now wearied him. The tedium of each day had him yearning for action, and Anna was tugging at his conscience. If only for the sake of decency, he felt he should be with her.

Mary and Francis had decided to move on to a more pleasant climate, and a hunting expedition was planned at Chenonceaux for the end of November. Bothwell planned to leave for Flanders then, too.

"It's time I left France," he told Mary one afternoon as they sat talking in her parlor. "If I delay, the storms at sea will keep me here until spring."

"When do you wish to go?"

"The end of this week—when you leave for Chenonceaux, madam."

She seemed angry, or was it disappointment? What difference would his going make to her? She had courtiers aplenty to surround her. Why should one more matter? France was her adopted country; it seemed she would remain here always. Doubtless they would never see each other again.

"Very well," she said, "make your plans. I had hoped you would stay a month more. The hunting at Chenonceaux is excellent this time of year."

She was called away suddenly; Francis was ill again. He had been ill constantly of late, and Mary fretted over him with a mother's devotion.

Bothwell was ready to leave by November 22. The house had been dismantled, and everything was piled on barges waiting to be transported down the Loire.

Bothwell went to Mary to make his last farewell. "Were it not for the threat of storms, it would pleasure me more to stay, madam."

"You would be of little use to me shipwrecked at the bottom of the sea. In any case, it is best you return to Scotland soon."

He hadn't told her about the detour he was taking in Flanders.

The door flew open and Beaton rushed in. She was flushed and breathless. "It is the King, madam," she said. "He is taken suddenly ill and complains of a violent earache."

Mary turned to Bothwell. "Will you come with me?"

There was no trace of command in her voice, only an urgency that begged for help. He followed her down the corridor to Francis' chambers, where he lay on the floor with only a coverlet under him.

Mary knelt down beside Francis and touched her lips to his cheeks. Bothwell saw her eyes cloud with fear as she pressed a hand to his forehead. Unable to speak, Francis lay moaning, his eyes glazed with the agony of pain.

She rose and drew Bothwell aside. "The King is burning with fever," she whispered. "I detected an odor of infection when I bent close to him."

Bothwell had also noticed the putrid smell in the chamber; it smelled faintly of decaying meat.

He said, "There is no sense in alarming yourself needlessly, madam. He has been ill like this before, and well again a day or two later."

Her hand tightened on his arm. "Never like this—the pain seems unbearable. I fear this attack is more serious."

"You cannot be certain until the physicians have made their diagnosis," he said, forcing dispassion into his voice.

His reassurances were beginning to calm her when Queen Catherine and the Cardinal rushed in with the Court physician. They waited in silence until the examination was over. When he had finished, the physician's expression confirmed Mary's fears. An order was issued for the furniture to be carted back to the house, and Francis soon had the comfort of his hastily assembled bed.

4

The household was thrown into an atmosphere of desolate gloom. It was rumored that Francis would never rise from his bed. Mary had asked Bothwell to postpone his departure, and she spent every minute at Francis' bedside. Everyone moved on tiptoe, hardly daring to speak above a whisper. Bothwell fumed inwardly at the useless delay—the boy seemed as good as dead already; he could do nothing to prevent it. He despised the Court for their spurious grief, for he knew how quickly they would desert Mary for the Queen Mother, once Francis was dead.

The mere sight of Catherine de Médicis hovering over her dying son, fairly licking her lips hungrily as she waited for him to die, brought the taste of vomit to Bothwell's mouth. Nor did the Cardinal's worried looks deceive him; he cared nothing for the suffering of Francis or Mary; his main concern was for himself. The Cardinal knew that when Francis died, the De Guise rule would end, and with it would go their exalted state in France.

Francis showed no improvement by the end of the first week. An evil-smelling, poisonous fluid kept oozing from his ear, and the pain had worsened. The stench of his chambers was unbearable—no one entered without a camphor-soaked cloth held close to his nose. All hope was gone, and on the last day of November, Francis fell into delirium.

The Court gates were closed to all visitors; only Mary, his mother, and the Cardinal were allowed in his chambers. Prayers were said throughout Orléans, but he was beyond help. And Bothwell could wait no longer. He sent a note to Mary asking that she see him for only a few minutes. An hour later she summoned him to a sitting room near Francis' apartments.

He was unprepared for what he saw. It was scarcely two weeks since Francis had taken ill, and only two days since he had last seen her, but she looked as though she herself had been ill for months. Her long hair had been hastily pulled back with some pins and hung lifelessly down her back; her eyes, usually so alive and beautiful, were dull and haunted now and cried out for sleep. She wore a simple black gown without adornment, except for a plain gold crucifix that sat in the hollow of her throat.

It was either her pitiful appearance or the growing feeling of confinement—whatever the cause—Bothwell felt suffocated with a sudden need to escape. And yet he wanted desperately to help her. He had the mad impulse to carry her away out to a fresh meadow, where they could both breathe freely in good clean air again.

"You have come to make your farewells," she said.

"My staying is of no avail, madam. I cannot prevent the inevitable."

"It is too late—" Her voice broke on a sob; tears spilled down her cheeks. "I know he loved me in his own way—and I have loved him. It may seem incredible, knowing he was never really a husband. But he was always so kind and thoughtful—he depended upon me so."

Did she think him incapable of pity? He was not so callous that he couldn't understand her tenderness for this dying boy.

"I am not heartless, madam."

"Forgive me, I did not mean to imply—"

Immediately contrite for his quick temper, he said, "It is I who should ask forgiveness."

She tried to smile. "I pray this postponement will not endanger your voyage."

"It will take more than a tempest to rid the world of me."

He got up and went to her, taking her hand in his. He held it for a moment, as though he wanted some of his own strength to flow into her. And for the first time in his life he experienced inadequacy. He could not offer her more words of solace—she had had enough of that.

Finally he released her hand and quickly left. For a moment the silent hall filled with the sound of his heavy boots, then silence returned—and he was gone.

CHAPTER IV

1

Bothwell heard of the King's death in Rouen; Francis' brother became Charles IX, and Mary, now Dowager Queen, stepped down to give her mother-in-law precedence during the young King's minority. But there was still Scotland where Mary could rule in her own right.

Bothwell knew that Mary's uncles would not permit her to stay a widow long; they were already negotiating a new match with another Catholic power. The De Guises had risen to power through Mary; now there were even greater prospects on the horizon—Spain perhaps—and the Cardinal could be counted upon to take advantage of the opportunity.

Bothwell was back with Anna before Christmas. He had expected to find her misshapen, for she was nearly six months with child, but when he saw her with only a light robe on she was slender as ever.

He eyed her suspiciously. "What's happened?" he asked. "Did you miscarry? Your belly is flat as the floor."

Anna laughed nervously. "I was mistaken," she said lamely.

His eyes turned hard and brittle; the little vixen had duped him. It had been a cleverly devised ruse, and he had been taken in by it. Rage came up hot in his throat; he fought the impulse to hit her, to strike out at the triumph he saw in her eyes.

"Did you also lie to your family? Do they think you are carrying my child?"

"No."

"Then why didn't they object to your going away with me?"

"You were leaving for France, and I went to my father to confess that I loved you. I told him that if he did not let me go with you, I would run away—and if he brought me back, I would wed no other man."

"He gave in to you that easily?"

"Not until I promised to find a way to make you wed me. He was worried about being saddled with an unwed daughter." She hesitated and glanced fearfully at him. "It was my final argument that won him over—I told him he wouldn't have to provide me with a dowry."

"Aye, there's something that would appeal to him."

She nodded, and tears flooded her eyes. "I did it because I love you. Even if you never wed me, I would sooner be with you than take one of those clouts my father would have me wed."

Suddenly he saw the situation as comical; he had always fancied himself as something of an expert on women—so sure he knew all their devious little ways, their deceptive minds. Now he had fallen prey to the oldest deception in the world; she had played him for a fool—and more power to her for succeeding.

He began to chuckle. His amusement grew until it became loud, raucous laughter. Believing the danger gone, Anna joined in. Great tears of relief spilled down her cheeks—but her laughter froze when she saw him come toward her. His amusement was gone—only a ghost of humor remained—and now Anna saw something in his eyes that made her shrink back in fear.

Swiftly Bothwell reached out and tore the robe from her. She stood there shivering, too frightened to move. He pulled her close, his kisses bruised her mouth, and one hand twisted her hair into a huge coil, holding her in a steel-like grip. Then, abruptly, he released her, flinging her backward onto the bed.

She started to cry out, but his body on hers smothered the sound.

"You came with me because you lied," he snarled. "For that I shall give you pause to think ere you deceive again."

It was over quickly; he had taken her violently—without emotion. Every touch had left a bruise; his satisfaction alone mattered. Yet, despite his brutality, she had not cried out or pleaded with him to desist.

He watched her cross the room to a table that held a basin of water. She was such an odd mixture; she had taken a great risk—he might have discovered her deception sooner and left her stranded, without sustenance. Even now she could not be certain he would not desert her. But she had been willing to chance it, and now that her scheme was known, she had taken the consequences without a whimper.

Anna dipped a cloth into the water and bathed a large welt on her arm; then she applied the cloth to her swollen lips. He had not intended to injure her. Now he thought he had been too brutal.

"Come here," he said.

She sat down on the bed while he examined the bruises; they were only pressure marks where his fingers had come down on her too hard—they would be gone by morning.

"There," he said, caressing her shoulder, "you'll live. In the future, however, you'd do well to remember that I do not take well to deceit." Then, because he was curious: "What would you have done if I had guessed the truth sooner? Didn't it occur to you that I might leave you stranded?"

"Aye, it occurred to me."

"Were you not afraid? How well do you think you'd fare alone?"

"Well enough. A clever woman needn't be lonely for long."

Incredulous, he asked, "Would you become a whore?"

She tossed her head defiantly. "Why not? What odds if I give my body to one man or many? Besides, even that would have been a welcome change from the watchful eyes of my parents."

"At last we come to the heart of the matter. You wanted to escape your family's domination."

"In part—but more because I wanted to be with you."

He laughed and pushed her away. "Fetch me some wine. Rape gives a man a powerful thirst."

She snorted. "Rape indeed!" She was halfway out the door when she turned and said, "If you think your brutal lovemaking has taught me a lesson, it has not—I loved every minute of it."

Agape, he stared at the closed door, then his laughter came bellowing out.

When she returned with the wine, he tossed a small felt pouch at her. "Here's a little trinket I found in Paris," he said. "Something you can add to your collection of gauds."

She undid the knot and took out a small silver medallion encrusted with seed pearls. Her eyes lighted with pleasure. "Then you did think of me while you were away."

"Now and then, but don't fill your head with meaningless fancies—it denotes nothing."

She went to kiss him. "One day you may regret that you could not care for me more," she said.

2

Bothwell returned to Scotland at the end of February. He had given Anna a choice, and she decided to go with him rather than return to her family. She wept, pleaded, then tried to cajole him when he told her they would not be living together, but she finally accepted his terms. She would have her own household, servants, and an allowance, and Bothwell would see her when he found the time.

Conditions on the Border had become chaotic during his

absence, and his first order of business was reestablishing his authority there. Next he tried to convoke a parliament in Mary's name, but it proved an immediate failure. The opposing party sent James Stuart to coax Mary back to Scotland, and Bothwell had no doubt that she would be an easy target. She was softhearted and wanted desperately to believe in her half brother's loyalty. And once James' mission had been accomplished, Bothwell knew his own influence with Mary would be on the wane.

Early in June, Mary summoned Bothwell to France; as her great admiral, he was to take charge of her return voyage to Scotland.

Mary was at the window looking out at the courtyard when he entered her chambers. She turned and smiled. Immediately, he detected a slight change in her. Strangely, sorrow had enhanced her loveliness.

She said, "When last we met you were in somewhat of a hurry, my lord."

"Aye, madam—certain matters of pressing importance called me away."

"Yes, we heard," she said. "I believe her name is Anna Throndsen."

"We must each judge the importance of our own affairs, madam. But I have been busy enough on Your Majesty's business in Scotland. Unfortunately, those of the opposition saw that with me in charge they'd not have their own way with things, so they sent Lord James to coax you back to rule—in their interests."

She stiffened and said abruptly, "What are your plans for my voyage?"

"How soon can you be ready to leave Paris?"

"Before the month is out. There is no reason to delay, now

my mind is made up." Then, sadly, she said, "I have come to think of France as my own country—I thought never to leave it."

"I grant you the beauties of France, madam, but your own Realm boasts of its own beauty."

"How can anything so savage be beautiful? Strangely, most Scotsmen share your pride of country."

"I fear you mistake greed and ambition for patriotism, madam. This pride you speak of has inspired your nobility with a fondness for anarchy. Scotland has a history of little kindness to its kings."

"History belongs to the past, my lord. The future appears more hopeful. My brother not only urges my return, but he also promises his party's support."

What he had feared was true—she had already placed her trust in the Bastard.

"May I suggest that you go cautiously before trusting anyone, madam? Lord James' sympathy with England makes a strange companion for your interests."

"Are you telling me not to return to my kingdom?"

"No, for I too urge your return, but take care whom you trust."

"I am aware of the enmity that exists between you and my brother. Like you, he makes no secret of his feelings. But I am certain that your differences can be dissolved in the interest of Scotland."

"Then I envy you your optimism, madam."

Impatiently, she said, "We will discuss this at greater length another time; for the present I am more concerned with my journey."

He made her an ironic bow. "As you wish, madam. I have three ships with me; they will serve as a spearhead for your French galleys."

"Do you anticipate trouble?"

"No, but there's no harm in caution, since Queen Elizabeth has refused to issue you a safe conduct. What reason does she give for it?"

"Because I have not signed the Treaty of Edinburgh. I've told her envoy, Throckmorton, that I have no one here to counsel me—therefore I can sign nothing without first consulting my ministers."

"Well said, madam. Let her know that she may not bully you."

Softly she said, "It is a chilling thought that before I even enter my Realm, I must spar with its closest neighbor."

Bothwell was ready to sail when Mary arrived in Calais on the eleventh of August. He was anxious to have her start, for he had had news that Elizabeth had dispatched a fleet in the Channel.

When he came into Mary's room at the inn, he found Throckmorton with her.

"Lord Bothwell," she called, "perhaps you can help Sir Nicholas to see that I can sign nothing without proper counsel. It appears that my safe conduct in English waters depends solely upon that issue."

She was obviously straining to appear gay and unconcerned. Bothwell wondered if Throckmorton's shrewd eyes saw through her pretense.

"Your Majesty misunderstands," Throckmorton said. "I do not wish to imply that my mistress has refused on those grounds—only that she would likely be more disposed toward hastening your letters of travel if the Treaty of Edinburgh were ratified. But more likely it is the fault of some underling that Your Majesty's letters have not come."

"I find it strange that an underling should have such a heavy hand in the affairs of Scotland's queen," Bothwell observed coolly. "Can it be that it was also this cipher who ordered the embarkation of your fleet?"

"I assure you, my lord, there is not the slightest connection between the two," Throckmorton said, avoiding Bothwell's penetrating glare. "It is mere coincidence that our fleet is at sea now."

Bothwell sent him a bland smile. "In any event, sir, *I* can guarantee Her Majesty's safe passage, if your mistress will not."

A din of silence filled the room. Then Mary said, "You may inform your mistress that the Queen of Scotland does not require her permission to cross the sea."

Throckmorton rose and went to kneel before Mary. "May the Almighty guide you safely toward your destination, madam," he said, waiting to be dismissed.

Mary waved him out. There were tears in her eyes when she turned to Bothwell, but he knew they were tears of anger—not fear.

"I could almost pity Throckmorton," he said. "He is embarrassed by Elizabeth's spitefulness."

"I suppose this is merely a taste of what lies ahead for me," Mary said. "Doubtless she means to frustrate me at every turn."

"Elizabeth is driven by many things, madam—insecurity for one, jealousy of you for another."

"Perhaps, if we met, she would realize that I wish her no harm. I have asked nothing unreasonable of her—only that she name me her heir."

"And she in turn asks that you relinquish all future claims to her throne. It's too great a concession for her. In her eyes naming you her successor constitutes a direct threat to her life."

"I shall never relinquish that which is mine by right." Then, brightening, she said, "Why should I dwell on what she might do? My next marriage may take me far from Scotland and England."

He knew she was speaking of the Cardinal's negotiations with Spain. Her uncle hoped to make a match between her and King Philip's demented son, Don Carlos.

"Would you enter into wedlock with another of God's deformities, madam, merely to escape your own Realm?"

She glanced up sharply. "How dare you suggest I am a coward? It is not escape I seek; Spain has power—Scotland has not. I could bring that power to my Realm through a union with Don Carlos."

"I grant you, Elizabeth would become a meek adversary with Spain to back you, but it would also bring the Inquisition to your Realm—a far greater horror to your people than England had ever been."

"I have never sought to rule men's consciences."

"Precious little you would have to say about it, once Phillip got a foothold in Scotland."

"Then what would you have me do? You tell me I cannot trust those who now govern in my name, and when I seek strength elsewhere, you find fault with that too. What alternative have you for me?"

"Take the reigns of government yourself, madam. Select a group of men who can be trusted to support you."

"With yourself at the head of that group, my lord?"

"You could do worse. English gold and interests do not guide me. A bare six months ago you appeared to share my opinion, madam."

"Do you profess to be the only honest man in Scotland, my lord?"

"No, there are still a few who remain loyal—but *damn* few."

"Your concern is touching, but I wonder why you trouble yourself so with my quarrels."

"I have risked too much already, madam, to abandon them now."

Exasperated, she said, "Your conceit is intolerable."

"Is your brother's faithlessness more tolerable, madam? While he pats your hand and murmurs assurances into your ear, he stuffs English pounds into his pockets. Perhaps you prefer that to the truth."

"For the moment, I would prefer that you go."

He was furious when he left her and walked the streets blindly. How could she be so witless, so blind to the past? How long would she allow Scotland to be torn and rent by traitors? Scotland was not a plaything to be tossed about in royal marriage beds. Her mother's struggles and sacrifices, his own, would all be for naught if she continued on this course.

He was still angry the next morning when he strolled down to the pier to watch the crew load Mary's belongings on the ships. The sun's coppery rays shone into a glass mirror that leaned against the rails, waiting to be stored below. Two men carried one of her ornately painted beds up the gangway; there were forty-five beds in all, besides chests filled with gowns and footgear and cloaks.

As he lounged against a mooring post, Bothwell's thoughts anchored on Mary. She had been spoiled all her life, she was used to being pampered, but Scotland would change her soon enough. He grinned maliciously as he envisioned the corpulent Huntly with his fleshy jowels, or Arran, slovenly and emaciated and half-witted, besides. They would not ply her with romantic verse like her French poets, nor would they speak the ugly truth to her as he had. They would lie and dissemble and plot her ruin every chance they had. But if she was so determined to trust herself to the wrong men, then let her!

Sleep evaded Bothwell that night; finally, he got up and went for a walk along the beach. The town was quiet, except for the sound of water slapping the wharf and the creaking of galleys bobbing on the current. Somewhere in the distance the town crier droned the hour as Bothwell went down to the beach.

He watched the waves lapping against the sandy shore for a while, until a slight movement up ahead caught his eyes. At first glance he thought it was a mooring used by the small fishing boats; then, approaching it, he saw it was the outline of a woman. She turned and stepped back, and he sensed her terror.

"Who's there?" he called.

There was a sharp intake of breath. "Lord Bothwell," she said, relief in her voice. "You had me frightened half to death."

What was she doing out here, alone, this time of night?

"This is a strange hour to find Your Majesty abroad. Is no one with you?"

"No, I am alone. I could not sleep, and a walk seemed better than tossing about in my stuffy room. And you, my lord, do you usually parade about at this hour?"

"Rarely, madam, although I will admit this hour is no stranger to me—often because I've not been to bed yet."

She laughed, and he thought: *She is quick to forgive.* Had she forgotten their quarrel of yesterday?

"Look!" she called suddenly. "A falling star. Is it true that a wish made on it will be fulfilled?"

"So they say—but it's nothing I'd count on."

"My wish is already made."

He smiled at her childlike belief. "What did you wish for, madam?"

"That I may return to France soon."

"Is Scotland so fearsome to you?"

"You yourself have told me what I may expect. Should those prospects cheer me?"

Gently, he said, "Come, madam, this brown study you're in can serve no purpose. You will likely have the lot of them eating out of your hands in no time."

He was thankful for the darkness that hid his face, for he

shared her doubts and wondered what the future held for her.

They walked along the shore in silence. Daylight began to appear far out on the water's edge. Mary stopped to look at a row of tiny stone houses that lined the pier.

"They will be my last view of France," she said.

"Your Majesty will find a more exciting view when we sail into Leith Harbor. You'll see no flatlands there; the land breaks away suddenly and thrusts itself upward in peaks, the waters run swift, and the moors with their bogs and bracken have an untamable beauty. I wager you will have forgotten France before winter sets in."

"There is a wager you are certain to lose, my lord."

"Of course, if you hold fast to your fancies...." He shrugged and let the words trail off. "But you must decide when we are to sail, madam. The English ships are still at sea; delay only increases the danger."

"I had hoped Elizabeth would give her safe conduct." She sighed. "I am finally reconciled that she will not."

"In that case, why not begin the voyage on tomorrow's early tide?"

She nodded. "Tomorrow then. Now I had best return to my inn before I am missed."

3

On August 19, five days after leaving Calais, Mary landed in Leith. Good winds and a calm sea had carried her ships to Scotland in record time. But Mary saw nothing of the view Bothwell had promised her, for the world seemed shrouded in a thick, gray curtain of fog that day. Even Bothwell, well accustomed to these heavy mists, confessed that he had never seen the like of this haar, and to make matters worse, not one of the nobility had arrived to welcome her. Only a few curious townspeople stood on the wharf to catch a glimpse of the elegantly dressed ladies and gentlemen.

"You had best wait for your escort indoors, madam," Bothwell told her. "This weather has been known to chill a body to death."

Mary glanced about the desolate seaport. "Where would you suggest? Every house appears to be in ruin."

"You can thank the English for that; they did a thorough job of it in the siege of '60. But there is still a house or two left in good repair. I've sent someone to Captain Lamb's house—it's small and boasts of few comforts, but you can keep warm and dry there."

He took Mary and her ladies to the tiny stone house and waited only long enough to see them settled before starting to leave.

"I thought you would accompany me to Edinburgh," Mary said.

"That was my intention, madam, before the galleys bearing your livestock and the one carrying Lord Eglinton were reported missing."

"Do you think they were captured by the English?"

"That's my guess. I am off to search for them now."

Bothwell did not see Mary again for three weeks, when he came to the Court to take his seat on the Privy Council. But after a few days of close contact with Lord James and his partisans, he had had enough of court life.

"I can do you more good on the Border, madam," he told Mary. "Besides, the company I am forced to keep here puts a strain on my temper."

"When do you wish to leave?"

"Before the week is out."

"I shall not keep you from your duties—even your enemies commend you for the miracles you have worked there."

"Do they now? And by way of reward, Lord James is to succeed me as lieutenant of the Border."

She colored. "I had hoped that you and James would share the duties amiably."

"I think not, madam. I doubt that he and I could share anything—outside of the enmity we now bear each other."

It rankled to think that in these few short weeks the Bastard had succeeded in robbing him of his post.

"This love of feuds among my nobles must cease," Mary said firmly. "How can there be unity in the Realm when the men who govern it will not unite amongst themselves?"

"You pose a difficult question, madam. I have no solution for it."

"There is something you could do, if you really had a mind to. Make peace with Arran."

"To what ends, madam? The man is clean daft—there is no dealing with him. Besides, we are presently embroiled in a heated dispute over the lands of Melrose Abbey."

She frowned. "So I am told. I would call it more than a dispute when armed men are employed to collect the rents."

"Less severe methods would scarcely bring the desired results."

"No doubt. But it occurs to me that the tenants may take another view since they are forced to pay rent to both you and Arran."

He grinned. "If the tenants have any objections, they've not ventured to enlighten me with them."

"And small wonder, too. In view of such strong-arm tactics, my lord, I too would be loath to object."

"Confound it, madam, am I to stand meekly by and let my enemies rob me of everything? Melrose Abbey was left me by your mother, and I'll not let it go without a fight."

She turned on him in fury. "Then you leave me no choice. I cannot have you and Arran bringing your feud to Court. You need not wait for the end of the week—you may leave now. And do not return until I send for you."

He knew that she could not banish Arran from Court, for he might not obey. But she could always be sure of James Hepburn.

Autumn came to the Border in a riot of color; the moors lay deep in purple-brown tufts of heather, bordered by hedgerows of scarlet rowanberries, and early frosts turned the leaves to russets and golds. On the dark lonely nights the earth trembled under the rude intrusion of galloping horsemen. As other men slept safe in their beds, Bothwell and his moss-troopers patrolled the Border from their far-stretched outposts.

Early in October, Mary summoned Bothwell to Edinburgh. During his absence he had kept in touch with her by letter, but now she needed him at the Council table.

His second day back, Mary asked him to attend an informal evening of music. After an early supper he went to the small turret room just off her bedchamber. She had set this aside to use as a supping room where she could entertain favored guests.

Holyrood had undergone many changes since his last visit; the evil-smelling rushes had been swept out, and in their place were the beautiful Turkey carpets that Mary had brought from France. Gracefully carved gilt chairs with brocaded cushions replaced the old oak chairs; exquisite tapestries covered the gray stone walls, serving the dual purpose of beautifying the halls and keeping out the drafts.

Mary greeted him warmly; she appeared to have forgotten their last meeting. "I have also invited James and Lethington," she told him. "If you are to work together successfully, past grievances must be set aside."

"I fear you have permitted sentiment to override good judgment, madam. Bringing us together could end disastrously."

"Will you not try—for my sake?" she pleaded.

He sighed hopelessly; would she never learn? But her plea had touched him and he gave in. "Very well, madam, tonight you shall see in me the most genial of guests. I shall make every effort to be civil to them."

"Given half a chance you and James may even become friends."

"Indeed? I would sooner cultivate the friendship of a wild boar, madam."

She gave a cry of exasperation. "Oh, you are intolerable. You will not do one thing to please me."

"Isn't it enough that I've given my word to behave tonight?"

She left him abruptly and went to speak with Lethington and Fleming. The music had begun, and Bothwell joined Mary Livingston at the window seat. The lute player's basso-alto voice lamented a young man's unrequited love for a beautiful maiden.

Thus far, the purpose of the gathering was a dismal failure. James sat in morose silence, speaking only when necessary—and that in clipped one-word sentences. Lethington, though not silent, gave his attention to Fleming. Bothwell kept his distance by showing sudden interest in Livingston. And Mary, in the role of mediator, made every effort to engage them all in conversation.

Finally, she threw her hands up in despair and had the musicians sent away. She turned on the belligerent threesome. "Is this the way you mean to keep your words? Not one of you has even attempted to ease the tension. We begin a new era in Scotland, but you, my lords, still choose to live in the past." She paused to look from one to the other expectantly.

Lethington said, "My lords, let us at least try to put an end to this enmity for Her Majesty's sake."

Grudgingly, Bothwell said, "I am willing."

"And I will pledge my friendship," James offered half-heartedly.

Mary smiled. "That is all I ask, my lords. Come, let us drink to this new friendship."

The musicians were called back, conversation flowed more freely, and to Mary's delight, Bothwell and James went off to talk.

"When do you go to Jedburgh for Justice Court?" Bothwell asked.

"Next month. I had thought to ride justice on the outlaws before winter frosts and the Christmas revels are upon us. Perhaps you will accompany me, since it is by your efforts these men were taken."

Bothwell nodded. He'd not trust his lambs to James' brand of justice.

Fleming came to tell Bothwell that Mary wanted to speak to him.

When they were alone, Mary said, "I know this hasn't been easy for you, but I felt certain that once you and James came together an agreement would be reached."

He smiled. "Your Majesty is a born optimist. One evening of civility does not make a lifelong friendship."

"This is only the beginning. Who knows but you and James may even come to like each other."

"I doubt that, madam. Our views are too opposite."

"Men are all alike; if they disagree politically, they cannot be friends. You might take an example from Queen Elizabeth and myself. We do not see eye to eye on many things—but we exert every effort toward amity."

And women, he thought, *they are always compelled to play the peacemaker.* Why could she not leave well enough alone?

"I'd not be too quick to trust in Elizabeth's overtures of friendship. Your Majesty had best go warily in dealing with her."

"You are suspicious of everyone. But never mind now; what of you and James? I saw you talking to him awhile ago."

"Aye, we have decided to attend Justice Court together."

"There, you see," she exclaimed triumphantly, "just as I

predicted. All it needed was someone to bring you to your senses. If only your enmity with Arran could be resolved so easily. This dispute over Melrose Abbey only widens the breach between you."

"I've already done something about that. My claim has been transferred to your half brother, Lord Robert, madam."

She rewarded him with a dazzling smile. "Now I am cheered, my lord. With the new year only two months off, we may all look forward to better times."

Again he was struck by her childlike faith.

4

Hoping to establish a more firm friendship between Bothwell and Lord James, Mary sent them on a diplomatic mission to England. Though somewhat strained, their truce continued, and the journey went without incident. But another of Mary's half brothers, Lord John Stuart, came suddenly into the foreground.

While on progress to the English border, he constantly jockeyed for a position near Bothwell. Mealtimes, he held the seat next to him and, on seeing Bothwell, would call, "Over here, my lord, I've saved a place for you."

Doubtless Lord John had good cause to behave so strangely, and Bothwell meant to find out what it was. Of Mary's three base brothers, Bothwell liked Johnnie the best; he was jovial, lighthearted, and always ready for a prank. But his odd behavior made Bothwell suspicious.

Lord John played host to the party the night before they returned to Edinburgh. At supper he reserved the seat of honor for Bothwell, who later took him aside to ask some questions.

"Look here," Bothwell said, taking a firm hold on Johnnie's arm, "what are you up to? What is this sudden attachment you've developed for me?"

Johnnie turned bright pink. "Why, I er—"

"None of your hedging—out with it."

"The truth is—it's about your sister—Lady Janet."

"Well—what about her?"

"I would like to court her—with your permission, of course."

Bothwell roared with laughter. So, that's what's been fashing the rascal. Well, he'd not make it easy for him.

"I don't know, Johnnie, my lad," he said hesitantly. "It's true there's royal blood in you—still, you're *natural* born." He paused to study him thoughtfully. "What will you do if I don't give my permission?"

"Wed her in spite of you," he said. "Besides, she has already accepted me."

"So, the two of you have talked it over, eh? Her promise is worthless without my consent."

"Good Christ, Bothwell—"

"Calm yourself man, I'll not stand in the way of such ardor. Wed her if she'll have you—and I'll give you a wedding to do you proud."

Johnnie let out a whoop of joy and called everyone to the table.

"I have an announcement to make," he said, letting his glance come to rest on his brother James. "Lord Bothwell has given his consent for his sister, the Lady Janet, to become my wife."

A loud cheer went up, and everyone raised his cup to the future bridegroom, glad for the excuse to down another drink. Only one man present appeared to dislike the news—Lord James. He remained seated, looking down his long nose as though he could not push the false geniality of the past three days another step. His hazel eyes betrayed his anger; his long, grasping fingers smoothed his thick beard with irritable strokes.

At first, Bothwell wished that Johnnie had waited to announce the betrothal; now that he saw James' reaction it suited him perfectly. It was a delicious piece of irony for the Bastard to bear. How it must rankle to have a Hepburn for his future sister-in-law.

"You are all invited to the wedding," Bothwell offered with an enormous feeling of well-being.

If Janet wanted Johnnie, then she would have him. He knew Mary loved matchmaking, and her approval would guarantee the union despite James' opposition to it.

Then, directing his attention to James, Bothwell said, "Where is the elder brother's blessing? Come, my lord, will you not drink to the couple's happiness?"

As though roused from a dream, James raised his cup to salute Johnnie. "Every happiness," he said through stiff lips.

This moment of triumph was too good for Bothwell to lose. Smiling, he nudged James. "The Stuarts could do with a bit of Border blood to strengthen them, eh, my lord?"

James' answer was barely audible. "Aye—a good match."

Mary clapped her hands delightedly. "Such happy news, my lord," she said. "Shall I be included among the wedding guests?"

"Indeed, madam. I had hoped Your Majesty would wish to attend."

"As though I would miss Johnnie's wedding. And I will stay the night—if you will have me."

"Crichton will be honored, madam. At least this trip has not been entirely wasted."

Mary arched her eyebrows quizzically. "Surely relations between you and James have improved."

"To some extent, madam. But we are not deluded by it."

"You *will* sign the truce we spoke of?"

He nodded. "I have also decided to leave next week with Lord James on his progress through the Border."

"Then I shall continue to hope. If you can work together in harmony, who knows what may happen next."

"I would rather not venture a guess, madam," he said, looking heavenward in mock horror.

Bothwell and James were gone a month and returned early in December. There had been an incident in their absence that gave the Court great alarm. Arran had come to Edinburgh with talk of kidnapping Mary and holding her prisoner. The palace guard was put on the alert and the watch at Mary's apartments doubled. But after an all-night vigil, Arran never appeared and everyone could relax.

"The man is plain daft," Bothwell said. "He should be taken in ward before he does real hurt to someone."

"He has been somewhat disturbed of late," James admitted, "but he is completely harmless."

"Just the same, he bears watching," Bothwell warned. "There is no telling what he may take into his head to do next."

Later that day Mary sent for Bothwell. He had heard that a solemn requiem mass was to be held for the first anniversary of Francis' death. He expected her to ask him to attend, but he had already made up his mind to refuse.

"Everyone will be there," Mary argued. "It is such a small request."

"You ask tolerance for your faith, madam; I ask the same for mine. I have always refused to attend the mass; why should I do so now?"

"Could you not make an exception this once? Every nobleman will wear mourning for the occasion—regardless of his religion—you will not even do that much for me."

Scornfully, he said, "Why should I prink myself in black to mourn a boy who has been dead a year, madam?"

"Oh, you are so—so intolerable," she cried.

"Your Majesty seems always to find me intolerable," he commented with infuriating humor.

Quietly, as though exerting every effort to control her anger, she said, "Go!"

Admittedly, he was irreligious, but in a fashion, he considered himself more steadfast in his beliefs than others who were willing to kill and destroy for the new faith, then attend a mass to ingratiate themselves with the Queen. They called him a Papist now, because of his loyalty to the Crown; what more did she want of him?

5

During Christmas revels, Arran again became a principal in another incident; this time it involved Bothwell. Aware of Arran's pretended piousness, and that he was one of Knox's prized adherents, Bothwell exposed him as a fraud by surprising him one night at a brothel.

Eventually it was brought to Mary's attention, and despite her vast amusement, she voiced her displeasure with both of them. In Bothwell's opinion, that should have ended it, but it did not. Now the Hamiltons felt the honor of their kinsman had suffered a serious blemish, and they sought reparation. On Christmas Eve, Bothwell had warning that Gavin Hamilton had rounded up three hundred men and was planning to waylay him. Bothwell in turn sent his regrets to Mary, with a full explanation, then he slipped out of the palace and managed to assemble five hundred men of his own—but his message to Mary saved the day.

Just as the bloody engagement was about to break, the common bell sounded and armed men, commanded by Lord

James and the Earl of Huntly, rode out of the palace to stop the onslaught. At first they tried to reason both sides to quietness, then realizing the futility in that, they demanded the street cleared under pain of death. Here was an argument that neither side could ignore, and peace was restored within half an hour.

Bothwell and De Châtelherault, Arran's father, were summoned to appear before Mary on Christmas Day. Bothwell all but laughed to see himself, a Protestant, standing at the head of so many Catholics, while his opponent, Gavin Hamilton, a Catholic, stood with as many Protestants. The Duke admitted that the attack had been organized by his kinsmen, but he professed ignorance of any foreknowledge of it.

Mary made several attempts to end the feud, but her efforts were useless. The Duke demanded that Bothwell withdraw all past charges he had made against Arran, "publicly, to the sound of trumpet."

Bothwell roared, "His demands are outrageous, madam. I will never comply with those terms."

It was an impossible situation; neither Bothwell nor De Châtelherault would give in, and the presence of armed Hepburns and Hamiltons would certainly end in battle on the streets. Mary's position was scarcely enviable, Bothwell admitted—one of them had to be banished from Court.

She turned to Bothwell; her eyes held a last-minute appeal. But he remained obdurate. At last she said, "You leave me no choice, my lords. Since you refuse to settle your differences peaceably, I am forced to a decision. I cannot permit both of you to remain—it will inevitably end in bloodshed. Therefore, you, my lord Bothwell, and your men, will leave town immediately."

A smile flickered on the Duke's lips. As always, Mary had taken the least troublesome way out. She knew that whatever her decision, Bothwell would obey—she could not be sure of the

Duke. And yet, her decision bore every indication of a farce, for everyone knew that Bothwell had intended to leave town in a day or two to begin arrangements for his sister's wedding.

If Mary's ineffectual severity amused others, it certainly did Bothwell, for he was seen to cover a smile as he knelt before her. But he was also enraged because she had used him again to placate his enemies.

Janet's wedding took place the first week in January; it was a grand affair, though Bothwell had nearly gone to staves to carry it off. Mary attended and stayed the night, as she had promised. And when Bothwell saw her off in the morning she made one last appeal to him.

"The incident of last month still disturbs me," she said. "I would rest so much easier if you and Arran made peace."

"Peace is such a dull existence, madam," he teased.

"Will you not give it some thought?"

He turned serious. "Aye, madam, I may indeed—if only to save the expense I must bear on account of it."

CHAPTER V

1

On a dark wintry night, early in March, a tall, heavily cloaked man made his way up the High Street. His boots crunched into the fresh-fallen snow, leaving a telltale mark of the path he took. He came to Warriston's Close, mounted the forestairs to a four-storied house and knocked loudly.

Slowly the door opened, and a thin, high-pitched voice inquired, "Aye, who comes to call at this hour of night?"

He peered into the dimly lighted hallway at a shriveled, middle-aged woman whose beaky nose and small, beady eyes put him in mind of a sparrow. "It is Lord Bothwell, to see Master Knox," he said.

"It is late, my lord. He is at work on Sunday's sermon."

He pushed her aside. "Announce me to your master."

She walked away mumbling about decent folk being in bed and disappeared toward the back of the house. Seconds later she was back, with Knox following close behind.

Knox's face registered astonishment. "Master Barron told me Your Lordship would seek me out," he said, "but not this soon."

"Now seems as good a time as any," Bothwell said.

The woman was still there scrutinizing Bothwell.

"Come, Your Lordship," Knox said, throwing her a reproachful look. "Let us go to my study where we can talk privately."

Bothwell took a stool near the fire and glanced about the room. It was small and cozy, furnished with a few stools and one oversized armchair that stood behind an oak writing table. A fire crackled in the hearth and threw its light on the opposite wall, which was hung with a small tapestry of Jesus delivering the Sermon on the Mount. He turned to look at Knox and was put in mind of a Hebrew prophet; he could vision him atop Mount Sinai, his long, scraggly gray beard whipped by winds, his thunderous voice prophesying doom.

Bothwell opened the conversation. "Since I am Master Barron's chief creditor, he is understandably anxious to see a good conclusion from this meeting."

"A most reverent gentleman, Master Barron," Knox said piously. "He told me something of Your Lordship's financial difficulties."

"Precisely why I am here. My feud with the Earl of Arran compels me to keep a large number of men in my employ. This, as you can see, will eventually destroy what is left of my estate—to say nothing of the losses Master Barron will suffer."

Knox clucked his tongue sympathetically. "My lord," he said, "would to God that I had counsel and judgment to comfort and relieve you. I have borne a good mind to your house; my father and grandfather have served Your Lordship's predecessors. Some of my kinsmen have even died under their standards. This is part of the obligation of our Scots kindness. Therefore, my counsel is that you begin at God."

It was quite a concession for Knox to admit that Bothwell was his overlord. Ordinarily he was quick to deny that any man ranked above him. But his advice was useless.

"It's not preaching I'm after," Bothwell said, getting up to go.

Knox raised a restraining hand. "As for me," he said quickly, "if you will continue in Godliness, Your Lordship shall command me as boldly as any that serves Your Lordship."

Bothwell sat down again. "Then I ask that you approach the Earl of Arran to see if he is of a mind to end our enmity. If Arran and I made up our quarrel I could live at Court with only a page and a few servants, and so save expenses."

"If Your Lordship is in earnest, I shall do all that is in my power to bring about a happy conclusion."

"A swift conclusion will be to my greater satisfaction," Bothwell said. He felt certain that if anyone could make Arran see reason, Knox was the man for it.

Toward the end of the month Knox performed the service asked of him. On the twenty-fourth of March, 1562, Bothwell and his kinsman, the Laird of Riccarton, went to the Hamilton town house in Edinburgh to make his peace with Arran. He was ushered into the common room ceremoniously, where Arran, Gavin Hamilton, and Knox waited to receive him.

Arran came forward and embraced him. "Words do little," he said, in a voice bordering on hysteria. "If the hearts are upright, no ceremony is needed."

Bothwell disengaged himself from Arran's hold and nodded.

Knox could not let his chance to speak pass. "Now, my lords," he admonished them, "God has brought you together by the labor of a simple man. I know my labors are already taken in evil part, but because I have the testimony of a good conscience, I the more patiently bear the misreports and wrongful judgment of men."

Gossip flooded Edinburgh within hours after the feud ended. No one believed his eyes when he saw Bothwell and Arran, so recently embroiled in hatred, walk down the High Street chatting amiably. A day later they were seen dining together, then hunting—they even paid a visit to Arran's father, the Duke de Châtelherault.

Three days following the truce, Bothwell asked Arran to his house for supper. They spoke of trifles during the meal, then after the table had been cleared they took their drinks to the fireplace, and Arran's manner changed.

"You have served the Queen well these past years," he said thoughtfully. "First her mother, now her."

"Aye, my loyalty to the Crown is no secret."

"But where has it profited you? Everything promised to you has been given to the royal bastards." He named it all, the lieutenancy, Dunbar Castle, Melrose Abbey, the lot. "Others enjoy the rewards that should be yours."

"I've asked no rewards."

"While you and I have risked our necks, those who are her enemies enjoy her favor. There is no one closer to the Queen now than Lord James and Lethington. They counsel her on all matters." Arran's voice had become shrill; he seemed to be losing control of it.

Testily, Bothwell asked, "Who else would you have advise her?"

"Myself, of course. Everyone knows the Queen is mad for love of me. You have only to see her when she speaks to me."

"Did she tell you that?"

"She didn't have to, I know. Oh, you will deny it; everyone does. Even she denies it—but I know, I know."

His eyes had taken on a wild look; clearly Arran was speaking out of his head. He raved about the Queen and his love for her; he kept repeating that she was too young to know her mind. Then he turned to Bothwell as though a thought had crossed his mind.

"She needs a husband—a man to order her affairs," he said. "You are my friend now, Bothwell. Will you help me win my suit with her?"

It was useless to argue with Arran in his present state. "We can talk of this later," Bothwell said. "Go home now, get a good night's rest—it will look different to you in the morning." He got up. "Come, I will see you safely to your father's house."

Fear clouded Arran's eyes. "No! Not my father's house. I don't want to go there," he pleaded.

Bothwell was losing patience; he longed to be rid of him. "Then where will you go?" he asked.

"To Knox—take me to Knox."

"It's late, you can see him tomorrow."

"No, I must see him tonight. There is something I must tell him—tonight."

Bothwell sighed wearily. "All right, to Knox then, but I'll not go in with you."

"No—no. I must see him alone—alone."

Bothwell called Paris to have the horses saddled and helped Arran into his cloak. Arran had sunk into deep silence; he permitted himself to be guided out to the horses. They rode up the High Street, dark and quiet at this hour. There were no people about, only the sentries at the Netherbow and a few loitering sluts.

They halted in front of Knox's house, and Bothwell watched Arran dismount and tether his horse. He waited for him to go inside, then he left. Arran was Knox's problem now; let him have the care.

2

The bay of hounds called ahead to warn the hunters of their find. Bothwell spurred forward.

"Pheasants, my lord," the falconer whispered.

Bothwell nodded and unhooded the falcon bound to his wrist. With swift fingers, he slipped the jesses and whistled her off. She soared into the air, took careful aim, and stooped her prey.

The falconer ran ahead to snatch the pheasant from the falcon before she tore it to shreds. Using his skill deftly, he hacked off the bird's head and fed it to the falcon for reward.

Bothwell galloped up. He lowered his wrist for the falcon and hooded her, noticing that one of her wings had been injured.

"Imp her wing when we get back," he said.

"Aye, my lord."

The hunt went poorly for the rest of the day; besides the pheasant they had bagged, there were only two plovers and a quail. Disgusted, Bothwell turned back to the palace.

He had ridden to Falkland to tell Mary of his truce with Arran. Now that it was done, he hoped that would be the last of her peacemaking, for he was inclined to think that enmities were less strenuous.

Entering the Great Hall he heard angry voices coming from the library's partially opened door.

". . . you cannot ignore this letter, madam. It's different from the rumors you heard last year at Holyrood," Lord James said.

Closer now, Bothwell recognized Lethington's soft, precise tone. "Lord James is right, madam. It would be wiser to investigate the matter fully, before dismissing it as a madman's raving."

Bothwell came in as Mary was about to speak. She seemed both surprised and relieved. "Now we can get to the nub of this," she said. "I am certain that Lord Bothwell can throw some light on it for us." She handed him a letter. "Read this, my lord, and tell us what you make of it."

It was a garbled mess of writing—almost impossible to read. Finally, he looked up, astonished. James watched him through cold, imperturbable eyes. Lethington stood at the fireplace in his favorite pose; one hand leaned delicately on the mantlepiece, the other stroked his meticulously clipped beard. The only note of friendship came from Mary. Her eyes told him that she trusted him—but they also pleaded to hear that it was all a horrible mistake.

At last he said, "Surely no one takes this drivel seriously. This is a madman's invention."

"Naturally you would like us to believe that, since this letter implicates you," James said. "It is quite clear now why, after years of hatred, you were so anxious to make peace with Arran. You would use him to seize the Queen and usurp her authority."

Mary said quickly, "I asked Lord Bothwell to end his feud with Arran."

Bothwell felt choked with fury; the words in the letter swam before his eyes. Why would Arran concoct such a tale? Why would he write that together they planned to kidnap Mary, keep her prisoner, and govern Scotland jointly in her place? Only Arran's madness could invent such utter nonsense.

He glared at James, and the thin veneer of friendship crumbled. "You have confused the role of usurper, my lord," Bothwell said. "It has been your game for years—not mine."

Lethington intervened. "Harsh words will avail us nothing, my lords. We have it all here in Arran's own hand—a complete confession. Likely he has had a change of heart and felt compelled to make a clean breast of his guilt." He turned to Bothwell. "How do you explain Arran's statement that together you intended to murder Lord James and myself—then leave the Queen in his keeping at Dumbarton Castle?"

"There is no explanation for madness," Bothwell said. "I saw it coming two nights ago, when he supped with me—"

"If you have any clue to this riddle, please tell us," Mary said. "What did he say to you?"

"He spoke of all he had risked for the Crown, then declared his love for Your Majesty, saying that everyone was against him. He wanted my help to wed Your Majesty."

Mary turned to James. "Obviously, this is all a hallucination of Arran's deranged mind. He should be brought in for questioning, then placed in ward to prevent future difficulties."

"Very well, madam," James said, "but I am not so easily convinced by Lord Bothwell's account. Until Arran is taken into custody—"

James' words were drowned out by a commotion outside. It was Arran's cousin, Gavin Hamilton. He too had been implicated in the letter; Arran had even named his father as an accessory.

"Let him come in," Mary said. "He has a right to be heard."

Hamilton dashed in and threw himself at Mary's feet. He was in tears; words tumbled from his lips. "Your Majesty, I know of the letter written by my cousin, and I beseech you not to give credit to any of it. It is all false—both of the Duke and the Earl of Bothwell—and myself. The Duke himself has commissioned me to tell Your Majesty that it is only his son's frenzied mind; twice before he has been ill like this—he takes it of his mother."

Gently Mary said, "Calm yourself, sir. If you are innocent there is nothing to fear."

But Mary's reassurances had little value. James took charge, and Bothwell knew that he was not likely to pass up a chance to exploit his enemies.

"If you and Lord Bothwell speak the truth," James said, "you should have little difficulty in proving it. But for the moment you will both be committed to safe custody."

Bothwell's fury overwhelmed him; his hand went to his dirk. James called the guards and ordered them to take Bothwell and Hamilton in charge. Bothwell started to throw them off; he turned to Mary in protest, but she looked away, letting her hands fall hopelessly to her sides.

They spent the night in cells below the castle, and in the morning a company of men came for them.

"Where are they taking us?" Bothwell asked.

"St. Andrews," Hamilton whispered.

"The Bastard's stronghold."

Hamilton moved closer to Bothwell. "The Queen said—"

"Don't count on anything the Queen said—it's Lord James we will have to reckon with."

They left Falkland under a gray, leaden sky, but after a few miles the sun came out. Bothwell squinted up into the wan March sun, his thoughts on the cell that awaited him. Panic seized him; how could he live cooped up, unable to come and go as he pleased?

Bothwell and Hamilton were ordered to dismount in the courtyard at St. Andrews Castle. They were taken inside and down a steep flight of winding stairs. They walked the length of a long, twisting corridor, shadowed by rushlights, and came into the guardroom. Their hands were untied, and Hamilton was prodded through a door toward a block of cells.

A guard thrust a stout rope that hung from an iron rung in the ceiling into Bothwell's hands and pointed to an opening in the floor. The Bastard had reserved the bottle dungeon for him.

Bothwell slid down slowly, and when his feet touched bottom, the rope was pulled up sharply. There was a deafening clank of metal as the opening above him sealed shut, plunging him into darkness. He took a few faltering steps and stumbled forward on the uneven floor. He felt like a blind man cast, unaided, into strange surroundings. Cautiously he half-crept along the ground, groping his way until he found the wall. Its jaggedness pierced his doublet, then he eased himself to the floor.

The cold clamminess of the stone crept through his clothes, but his body was bathed in sweat. He smelled excrement, and there was a sickening sensation in the pit of his stomach. Outside he heard the sea crashing against the walls, reverberating through the dungeon, pounding in his brain.

Gradually, he became accustomed to the dark; he could see the stalactites that hung on the vaulted ceiling like unsheathed dirks. One side of the dungeon had the outline of chains hung from the wall, and there was a post, sunk deep in the floor, with shackles dangling from it the size of a man's neck.

He closed his eyes to shut out the sight and fell into merciful sleep. He had no way of knowing how much time had passed when he heard the metal trapdoor above open and a dim ray of light illuminated the dungeon. He preferred the dark, for it hid some of the gruesomeness. A bucket containing meat and a flagon of water was lowered down—this was the first of his three daily meals in prison.

3

The Privy Council had been called together at St. Andrews to hear the evidence in Arran's fancied kidnap plot. It took a while for Bothwell's eyes to accustom themselves to the light again, and he stood at an open gun loop to fill his lungs with fresh air.

An escort of four guards brought him to the Great Hall where the Council had assembled. He glanced at the men seated at a long table; not all the members were there—but enough to pronounce judgment. More important, they were all James' partisans, but he assured himself there was no cause to worry. There was no evidence against him; they would have to find him innocent.

Mary sat on a raised dais under a canopy of state, James stood beside her, and Lethington was seated at a small table next to him. She had looked up when Bothwell came in, but she gave him no sign of encouragement.

Bothwell thought of how he must look, disheveled and filthy. A four-day growth of beard covered his face; his clothes, the same he had worn for hunting at Falkland, were blood-stained from the falcon, creased, and bore the lingering smell of the dungeon.

Arran was brought in, his clothes in disarray, his hair matted and tangled; his skin had the pallor of yellow wax. He glanced about nervously until he saw Bothwell, then he looked away quickly and hurried to the opposite wall, where he sat down mumbling incoherently.

Lethington called the Council to order, and the charges were read. Arran was questioned first. There were a few brief periods of lucidity in his testimony when he denied having authored the letter. At such times he exonerated Bothwell, the Duke, and Gavin Hamilton, saying, "All those things were but fantasies." Then his mind clouded again, and he confirmed the charges of before.

"What would you have done with the Laird of Lethington and myself, if your scheme had succeeded?" James asked.

"Hack you both to pieces and leave your carcasses to the vultures."

"And my Lord Bothwell?" James coaxed. "What was his involvement?"

"He was to have taken charge of the Queen, then delivered her to me at Dumbarton Castle," Arran said.

James gave him a nod of satisfaction and turned his attention to the Council. "There you have the proof, my lords. It is a simple case of the strong man forcing his will on this pitifully distraught creature," he said, placing a consoling hand on Arran's shoulder.

"We all know of Lord Bothwell's reckless nature," he resumed. "His daring would stop at nothing—not even placing the person of Her Majesty in the hands of a madman."

Bothwell lunged forward. Blinded by insensate rage, his only desire was to tear Arran apart, limb from limb.

"Let me at him," he shouted. "I'll force the truth from him."

It took several men to restrain him; in his fury and frustration, Bothwell would have killed Arran with his bare hands.

"Do you still deny the charges, my lord?" Lethington asked.

"Yes, I deny them," Bothwell roared, "and I'll fight to the death any man who claims otherwise—beginning with you—if you've the stomach for it."

"I fear your sanguinary tendencies will afford you little here," Lethington said unctuously. "It would seem that your anger bears proof enough of your guilt. An innocent man would be less inclined toward violence."

Lethington's words had a calming effect. "Very well," Bothwell said, thinking more clearly now, "I demand a trial in a court of law. Let a jury of my peers hear the evidence, if you have any. Let them decide if I am guilty."

Arran was clean mad, and anything drawn from him, forcibly or otherwise, would hold no weight. An open trial was Bothwell's only hope.

Lethington's eyes narrowed. "That is quite impossible, my lord. The Earl of Arran is next in line to succession. Should he be found guilty the scaffold would be his fate—" He paused dramatically to allow the Council to absorb his meaning. "Which is, to say the least, a circumstance that could provoke dangerous repercussions."

"Take them away," James said, gesturing toward Bothwell and Arran.

As long as James remained in power there would be no trial. The evidence, or lack of it, would never be heard before an impartial jury. Bothwell could have no hope of clearing himself, and if James had his way, he would rot in the foul pit reserved for him forever, forgotten and alone.

Back in the dungeon, Bothwell laughed scornfully; so much for his loyalty. In the darkness he saw Mary's face, pale and tight-lipped, as she had sat upstairs in the Great Hall. Several times she had leaned forward, about to speak, then decided against it. She had been silent throughout the proceedings—living proof of her brother's ascendency over her. And now those who had kept faith with her would be forced to yield to James' revenge and ambition.

April passed slowly, and the days of imprisonment dragged on—days filled with emptiness, except for the fury that ate at him. Bothwell had never known confinement before; the walls began to creep in on him, and he longed for the sound of a human voice.

Heavy rains soaked the earth and seeped in through the stones, forming small puddles on the pocked floor. Through a privy, dug in the wall, he heard the steady tapping of rain until he thought he would go mad for the feel of it on his face. He envisioned himself riding on the muddy moors and paced the pit from end to end. At times he fancied the scent of damp spring grass and cherry blossoms—and he imagined the orchards in bloom at Crichton. . . .

Early in May he was moved from St. Andrews to Edinburgh Castle for "an indefinite period of confinement." His cell was in the topmost part of the prison, overlooking the Grassmarket. They called this section the Devil's Elbow, for the wind howled relentlessly day and night. But there was one consolation; he had a stanchioned casement with air to breathe and the sky to tell him if it was day or night.

The strictness of his confinement was relaxed, and he had been able to bribe the guards into letting him have a bath and a fresh change of clothes that had been smuggled in to him. He was also permitted to exercise once a day on the narrow passage between the cells and battlements that looked down on a sheer drop of jutting rocks.

News trickled in; he heard that James had visited his wrath upon the Border, "to discourage those who might be inclined to help their overlord." Even in prison the Bastard feared his influence.

In the Highlands, Bothwell's great-uncle, the Bishop of

Moray, was pressing for his release. In a letter to Bothwell, the Bishop wrote, "Young Lord Hugh of Lovat has designed to go south to take a view of the Court for you." But his enemies were too strong, and nothing ever came of it.

Then, early in August, something happened to make him realize that any motion for his release would have to be self-initiated. Mary had begun a progress to the Highlands with James. It was called a routine visit, in order that she might become better acquainted with the northern part of her Realm. But Bothwell surmised it was more of James' avarice—that he was lusting after the rich earldom of Moray.

It seemed a safe guess that the old Earl of Huntly was James' next victim, and Bothwell had no intention of waiting for the outcome in prison. But before taking matters into his own hands, he wrote to Mary to know her true mind. For answer she told him that she had believed in his innocence from the start, but that she was powerless to help him. "Therefore," she wrote, "do the best you can for yourself."

That she had allowed him to be imprisoned, knowing all along he was innocent, made him go white with rage. All those years spent in fighting her quarrels, defending her Crown, winning for himself the enmity of half the nobility in Scotland because of it—and this for thanks. Aye, she bore the stamp of royalty—who but royalty would repay service with betrayal?

Mary's letter was the deciding factor; she had told him to do the best he could—and he would do that. On a dark, moonless night, only a few hours before dawn, Bothwell slipped through an opening he had made in the bars of his casement window and began his descent from Castle Rock. He had only a rope between himself and sudden death among the jagged rocks below. One slip, and he would be impaled on a jutting peak at the base.

He took a firm hold on the rope and inched his way down.

The screaming wind tossed him about; he strained every muscle to avoid being crushed against the granite mountainside. Slowly, so slowly, he put one foot in back of the other, desperately attempting to get a foothold on the slippery rocks.

Grasping the rope more tightly, he looked down at the razor-sharp peaks. His hands were sweating profusely, making it difficult for him to hold on. Then he realized it wasn't sweat—it was blood. His hands were sore from the work he had done on the bars; now the rough hemp rope had torn into the flesh, leaving a sticky, slippery mass of blood. He couldn't hold on much longer; his arms ached, and his grip was loosening. He looked down again and saw that he hadn't even reached the halfway mark yet.

He told himself it had been madness to attempt this; in its entire history only one man had ever succeeded in escaping from the castle. Why had he thought his luck would hold out? He felt himself slipping, the rope burned into his raw flesh, a gust of wind swung him to a side violently, and his right leg stung with pain. A jutting rock had torn through his hose, piercing the skin of his calf.

Suddenly his foot seemed to touch something solid. Turning slowly, still clutching the rope, he saw that he had reached the bottom. He sank to his knees in the wet mud and dug his bleeding hands down into it to cool them. Then, getting up, he scanned the area for the horse that someone had promised to leave for him. He saw it grazing only a few yards away.

He ran to it, mounted, and rode off swiftly, for the guards would be making their early morning check on prisoners soon. This was his first taste of freedom in five months; exhilarated, he raced across the Grassmarket onto the High Street and up to the top of Calton Hill. Dismounting there, he tethered his horse to a tree and watched the gray dawn stretch across Holyrood and Arthur's Seat.

4

That was the night of August 28, and by the following day news of his escape was all over Edinburgh. He heard later that Knox had implicated Mary, accusing her of having paved the way for Bothwell to walk out of prison.

At the end of that week, Bothwell paid a visit to his mother at Morham Castle. He found her in a strange mood; she seemed more angry than glad to see him.

"Where have you been all this time?" she asked.

"You needn't fret. I am well able to take care of myself."

"Would you call spending these last five months in prison taking care of yourself?" she asked. Then she insisted on knowing. "Where have you been, with your Norwegian lady?"

"No, not with my Norwegian lady," he mimicked. Whenever she spoke of Anna, she always used that same acid tone. "I stayed close to Edinburgh—this confinement did my finances little good, and I was obliged to see Master Barron. He was good enough to lend me the cash I needed."

"More mortgages?" she asked wearily.

He shrugged. "I have to live."

"It's a wonder you have anything left."

"Enough," he said impatiently. He'd been on his own too long now and didn't like having to answer to anyone.

"What will you do now?"

"Stay here for a few days, then I'm off to Hermitage. That's the safest place, in case of trouble."

She frowned. "Do you expect any?"

"I don't think they'll come after me. My innocence was apparent from the start. And if they try to take me again, they'll have a fight on their hands this time. I'll not be caught off guard again."

"Would you go against the Queen's authority if she ordered you back to prison?"

"She won't. Only last month she sent word to me in prison that she knew I had been confined unjustly."

"Just the same, she was willing to let you go to prison."

His mother had good cause to speak against her, yet he refused to listen—even if her indignation was just.

"That's clean different," he said. "It's James Stuart, not the Queen, who wields power these days, and from the look of it in the north, he will come back the Earl of Moray and more powerful."

He was gone a few days later and off to Liddesdale to round up his Borderers. He traveled alone, riding miles over desolate moors and hidden valley roads. There were no farms here, no fields of oat and barley, only barren heaths and grazing haughs. He saw no signs of life, except for sheep high in the hills and peel towers spaced miles apart with thin black streamers of smoke rising from their chimneys.

Ancient fortifications, dug into the earth by Romans centuries ago, still pockmarked the hills and brought to mind the early conquerors. As he neared Hermitage, a bright orange sun was going down over the Cheviots, splashing their great humps with gold and bronze. Mountainous clouds, piled one on the other in a blue-gray sky, competed with the rolling hills in their endless struggle for supremacy. And as twilight approached, a soft gray carpet of mist spread over the land.

At last Hermitage's great hulk came into view—it was like coming home. The ancient fortress, set in the midst of a bleak, godforsaken stretch of borderland, seemed to open its huge arms to embrace him. It was ugly and worn, and boasted of few comforts, but this is what he had craved most during those five torturous months in prison—he had been desperate for this open stretch of land.

From the time he arrived, men began pouring into the castle, until their number swelled to five hundred. They slept in the courtyard and in the halls; they lay on rag pallets and on straw, and some on the bare oxblood floors. He filled with pride to see their devotion, their willingness to lend a hand when he needed it.

Willie Hepburn was the first of his kinsmen to arrive, and they greeted each other warmly.

Bothwell laughed when he spied Willie eyeing him from head to toe. "A man's not apt to waste away so quickly in prison," he said.

"You're thinner, Jamie, but it's not that I'm thinking of. You could never bear fences; was it sore hard to take?"

"Aye."

Willie nodded. He knew the hell it had been for Bothwell, for no one knew him better.

Brightening, Willie said, "I doubt there was ever a more leisurely fugitive. Here you are flitting about the countryside instead of staying put."

"Would you have me cowering in the bushes for fear?"

Willie shook his head skeptically. "Eh, well, I'd not be in your boots for all the world. You've a mess of woe staring you in the face."

"It could be worse. I have a goodly number of men and horses stationed within these walls—and fifteen hundred more on call. So, if my enemies are planning a siege, I can withstand it."

"And how do you propose to feed these men? There are not enough provisions here to last you a week."

"We'll make out."

But Willie's question had been an echo of his own thoughts. He knew the situation was near desperate without being told. There was not even enough straw to feed the horses; somehow he had to victualize the castle, or defense would be useless.

There was no sleep for Bothwell that night; he roamed the drafty corridors restlessly. Five hundred men slept under his roof, and tomorrow five hundred bellies had to be filled. He climbed to the ramparts and looked out to the moors.

It was a black, moonless night; he saw only the crests of the Cheviots silhouetted against the sky, heard the rush of Hermitage Water and the light hoofbeats of a deer in flight. A sentry passed, ghostly and silent, huddled in his cloak. Then he disappeared into the enveloping darkness that hid the northern embankment wall.

Bothwell was aware of an uneasiness, a lack of peace and a strangeness, as though Hermitage had a life and heartbeat of its own. Something—from the past, perhaps—reached out to him. Something horrible and unknown seemed to walk the fortress' shadowy recesses.

Then he brought himself up short, chiding himself. A fine thing! He was behaving like a skittish spinster left alone in the dark. It was then he heard a cry; it was wretched and despairing, rising from the castle's vaults. It didn't resemble anything human—it was more like some great felled beast—and yet nothing he had ever heard or known before. He felt torn apart with pity for the suffering of this nameless creature.

Hurrying to the northern wall, he found the sentry. "Who cried out?" he asked.

The sentry's face was hidden, but his voice betrayed amazement. "I heard no cry, Your Lordship."

Bothwell gripped the man's arm. "You must have, it came from the dungeons. Who is imprisoned there?"

"No one. The last prisoner was released months ago."

Incredulous, he said, "Surely you heard the cry!"

"I heard nothing. I will ask the others, perhaps—"

"Never mind," he said gruffly. "Go on with your duties. I'll discover the source myself."

He walked away, feeling the sentry's eyes boring into his back. Doubtless the man thought he was daft. Could he have imagined it? No, he *had* heard something; it had left him so utterly depressed. And because his reason demanded an explanation, he told himself it was a screech owl calling to its mate.

He turned and raced down the winding stairway. Everyone was asleep; only a guard walked duty at the arched entrance. Bothwell went to the stables, saddled his horse, and rode off toward the hills. He gave no thought to direction—he had to go. Something drove him on as he spurred his horse into the thick dark. He knew every inch of territory here, every rabbit hole and tree stump, every bog and ditch. Still troubled, he turned once to glance back at Hermitage. What had made that unearthly sound?

Finally, because his horse's sweat-glistening hide told him he had ridden far enough, he stopped. The early morning dampness crept in and told him dawn was near. He sat down on a flat rock that jutted up from the bank of a small brook. A gentle wind rustled the foliage like the whisper of silken skirts, the ground under his boots felt springy soft, and he reached down to touch the tangles of dried heather and bracken.

Above, the inky sky faded sluggishly into a slate-gray dawn, and he walked ankle deep in curling mist. A hawk swooped down with poised talons in search of breakfast, then soared skyward again in favor of better prey. Bothwell glanced up into the bird's rapacious eyes and felt a surge of compassion for its victim, unaware that soon it would be locked in the vise of those grasping talons. Try as it might, that luckless thing could not escape its fate; the hawk would feast on its flesh, then fly off before the blood had dried on its beak.

It was bright daylight now. The curtain of mist had disappeared as mysteriously as it had come, and with it was gone the fogging in his brain. Likely he had always known his destiny, but he had floundered about stubbornly refusing to accept what he knew he must. At last he knew what he had been striving for; he would no longer deny it.

Little did it matter what Patrick had been, or that the Queen Regent had been a woman alone—even now it didn't matter if Mary Stuart kept faith with him or not. Enough that he knew what he must do. He had to fight to free Scotland from the treachery that threatened to destroy it.

He saw James Stuart and others like him as hawks, casting a great shadow over Scotland, tearing it apart with their greed. Somehow he had to prevent that destruction. As long as he lived he would defend Scotland against its would-be murderers, for he loved this land with its bleak, stony crags and desolate heaths, its sodden earth and sea-washed shores. He loved and treasured it as some men do a woman. Scotland was his pride, his fierce passion, which inspired in him a protectiveness.

Aye, he would fight to keep Mary Stuart on her throne— alone if he must—but not because she was a woman—that was for empty-headed lads who dreamed of championing the cause of fair damsels for the sake of chivalry. To him Mary Stuart was Scotland. Long ago the Regent had said that every man must have a course to follow—this was his. Blessed or cursed, this blind compulsion would always drive him. He was part of the land—as though he had been spawned from it, instead of woman.

He felt suddenly lighthearted; a heavy burden had been dropped from his shoulders. Whistling for his horse, he mounted and turned back for Hermitage. Now he glanced up at the sky and saw it with new eyes—eyes that had never seen that wondrous sight before. Chilling winds rippled the water and blew clouds into distorted shapes, as the sun crept through white and wan. He knew that nothing had changed since yesterday; yet the grass seemed greener, the hills were possessed of greater majesty—even the moors seemed less barren. He breathed deeply, inhaled the intoxicating air, and threw his head back, laughing exultantly into the wind.

5

Bothwell changed to a robe and slippers and took his breakfast in the Great Hall. Usually he had his meals with the castle's garrison, but it was a pleasant change to eat without their noise and clamor. He ate slowly, savoring every bite, then leaned back contentedly, nibbling the last bit of meat from a bone before tossing it to a deerhound at his feet. His glance roamed the hall lazily and came to rest on a wall hung with armor and swords. He frowned at the heavy breastplates and felt their weight unconsciously. His thoughts were broken suddenly by the sound of hurrying footsteps on the stairway. They hesitated at the door, then a guard entered.

"A party has been sighted approaching from the west, my lord."

"Soldiers?" Bothwell asked, jumping to the conclusion that a troop had been sent to retake him.

"They are still too far off to tell, my lord. Should I sound the alarm?"

"Not yet. We'll wait until we know who they are." He had enough confidence in his men to know they would perform their duty on a moment's notice. They had been trained by him and they knew their jobs well.

He got up and followed the guard to the west tower. The cavalcade was approaching at a steady pace, but he wondered at their slow progress. The sun blurred his vision, but it seemed a fair-sized party. If they were soldiers, there would be a bloody battle soon.

They were closer now. Their mounts appeared small; Border ponies, Bothwell thought. Then he blinked in disbelief. Either his eyes deceived him or most of the horses were riderless—men

on foot were leading them. If this was a troop come to attack
Hermitage, their method was indeed strange. He narrowed his
eyes to slits, hoping to catch a reflection of their weapons or
armor.

The pebbled roof floor dug into his thin-soled slippers. He
paced up and back to relieve the pressure on his feet, then
turning, he caught a glimpse of their banners flapping in the
breeze, and he saw that what he had thought were ponies were
in fact livestock.

The cavalcade approached a hill; when they reached the
bottom he would be able to read the crest on their banners. He
breathed easier now, for he was certain they were not
invaders—more likely they were a party of farmers driving their
herd to market.

Two riders came galloping over the hill ahead of the others;
one was the standard-bearer, the other a woman. Bothwell saw
the familiar Buccleugh crest and dashed down to greet them as
they picked their way over the earthworks. Barking hounds
pranced ahead as he ran across the flagged stone hall and came
out of the high-arched entrance in time to see Janet Beaton ride
up.

She smiled to him in that special way he remembered so
well, and he swept her out of the saddle into his arms. She was
still feather light, but he saw the changes in her at a glance.
Sadly he noticed the graying hair that showed from her coif;
although her eyes were still the same deep shade of green, there
were lines around them that had not been there before. But the
years could not mar their beauty, nor the promise they held,
and he felt a ghost of the old excitement in her touch.

"I bring you gifts, my lord," she said. "No gold or silver, but
commodities of a more practical nature." She ticked off on her
fingers: "Two cows, three suckling pigs, a healthy sow, and a
goat for milking, some oats and barley and ale."

He was overwhelmed; he had no words to express his

gratitude—nor were any needed. "My lady bountiful," he said, putting her hand to his lips reverently.

"Will you keep me standing here forever?" she chided.

He came out of his reverie. "Damn me for my bad manners. Come, we'll go to my apartments," he said, taking her arm.

When they were alone, she said, "You've stirred up a hornet's nest, my lad."

"Aye, it was the devil's own luck for this to happen—now, of all times."

"Trouble of this kind is always bad, no matter when it comes."

"Granted. But with the Bastard's fortunes mounting as they are, there is no telling where he will stop. Who knows but what his next step will be the throne."

"Long ago I warned you to make peace with your enemies. They've never forgiven you for supporting the Regent, and no sooner were they rid of her when you came out openly for her daughter. Only your ruination will satisfy them now—and it seems they have all but succeeded."

He snorted. "Make peace, you say! I'd sooner leave things as they are and let the devil take it all."

"He may that where you are concerned." She leaned forward suddenly and took his hand in hers. "Look now," she said, "I've not much money, but I can let you have a little, if you need it."

He smiled. "I'll take your food, but not your money. There is always Master Barron. He has already invested so much in me, a little more can't matter."

"You took money from Anna Throndsen when you had need."

"Aye, but the circumstances were clean different. I was desperate then; it was that or remain stranded in Bergen for God knows how long. But how did you hear of it?"

"Everyone in Scotland has. She never tires of telling it."

"Doubtless it is her favorite topic," he said. "But she has no cause to complain—I've repaid the loan ten times over."

"I thought as much. In any case, it is of scant interest to me."

He nodded ruefully and thought of all the furniture and gauds he had given Anna since he had brought her to Scotland. Then, dismissing her from his mind, he remembered that Janet's hands had felt cold, and he got up to stoke the dying fire.

"What are your plans?" she asked. "You can't remain here indefinitely."

"I'll wait it out here for a while at least, and pray that a change of fortune will come. If not"—he shrugged—"I'll be forced to go abroad."

"You would go into exile?"

"Unless my affairs improve I'd have no recourse. Whether the sentence was just or not, I *have* broken prison, and I am a fugitive."

"But to leave everything—"

"Only if there is no other way."

"Where would you go, France?"

"Aye, I have friends there. The Duc de Guise once promised me a position at the French Court if I ever had need."

Tears gathered in the corners of her eyes.

"Come now," he said, "it's not so tragic. I could think of worse places—all those dazzling Court ladies. And if I go, it won't be forever. Do you think I'd leave Scotland to its enemies for long? Sooner or later the Queen will recognize her brother's duplicity, and I'll be back to take up where I've left off."

She smiled sadly. "It's a pity that the Queen of Scotland is such a piddling child that she can lightly toss aside a man of your worth. Is there no gratitude in her after all you've done?"

"She's not to blame," he said. "She is little more than a pawn in her brother's hands. He has grown so powerful of late that even she cannot stop him."

"Who gave him that power, if not she? Will you never learn? How many times must you be sacrificed before you see the truth? Have you no pride?"

He laughed triumphantly. "None where Scotland is concerned. Once you confounded me with such arguments—but no more. Now I know what I must do. I may be cast down now, but mark me well, Mary Stuart will yet have need of me."

Incredulously, she said, "You would continue to serve a cause that mocks your loyalty?"

"Aye, but not for her—for Scotland. And when the time comes, I am not likely to let the power that comes with it slip through my fingers as before. I was too much at war with myself in the past to see that without power I could not help Scotland."

He had frustrated her. "I confess this is beyond my ken. I see before me either a truly honest man or a child living on dreams. But I know you well enough to realize that any attempt to dissuade you now would be like screaming into the wind."

He made no further effort to explain; she could never understand. Doubtless she thought him a fool; more talk would only serve to make him a bigger one in her eyes. Abruptly, he led the talk to other matters, and they were soon laughing again. She left late in the afternoon, promising to return. He watched her ride away, wishing she had stayed longer.

Janet kept her word; she came often and never again mentioned their differences. There were times during those visits when Bothwell felt the old desire to make love to her, for he continued to see beyond the years that separated them. But he knew that any attempt to resume the past would jeopardize her friendship, and he treasured that too much to risk losing it. He realized that Janet would always mean a great deal to him—she was the first woman he had loved.

Then on a rainy, wind-swept day in mid-October, Bothwell had another visitor, Lord George Gordon. He was the Earl of Huntly's eldest son, and he had ridden south from his father's stronghold. Bothwell had heard that Huntly's fight against the Queen's troops was going badly, and he surmised the purpose of Gordon's visit.

"We are in desperate straits," Gordon told him. "If this battle is lost we are ruined."

This was scarcely news to Bothwell; he knew their situation and pitied them for it. And all this because young John Gordon had refused to place himself in ward at Stirling Castle for brawling on Edinburgh's High Street. He had no particular love for Huntly, but he sympathized with him now. Sir John's warder at Stirling would be Lord Erskine, the Bastard's uncle, and any number of mysterious mishaps could result in the prisoner's forfeiting his life.

Yet Bothwell could not believe that Mary would hold Huntly accountable for his son's actions. More likely it was the Bastard's doing that she had marched against Huntly, for he was the last of her Catholic supporters with any real strength.

Bothwell said, "I doubt the Queen will remain inexorable. If your father went to her and asked for mercy, a solution would be reached to satisfy both sides."

"Do you think we've not made the effort?" Gordon said bitterly. "No one may see her without first gaining approval from Lord James or Lethington. Surely you are well acquainted with the mercy they show their enemies. Besides, did you know that she has already invested Lord James with the lands and titles of Moray?"

"Has your father relinquished his claim to it in favor of the Bastard?"

Gordon laughed. "No, but legalities never fash the Bastard. He has his own means of dealing with such matters."

"Aye," Bothwell murmured thoughtfully, "doubtless he's so rattled her brain with his shrewd schemes that she's not had the chance to grasp the wrong."

Gordon looked at him strangely. "Now will you help us?" he asked. "Your Borderers are loyal to you, they would follow you anywhere. It's said they'd follow you into hell—if you led them."

"Likely they would—and for that reason I'll not lead them into a rebellion against the Crown. In any case, I've had my own share of trouble of late. I'm not inclined to borrow more."

Gordon hammered his fist on his thigh. "Can't you see it's no more the Queen's authority we flout than it's her troops we fight! Everything belongs to Lord James—he alone wields power now."

"Granted. Nevertheless, his men march under the royal standard, and opposing them can be interpreted only as treason—I'll not ask my lambs to do that."

"Very well," Gordon said, "I'll press you no further. You do what you must, and I bear you no grudge for it."

"What will you do now?" Bothwell asked. He had no regrets for refusing Gordon, but there was a desperate look in his eyes, and he didn't like seeing him go this way.

"To Keneil Castle. Perhaps the Duke de Châtelherault will lend a hand."

"I fear it will afford you nothing to go there. The Duke's lot is scarcely better than mine."

"Even a slim chance is better than none," Gordon said, getting up to go.

"Why not stay the night here? Then you can get a fresh start in the morning."

"No, that would delay me a day—I must return to my father as soon as I am able."

Bothwell urged him no further and walked out with him. Gordon disappeared into the evening's twilight, lost in the curling fog. Bothwell stood there for a while, wondering what the future would hold for them before they met again.

Shortly after Gordon's visit, Bothwell had a letter from his uncle, the Bishop of Moray. Mary had spent a night at Spynie Castle, and the Bishop had spoken to her in Bothwell's behalf. Now he suggested that Bothwell write to James with an offer of friendship.

Trusting to his uncle's advice, Bothwell wrote the letter, but his offer was rebuked with an added reminder that he was still a fugitive from justice, and therefore he should return to prison immediately. Two months had gone by since his escape from Edinburgh Castle, and aside from his freedom, he was no better off than before.

Mary had returned to Edinburgh after Gordon's defeat in November. The old Earl of Huntly had died mysteriously at Corrichie, and it was bruited that James' dagger had done the deed. Young John Gordon had been captured and hanged at Aberdeen; George had been taken prisoner, his titles and possessions confiscated by the Crown.

Realizing that his situation was rapidly deteriorating by remaining at Hermitage, Bothwell decided to see Mary. Either she would have the false charges against him dropped or he would be forced to leave Scotland to seek his living elsewhere.

CHAPTER VI

1

When he entered the West Bow Port, Bothwell had an immediate sense of something wrong. It was early afternoon, when the streets usually bustled with townsfolk, but no one was about. A strange stillness hung over the town as he rode through the Grassmarket and up the High Street. He wondered at the quiet; the food stalls were closed, no merchants hawked their wares, and were it not for the smoke rising from chimneys, Edinburgh would have seemed deserted.

He heard the tinkle of bells and turned to see a black-shawled woman enter the apothecary's shop. A mongrel dog howled under a window and received a sound dousing from above. At the Netherbow Port he pulled his wide-brimmed hat down over the side of his face so he wouldn't be recognized.

A sentry came forward and Bothwell dismounted. He asked, "Has the plague overrun the town?"

The sentry crossed himself in horror and glanced furtively at St. Giles, lest someone had seen him imitate that papist trait. "Merciful God," he said, "make no jest of such matters."

"Then why is everything steeped in gloom?"

"It is the new acquaintance. Every house has been struck— the palace, too. Aye, even the Queen and her Court have taken to their beds with it."

"The Queen, eh?" What foul luck! She might be too ill to see him. "This new acquaintance, is it fatal?" he asked.

"Rarely, except when it strikes the very old or young. Most folk recover, though it's a slow and loathsome process, for it brings with it an aching head, a wretched cough, and a soreness in the stomach."

"Take care you don't fall victim to it yourself," Bothwell said, mounting his horse again.

The sentry reached into the neck of his cloak. "This camphor bag and red scarf will ward off the evil," he answered.

Bothwell looked into the man's earnest face and stifled the impulse to smile; the ignorant believed in their good luck charms almost as much as they did in God. He jerked the reins and passed through to the Cannongate.

Here too the streets were deserted; most of the nobles' houses were boarded up. Likely they had retired to the country to avoid the epidemic. He turned into his street and tethered his horse in the back garden of his house.

In the morning Bothwell sent a message to Mary at Holyrood, but Lord James answered him with a note delivered by one of his heavily armed henchmen. Bothwell admitted the surly messenger, glancing past him to make certain he was alone. He sized the man up and knew instinctively that he stood face to face with an able cutthroat—a fit lackey for the Bastard.

The messenger thrust a paper forward and said, "For the Earl of Bothwell, from my lord, the Earl of Moray."

He turned to go, but Bothwell stopped him. "Wait, there may be an answer."

"I think not, my lord."

Bothwell waited until the man had gone, then he bolted the door and returned to his study to read the note. It was brief and to the point, stating that Mary was too ill to see him. "However," James concluded, "I strongly recommend that you return to prison, for you remain at liberty under pain of treason."

Bothwell crumpled the note and threw it into the fire, watching the flames lick at the paper until it was only ash. So, he was expected to return to prison, dismissed like a petty criminal to rot behind bars. He slammed his fist on the mantelpiece. By God, he would see them all in hell first. Treason or not, liberty was too precious to give it up that easily.

Aye, he had broken prison, but only because they would have left him there indefinitely, without hope of ever having a fair hearing. If he obeyed James' order, he had nothing to look forward to but more endlessly passing days and nights—he could not live without freedom.

He remained motionless, staring into the fire. The room was icy cold, but sweat poured from him as he thought of prison. The stench of decay was in his nostrils, and there was a foul taste in his mouth. Then the sound of rain pelting the mullioned windows reached him and he brought himself up short. What use to bemoan fate—he had been prepared for this eventuality.

Barron admitted him with a greeting that was both guarded and respectful. Doubtless he had already guessed the nature of the visit. And since Bothwell was not one to waste words on formalities, he came straight to the point.

"I have further need of your services," he said. "Circumstances compel me to leave Scotland for a time, and as usual, I find myself in need of cash."

"Do you anticipate a lengthy stay abroad, my lord?"

"Not if I can help it. But to be frank, my plans are somewhat vague at the moment."

Barron was a meticulous man, as fastidious in business as he was in his dress. He cleared his throat and made a pyramid with his fingertips. "I am reluctant to point out that with so uncertain a future, my lord, it would be no small risk on my part to advance you further money. I fear you have already mortgaged everything you own to the hilt."

"Not quite. There is still some land belonging to Hailes Castle."

Barron showed renewed interest.

"Here are the deeds to it," Bothwell said, tossing the papers on the table. "Examine them and tell me how much you can let me have. I expect they will bring me a tidy sum."

Barron looked up and murmured absentmindedly, "To be sure, my lord, to be sure."

Bothwell waited, an impatient frown puckering his brow.

Finally, Barron said, "I think we can come to terms, my lord. Of course, it is my earnest desire that you will redeem these mortgages in the not too distant future."

Bothwell nodded curtly and got up to go.

After leaving Barron's house, he booked passage on a ship bound for France, then he took the road out of town for the Border.

2

He made a detour through Calder before returning to Hermitage; now that he was leaving Scotland, he felt duty bound to tell Anna. It was past ten o'clock when he reached there; most of the houses were already dark, but there were still some lights on in the lower floor of Anna's peel tower.

He sent a servant to tell Anna of his arrival and went into the common room to wait for her. There was a flurry of excitement outside the door, then Anna burst in, dressed in a fur-trimmed, brocaded robe. Her long black hair hung in a thick braid down her back and bounced merrily as she ran to embrace him.

Then she stood back, pouting. "I should not even admit I am happy to see you. You neglect me so. I could be dead, but you would not hear of it for months."

Her complaints wearied him. "Haven't I enough grief

without your adding more?" he said. "I am scarcely in a position to flit about the country paying social calls."

"But I have not seen you since your escape from prison. You might at least have sent for me. You care nothing for me—I am weary of this place," she said, tossing her hand aside in disdain.

Bothwell glanced about carelessly; he had provided her with the finest furnishings, brocaded couches, upholstered chairs, carved tables. . . . She had everything she could need or want to make her comfortable; still she was dissatisfied.

"You are such a selfish little minx," he said. "Much as I give you, you ask for more. Besides, Hermitage is hardly suited to your tastes—it is a fortress and not equipped to accommodate women."

She tilted her chin defiantly. "The lack of accommodation does not prevent the Lady of Buccleugh from visiting you there. She appears not to mind the inconveniences."

"She came as a friend, to give what she could—not to take."

"But I am lonely."

"Are you now?" he asked, his voice heavy with sarcasm. "Not from the tales I have heard."

"And what did you hear?"

"Did you think your little affairs would remain secret, my dove? Servants, you know, are a gossiping lot."

She went to him, swinging her hips provocatively. "Why should you expect otherwise, neglecting me as you do? I must have companionship. I cannot live isolated, waiting for you to come."

He laughed. "You needn't make excuses. I have no complaints. What you do with your time is of no concern to me. However, if it's companionship you crave, why is it never from other women?"

Furious, she lunged out to claw his face. "Oh, how loathsome you are," she screamed. "You are not even jealous."

He caught her by the wrists and pushed her into a chair. "Calm yourself," he warned.

She quieted, and he saw a flicker of fear in her eyes.

"I haven't come all this way for the mere pleasure of quarreling with you," he said, returning to his chair. "I am leaving Scotland for a while. I've already booked passage on a ship that sails the end of this month."

His announcement stunned her. At last she said, "That is scarce three weeks away. You do not allow me sufficient time to pack."

"Pack? Where are you going?"

"With you, of course."

"Whatever gave you that notion? It will be difficult enough for me without you there to plague me."

"If you had wed me before we left Flanders you might never have come to this—and you could not dismiss me as simply as you do now."

"Wives have been left behind before," he said. "But for the life of me, I cannot see how being wedded to you would have spared me."

"What shall I do now?" she asked, ignoring his last remark. "With no one to look after me I shall be lost."

"I doubt that. In any case, you are free to return to your family. I haven't much, but I can give you some money, enough to pay your passage home or to enable you to live on here—if you don't squander it all on new gauds."

This seemed to appease her, and her manner softened.

In the morning Bothwell awakened to the tinkle of glass. He looked out from the bed-curtains and saw Anna seated at her dressing table applying scent to her shoulders. Her robe hung loosely from her hips, draping to the floor carelessly. He watched her dab a last bit of perfume to her breasts, then she stood and went to the wardrobe.

The room filled with her sweet, exotic scent. His glance followed her as she moved in sleek, animal-like strides across the room. Her flesh was soft and pliable to the touch, yet it was also firm and smooth as marble. She reminded him of a cat, taut and lean; her movements were deliberately sensuous with the studied care of a courtesan, and he was brought to mind of a huntress.

She was aware of his studied gaze, for she turned suddenly. "Does it please you?" she asked, running her hands lightly over her body.

He shrugged. "I haven't decided yet."

She came toward him smiling, undulating her hips. The muscles in her legs and thighs swelled rhythmically, and as always, he was struck by their marvelous strength. She lay down beside him, arching her back to mold her body to his, drawing him upon her. His hand went to rest on the curve of her hip; the other teased her breasts and throat.

She moved closer, placing her mouth hard on his; her nails dug into his shoulders as she twisted convulsively under his touch. She pulled him closer, as though she would blend their bodies into one, her ultimate desire, possession. She was insatiable in love as in all things, always wanting more than he could give—himself.

Slowly, he felt her body relax against him and she dozed in his arms. He disengaged himself, edged out of bed, and started to dress.

Her mood had changed when she came downstairs later. She seemed petulant, even reproachful, and he realized that she had used their lovemaking as a stratagem. In a moment he knew she would begin to badger him about taking her to France, and when he refused, she would make another scene. But he had had enough of her shrewishness. Finishing his breakfast quickly, he ordered his horse.

Now her face reflected another change in mood; she recognized her defeat. She went as far as the door with him; her farewell was tearful and full of protestations of love. But he was vaguely amused to see how soon her tears dried when he pressed a money pouch in her hand. Her eyes betrayed her greed as she bounced the pouch up and down in her hand to guess how much it held.

He turned away, knowing that she was already running to her chambers to count the money. He looked up at her window and thought that leaving Anna was by far the easiest part of this business.

3

On Christmas morning Bothwell rode out of Hermitage. He was sailing in three days, and if luck went against him, he might never see Scotland again. His horse had taken him only a few yards when he turned for a last look. Paris too came to a halt beside him and sat huddled in a wool cloak many times too large for him, holding the reins of a packhorse loaded with two small leather trunks.

Everything around them was covered with snow, with drifts high as a man's shoulders. A freezing wind blew sheets of blinding flakes into their faces, and Paris shivered. Bothwell felt neither cold nor wet; his eyes were fathomless, staring into space at nothing and at everything. He was aware of a dull ache in his chest and he swallowed hard to dissolve the pressure.

He saw the moors as they would look in spring: yellow with gorse and whin, stretching out to meet the sky. The mere thought of never seeing these hills again, or riding their crests, or hunting in the forests, shot through him like a flash of flame, and the pain in his chest grew sharper. How could he leave it?

Mutely, he cried out: *I cannot go.* His thoughts whirled. What right had they to drive him away? He jerked at the reins and made ready to turn back, then he remembered St. Andrews—it had been like being buried alive. He couldn't forget his desperation in prison, hungering for the freedom he had always known. No! He would risk anything sooner than relive that agony. Abruptly, he turned to Paris, nodded, and galloped off.

More than once, Bothwell deliberately hung back to savor a particular scene. Those things that he had always taken for granted seemed so precious now: a doe and her fawn leaping over snowbanks, a brook stilled in the sleep of winter, a fox slinking through bare, snow-tipped hedgerows. . . . He wondered which of these things he would take with him if he could—it was like asking a man to save only one of his many treasures from a burning house.

Reluctantly, he pushed on; dusk came early in December, and Morham was still a long way off. He had sent a messenger ahead two days ago to inform his mother of his coming. At midday they stopped at an inn near Lauder to refresh themselves and the horses; they were back in the saddle an hour later, and it was well after nightfall when they finally rode into Morham.

"I had about given up hope of your coming," his mother said.

Bothwell stood with his back to the fireplace, warming himself. "I would have sent word, then, not to expect me," he said tonelessly.

"The roads are bad; I thought you might bypass Morham."

He turned away. "Would it have mattered if I had?"

He was in the grip of an overwhelming bitterness, wondering if anyone really cared what happened to him. If he were to die suddenly, who would mourn him? His mother? What were they to each other more than strangers? He respected her as a son ought, but he scarcely knew her.

Certainly, Anna would not care; but why should she? He had never given her even the smallest part of himself—nor to anyone else for that matter, except Janet. He knew she would remember him now and then, but she scorned the past and had her own life to live.

Then the bitterness left him as quickly as it had come. He had always despised self-pity in others; now he had allowed himself to become steeped in it. His mother was speaking and he turned to her.

"It would have mattered greatly to me," she said. "I might never see you again."

He reproached himself for the hurt in her voice and felt a sudden surge of tenderness for her. But he could not bring himself to tell her of it. To cover his discomfort, he went to the table and filled a plate with food.

His mother asked, "When does your ship sail?"

"Tomorrow, on the evening tide."

He pushed his plate away, his appetite gone.

"You've still a long ride ahead," she said. "A night's sleep will do you good."

He nodded. He was thoroughly warmed now and suddenly overcome with drowsiness. "I'll be grateful for the feel of a soft bed under me tonight."

They went upstairs together. Before going to his chambers, he said, "Should anything befall me, my lawyer has been instructed on the disposition of my estate. Since I have no legitimate heirs, William Hepburn of Gilmerton will succeed me, but I've left some property and a few small possessions of value to little Willie."

"Morham will be his some day," she said. "He is my sole heir. Legitimate or not, he is my grandson and a part of you."

"It appears that you have grown right fond of the lad. To be frank, I had my doubts on bringing him here for fear a child might be troublesome to you."

The stern lines in her face softened. "I was denied the pleasure of seeing you grow to manhood—now I am somewhat compensated through your son."

She had never spoken about the past before. Now he realized how deeply she had been hurt, and he was glad that he had this child to give her. It had been his intention to discuss the boy's future with her, but there was no need; she would do her utmost for the lad.

In his bedchamber, Bothwell lay staring up at the canopied hangings. He thought of his mother and how different his life might have been if the past had been different. He had never had a sense of belonging, until his succession to the earldom; he had never even lived anywhere that he could call home.

Sleep claimed him and his thoughts were lost in dreamless peace. Through a haze he heard the door open, and footsteps approached his bed. He felt the weight of another cover and heard his mother's voice whisper, "Sleep well, my son." But he was too drugged in slumber to rouse, and he snuggled deeper under the covers.

4

A thick fog swirled around the *Abercon's* torchlit gangplank and rose to the deck in ghostlike wisps. Paris went ahead with the baggage, while Bothwell stopped to show their letters of travel to the captain.

"I feared we might sail without you, Master Andrews," the captain said, handing the papers back to him.

"I'm damn glad you didn't. I'd have had a devil of a time finding another vessel this time of year," Bothwell said.

"I mind your man remarking that you had urgent business in France."

The first mate shouted the call to raise anchor. Bothwell stepped back as the gangplank slid past them and the sails unfurled above their heads with a roar. An overpowering gust of wind came in from the sea and rocked the *Abercon* with a sharp jolt. The captain looked up uneasily at the creaking masts as the sails ballooned out like a full-bosomed matron.

They headed into a violent storm. The *Abercon* pitched and swayed for hours, until they were forced on the rocks at Holy Island, a place heavily garrisoned by English soldiers. Bothwell and Paris managed to escape over the side undetected and swam ashore.

They sat in the cover of rocks far off on the beach and watched the other passengers rowed to shore where they would find the safety and warmth of a house. Bothwell knew he was in a fine mess now; ahead lay Holy Island, England, and the risky unknown; behind him lay the frozen sands, Scotland, and the likelihood of another imprisonment.

There was only one hope open to him now; Coldingham was the closest place of refuge—his sister Janet and her husband were spending the Christmas holidays there. Of course, Johnnie Stuart might not want to shelter a fugitive, but he had always shown himself a friend—and he had openly sided with Bothwell against his own brother.

Coldingham was twenty miles away, and they would have to go on foot, since the purchase of horses would attract too much attention. It took the entire day to cross the frozen sands, then toward evening, their faces blackened with cold, Bothwell and Paris reached the gates of Coldingham.

The great wooden doors were locked, and Bothwell hammered on the iron knocker with stiffened fingers. A few minutes passed before he heard the bolt scraped out of place and the door parted halfway. A servant looked out inquiringly.

"Is your master at home?" Bothwell asked.

"Aye."

"Then summon him," he said, pushing the startled man aside.

The servant stood his ground, peering at them suspiciously.

"I am His Lordship's brother-in-law," Bothwell snapped. "Fetch him here immediately."

Bothwell took off his cloak and sat down on a wooden bench to remove his wet boots. The soles of his feet were blistered and deadened with cold. He divided his time between rubbing his hands and massaging his toes to restore their feeling. Then he heard Johnnie's cry of amazement.

"Good God, is it really you, Bothwell?"

Smiling, Bothwell stood. "When I've thawed out, I'll pinch myself to find out."

Johnnie slapped him on the back affectionately. "What are you doing here, man? When last we heard you were on your way to France."

"So I was, but we were stormwrecked off Holy Island—and well you know the reception I'd have had there."

"Aye, you'd be in a sorry state now if they'd caught you."

Bothwell stepped back in assumed indignation. "A fine host you are to keep me standing here in this drafty hall when it's a fire I need," he said. "Where is my sister—and your son?"

Johnnie's face clouded, a strange look came into his eyes, and he glanced away uncomfortably. "Janet's in the study," he said hesitantly. "But there is something you should know before—"

Bothwell ran ahead without waiting for him to finish. He thrust open the study door and the smile on his face froze. His glance swept past Janet and came to rest on the equally startled face of Mary Stuart. She was the last person he had expected to find here, and his attempts to see her—all ending in disappointment—flashed before him.

Slowly the shock wore off, and his thoughts came in rapid succession. How would she receive him? How did she really feel about his having broken prison? Would she be angry because he had attempted to leave the country without her permission? Then he saw that he had no cause for concern—she was smiling.

"I had heard that Christmas in the country is informal," she said, "but this—and you a fugitive from the Queen's justice."

He laughed and knelt at her feet. "I bow to Your Majesty's mercy."

She glanced down. "In stocking feet!"

"A humble penitent, madam." Now he understood Johnnie's apprehension, but he felt certain there would be no reproaches. Johnnie heaved a sigh of relief and became the genial host again, and Janet hurried off to the kitchen for hot possets.

Bothwell sat by the fire sipping his drink; his hands and feet were finally thawing, and a slow, comforting warmth started to engulf him.

He finished the heated brew and extended his empty cup to Janet. "Is this all you can offer a starving man?"

"Mind your manners," Janet scolded. "You will be fed."

The words had scarcely left her when a kitchen maid brought in a tray of food. Bothwell didn't wait to be served; he was ravenous, and this was his first meal since last night's supper at Leith.

They hurled questions at him. Where had he been since the end of November? Why hadn't he gone to France as he had planned? He told them everything, answering between mouthfuls, but his eyes never left Mary.

She seemed unchanged; her face still betrayed the indolence of youth. He marveled at the aura of innocence that still clung to her. Her eyes met his, clearly and unveiled, eyes that had looked on at injustices without flinching. And he wondered what thoughts lay beyond those dreamy, lash-curled lids.

He let his glance travel over her straight, childlike figure—she wasn't a woman yet. Her breasts lay flat against the soft velvet bodice of her gown; her hips were narrow as a lad's, and he knew that love was still a stranger to her. She met his gaze; he looked away quickly, like a bairn caught at the honeypot.

Suddenly he was seized with a desperate need for sleep; his eyelids felt weighted with lead, and he was aware of a lightheadedness. He rose unsteadily and bowed to Mary.

His voice sounded unnatural and thick. "With Your Majesty's permission. I'll be off to bed."

Mary nodded. She spoke, but her voice reached him in a blur, and he found himself unable to grasp her words. The hot possets had been generously laced with brandywine—too generous for an empty stomach. That, added to a twenty-mile walk and no sleep for two days, would account for the strange way he felt.

Johnnie got up and took Bothwell by the arm, and the room seemed to whirl. They climbed the stairs to his chambers.... Strange fingers fumbled with the laces on his doublet, and somehow Bothwell managed to struggle out of it. He sank into bed with the sensation of drifting weightlessly into space.

He slept through the night and half the morning without stirring, then someone knocking at his door roused him. He sat up and leaned back against the headboard.

The bed-curtains parted and Johnnie asked, "Are you ill?"

Bothwell pulled the curtain farther back and blinked at the bright sunlight. Yawning, he asked, "What is the hour?"

"Past eleven o'clock. Do you want breakfast?"

There was an unpleasant, cottony taste in his mouth. "Not yet." He got up and stretched. "Where is Paris?"

"In the kitchen, no doubt. We've a pretty little scullery maid there, and he is likely exploring her charms."

"Aye, he has a weakness for anything in petticoats, that one."

Johnnie hooted. "You're a fine one to talk, with the example you've set him."

For answer, Bothwell flung open the door and bellowed for Paris.

When he came down later, Bothwell was clean-shaven and dressed in fresh garments. The long sleep had done him good; he felt a surge of energy and swaggered in his step even more than usual.

Mary and Janet were in the study cooing over the baby when he came in.

He looked down at the infant and frowned. "I confess, women never cease to puzzle me. How can you find that red-faced, wrinkled mite attractive?"

"And how can you be so insensitive as to make sport of your own nephew?" Mary snapped.

Janet made a face at him. "He is not my real brother, madam. A bear left him as a cub with my mother, and she raised him out of pity. Actually he is a great grizzly bear, prinked out to look like a man."

Mary giggled. "That would account for his bad temper."

"Aye, madam. He has been a scandal to us from the start."

Ignoring their taunts, Bothwell asked, "What do you call this scrawny lad?"

"Francis, after Her Majesty's late husband."

"A regal beginning, eh, my lad?" Bothwell said, tweaking the baby under the chin. "Well, why not? His father has half a king's blood. That makes his son part royal—though I warrant it's his Hepburn blood that will make a man of him."

Later, Bothwell asked Johnnie for the loan of a horse.

"May I join you, my lord?" Mary asked shyly.

"I would be honored, madam. But let me caution you to dress warmly; there's a bite to the air."

"I shan't be a minute," she promised.

Janet followed her out, and Johnnie went to order the horses. Bothwell sat down to wait for Mary. Tomorrow night was New Year's Eve, and instead of spending it at sea, as he had expected, he would be with the Queen.

Nevertheless, he knew that he could not remain here long; news of his visit would reach the wrong ears, and he had to be gone before that. In a day or two he would send for David Chalmers, who had contacts in this area—he might be able to arrange for Bothwell's passage on another ship.

Mary returned. "I have kept you waiting overlong, my lord," she apologized.

"It's a small price to pay for such charming company, madam."

She laughed. "A courtier's compliment from you, my lord?"

"Aye, madam. Even a ruffian like myself can toss one off on occasion."

She was dazzling in a dark-green riding dress trimmed with a shawled collar and deep cuffs of sable. A sable coif covered her head and tied under her chin with furred pompons.

Bothwell tossed a wool cloak over his shoulders and followed her out to the courtyard. Johnnie had chosen a dappled mare for Mary and his own chestnut stallion for Bothwell.

They turned away from the sea and rode in silence for a while. Blue vapor streamed from the horses' nostrils; flocks of snow danced in the air to their flying hooves. Bothwell glanced sideways at Mary and saw her spring to life before his eyes.

Her skin, usually so pale, came alive and tinted pink with the cold, her eyes sparkled brilliantly, and she threw her head back laughing. He sensed her joy and knew the exhilaration she felt.

They slackened pace and she said, "What will you do when you reach France?"

He shrugged. "Make myself useful to those who will pay for my services."

"I shall write to my uncles. They will see you are well situated there."

He was on the verge of asking if she hoped to salve her conscience with that. Instead, he murmured, "Thank you, madam."

She seemed thoughtful. Then she asked abruptly, "Did you know that Lady Fleming and Lethington are betrothed?"

Did she think he had wanted Fleming for himself?

"Aye," he said, "though I can't for the life of me see why she chose that prick-me-dainty. Laying aside my personal dislike for the man, he is old enough to be her father."

"Why, he is scarce thirty-five!"

"That proves my point."

She looked puzzled. "How so?"

"He even seems older than his years—Fleming is too vital a lass for him. He brings to mind a fragile piece of old parchment. He is wily and smooth, with a cunning wit. His policies are shrewd—but lay hands on him and he will crumple to nothingness."

"Are you certain your opinion of Lethington is not goaded by jealousy? For a time I thought you would ask Fleming to be your wife."

"Frankly, it never occurred to me. She is the prettiest and the most amusing of your ladies—but not the kind of wife I would choose."

"What kind would you choose?"

"I've never really given it any thought—and a good thing too, considering how bleak my future seems now. Pity the wife who waits at home while her husband sits out a term in prison and exile."

"Your parents were separated by like circumstances."

"Aye, my mother had it that way for ten years off and on. My father was gone a year or two at a time—in prison or exile—to await your father's displeasure to pass."

"Would you say my father was unjust?"

"No, the punishment was deserved."

Without warning she brought her riding crop down on the mare's rump and galloped off, leaving him far behind. He laughed. "So it's a game of tag she wants," he said, digging his spurs in deep and racing after her. He caught up to her a quarter of a mile down the field and cut her off sharply by blocking her path.

Her horse reared and threw her to the ground, where she landed in a snowbank. He dismounted quickly and ran to her, cursing himself for allowing her to play this dangerous game. She hadn't moved since her fall, and he knelt down beside her worriedly.

Her hand shot out, and laughing, she pulled him down into the snow with her. Their faces nearly touched, and he was struck with the impulse to take her in his arms. Instead, he pulled her sharply to her feet.

"Have you forgotten that you were ill a month ago?" he said gruffly. "Lying here in the wet could put you back in a sickbed."

"Forgetfulness is often the best medicine," she said.

"What is it you wish to forget, madam?"

"That I am so badly used by others—and always have been. At night when I am alone memories prick my conscience and I am reminded of Huntly and his family—and you . . ."

He longed to shake her—shake her and shout at her, until she saw the danger in her passiveness. Would she never wake from this dream of hers? Even now she need only ask and he would ride to rally an army to support her. If only once she would take a positive stand.

But the words never left him; he turned away from her and went to gather their horses. They rode back in silence, and when they returned to Coldingham, Mary went directly to her chambers.

They were both strangely quiet that evening. They made up a foursome at primero for a while, but Johnnie sensed that neither one of his guests seemed able to concentrate and suggested they do something else. Mary and Janet left him with Bothwell and went to the sitting room to work on their embroidery.

"Shall I set up the chess pieces?" Johnnie asked.

Bothwell shook his head. "My mind is not for it tonight."

"Dice?"

"No."

"Then we will talk," Johnnie said, settling himself in a chair. "Did something happen during your ride this afternoon?"

Bothwell shook his head; he was in an odd mood and wanted to be left alone. "Look here," he said with forced pleasantness, "you needn't feel obliged to amuse me. Do whatever pleases you. I want some air and I'm about to take a stroll on the beach."

He left quickly, before Johnnie could offer to go with him.

5

Janet had a small feast prepared for them to celebrate the coming New Year. Three kinds of meats were served, baked and roasted. There were roasted pheasants, glazed and garnished with fruit, and puddings and cakes with fruit tarts for dessert.

Everyone, including the servants, gathered in the Great Hall. Mary had the seat of honor on Johnnie's right, and Bothwell sat next to Janet. The servants were given seats on a lower tier, below the salt, in order of their importance. Johnnie, filled with camaraderie and brandywine, toasted everyone, even the chimney sweep and his future heirs. Bothwell's mood had improved, too, and he matched Johnnie cup for cup, though he was less boisterous, for he had a better head for drink.

Amid the gaiety, Bothwell saw that Janet's adoring glances

were always on Johnnie; she seemed more in love with him than ever. She had matured amazingly after only a year of marriage. She was very appealing in a gown of peacock-blue silk with her reddish-gold hair done up in a crown of curls. He would not have known her from the scrae lass she had been before.

But Mary was the crowning touch; she was like a glittering ornament that lent its radiance to the somber gray stone walls. She wore a persimmon satin gown, cut to bare her shoulders and accentuate their sloping gracefulness. Her chestnut hair was caught up in a snood, dotted with tiny splinters of emeralds and diamonds, and her jewel-flecked eyes shone to the flicker of rushlights. She laughed at Johnnie's nonsense and at Bothwell's antics, taking special delight in everything.

After the sweets, a trio of pipers and some fiddlers came in to play for them. Johnnie got up and pulled Janet to her feet, and they danced out to the floor.

Bothwell went to Mary and bowed. "Will you do me the honor, madam?" he said, offering his arm. "My sister's husband appears to have forgotten his manners."

She took his hand and walked to the floor with him. "Please don't blame Johnnie," she said. "I told him I wanted no special attention tonight."

His arms encircled her loosely and they danced off. The top of her hair touched his cheek and he inhaled her fragrance. He had held her like this before. . . .

"You dance well, my lord," she said.

"Your Majesty remarked on that the last time we danced."

"So I did. I marvel you still remember."

"It was a farewell masque at St.-Germain, before the Court journeyed to Orléans. I was your partner to the Highland fling."

"It seems so long ago," she said wistfully. "The girl you danced with seems to have existed in another world. She moved about as in a dream—"

"Are you so different now, madam?"

Her answer was lost, for Johnnie swept her away and Janet took her place.

On New Year's Day, Bothwell began to make plans for his departure. A man in Berrington offered him refuge in his home—for a price—and Bothwell accepted. But if it had been difficult before, it was doubly hard to leave Scotland now.

In the past, he had never felt close to anyone, or anything—and he was the first to admit the fault lay with him. He thought of himself as part of the Border and its people, but even that was not quite true. He had never really established roots anywhere—something prevented him from doing so. He had touched many lives, but none had touched his, no one had ever penetrated him deeper than the surface.

He knew the opinion others had of him; they called him a bold adventurer, arrogant and vainglorious, and thought he lived for the sport of battle and the favor of women. But they saw only what he wanted them to see, for he cared nothing for their opinions. Admittedly, he was proud of his skill on the battlefield; the first clash of steel always thrilled him. And he reveled in the attention women paid him. Now suddenly those things were not enough.

He had never given any part of himself to anyone, but after this week spent at Coldingham, an infinitesimal part of him would remain here always. It may have been the friendship he had found here when he needed it most. Whatever the reason, he had begun to sprout roots, and he longed to plant them—to belong. Scotland, Mary, Janet, Johnnie—even their baby— something of himself had gone out to each of them.

These were his thoughts when, heavyhearted, he left Coldingham, expecting to sail for France. They were still in his mind when he was betrayed a few days later at Berrington and taken a prisoner to England.

There were times in the next eighteen months when Bothwell would look back on this Christmas holiday with bitterness and longing, for although she had no legal right to hold him, Queen Elizabeth kept him a prisoner for that length of time.

Shabby, suffering every privation, without funds and friends in a belligerent country, Bothwell alternated the time in prisons, watched over by warders, and at the mercy of anyone who wished to make sport of him.   .

Then, at last, more than two years after the Arran kidnap plot, Bothwell gained his release. France held little hope for him, except as a means to live, but there was no other place to go. Even there his enemies worked toward his ruin. In keeping with his scheming wit, rather than the courage to do the deed himself, Lethington bribed some of Bothwell's servants to murder him. But at the last minute, despite Bothwell's ignorance of the plan, the forceful personality of their master rendered them incapable of carrying it out. It was apparent that as long as his enemies remained in power, Bothwell could never return to Scotland.

CHAPTER VII

1

Mary was in love and had taken another husband. She had fallen madly, deeply and unreasonably in love with her distant cousin, Henry, Lord Darnley. Bothwell had met him while in England and remembered him as an exceptionally tall lad, fair-haired with a peaches-and-cream complexion, and somewhat feminine in manner.

Darnley was younger than Mary and a Catholic, and he had some vague claim to the succession, for they shared the same grandmother. His religious affiliations were odious to the Protestants, and Mary's nobles were strenuously opposed to the match; James and his adherents had threatened open rebellion if the wedding took place, and when she married her "lang love," they made good their threat.

Although the people refused to support James' rebellion, he was too powerful for the meager army Mary had assembled. Her new husband's talents lay in reading poetry, lute playing, and the latest fashions, not in warfare. And Mary immediately thought of the one man on whom she could depend—Bothwell.

She summoned him back from exile, and Bothwell made a swift departure from France. Despite England's desperate attempts to stop him, Bothwell arrived safely in Eyemouth Harbor with a store of munitions he had gathered on the Continent.

He climbed the broad stairway to Mary's apartments and paused outside her door to beat the dust of travel from his clothes, for he had only landed that morning in Scotland. Three years had passed since he had been in Holyrood, yet nothing seemed changed, except himself.

Imprisonment and exile had taken their toll; the changes were small but evident at first glance. He had never been fleshy, but he was thinner now; his body had become harder and more muscular. The skin at his temples was pulled taut, his eyes were more tense and deeply set, and there were new lines of hardness around his mouth.

Music came from Mary's audience chamber, and when Bothwell entered, he saw her half-hidden in shadow. Dancing flames from a candelabrum played on her face, and he was struck by her absolute serenity as she listened to the lute player's love song.

Seton was the first to see him; she started to rise, but he motioned her still. Then Mary looked up and smiled. She rushed to her feet and started toward him, but he was with her before she could take a step.

He knelt and kissed her hand.

She clapped her hands for silence and said to the others, "Leave us."

The music came to an abrupt end and the room emptied. Bothwell stepped back and came to the sudden realization that she was finally a woman. That time at Johnnie's house, more than two years ago, she had still been a mere slip of a girl. But she had emerged from the unsure awkwardness of girlhood into a woman—a woman in love.

Everything about her spoke of change; her eyes held a secret that her body revealed. She was possessed of a quiet confidence that comes of being in love. He had sensed it immediately and resented it. But his practical side told him that she might at last begin to rule as she ought. The thanks, of course, would go to

Darnley; for him she had lifted herself from torpidity to defy her brother. But the reason didn't matter, as long as Scotland benefited.

Mary returned to her chair. "Welcome, my lord," she said. "You travel fast."

"Thanks to the English, madam. But I gave them a merry chase through Europe for their trouble."

"Thank God they didn't succeed in stopping you, for I have need of you."

"You have only to command me, madam."

Relief flooded her eyes, and he wondered if she had been afraid that he would refuse to come.

"There is so much to be done, I scarcely know where to start."

He smiled. "The beginning is always a good start. Where are the rebels now?"

"At last report they were camped in the west, near the English border."

"Then we must move quickly, lest they escape to safety. I've managed to assemble a quantity of arms—and a promise of two thousand fighting men from Sarlebous in France, if they are needed."

"You've not been idle, my lord. I am already comforted."

"It's too soon to take comfort. There is still the Border to amass—without them your campaign lacks force."

"I am depending upon you for that. You shall be restored to your post as lieutenant of the Border, and you will have command of the troops."

"It takes time to raise an army, madam. Old alliances must be resumed, new ones formed."

"How much time will you need?"

"A week—perhaps less, with luck."

She laughed. "I should have known that you would measure time by a shorter ruler than most."

Her bedchamber door opened, and Darnley appeared in a maroon velvet robe. "Must I wait forever while you chatter the night away?" he said peevishly.

Color sprang to her cheeks, but her eyes betrayed her pleasure. "I thought you were already asleep, sire. Lord Bothwell arrived only a while ago. We have been discussing the coming campaign."

He put his arm around Mary's waist and drew her close. His manner changed to graciousness. "Bothwell, eh, damn glad you're here at last. Her Majesty has awaited your arrival as anxiously as she would the Messiah's."

"Pray don't confuse me with that exalted being, sire. I could never measure up to the image."

"From the tales I've heard, you would have a deuced time of it in the attempt."

Bothwell laughed. "Frankly, the prospect of saintliness fills me with dread."

Mary chuckled softly and Darnley's grasp on her tightened. His glance strayed about, as though searching for something.

"Where is the wine?" he asked. "Lord Bothwell's homecoming should be toasted in proper style."

"It is late, Harry."

Bothwell said, "Another time, sire. I plan on an early start for the Border in the morning."

His tone peevish again, Darnley nodded. "Very well, one time is as good as another."

Mary disengaged herself and offered her hand to Bothwell. "Until next week, my lord," she said.

Before the door closed behind him, Bothwell heard Darnley say, "Come to bed, Mary," and he pulled the door shut with a bit more force than he had intended.

In the courtyard, Bothwell met Captain Erskine, who had charge of Mary's guard. "When do we march against the Bastard?" Erskine asked.

"At the month's end. It will take me that long to rally forces."

"I knew we'd see some action once you were back, my lord."

"Aye, the shoe is on the other foot now. It's my enemies who are on the run."

"Did you see the King?"

Bothwell nodded.

"How did he impress you?"

"No different than when he was a lad in Queen Elizabeth's Court. But he is still new to his position—it's too soon to say what he will do with it."

Erskine took a pouch from his belt and shook out a coin. He handed it to Bothwell. "Have you seen the new coin of the Realm?"

Bothwell held it up to the light. The newly minted metal reflected the flames, and in coppery glow he saw the etched profiles of Mary and Darnley.

"Two prettier faces I've never seen," he commented dryly.

Erskine snorted. "Aye, he's a dainty lad, for all his height. The Queen heaps him with honors galore, as though she need call down the stars from heaven to prove her love."

"God grant he is worthy of it," Bothwell said.

2

Good as his word, Bothwell was back at Holyrood within the week. He had the Johnstones and Jardines, the Kerrs, Turnbulls, and Rutherfords, all on his side. Liddesdale and Teviotdale were his too—after a slight skirmish with a few stubborn Elliots. Mary had reinstated him to the Privy Council and declared her intention to give him command of the troops.

There was only one dissenting voice—Darnley. He stood and faced the Council. "Dumfries is part of the western marches;

my father is lieutenant there, and the command should go to
him."

"But, sire," Mary said gently, "your father is occupied in
preventing Argyll from joining forces with my brother. It will
take him at least another week to secure matters there."

"Then we will wait," Darnley replied haughtily.

Concealing his anger, Bothwell said, "I have fifteen thousand
men standing ready to fight now, sire. Waiting might cost us the
campaign."

The other members added their agreement.

"I'll not see my father robbed of an honor that is his by
right."

Lord Mar injected angrily, "Would you sooner permit the
rebels to escape for the mere satisfaction of one man's glory,
sire?"

The Earl of Morton gave his backing. "That foolhardy delay
would keep an entire army idle. Do you propose they wait on
the pleasure of one? Besides, my lord Bothwell is a better
general of the two."

They argued for an hour; in the end Darnley's obstinacy won
out.

Avoiding Bothwell's scathing glance, Mary said, "We will
wait until the Earl of Lennox is free to take command."

One by one they filed out. Only Bothwell remained. He was
determined to face her with his justifiable fury. He was both
shocked and disappointed to discover that she had freed herself
from James' influence to be led by an empty-headed youth.

His voice betrayed his disgust. "Was it Your Majesty's
intention to recall me for this?"

Mary sat frozen, twisting a lace handkerchief in her hands.
"You know it was not," she said miserably. "*You* were to have
command."

"Then why in God's name did you agree to your husband's
demands?"

"He is still such a child in many ways—so unsure of himself."

"And so you indulge him." Fury choked his words back, and the damage had already been done. But he made a silent vow that he would not let her destroy Scotland for a golden-haired lad—not even if he had to fight Mary herself.

He started for the door, then paused and turned. "Your Realm is a dangerous plaything to trust to a child, madam."

He stormed out, past the guards, past a group of lords, and went to his waiting horse. Mounting, he jerked the reins savagely from his groom's hands and rode off. Fresh fury overwhelmed him; it was her nature to be led—and she would always choose the wrong man to lead her.

Bothwell was late in arriving at the palace; he had almost decided not to come at all. Before their quarrel that afternoon, Mary had invited him to sup with her. He had accepted but had changed his mind after the Council meeting. Then, at the last minute, he dressed hurriedly and went despite his anger.

It was a private party, held in Mary's small supping room. Only Mary and Darnley and a swarthy, hunchbacked little man, whom Bothwell had never seen before, were there. The stranger had caught his eye immediately, and from the look of him, he was no Scot.

Judging by his doublet of red velvet, decorated with diamond-shaped inserts of gold silk, he could have passed for a jester. But jesters did not take supper with the King and Queen, nor did their fingers gleam with magnificent jewels, nor were their shoulders adorned with heavy gold chains. No, Bothwell thought, this was no ordinary buffoon; those shining black eyes revealed intelligence, and the ease with which he spoke to Mary showed him to be much more than that—much more. . . .

Darnley rose and greeted Bothwell amiably. He could afford to be agreeable now that he had had his own way.

"The guest of honor has arrived at last," Darnley said.

Bothwell glanced at the mantel clock. "A little late, I fear, sire."

Darnley waved his hand aside magnanimously. "No matter, you are here now. Come, take your place, there is someone I want you to meet."

Bothwell bowed to Mary and took his seat beside her.

Darnley said, "This is our very good friend, Signor David Rizzio."

Rizzio stood and bowed. "We meet at last, Lord Bothwell. Her Majesty has paid you many compliments."

"Then you have me at a disadvantage, Signor Rizzio, for I've heard nothing of you."

Mary said, "Davie came to us three years ago in the train of the Savoyard ambassador, Moretta. He has been with us ever since."

Rizzio smiled. "I began as a bass in Her Majesty's quartet, and when Her Majesty's French secretary vacated his post, I succeeded to it." He looked at Mary affectionately. "Is it not fantastic the heights a poor man may attain in this wondrous Realm?"

"I pray you never find it otherwise, for here in this *wondrous* Realm, men may fall as quickly," Bothwell said, glancing at Mary.

She looked away and said, "Davie is invaluable to us. He was especially brilliant in negotiating with Rome and Spain. The King and I were wed before Rome sent the dispensation, but Davie won their approval, thereby saving us great difficulty. But more, were it not for Davie, we might never have wed at all."

Darnley bristled. "I should like to think it was for love alone you wed me."

She reached across to pat his hand. "Of course, dearest, I cannot credit Davie with that."

"I should not wish Lord Bothwell to be misled."

Amused, Bothwell said, "Rest assured, sire, there was never a doubt in my mind."

They ate amid a flow of light conversation. Bothwell watched Darnley heap gluttonous portions of fowl and meat on his plate, but he scarcely touched any of it. He filled himself with wine instead, and by the time dessert came, he was slumped over in a druglike stupor, his leaden weight resting against Mary.

The table was cleared, and Rizzio took up his lute. Darnley slept while Mary and Bothwell listened to the music. Bothwell felt a relaxed contentment—the first he had known in three years. Rizzio's love song added a subtle flavor to the mood, and when Bothwell glanced at Mary, she seemed lost in a dream.

She looked at Darnley and her eyes warmed. Bothwell sensed that a part of her had drifted beyond the boundaries of the room, as though her spirit roamed free, and he wondered at the fantasies her mind was spinning.

Darnley stirred and woke; the magic of a moment ago was gone. He struggled to his feet and his attendant hurried to support him, but Darnley shook him off and went to Mary.

He bent to kiss her. "Pray excuse me, dearest," he slurred. "I am not well—perhaps if I slept . . . "

She smiled up at him and touched his hair lovingly. "I shall look in on you later," she promised.

Darnley staggered out, leaning on his attendant.

Rizzio put his lute aside and joined them. "I have heard that you are an excellent judge of horses, Lord Bothwell," he said.

"I've made some fortunate buys from time to time. Are you in the market for one?"

"In a manner of speaking. Her Majesty has graciously rewarded me with my pick of any mount in her stables. Frankly, I am at a loss to choose."

"Will it be a battle steed, one suited for the chase, or an ambler?"

Rizzio made a humble little gesture. "You flatter me, my lord. With my deformities, I am thankful for a gentle trotter."

"Davie is too modest," Mary said. "At the hunt he rides with the best of us."

Bothwell paused to take a long look at Rizzio and decided that he could like him. He didn't believe the role Rizzio played, that of an amusing but thoughtless fellow. On the contrary, he would be willing to wager that beneath the little Italian's carefree good humor lay a quick-witted brain. A brain more keen than Rizzio wished to have known. And to his credit, he seemed devoted to Mary.

"Meet me at the stables tomorrow morning," Bothwell said. "You shall have the gentlest of Her Majesty's amblers."

"You are too kind, my lord. A pity all Her Majesty's nobles are not more like you."

"What quarrel have you with them?"

"They think it an outrage that she befriends a low-born creature like myself. That, and the fact I am Catholic, appears to have inspired their hatred."

"Then let me warn you, signor, being seen in my company will only add to that hatred."

Rizzio laughed. "Her Majesty seems willing to take that risk, and I wear their hatred as a medal of honor." He returned to his lute and struck up a melody.

Bothwell whispered, "A talented fellow, your Davie, madam. Musician, secretary, and heaven knows what more."

She said, "He is a friend, counselor, and always a great source of comfort to me."

"Then I advise you to see that he acquires no new enemies among the nobles. They are a broody lot—it's their nature to begrudge even the meanest favor to others."

"Davie is under my protection; he needn't fear anyone."

Unable to resist the twit, Bothwell said, "Then I envy him,

for who knows better than I what the lack of that may bring."
He rose. "With your permission, madam, I bid you good night."
She nodded stiffly. "Good night, my lord."

The courtyard at Holyrood was packed with armed men:
white-leather-jacked Borderers, hackbuteers cased in mail,
morions gleaming in the October sun, the glint of steel pike tips,
and the restless stamp of horses' hooves. Mary came out and
mounted her palfrey; she wore light armor under her heavy
wool cloak and carried a steel helmet. Her face glowed with
excitement, and Bothwell recalled that she was always at her
best when danger threatened.

She glanced at the empty mount beside her and looked up at
Darnley's windows. Impatience flickered in her eyes, then it
was gone when the heavy wooden doors parted and Darnley
came out. Three servants followed at his heels, carrying his
helmet, gloves, and whip.

Darnley swirled his fur-trimmed cape over one shoulder, and
the sun bounced off his armor blindingly. He was resplendent in
a gilt breastplate. He mounted, put on his helmet, then his
perfumed gloves, and two grooms ran forward to adjust his
stirrups as the sound of muffled laughter rose from Bothwell's
battle-scarred moss-troopers.

The trumpets sounded, a tuck of drums, and the procession
marched to a piper's tune. Morton came abreast of Bothwell as
they rode up the Cannongate. Hackbuteers separated them from
Mary and Darnley in the swill-splashed roadway.

Smiling, Bothwell turned to Morton. " 'Twould be a pity to
see the King's finery spattered," he said. "He makes such a
pretty sight."

Morton snickered in his red beard. "I pity the horse more,
for the weight of his armor. Only a miracle will prevent them
both from sinking in the bog."

Bothwell laughed and glanced sideways at Morton, whose own armor, though lighter than Darnley's, was no less cumbersome. Morton still clung to the standard battle dress and bore the extra weight of a heavy two-handed broadsword. Bothwell favored the freedom of a leather jack and the maneuverability of his rapier. His only armor was sleeves of linked chain mail.

They met Lennox at Biggar, then extended the march to Castle Hill for a council of war. They were all day planning their strategy; Lennox seemed more concerned with ceremony than battle, and Darnley hampered them with useless suggestions.

It was long after dark when they finally agreed on a course of action. Lennox elected to lead the vanguard, Atholl would take the rear guard, and Darnley would ride at the head of the main body of men—but all decisions in the field were to be made by Bothwell, with Morton and Mar to assist him.

Last reports had the rebel army camped at Dumbries, but that had been four days ago; now they found only a deserted campsite. James and his allies had fled, unmolested, to the safety of England.

Mary called the lords together for another meeting. She seemed disappointed and, Bothwell thought, relieved as well. It occurred to him that she might not have been too anxious to bring complete ruin upon her errant brother after all.

Lord Mar asked, "What of the rebels now, madam?"

"Since we cannot cross the border to engage them, they may remain exiled in England."

Bothwell glanced at the others. They seemed content that no battle had been fought; he seemed to be the only one who felt impotent rage because of this Chaseabout Raid. He pushed his way forward.

"Do you think it wise to leave this territory unguarded, madam?" he asked. "Your rebels need only wait for us to go before they cross back into Scotland undetected."

"What do you suggest, my lord?"

"Leave a force of men here. That way you are assured they cannot return or communicate with any followers left behind."

"An excellent thought," she said. "You shall have charge of that. Keep as many men as you need to see the matter done; the rest may return to their homes."

Two hundred hackbuteers and eleven hundred Borderers stayed with Bothwell. Mary and Darnley returned to Edinburgh. Left to his own, Bothwell went straight to work, determined to block every effort the rebels might make to reenter Scotland.

Dividing his men into groups, he spread them across the western Border with instructions to watch for any unusual activity on the English side. Outposts were set up to intercept communications, and within two weeks not so much as a bird crossed into Scotland without Bothwell's knowledge and consent. His network complete, he put the Master of Maxwell in command and returned to Edinburgh.

3

On Christmas Eve, Mary gave a banquet in Bothwell's honor. As he entered the Great Hall, the first familiar face Bothwell saw was George Gordon. He was the Earl of Huntly now, for Bothwell had urged Mary to reinstate him on his return from France. The last time they had met both had been on the verge of ruination. Now Bothwell wondered if Huntly had forgiven him for refusing to join his father's quarrel with Mary.

Others had said that Huntly was a changed man; now Bothwell realized sadly that it was true, for Gordon's fiery ways seemed gone. He stood off to a side, stoop-shouldered and ill at ease. His eyes, once so clear and defiant, bore a look that trusted no man and doubted all.

Huntly smiled dimly at Bothwell. "It appears that your recent difficulties have in no way changed you, my lord."

"And you," Bothwell asked, "are there ghosts that still haunt you from the past?"

"A few perhaps—but I have reconciled myself to live at peace with them."

"Better that you dislodge them, my friend. They can only serve you ill."

Huntly shrugged. "The future may provide me with the means."

"Aye, the future offers a remedy for all ills. Come, join me in a drink."

They went to the refreshment table. Bothwell raised his cup. "To the future—may fortune always smile upon us."

They spoke of old times, then Bothwell asked, "What of your family? Are they well?"

"Aye. My mother and younger brother, Adam, reside with me. My sister, Jean, is lady-in-waiting to the Queen. There she is now, dancing with Lord Robert," he said, pointing across the floor.

Bothwell looked in the direction Huntly indicated. He had seen her before in Mary's company, but she was scarcely the type of woman to interest him. She was unattractively plain with sandy hair, pale blue eyes, and a nose and mouth too large for her thin face. Her gown of rose satin did nothing to add the color she needed, nor did it enhance her straight, narrow figure.

Huntly followed his glance, possibly even his thoughts. "Jean is not pretty, I grant you. But she has a keen mind and many admirable qualities. The man who weds her will be fortunate."

"No doubt," Bothwell said disinterestedly. "As I recall, the Queen said she is betrothed to Alex of Boyne. When is the wedding to be?"

Huntly scowled. "Never! It is broken off—another of the Queen's ladies, Mary Beaton, has won his heart. And Jean, the little fool, is overcome with grief for the loss of her true love."

Bothwell shrugged. "A woman's grief is more fickle than weather. Give her something new to fill the void and her unhappiness will soon be forgotten. Find her a husband, that will dry her tears."

"Jean is not like most women. It will take her longer to forget. In any case, all the younger men are already spoken for, which leaves only the elderly widowers—and Jean will never have one of those." He paused, then slyly he said, "Of course, the most eligible of our young noblemen has not been claimed yet."

"Who?"

"Yourself. You could do worse than Jean. She will bring a handsome dowry to the man she weds—something you cannot afford to sneer at."

The proposal had taken Bothwell off guard; he could not refuse without offending Huntly.

Vaguely, he answered, "Aye, it's something to think on."

"Why wait? You are almost thirty with only the turbulence of your youth to look back on. It's high time you took a wife—a union of Gordons and Hepburns is no mean thing. One of your own ancestors deemed it a fit match."

The first Earl of Bothwell had wed a Gordon in James IV's time.

Smiling, Bothwell said, "Gently now. You'll never get a horse to the stall by pushing from behind."

Later everyone repaired to the Banquet Hall. When they were seated, Mary rose from her place on the dais and clapped for silence.

"My lords and ladies," she said smiling, "I have happy news for you. With God's grace, the King and I will present Scotland with an heir, come next June."

A loud clatter of applause and congratulations rang out; cups were filled and toasts proposed. Only Bothwell, seated next to Mary, remained curiously quiet.

For some unexplainable reason Mary's announcement left him numb. He felt as though the blood had ceased to flow through him, then suddenly it gushed to his brain and his head seemed about to burst. The scene before him turned to mist, and he was blinded by anger.

His glance fell on Darnley, who sat smiling proudly; he held himself even more haughtily than usual, as though he were the only man capable of begetting such miracles. Bothwell found the sight of Darnley's pink and white face intolerable, and he turned away.

Bewildered by his strange reaction, he shook his head to clear it—there was murder in his heart without his knowing why. The hall felt unbearably hot; the shouting grated on his nerves. The arras behind him flapped, and he felt a cold draft on his back. He thought some air might help—he might have had too much wine. If he could slip away—out to the courtyard. Slowly he eased his chair back and started to rise.

Mary glanced at him questioningly.

He said, "With your permission, madam. I am taken with a sudden need for air."

She got up with him and took his arm. They walked to a quiet corner, away from the others.

"You have been strangely silent since my announcement, Bothwell," she said. "Have you no good wishes for me?"

"The very best, madam."

"Then why are you so withdrawn this evening? I am giving this banquet for you, yet you are the most solemn one here."

"In the past Your Majesty expressed the desire that I conduct myself with more austerity. Now that I do you complain."

She laughed. "If this is the new you, then I need time to accustom myself to the change."

Her teasing infuriated him. He blurted, "Since it is my intention to wed soon, I must practice a more sober countenance."

Her smile faded. "You are to be wed?"

Although the words had come from him, he was no less surprised than she. Yet her astonishment baited his anger. "Why not, madam? Is it so difficult to believe that a woman will have me?"

"On the contrary, more the wonder that you are willing to settle down with *one*. Somehow I have never thought of you as a—"

"Husband, madam? Am I so different from other men? Scotland is at peace, and so should I be."

Her voice turned oddly husky. "Who is it to be?"

He blurted the first name that came to mind. "Lady Jean Gordon."

"I thought you barely knew each other. Jean said nothing to me."

"I doubt she knows herself, as yet, madam. Her brother and I spoke of it only briefly, earlier this evening."

"Then how can you be certain with so scarce an acquaintance?"

"I can think of nothing to hasten friendship sooner than marriage."

She smiled again. "You are outrageous. Is nothing sacred to you?"

He shrugged. "I am credited with two wives already—a third cannot hold much excitement for me. There is Janet Beaton, who folk say is handfasted to me, and a French lady that I am alleged to have left behind in Paris. In a manner of speaking you could say that Lady Jean will be my third victim."

"If you were never wed to these women how can they be called your wives? Such rumors should be dispelled."

"It's scarce worth the effort, madam. Let them think what they will—it's of no consequence to me."

"Perhaps you are right to ignore them. Jean's love is all that will matter. I am certain she will pay scant attention to such talk."

"Love, madam? Have I spoken of love?"

"No, but it is natural to assume—"

"Not at all, madam. Lord Huntly tells me that Jean still loves Alex of Boyne, despite his betrothal to Lady Beaton."

"And this knowledge does not disturb you?"

"Not in the least. Prudent folk do not confuse love with marriage. My demands in a wife are few; I care nothing for Jean's affection, as long as it doesn't interfere with her duty to me. Besides, a loving wife could prove a hindrance to a man like myself."

"But to wed without love. Even I, who had first to consider political wisdom, made a match of the heart."

"Love is a fancy one merely contemplates, madam." He frowned. "Can it be that you do not approve of my choice?"

She colored. "Of course not. Jean will make you an ideal wife. She is intelligent and staid—more so than most girls her age. Who knows but she may have a sobering influence on you."

He laughed. "Heaven protect me from that horror."

Once Bothwell had committed himself there was no way of backing out. He called on Huntly the following day and asked for Jean's hand. Huntly was delighted; they toasted the match, then he called his mother and Jean to tell them the news.

Jean's attitude was cool but resigned. The elderly Lady Huntly shared her son's pleasure; she beamed at the couple and gave them her blessings. Then she made a clumsy exit, dragging Huntly with her.

Left alone with Bothwell, Jean sat stiffly in a high-backed chair without speaking; her hands lay primly in her lap, her eyes lowered demurely. She seemed even less attractive to Bothwell now than she had last night. He noticed that she didn't paint her face; her lips were pale and bloodless, her complexion pallid.

He waited for her to speak, but she remained silent. The prospect of wedded life with this dull creature appalled Bothwell; he could envision their nights together—Jean in one chair, he in another, a book in his hand, perhaps, a piece of embroidery in hers, and a heavy wall of silence between them. He might comment on the weather, she would nod, he might make mention of a recent foray, or an incident at Court, and she would nod. He vowed that unless Jean changed drastically after marriage, he would avoid such agonies—or die of galloping boredom.

He went to the window to peer out. "Does the betrothal please you, my lady?" he asked.

"I am a dutiful daughter and an obedient sister, my lord. My brother heads our family now, and I must wed whom he chooses."

A good beginning, he thought; her romancing may turn my head.

"Then I may expect in you a dutiful and obedient wife," he said.

"You may, my lord."

He felt a chill and thought: *She is cold as the sea.*

Twelfth Night revels followed Christmas, and Bothwell and Jean were often together. Jean brought little warmth to their meetings; her manner remained always coolly distant. Nor did Bothwell ask, or want, more of her.

He felt neither pleasure nor disappointment in their betrothal, for his outlook was coldly realistic. His estates were going to ruin and were sorely in need of a woman's touch. If Jean was quiet and distant, then so be it; the past had been adventuresome enough—if the future proved too dull he could provide diversions enough for himself. Besides, there was no woman he preferred to Jean; women, in fact, had begun to bore him of late. Jean would do as well as any for him.

4

The wedding day was set for the twenty-fourth of February. Huntly sealed the union by providing Jean with a dowry of twelve thousand marks, but the money would do Bothwell little good since all but one thousand of it had been set aside for the redemption of Crichton.

Huntly made a solemn affair of signing the marriage contract, and Bothwell forced himself to follow his example. But he could not entirely conceal his amusement when he read the clause concerning Crichton, investing Jean with "the towns and mains of that property for all the days of her life."

Later, when he strolled with Jean in the garden, Bothwell said, "You appear quite taken with Crichton, my lady."

She smiled. "I have always thought it one of the loveliest estates."

"Have you ever been there?"

"Yes, when I attended your sister's wedding."

He had suspected Jean's influence in that special clause. Now he was certain of it—she came alive at the mere mention of Crichton. Glancing at her now, he saw that her normally lusterless eyes sparkled.

"It has changed since my father's time. Thanks to my enemies it is sorely in need of repair."

"After we are wed, perhaps you will allow me to take charge of restoring it."

This was the first time he had heard her allude to their wedding.

He nodded indifferently. "If it pleases you. My duties allow me little leisure; you may find it a pleasant way to spend your time."

"The Queen depends upon you a great deal. It is said that you rank highest in her favor." She hesitated. "Frankly, my lord, I marvel that you find time to take a wife."

"I serve Her Majesty as best I am able. But royal favor is often short-lived—a wife is said to be more faithfast."

"She is indeed, my lord."

They had walked the length of the garden and back. He stood aside to let Jean precede him into the house. "You will excuse me, my lady; I am expected at the palace," he said, taking his leave.

The instant Bothwell saw Mary he knew that she was in a prankish mood and bursting to tell him something. Reluctantly, he had to admit that motherhood was becoming to her—she was radiant and lovelier than ever.

He had seen this change in other women, but he had refused to recognize it in Mary until now. In fact, he had refused to think about it at all since her announcement on Christmas Eve. At first, he had wondered at his angry resentment, then it seemed best not to probe too deeply.

Mary tapped the arm of her chair impatiently. "You are late, my lord."

"My apologies, madam. I have just come from signing my marriage contract."

"Then I forgive you. I regret having to tear you away from your future bride at so tender a moment. No doubt Jean is all aflutter, now the wedding day is scarce two weeks away."

"As always, Jean is entirely cool-headed, madam."

She got up and went to the door. "Come with me. I have something to show you."

He followed her out, and they climbed a circular stairway that led to a small turret room where her personal belongings were stored. Bolts of cloth stood propped against the wall, and she selected one of silver, unrolled it, and draped a length of it over her shoulder.

"Do you think this worthy of your bride?" she asked. "She may have it for her wedding dress."

The effect was bewitching; the shimmering silk gave her skin the translucence of pearl—he couldn't bear to think of Jean gowned in it.

He looked away and rasped, "Jean is too plain for it, madam."

"Nonsense. I want Jean to have it. There is more. Harry and I will give you a banquet after the wedding."

Stiffly, he said, "Your Majesty is too kind."

She touched his hand. "It is the least I can do." Then, gaily, she said, "I adore weddings, and I am especially pleased to have a part in yours."

She put the material back and they left. Bothwell started down first to lead the way. Mary stumbled; he turned quickly to break her fall with his body. She fell against him, and his arms closed unconsciously around her trembling body. He inhaled deeply the faint fragrance of crushed rose petals in her hair. Then abruptly he put her from him.

She covered her embarrassment with a smile. "How clumsy of me. Thank God you were here."

"Happily you are hale-scart and none the worse for it," he said gruffly.

"Nevertheless, you shall see me light an extra candle of thanks at mass tonight."

He held the door open to let her enter the audience chamber. "I, madam? Have you forgotten that I will not attend your mass?"

"How could I forget with your constant reminders? But this

is Candlemas, the Feast of the Blessed Virgin. Surely you will not refuse."

"I'm afraid I must, madam. It is my intention to hear Master Knox preach at St. Giles this evening."

He had heard that Knox was preaching dangerous sermons from the pulpit and wanted to investigate.

"I wonder if it is more fear than your professed hatred of the mass that prevents your attendance, my lord."

"Can you honestly believe that mere superstition is the cause, madam?"

"Why else would you oppose anything so harmless?"

"I assure you, my reasons are sound."

"Then it is mere stubbornness. Frankly, I am at a loss to understand. I might expect this from others, but you have shown such tolerance for all religion—that is what puzzles me so."

"I learned to despise the mass during my student years in France, madam. A Huguenot youth made the grave error of speaking out against Catholicism. He was silenced by three priests who whipped him half to death and left him in a pool of blood.

"I can still remember standing there in the midst of the crowd that had gathered to watch. They shouted encouragement to the priests and cried for more blood. Then they moved, and I found myself pushed along into church. A priest stepped up to the altar and began the mass. He was one of those gentle men of God who had whipped the boy. The hem of his robe was still damp with blood, which left a hideous smear on the altar rug when he knelt. I shall never forget my revulsion—I've not heard the mass since, nor do I intend to."

Her anger had abated. "You give me an isolated incident. The hems of my priests' robes are immaculate."

"Granted, madam. Nevertheless, I made a vow that day, and I shall not break it—not even for you."

Knox mounted the stone pulpit and looked out over the congregation seated on benches and stools that faced him. The great pillars appeared black and shadowy in flickering candlelight and stood like giant sentinels among the hushed, rapt faces. He began mildly with gentle exhortations, then slowly his voice gathered strength and each word became a clap of thunder.

His scraggly gray beard bobbed up and down on his black frock coat; his eyes glowed like burning coals. He was like a man possessed, shouting, ranting, pounding his fist in fury. He threatened all nonbelievers of the *true faith* with eternal damnation, cursed his enemies, and prayed for their ruin. He had worked himself to a pitch of hysteria.

Despite the spectacle, Bothwell found himself growing increasingly bored. He glanced at the door, contemplating a hasty exit. Then Knox's sermon took on a new flavor—suddenly Bothwell listened with renewed interest.

Knox shouted, "Shall we suffer that horrible regimen of women?"

This was Knox's favorite reference to Mary. Bothwell looked sidelong at Huntly seated next to him. Huntly seemed only mildly interested, not in the least disturbed by what he heard.

The voice in the pulpit thundered down, promising revenge. He accused Mary of wantonness and debauchery, and warned that her mass was more dangerous to Scotland "than an army of ten thousand enemies landed in any part of the Realm."

He screamed, "Shall that idol be suffered within this Realm?" He paused dramatically, then shouted, "No, it shall not! Death to the idolatress and to all her corrupted followers."

Bothwell sat rigid, afraid to move, lest he bolt from his seat to tear Knox from his perch.

Knox pounded out his denunciations, pledging himself against all offenders. He demanded punishment for those "who had grown to such greatness of late without merit, which will not be borne by the honest men of this Realm."

When it was over, Bothwell watched the people leave. Their eyes burned with hatred, their ears still rang with Knox's sedition, and their hearts were bitter with a rancor that brewed a deadly poison. Suddenly he was afraid for Mary.

Mary was at breakfast when Bothwell called on her the next morning. He told her about last night's sermon at St. Giles. "This treachery cannot long prevail without ending in disaster, madam," he warned.

"How can I prevent it?" she asked. "Shall I demand his expulsion from Edinburgh?"

"Do that and you make him a martyr."

"You say he threatened some of my people. Did he mention names?"

Bothwell shook his head. Before he could answer, Rizzio's voice came from the doorway.

"Knox is forever threatening, madam. But his words amount to nothing," he said. "It would take a braver man than he to put his words into deeds."

Bothwell said grimly, "I admire your confidence, but I cannot share it. Call it a premonition, but this accursed feeling I have kept me awake all night."

Mary rose from the table. "James and his allies are still in England, and I cannot recall when there has been less discord in the Realm."

Rizzio said, "I am inclined to agree with Her Majesty. The nobles have never been in greater accord."

Bothwell frowned. Despite their confidence, his uneasiness persisted. He wished that Rizzio were not always so quick to supply the balm for her wounds—it was difficult enough to make her face reality.

"Precisely why I am suspicious, madam," he said. "Experience has taught me to take heed most when my enemies appear amiable."

Then he stopped himself—perhaps they were right. Knox had been preaching sedition for years; why should his maniacal ravings seem more dangerous now?

He smiled. "Curse me for a worrisome old crone, madam. Likely I borrow trouble where there is none. It may be the approach of my wedding that makes me so."

"All bridegrooms are entitled to jangled nerves—even you, my lord," Rizzio said.

Mary teased, "It may be the prospect of bidding farewell to your past amours."

"My wedding can scarce bring me to employ such drastic measures, madam."

She laughed. "I pity Jean her efforts to mold you to the role of husband."

"Many's the man speaks that way before the wedding," Rizzio said. "But after the honeymoon—"

Bothwell reached for his cloak. "I have provided you with enough sport for one day, madam. It's a cross all bridegrooms must bear—I've been guilty of it myself."

"And so you escape to avoid it?"

"On the contrary, madam, it would pleasure me to remain, but I am due for the final sitting of my portrait. It is to be my wedding present to Jean."

5

It was a rare day for the twenty-fourth of February; the sun was out bright and clear in a very blue and cloudless sky. For his wedding clothes, Bothwell had chosen a gold silk ribbed doublet with velvet breeches and hose to match. His slashed sleeves were tailored to display the embroidery on his buff-colored lawn shirt underneath. His velvet cape was short, in the

Spanish style, trimmed with thick gold braid. He paraded up and back awhile to work the stiffness out of his new kid boots as his valet fussed with some last-minute touches on his ruff. His dressing completed, he took his velvet toque from Paris and started out to his horse.

Mary had wanted the ceremony held in the Chapel Royal at Holyrood, but he had refused. He would be wed in the Protestant faith or not at all. He had made one concession to the old faith, and that to Jean's mother; since he and Jean were related within the fourth degree, Lady Huntly had insisted on their obtaining a dispensation from Rome. It had come a week ago, but it was of questionable authenticity, for an error in the Pope's name made it smack of forgery.

Bothwell's decision to be wed at the Cannongate Kirk prevented Mary from attending; she would not lend her presence to a Protestant ceremony, and he regretted that. Despite her disappointment, she had accepted his decision without a word and had gone on to discuss plans for the banquet that was to follow at Kinloch House.

Bothwell climbed to his mount, caparisoned in gold trappings, and signaled his retinue to start. Hoards of people crowded the streets to catch a glimpse of the wedding party and their guests. He entered the church by a side door and waited there with his attendants. Guests were packed in to capacity; some had brought stools to stand on for a better view of the ceremony.

From the excited whispers and craning necks, Bothwell knew the bridal party had arrived. Jean came down the aisle on Huntly's arm, looking pale and solemn. Mary's gift of the silver cloth had been exquisitely fashioned; twelve yards of fabric had gone into the extra-wide sleeves and train, and six more yards of white taffeta had been used in the lining. Jean's veil of French Alençon lace was crowned in tiny seed pearls and fell to the floor in a graceful sweep.

Bothwell went to meet her; they stood side by side at the altar and joined hands. Her uncle, the Bishop of Galloway, officiated. Jean's hand, cradled in Bothwell's, felt cool and limp. He glanced sideways at her and remembered the silver cloth as it had looked draped over Mary's shoulder.

At Kinloch House guests rushed forward to pelt them with wheat and give their congratulations. Mary came to offer her good wishes; she seemed troubled, and glancing about, Bothwell found the source.

Darnley sat sprawled in a chair, his legs outstretched to their enormous length. He stared into space through glazed eyes, one hand dangling over the arm of his chair, holding a tipped cup that dribbled wine to the floor.

Mary followed Bothwell's glance. Quickly, she said to Jean, "You are an exquisite bride, my dear."

Jean curtsied. "It is the gown, madam."

"Nonsense, your own loveliness enhances it." She appealed to Bothwell. "What is your opinion, my lord?"

"All bridegrooms are prejudiced, madam. Therefore, I cannot but agree."

His answer had been gallant, but his eyes paid tribute to Mary alone. He thought her the most beautiful woman in the room; she wore a gown of crimson silk trimmed with gold fringe. Her hair was piled high with curls and dabbed with rubies here and there.

Jean left them to mingle with the wedding guests. Bothwell led Mary to a table set with wine and sweet cakes. He filled a glass for her.

"I marvel that I can bear the taste of this," she said, glancing at Darnley in disgust.

"All men drink, madam. You have only to observe your

nobles. It's not uncommon for them to sit at table and vomit into the rushes from drunkenness."

"But they cannot follow me to my apartments—Harry does."

He shrugged. "You embroider altar cloths, the King drinks—each to his own pleasure."

Exasperated, she said, "How can you be so casual? How can I hope to win the respect of foreign nations when the man I have elevated to the highest position in the Realm is a drunken sot?"

So Darnley was no longer her fair-haired charmer, Bothwell thought, with a stab of pleasure. He wondered what more, besides his drinking, had disenchanted her. Had she heard of the pages he took to bed, or the brothels he frequented?

"Why take your anger out on me, madam? May I remind you that you were forewarned. I was with the Cardinal when he wrote warning you that Lord Darnley was only a pretty young fool. Had you consulted me before you wed him, I would have said as much—and more."

He saw her misery and regetted his taunts. Gently he said, "Why fret yourself? If nothing else, he has served his purpose—you are bearing his child, and Scotland will have an heir."

Tournaments and banquets were held in honor of Bothwell and Jean for five days. The nights were filled with jesting and dancing until the early hours, the days with games and jousts in which Bothwell took the foremost role. But the most splendid banquet was held at Holyrood the night before they left on their honeymoon for Seton House.

The Great Hall had been lavishly decorated with gossamer draperies hung over shots of silver and gold silk. Musicians had been engaged to play all night, and at midnight the guests sat down to a supper consisting of ten varieties of meats and fish.

Mary was at her gayest; she seemed determined to enjoy herself. Even Darnley was on his best behavior; he had remained sober throughout the evening. But as supper progressed, Bothwell saw the usual pattern repeat itself.

Darnley's food remained untouched on his plate while he downed cup after cup of wine. Bothwell watched Mary's face and saw that she strained with mounting anxiety. Finally, as though she could bear no more, she leaned back and whispered something to Darnley's attendant.

Instantly Darnley came alert. He turned on her in fury. "How dare you meddle with my servants, madam?" he shouted. "I shall take as much to drink as suits me."

Lord Fleming sprang to his feet. "I give you a toast to Scotland's unborn heir," he said.

Darnley's shrill voice froze the cups in their hands. "There is a fair guess that the Queen bears no child of mine—more likely it is Solomon, son of David."

Mary turned ashen gray. Those nearest Darnley sprang to their feet, ready to pounce on him. Bothwell leaped up, overturning his chair, his hand gripping the hilt of his sword. Mary rose quickly and put her hand on his, her eyes pleading with him to desist.

She struggled for control. Her trembling voice came in a dry whisper. "My lords and ladies, I ask your indulgence. The King has had too much to drink and speaks out of his head. Please excuse me, I must see he is put to bed."

She left the hall with Darnley following, assisted by two servants. A deadly silence prevailed. Bothwell set his chair to rights and sat down. He wanted desperately to go to Mary, but he couldn't trust himself with Darnley.

"Would you rather that Jean and I remain in Edinburgh, madam?" Bothwell asked.

He had gone to Mary early the next morning, hoping in some

way to help her. She was hollow-eyed and worn, and he knew that she hadn't slept at all last night.

Tears threatened to spill down her cheeks. She touched his arm gratefully and shook her head. "I couldn't let you do that. Harry has spoiled so much already; he'll not add your honeymoon to the list. I have dealt with his drinking this long . . . "

"The situation is clean different now, madam. Mere drunkenness is one thing; that he insults you is another—and in public."

She dabbed a handkerchief to her eyes. "How can I ever face those people again? He has insinuated that filth before—but never for others to hear."

He was with her in two strides, spinning her around to face him. Incredulously he said, "And you did nothing to stop him?"

"What could I do? He said it out of drunkenness; in the morning he was always contrite and promised to never even think it again."

"What put the notion into his head? Why Rizzio?"

She looked away. "I don't know. Harry has become madly jealous of the one man in Scotland who is truly his friend."

Bluntly, he asked, "Have you given him cause to be suspicious?"

"How can you ask? Rizzio is my friend—but only that. We sometimes sit up working late into the night, or for an occasional game of cards. But never more—"

"Aye, it's innocent enough, I know. But you have allowed him such liberties as none other enjoys. It's the manner he takes with you. I myself have heard the lords grumble over his familiarity. You've used poor judgment in elevating someone they dislike so to such a high position. It's not safe for either of you."

"But to suspect Rizzio. Surely they cannot think I would

carry on an affair with a man of Rizzio's birth—if I wanted to take a lover, there are more attractive men to choose from."

He marveled at her naiveté. Had she thought that Rizzio's low-born rank or appearance would protect her?

"Logic has no place in small minds, madam. Folk think what they will—and most times I say let them. But in your case it's too dangerous. This child you bear is the future of Scotland, doubly so because it strengthens your claim to the English throne. You dare not risk even the slightest question as to its legitimacy."

"What difference does it make now—after last night? Everyone must be gossiping about it."

He wanted to comfort her, to pet her—instead, his tone held a cold command. "Dispel his suspicions any way you can. Lie to him, tell him you love him—even if it sickens you. No matter what means you employ, your husband must be made to trust in you again. And above all, never again permit Rizzio to be alone with you."

"I pray it is not too late to undo the damage." Then, with a wan smile, she said, "You must go now—you have kept Jean waiting too long already."

"Aye, Jean," he murmured.

6

Jean said nothing of the delay; she seemed pensive and uncommunicative, except for an occasional remark on the scenery as they rode along. Her silence suited Bothwell, for his thoughts were of Mary and the tempest that Darnley had stirred up with his vile accusations. Yet Jean's cold withdrawal irritated him.

He had entertained no romantic notions about their marriage, but Jean's behavior was difficult to fathom. Whether in the company of others or in the privacy of their bedchamber, she was always politely indifferent. She had yielded to him on their wedding night, doubtless out of a sense of duty, but not since. Suddenly he found himself in the role of a patient husband.

He attributed her lack of responsiveness to shyness; it had even crossed his mind that she feared him. She must have heard of his reputation with women. That could account for her pretending sleep every night, even before he got into bed. They were nearing Seton House, and he thought once they were settled and away from prying eyes, her shyness, or whatever else was bothering her, would pass.

Lord Seton had provided them with complete privacy; of the household, only the servants remained. The bridal chamber was large and airy with a sitting room attached that looked out on the beach and the Firth of Forth. It was a perfect setting for a honeymoon—all that it lacked was ardor.

Bothwell had the trunks carried up to their chambers so Jean could change from her riding clothes to something more comfortable. Out of consideration for her modesty, he waited downstairs in the library until she had completed her wardrobe. Then he joined her, totally unprepared for the sight that greeted him.

Jean had changed from her peacock-blue riding clothes to an outfit of black. Her gown was of plain black silk, devoid of any ornaments; her hair was covered by a black coif with a veil that reached to the floor. She looked more drab and unattractive than he had thought possible—even for her.

Recovering his speech, Bothwell asked, "Why the somber attire, my lady? Such garments are for mourning—they ill become a honeymoon."

She raised her head defiantly. "They are indeed dole weeds, my lord. I mourn the loss of my love, Sir Alex of Boyne."

He stared at her in disbelief. The insult was intolerable; he was infuriated past reason. He felt sorely tempted to beat the insolence out of her. But he saw the pleasure she took in his fury; her glance met his in triumph, her mouth twisted in a smirk.

His temper cooled; plainly, she wanted him to rip those hideous garments from her back. She may even have thought he would drag her to bed against her will—he could imagine how she would enjoy the part of a wronged, ill-treated wife. She could tell herself that he was a brutish beast, deserving her scorn. Aye, but he would not give her the chance.

Without another word to her, Bothwell flung open the door and shouted for Paris, ordering him to move all his possessions to another apartment.

When the last of his things had been removed, he bowed to her and said, "I've no wish to intrude on your privacy, my lady. You will no doubt be more content alone in your bereavement."

Her triumph melted to confusion as she watched him go in her mute bewilderment.

Not once during that week did Bothwell enter her chambers. He had decided to let her work out the problem in her own way. They saw each other only at mealtimes, and these were solemn affairs. After two days of this treatment, Jean showed herself inclined to make amends. She made pathetic little attempts to draw him into conversation, but he would have none of it. He sat at his end of the table in morose silence, eating with painstaking concentration, taking enormous delight in her misery.

At the close of that week Bothwell took Jean to Crichton and announced his intention to leave for Edinburgh.

"Will you not stay at least for the midday meal?" she asked.

He shook his head stubbornly. "If I leave now I can be there before dark. In any case, you have shown such fondness for solitude, I dare not intrude on you further."

Hesitantly, she asked, "When may I expect your return?"

"A week, two, perhaps three. If you are in need of anything, send a servant."

He rode off, leaving her standing forlornly in the courtyard. Her look of desolation had touched him, and he even felt a spark of admiration for her. It had taken courage to defy him; she had shown spirit where he had thought there was none. But even defiance could be tiresome when carried to extremes. It was his intention to stay away until she asked him to return—doubtless he would find her more malleable then. He vowed he would be either a proper husband to Jean—with a husband's rights—or no husband at all.

CHAPTER VIII

1

Mary was uppermost in Bothwell's mind as he rode toward Edinburgh. Her marriage to Darnley was a dismal failure; thinking back, Bothwell traced their difficulties to the Christmas holidays. He had paid it scant attention, but it seemed to stem from Darnley's excessive drinking—Mary was revolted by it. Others at Court had noticed too; he had seen their meaningful glances and had heard their whispered comments.

The fool, he thought, *the dull, stupid, mad fool.* Darnley was a mere stripling of a boy, with nothing to recommend him but a pretty face—and for that he had been raised to the highest position in the Realm. That Mary should have deigned to look twice at Darnley seemed remarkable to Bothwell. And how had Darnley treated his good fortune? He had abused it, trampled it—more, he embarrassed Mary beyond endurance and had dragged her name in the slime.

Horsewhipping was too good for him, but she had elevated the proud fool to a position which put him beyond anyone's jurisdiction—no one in Scotland could punish him. And yet, Bothwell thought, he could still change. Darnley was young; with proper guidance he might yet prove himself worthy.

A violet dusk had settled over the town when Bothwell rode up the West Bow; lights gleamed from houses on the High

Street, the Tolbooth clock chimed the hour of five, and as he passed Grievie's Tavern a ballad singer's voice filtered out to him.

Mary greeted him warmly. She offered him wine and asked him to sup with her.

"The honeymoon went well, I trust," she said.

He hadn't the slightest intention of confiding the truth. "As honeymoons do, madam."

"Did Jean come with you?"

"No, she preferred to remain at Crichton."

"I can scarcely blame her. The opening of Parliament is a dull business, and she would have seen little enough of you. I must apologize to her for taking you away so soon after the wedding."

"I am certain she expects none, madam."

"Nevertheless, it does not lessen my guilt. Perhaps she will be more apt to forgive me when she sees the surprise I have prepared for you."

"You have given us too much already."

She frowned. "Why must you always protest when I wish to give you something? Others far less deserving ask favors constantly—you never do."

"Then I shall badger you for favors from this moment hence."

She laughed. "You are impossible. Though you don't deserve it now, I have arranged quarters for you here in the palace."

Only those closest to her lodged at Holyrood. "I've no wish to appear ungrateful, madam. But with a house of my own on the Cannongate—"

She shrugged. "Call it a whim. I will feel safer, knowing you are this close."

The quarters Mary had set aside for him were large enough to accommodate himself and Jean. From the bedchamber window Bothwell had a perfect view of Arthur's Seat; from the study he could see part of the gardens and the less appealing view of the lions' pit, where two gigantic beasts prowled within the confines of their chains. These were Darnley's whim, given him by Mary soon after their wedding, when she had been unable to deny him anything. Now, looking down at the tawny beasts, Bothwell felt a surge of pity for them. He felt the injustice keenly—as he would for anyone to whom freedom had been denied.

At eight that evening, Bothwell returned to Mary's apartments for supper.

"I have asked Davie to sup with us," she told him. "You can chaperon us."

He laughed. "There's a role new to me, madam. My presence has been known more to tarnish a lady's reputation rather than save it."

"Being married recommends your respectability now."

"The sated husband, eh, madam? In any case, I am pleased to see you've taken my advice about Rizzio."

"Frankly, such deceit appalls me. Why should mere friendship between a man and woman suggest lewdness?"

"I share your distaste, but with Knox and the others seeking to discredit you, it would be foolhardy to pander to their wishes."

She nodded wearily, and he thought she looked worn. Childbearing and Darnley's beastliness were taking their toll on her. He wondered if she was strong enough to endure it.

Rizzio joined them and they sat down to supper. Platters of food were set before them, and to Bothwell's surprise he saw they contained meat and fowl.

He looked quizzically at Mary. "This is the Lenten season, is it not, madam?"

Rizzio chuckled. "Indeed, my lord, but Her Majesty has a dispensation from the Pope. His Holiness knows that childbearing is taxing and that women need their strength to overcome it."

Bothwell took a sip of Malmsey. "How are you getting on at Court these days?" he asked Rizzio.

"Not well, my lord. I can scarcely claim a civil word from the nobles."

"They treat Davie abominably," Mary said. "They rudely push and jostle him about without cause."

"Have you never attempted to defend him, madam?"

"On several occasions, but it only serves to make matters worse. They taunt him and call him my pet monkey."

"I seem to be a bone in their throats. They despise me more every day."

"I'd not regard their hatred lightly," Bothwell warned. "The lords seem in a broody mood these days. They are apt to chance anything. You might be wise to keep out of their way."

Alarmed, Mary asked, "Do you think Davie is in any real danger?"

"Now you have frightened Her Majesty," Rizzio said. "Their threats are empty words. Besides, I've nothing to fear from them; only yesterday a seer told me that I need only fear the prick of a bastard's treachery—and since the Earl of Moray is still in England, it appears I am safe."

Bothwell reached for a chicken leg. "He's not the only man in Scotland to claim the distinction of bastardy," he said.

Mary shuddered. "Your words chill me," she said. "It is as though you had a presage of the future."

"Rest assured, madam, I have no extraordinary powers—only a fair understanding of your nobility. However, I doubt you need worry, for you've begun to remedy the matter."

"Then let us talk of more pleasant matters," Mary said. "This subject depresses me so."

"It was not my intention to upset you. What shall we talk about?"

"There is tomorrow—I have decided to ask Parliament to proclaim James and his adherents outlaws before the Realm. Their lands will be forfeited and revert back to the Crown. I have had them notified to that effect and have given them until the twelfth of March to answer the charges."

Bothwell nodded his approval. "It will serve as good warning to other would-be traitors."

Then, smiling, she said, "In the procession tomorrow, you will bear the scepter before me, Huntly the crown, and Lord Crawford the sword."

She was giving Bothwell the Realm's highest honor—given only to the first noble in the land.

2

Saturday the ninth of March dawned gray; heavy clouds hovered overhead, and there was a promise of snow in the air. A bone-chilling east wind flurried up from the Nor' Loch as the procession prepared to leave for the Tolbooth. Mary came out gowned in crimson and gold robes of state. Bothwell helped her into the litter and took his place with Huntly and Crawford at the head of the procession.

They clattered over the moat and out onto the Cannongate, where townsfolk had gathered to catch a glimpse of the Court. They shouted joyfully as Mary's litter approached, blessing her, cheering, and calling her name. They abhorred her religion, but she had won their hearts. She smiled and waved, throwing kisses to the right and left. Sentinels at the Netherbow Port stood at attention and saluted as the cavalcade passed through to the High Street.

Here the atmosphere suddenly changed; the cheers faded into ominous silence. Bothwell glanced down at the sea of faces and felt the chill of their dourness. Then he saw the reason; Knox had placed himself at the entrance of St. Giles in open defiance. He stared at Mary, his eyes ablaze with hatred, his lips moving in soundless prayer—as though to ward off her evil.

Bothwell tensed as Mary stepped from the litter; she waited as attendants lifted the train of her gown from the floor. Ignoring Knox, she walked into the Tolbooth, her head held high.

Mary opened Parliament with a speech in Scots, tinged with her French accent. Bothwell listened, half-amused as always when she used the Scots tongue, for it had a charming ring. She concluded by asking the Council for an assenting vote on the proclamation and forfeiture of her rebels. They agreed unanimously.

Bothwell had asked Huntly and Atholl to sup with him that evening, and since they were not due for an hour yet, he used the time to study Étienne de la Roche's book on higher mathematics and geometry—one of his interests that caused simple folk to accuse him of necromancy.

Winds rapped noisily at the casement, rustling the arras, fanning the fires. It was a bitterly cold night, but he laid his book aside, went for his cloak, and started out for a walk. He was unaccountably at odds with himself; a strange uneasiness had overtaken him soon after he returned from Parliament that afternoon.

On the stairway he collided with Rizzio, who was decked out in a russet doublet with velvet breeches and hose to match.

Rizzio doffed his plumed hat merrily. "Good evening, my lord."

"Where are you off to in such haste?" Bothwell asked.

"To sing for my supper," he said, extending his lute. "Her Majesty has invited me to take the evening meal with her."

"Alone?"

Chuckling, he shook his head. "There will be others; the Countess Argyll, Lord Robert—"

"Not the King?"

"No, he dines with friends on the Cannongate."

"Then run along. Don't keep the Queen waiting on my account."

Rizzio waved and hurried away.

From the garden Bothwell looked up at Mary's windows. The cold stung his face and chilled him through. A wolf howled in the distance, its cry a bloodcurdling sound in the night. Two priests walked ahead in their long black robes and disappeared into the abbey. Hedgerows and trees swayed to the wind's command, casting grotesque forms against a snow sky.

The penetrating cold finally turned him indoors. Walking along the inner quadrangle, Bothwell heard Rizzio's soft basso voice in song, then it died away as he turned into the southeast wing.

Huntly and Atholl were already waiting in his apartments.

"A fine host," Huntly chided. "Asking us to supper, then running out to let us wait on your pleasure."

Atholl said, "Aye, if I were not so famished, I would leave you to your roast lamb and sup elsewhere."

Bothwell made them a low bow. "My lords, I offer my most humble apologies, and plead guilty as charged."

"A wench, no doubt," Atholl said, winking at Huntly.

"And my poor, poor sister, his wretched bride of only two weeks."

"You've only yourself to blame for her piteous plight, allowing this spoiler of women to wed her," Atholl said.

Bothwell affected an air of wounded innocence. "I protest, my lords, you malign me unjustly."

Huntly and Atholl snickered.

A servant came in carrying a trencher of lamb that still sizzled from the spit. Bothwell did the honors and served them with all the ceremony of a majordomo.

Huntly speared a piece of meat with his dirk. "If your food is palatable, we may forgive—"

"Wait," Bothwell said, turning to listen. "Was that a scream?"

They listened, but heard nothing.

Atholl said, "Likely a serving wench in the kitchen."

They resumed eating, then Bothwell heard a crash, this time followed by an unmistakable scream. It seemed to come from the northwest wing—the others had heard it too, for it had echoed through the quadrangle.

"Something is amiss," Bothwell said. He thought of Mary. "The Queen—the commotion is coming from her apartments."

They ran out. There were more screams, the cries of a woman in terror. Bothwell dashed ahead; he turned a corner of the stairway and stepped back, motioning the others to stop.

"Stand back," he whispered. "The palace is packed with armed men."

They retreated to his quarters and bolted the door.

"How many were there?" Huntly asked.

"More than we can handle."

Bothwell did some quick calculating; they were hopelessly outnumbered. He had only half a dozen men in attendance; Huntly and Atholl had perhaps double that between them. It would be sheer suicide to attempt anything so foolhardy. But those screams plagued him—they had held such terror and despair. It might have been Mary; she could be in desperate peril—he would take the risk at any cost.

He rememberd the kitchen help; most of them were French and loyal to Mary. He glanced at Huntly and Atholl; they were bewildered, waiting for him to decide.

He said, "Summon your attendants. Tell them to bring what weapons they can find."

He went to his bedchamber, grabbed for his dag and rapier,

and ordered his servants to gather up the fire pokers and an ancient battle-ax that decorated the wall.

"We'll take the back stairs to the kitchen," Bothwell said when Huntly and Atholl had returned.

The way was still clear, and they took the terrified kitchen help by surprise.

Bothwell told them his plan. "We'll charge our way up to the Queen's apartments. Take anything in hand that will serve as a weapon and follow me."

He started up and glanced back at the pitiful group: cooks, turnspits, butchers, carrying meat cleavers, carving knives, logs, and huge iron pots. He thought: *God, what an army!*

Noiselessly they crept from the kitchen, out to the main stairway crowded with invaders. Bothwell recognized some of them. They were Douglases, the Earl of Morton's men—the palace was filled with them. They tried to prevent his advance, yet seemed puzzled whether they should or not.

He snarled, "Out of my way—let me pass."

His tone cowed them momentarily, and he motioned those at his back to follow. Together, Bothwell, Huntly, and Atholl tried to force the door, heaving their weights against it, but the solid oak didn't budge. Bothwell put his ear to it and listened; he heard a man's frantic voice over scuffling feet—and a woman's sobs.

Suddenly the door flung open; someone from the other side held it partially ajar. Deep, horrible retching came from a part of the chamber hidden from Bothwell's view. Certain that it was Mary, his hand jumped to his sword hilt.

Mary called to him and rushed forward, disheveled and wide-eyed, her skirt smeared with blood. Unseen hands dragged her back out of sight. Bothwell lunged forward; the door slammed shut in his face, and he stood there, helpless.

The door opened again and Lord Ruthven came out. His face

a death mask, he gasped for breath. The hem of his tunic was blood-drenched and torn.

"Go back, my lord," Ruthven said. "We are too many for you."

Bothwell clutched his arm. "The Queen, is she hurt?"

"She is unharmed, but your presence here places her in great jeopardy. A servant of the Queen has been slain—only that. Return to your quarters. I will seek you out later to explain."

Ruthven's threat was enough to convince Bothwell; he couldn't place Mary in greater danger than she already was. He nodded to the others, and they retreated slowly down the stairs.

Back in his apartments, Bothwell paced the floor restlessly. No one spoke; each had his own nightmarish thoughts. From the courtyard they heard the dim clamor of boots and horses—then a blood-chilling cry: *"A Douglas!"* The murderous Douglases were on the warpath.

The door flung open and Ruthven staggered in. He looked even worse than before, and Bothwell recalled that only a week ago he had heard Ruthven was ill and said to be dying. He wondered what hideous deed had been in the offing to pull the wretch from his deathbed.

Ruthven dragged himself to a chair and sank down into it. "Some wine," he gasped. "For God's sake, some wine."

Huntly poured some into a cup and gave it to him. They waited in suspense while he drank. Slowly he gathered strength to speak.

He inhaled deeply. "A mere varlet has been slain."

Bothwell said, "The Queen—"

"Well enough—better perhaps than she deserves."

Huntly started forward. "Have a care, my lord—"

Bothwell put his hand out to restrain him. He kept his own

temper merely to know more. Ruthven had the upper hand for now; there was nothing to be gained by antagonizing him.

"Why are you holding the Queen prisoner?" Bothwell asked.

"Not a prisoner," Ruthven said, taking another gulp of wine. "She is in her hsuband's keeping. We've done nothing without the King's consent. Come, let me show you."

He struggled to his feet clumsily, encumbered by the weight of his armor. He led them down to the kitchen and pointed to something that appeared to be a full sack, carelessly thrown at the foot of the back stairway. But on closer examination, it showed itself to be the body of a man lying face down.

Bothwell went to see who it was. Daggers protruded from the back of the blood-soaked doublet; the body was a bleeding mass of wounds too numerous to count. Kneeling beside it, he attempted to pull the daggers loose, and new rivers of blood began to flow. One dagger fell to the floor; it was of silver with a sapphire hilt. Bothwell recognized it as the one Mary had given Darnley last Christmas. He rolled the corpse over on its back and stared in horrified disbelief.

Death was nothing new to him. He had seen it in all forms—but never like this. Wild beasts were more humane with their victims. The dead man's eyes were open wide and bulging; they reflected all the terror of his last moments. The lips were stretched tight across clenched teeth and locked into position by his jaw.

Gently, Bothwell lifted the body and carried it to a table. His hands came away sticky and wet. He went to retrieve a fallen boot and put it on the velvet-hosed leg. Then he straightened what remained of the russet doublet and buttoned it.

At his back he heard voices, muffled, scarcely audible. Huntly and Atholl were talking to Ruthven. Vaguely Bothwell wondered what they were saying—what could anyone say now?

He took an apron from the wall and dipped it in water to

wash the bloodstained face, then he pulled the eyelids shut. A hand touched his shoulder, and he spun about sharply.

Huntly looked past him at the body. "Come away, my lord," he said softly.

Bothwell nodded and crossed the dead man's hands over his chest. "If the Queen were here, she would do this for Rizzio," he said.

In the passageway Ruthven said to Bothwell, "You saw the King's dagger?"

"Aye."

"Then you have proof enough that we had the King's consent."

Atholl stared with glazed eyes. "But why Rizzio?" he murmured.

Ruthven spat viciously. "He usurped the King's place with Her Majesty—a disgrace we could no longer allow."

Bothwell clenched his fists to keep himself in check.

Huntly said, "You did this for the sake of mere gossip?"

"If it were that alone we might have let him live—but we know also of his plots with Rome. That would surely have ended in the ruination of the Protestant cause."

Bothwell thought: *always the excuse of religion for their treacheries.*

Ruthven broke into a violent fit of coughing, his knees buckled, and he leaned against the wall for support.

Finally able to trust himself to speak, Bothwell said, "Take care you are not the second victim tonight."

Ruthven shook his head. "Not the second—though soon enough, I fear."

"When may we see the Queen?" Bothwell asked.

"In due time. For now, all three of you must remain in your quarters until order is restored—it's for her safety, and yours as well. The King has issued warning, under pain of death, that Parliament adjourn. All members must be gone from town within three hours. As for yourselves, no harm will come to you if you do not interfere."

Bothwell nodded. "A good general knows when to retreat."

Ruthven seemed relieved. "Then I bid you good night, my lords."

Huntly glanced at Bothwell; his puzzlement bespoke his thoughts. *Will you do nothing while the Queen's life is in danger? You, the man of action, the man who would dare anything. Will you stand idly by and let them have their will with her?*

Atholl left them to return to his own apartments. The palace was surrounded outside and in by the conspirators. Any sudden move would certainly endanger Mary's life, and their own as well. Bothwell went to the door and listened; he heard the heavy tread of boots in the hallways. He opened the door a slit and saw that guards had been posted outside. There was no hope of exit that way; he closed the door and turned to Huntly.

"We've got to get out of the palace," he said. "We are of no use locked in here."

"How? We would get no further than the hall," Huntly said. "The guards may even kill us. It may be more practical to wait."

"Wait for what?" Bothwell snapped. "Do you imagine we will fare any better than Rizzio? Even if they don't kill us, our presence here will signify approval for their detestable treachery."

Huntly nodded. "They are like beasts who have tasted blood—they will thirst for more."

Bothwell crossed to the window and looked out. He could barely make out the lions below in the murky dark. They seemed unusually restless, and he wondered if they had caught the scent of blood. Then he hit his fist against the wall, opened the window, and looked down.

"There's our way out," he said. "We'll escape through the window."

Huntly blanched. "Are you mad? We are certain to break our necks in the fall. If by some miracle we don't, the lions will tear us to pieces."

"Then please yourself. Stay if you like; for myself, I am taking the one chance left. Risky or not, it's better than sitting here to wait for God knows what."

Since that first horrible scream, Bothwell's thoughts lay anchored on one fear. Rizzio's murder—even his own safety was of no consequence now; Mary alone mattered to him. It was intolerable having her at the mercy of those inhuman fiends.

Quickly he fastened on his sword and reached for his cloak. He swung a foot out the window. "Are you coming?" he asked.

"Aye."

"Then hurry. Take one of my cloaks and follow me." He waited until Huntly returned. "When you jump, veer to the left," he said. "With luck, we'll fall beyond the lions' reach."

He jumped and held his knees up to his chest; the descent was rapid and dizzying. He landed hard on his feet, but unhurt. The lions lurched forward, growling fiercely, but their chains fell short of reaching him. He looked up and saw Huntly jump and land only a foot away. They climbed out of the pit and ran for the abbey.

Bothwell went first and peered in cautiously. It was deserted, and he motioned Huntly to follow. The candles burned at the altar, casting eerie shadows on the great stone columns. Then his attention was drawn to something on the altar.

He went to it and saw that it was the black-robed figure of a priest kneeling at the Virgin's statue. He leaned forward and tapped his shoulder. "Father," he said.

The figure swayed and toppled over. Stunned, he saw the altar carpet drenched in blood—Father Black had suffered Rizzio's fate. The front of his bloodied robe was torn with dagger cuts, and clutched in his fingers was a gold crucifix. Bothwell looked sadly at the aging man who had been Father Confessor to both Mary of Guise and her daughter. Now he understood Ruthven's meaning when he had said that he would not be the second to die that night. There seemed no end to this trail of blood.

But there was no time to stand here and mourn the dead; he had the living to think of. He snuffed out the candles and ran to the front door, opening it just a crack. Voices came from the garden. He waved Huntly on and doubled back the way they had come. They ran back across the sloping foot of Arthur's Seat and came out on Horse Wynd.

"We can go to my house," Huntly said.

Bothwell shook his head. "The provost's house first. We'll tell him what's happened and have him rouse the town."

It took a while to coax the provost from his warm bed, but their pounding finally roused him. He was reluctant at first to take a hand, but Bothwell hustled him back into the house and gave him just time enough to throw a cloak over his night robe.

Gradually the clamor of the common bell brought results; one by one lights came on in the darkened houses. Casements opened and nightcapped heads appeared. The bell continued to ring; folk poured into the street with only shawls to cover their nightclothes.

Bothwell and Huntly stayed to see the provost and the town guard march off to the palace. Bothwell knew they would never gain access to Mary—they were too few and no match for her captors—but they might in some way ensure her safety. Men like Morton, Ruthven, and Lindsay could browbeat a helpless woman and murder a poor cripple easily enough, but their courage would likely fail them if they knew the entire town was against them.

He waited until the crowd began to disperse; then, with Huntly, he doubled back to the Cannongate and climbed the wall into Huntly's garden. The house was dark, its occupants asleep. They entered quietly and went into the study. Huntly poured some brandywine into glasses and gave one to Bothwell.

Bothwell sat down; his fingers gripped the arm of his chair tightly. He had the wild impulse to rush headlong to Holyrood—even if it meant attacking the palace single-handedly.

Visions of Mary in those brutes' power tortured him; he knew he should be making plans for her rescue, sensible plans, but his mind seemed unable to function. Ruthven had told him that Mary was unharmed—but he could have lied. She could be ill with no one to tend her; women had been known to miscarry for less than the horror she had just witnessed.

An hour passed, and still he could think of nothing to do. Then he hinged on a workable plan and used old Lady Huntly to lay the groundwork. Since he could not get near the palace, Mary had to effect her own escape from there. She could meet him on the road, where he would be waiting for her with troops.

By some miracle Lady Huntly managed to gain access to Mary and told her what Bothwell had in mind. But Mary was in desperate straits; not even her tiring women were allowed near her. The rebels controlled everything, and Darnley was with them. He was mad for power; since their marriage he had been plaguing Mary for the crown matrimonial. Now the rebels promised him that and more, and he was willing to sacrifice his wife and unborn child for that.

Lady Huntly told Bothwell the townsfolk had stormed the palace the previous night, demanding to see the Queen. But Darnley had spoken to them instead, while Lord Lindsay threatened to "cut Mary to collups" if she showed herself. Earlier, while they had butchered Rizzio, Kerr of Fawndonside had held a dag on Mary, lest she try to prevent them from doing as they wished.

Bothwell swore; he would not have treated a whelping bitch so cruelly. Darnley earned his greatest fury; how could he have allowed it—and, God, at such a time? Was there no decency in him?

He blurted, "We'll not wait to rally men. She must be brought out of there now."

Huntly shook him roughly. "Think, man—don't let anger govern your brain. They'd put an end to her before we'd get past the gates."

Bothwell nodded wearily. Huntly was right, they would kill her for certain. She was safe enough for the moment—the Bastard was returning. He had likely engineered the entire plot. But he relied more on his brains. Whatever his scheme, her blood would not be on his hands—he would be too smart to share in the guilt.

There was no point in remaining in Edinburgh. Bothwell had to get to the Border to rally his men. They waited until nightfall, then they slipped quietly out of town.

3

They headed straight for Chrichton, and when they arrived Bothwell sent a servant to rouse Jean. Her expression was a mixture of pleasure and consternation. She stood at the door, clutching her furred robe to her, studying their solemn faces.

"What is amiss?" she asked.

Huntly attempted a weak smile. "You are so quick to presume the worst."

"Your faces betray you."

Bothwell told her briefly what had happened, then, yawning,

he said, "You will pardon us, my lady, we have had no sleep in two nights."

They took Jean to her chambers; Huntly gave her a brotherly kiss and bade her sweet dreams. She waited expectantly; Bothwell knew her thoughts and settled the matter by going to his own apartments. He was aware of Huntly's quizzical stare, but he was too weary for explanations. If Huntly wanted to know, he could damn well ask Jean why her husband did not share her bed.

The scent of fresh cedar greeted Bothwell in his bedchamber. He had expected to find it musty and thick with dust and cobwebs—instead it was freshly aired and clean, as though it had been used the night before. He suspected Jean's touch and smiled; if she was a disappointment to him in some ways, at least she proved herself the ideal mistress for his estates.

It was a mad ride Bothwell and Huntly took from Crichton that Monday morning. They cut through the Moorfoot Hills, intending to make Lauder their first stop.

When they had gone only a short distance, Huntly said, "All is not well between you and Jean. Am I presumptuous to ask why?"

Bothwell shrugged. "Your sister appears to prefer the ghost of what might have been to reality."

"Alex of Boyne?"

"Aye. She mourns her 'lost love,' and I respect her bereavement."

"I would never have thought her capable of such foolishness. Perhaps if I spoke to her—"

"I'll not have it. If there is to be a reconciliation, it must come from Jean. She will either make amends for her conduct or matters will stand as they are."

"Surely you want an heir to succeed you?"

"Aye, but there's a limit to the price I'll pay for one."

The finality of his tone discouraged Huntly from probing further.

The sky began to brighten in the east, and the morning turned to pearl gray. Their horses plodded over wet, slippery ground, their hooves ankle-deep in mist. This was the cold, unfriendly hour when night and day clashed; dawn broke as a violent intrusion.

They roused the Lauder bailie and all available men who were loyal to Bothwell—the district yielded one hundred and fifty men. It was the same everywhere they went; through Galashiels and Melrose, farther east to Kelso and Duns, over the Lammermuirs, on to Seton. Bothwell had nine hundred Borderers at his back, and he sent a message to Lady Huntly for Mary to meet him on the road out of Edinburgh.

They supped that night at Seton House, where they were joined by the Lords Fleming and Livingston. Later they set out to meet Mary.

They brought the troops to a halt on the outskirts of town to watch the road for approaching riders. Bothwell and the other lords rode on with a small party of men, but they dared not go too far, lest they be discovered. They waited in the numbing cold with the wind from the Firth of Forth at their backs.

Bothwell sat his mount in broody silence; the frail defenses of Seton House preyed on his mind. Mary would find no safety there to his satisfaction. He wanted her within the walls of a strong fortress, somewhere less vulnerable.

Resolutely, he said to Huntly, "We'll bypass Seton and take the Queen to Dunbar."

"But it's farther by fifteen miles," Huntly protested. "It may be too much of a strain in her condition."

"Seton can't withstand an attack if the conspirators pursue."

He went to tell the others. Some gainsaid him, but in the

end Bothwell won out—they would take Mary to Dunbar Castle.

Bothwell was the first to hear the pounding hoofbeats. He realized the perfect silhouette they made against the Forth's background and regretted the lack of trees and hedgerows. If those were enemy horsemen they could be picked off one by one.

The riders were closer now and coming hard. He heard a man's agitated voice—then a woman's. It seemed they were quarreling, then a lone horse galloped off in another direction and three riders appeared suddenly out of the dark.

Bothwell recognized Erskine, Mary's captain of the guard, and riding pillion behind him was Mary. He felt grateful beyond words to see her safely out of the rebels' hands. He longed to snatch her away, to cradle her in his arms, to pet and fondle her—and because of that he hung back, letting the others go to her.

She called to him. "The lords tell me you have decided on Dunbar."

"Aye, madam. It's fifteen miles more, but you'll be safer there. Can you ride that far?"

She smiled. "After what you have accomplished here tonight, I can do that and more." Then, hesitating, she said, "The King mistook you for enemies and galloped off in fright."

So the lone rider had been Darnley.

Bothwell said, "A hero to the last, eh, madam? I'll send some of my men after him; they'll bring our lost lamb back."

They galloped along the frozen beach, and Bothwell marveled at the quiet. So many hundreds of men; their silence seemed a tribute to their valiant Queen. He glanced at Mary, still mounted behind Erskine, her head held erect. He imagined her weariness, the strain of riding pillion for so many miles. But she had not complained once, nor asked for respite.

He felt the intense cold and wondered if she were warm

enough. Weaving his horse in and out of the other riders, he came abreast of her and whipped off his cloak to put over her shoulders. She looked at him gratefully, but he galloped off before she could thank him.

They were still miles from Dunbar, but every mile they covered brought her that much closer to safety. He envisioned the fortress built on the sea; it was sturdy and impregnable, yet he worried because it was a fortress. Dunbar had not been intended to accommodate women. It was an arsenal built for war, barren and bleak, and he doubted that it could offer Mary even the comfort of a bed.

He paused; why did he concern himself with such trivialities? Doubtless no one else fretted over her comforts—enough that she was safe. But he fashed himself like a mother hen over her chicks. The agonies he had suffered since Rizzio's murder—nothing could reassure him until he had seen for himself that she was safe and unharmed.

Then everything became suddenly clear and the truth struck him a stunning blow; he had fallen in love. Now he knew why he had remained loyal to her despite the times she had sacrificed him to placate others. Here was a side to love that had been a stranger to him: the willingness to give himself fully, unselfishly, to another.

Aye, he had given equally faithful service to her mother, without such emotional entanglements, but he would never have forgiven Mary of Guise for the injustices he had suffered at her daughter's hand. He had attributed his unflagging loyalty to his love for Scotland; now he realized that Mary *was* Scotland—the two were hopelessly mingled in his blood; he could not tell them apart.

The sound of gulls overhead brought him sharply back. It was nearly daybreak. Dunbar lay just ahead, silhouetted like a crouched monster against a leaden sky. Creamy waves lapped the shore, and the frosty morning air had a strong salt tang. He could see Mary clearly; she put him in mind of a weary child, determined to elude the sleep she craved. Resting her head on Erskine's shoulder, she gazed trancelike into the distance.

4

They crossed the moat and entered the courtyard. Bothwell dismounted and went to lift Mary down. She swayed and gripped him for support. Her exhaustion was apparent. She leaned against him and permitted herself to be led into the castle.

Some of Bothwell's soldiers were lighting a fire in the Great Hall. Shadows danced on the bare stone walls; a tomblike chill hung over the drab surroundings. Mary shivered and huddled closer in Bothwell's cloak. He took her to the fire and found a stool, and she sat down wearily.

The others came in, but no one approached her. She sat rubbing her hands, staring into the flames. Then she threw off both cloaks and came to life; she seemed refreshed after her short respite and fortified with new vigor. Her glance swept the faces before her—Seton, Livingston, Huntly, Fleming—then came to rest on Bothwell.

"How can I thank you, my lords?" she said.

Huntly said, "Your Majesty's safety is all the thanks needed."

"Safety is not enough. The conspirators are still at large."

Pride in her surged through Bothwell; he had always admired her spirit. "But not for long, madam," he said. "Within a few days I can raise three times the men I have here now. We can turn your escape into a victory by drawing the traitors out of Edinburgh."

She nodded. "I must send dispatches for all loyal followers to join us here. But first"—she paused and smiled at Bothwell—

"your men have proven their dexterity in battle, but how are they at finding us some breakfast?"

"If there's a morsel of food in town, they'll find it, madam."

He left to send a party out to forage about; they were back shortly, carrying helmets filled with eggs.

Mary laughed delightedly. "Your men are pure marvels, my lord."

Amused, Bothwell said, "Imagine the townsfolk's consternation when they awake to find all their hens have been lax in their duty, madam."

They cooked the eggs in helmets and sat around on barrels and crates to eat them. They had barely finished when a small commotion started up in the outer hall. Darnley came in, red-faced and complaining shrilly.

"Why did you not wait for me on the road?" he demanded of everyone there.

Mary said, "Because our enemies may have been in pursuit."

"All the more reason for you to have waited. They might have captured me. With no one there to defend me, I dread to think of the consequences."

She eyed him coldly. "You chose to run."

He colored and looked away. "I am famished."

Mary indicated the uneaten eggs. He took one, then dashed it to the floor, yolk spattering the hem of her dress.

"I abhor cold eggs," he said.

"Then fix yourself another."

Arrogantly, he said, "Whoever cooked these will do that."

"*I* cooked them," Mary said.

Summoning what dignity he had left, Darnley turned away. "Never mind, I would prefer to rest. Where are my quarters?"

"Take any that suit you," Bothwell said. "No chambers have been prepared—except for Her Majesty."

"Then I will share the Queen's chambers."

Mary rose abruptly. Her voice held the coldness of death. "You will not."

He stared at her blankly. "After last night, I thought—"

"Last night you were a necessary expedient."

Mary faced the fire. Her body trembled convulsively; she slumped forward; her strength suddenly failed her. Bothwell went to her, lifted her in his arms, and carried her upstairs. She leaned her head on his shoulder wearily and closed her eyes.

A floor pallet had been laid near the fireplace for her. Bothwell set her down on it gently and covered her.

"Try to sleep," he said. "It will do you good."

"If only I could. My dreams are filled with blood and Davie's screams. He died at my feet, clutching my skirt."

"Though you doubt me now, the horror of that night will eventually fade. There are yourself and the child to think of."

The thought of Darnley's child in her womb enraged him—more because he knew that child would be Darnley's means of escaping punishment for his part in Rizzio's murder.

She sat up. "When I think of how the father betrayed me, I could rip it from me. I gave him everything—nothing was too dear—this is how he has repaid me."

"Forget him, madam. There are others more deserving of your scorn—James, Morton, Lindsay, and unless I miss my guess, Lethington, too."

She nodded. "I detected his hand in the pardon drawn up by the traitors."

"They dared ask your pardon?"

"I waited until James arrived, then I promised to sign it—if Ruthven and Morton would withdraw their guards."

"They believed you?"

"Harry saw to that. He told them he would take me in charge and secure my signature on the pardon. They agreed, then retired to Morton's house for supper. The rest you may imagine; I had to win Harry over by much dissembling and fair words."

"Aye, vanity would win him over. But he's not to be envied; he's betrayed not only you, but his fellow conspirators as well. He's made some dangerous enemies for himself."

"They promised to confer the crown matrimonial on him," Mary said. "For me they planned imprisonment—if their violence did not cause me to lose my life in miscarriage."

"Thank God you gave them neither pleasure. You must begin to plan for the future. It's imperative that you return to Edinburgh immediately. The traitors must be brought to justice. As for your brother—"

"James shall be pardoned. His part in the murder is so well hidden I cannot charge him with it."

He marveled that they had shared the same thought.

"Aye. Alone he'll not committ more treachery. He must be kept apart from his allies—Lethington above all."

She nodded. Her eyes grew heavy with sleep.

Softly he said, "We can talk later. Go to sleep now."

Obediently she lay down and closed her eyes. "Stay with me," she murmured.

He leaned against the wall, drawing his knees up to his chest, resting his chin on them. Her face was turned toward him; he watched it intently, treasuring her with his eyes, tracing an imaginary finger over her incredibly pale skin, past her rose-tinted lips, across her slanted lids. A heavy strand of hair had come loose from its pin and lay curling on her shoulder—he longed to touch it. Her breath came steadily, and he knew that she was finally asleep. Loath to go, he stood and tiptoed out.

Downstairs, he summoned a handful of Hepburns with orders to ride. Bothwell wanted Mary to march back into Edinburgh in triumph. He would have a great force of men to stand at her back, and in his mind he saw thousands of spears raised as far as the eye could see.

5

He was back in three days; his route had taken him through Jedburgh and Hawick to Hermitage, into Teviotdale and Liddesdale, returning by the east coast. When he rode into Dunbar he had amassed more than three thousand men.

Mary's dispatches had borne fruit too; the halls echoed with the heavy tread of spurred boots, for nobles had gathered from the west and from the Highlands, with more reported on their way. On his way up to her chambers, Bothwell saw two recent exiles from James' rebellion of last fall, the Earls Glencairn and Rothes—even past enemies were joining them now.

Mary had fresh news from Edinburgh. The rebel forces had been depleted when word of Bothwell's strength had reached them. Morton, Lindsay, and Ruthven had skulked off to the English at Newcastle. James waited at St. Andrews for her pardon, Knox had retreated to the safety of Ayrshire, and Lethington had discreetly taken himself to the Highlands.

Bothwell laughed. "Your victory is complete, madam."

"There would have been no victory at all without you."

He shrugged. "No matter, we've accomplished what we wanted to."

He glanced at the drab wool dress she wore and regretted that she had no royal robes to wear for her reentry into Edinburgh.

For appearance's sake, Mary and Darnley rode side by side at the head of the troops. But it was a cowed and sullen-faced Darnley now, instead of the princely robed figure he normally displayed. Bothwell followed at the head of his Borderers and four companies of professional infantry.

At Haddington they were met by Mary's foreign envoy, Sir James Melville, who pleaded James' case before her. To prove his innocence, James had severed relations with "such as had committed the vile act." And Mary, in turn, coolly assured Melville that she held her half brother in no way responsible for Rizzio's murder. "But," she added, "in view of his past offenses he had best absent himself from the Court for a while."

Mary had the triumph Bothwell had promised her, and the townsfolk cheered her madly from the West Bow to the High Street. She refused to return to Holyrood, for the horror of a week ago was still fresh in her mind. Rizzio's blood still stained the spot where they had thrown his body just inside the audience chamber door. Fifty-six stab wounds had been counted on his corpse; no matter how they tried, no one could remove the spot made by the river of blood they had drained from him.

It was decided that Mary would spend the remaining months of her confinement in Edinburgh Castle. In the meantime she was taken to the Bishop of Dunkeld's house until the castle was made ready for her. To ensure her safety, Bothwell had field guns placed at the doors, and three shifts of guards posted on duty there.

Early the next morning, Mary called a special Council meeting to charge the conspirators with their crime. Darnley, too, was present, and he played his farcical role to the hilt, protesting his complete innocence in the conspiracy before a contemptuous assembly of lords. He extended himself further by claiming that he had "never counseled, commanded, consented, assisted, nor approved the same." This might have been easier to swallow had Ruthven not shown Bothwell the murder bond with Darnley's signature on it.

CHAPTER IX

1

For appearance' sake, Mary pretended to believe Darnley's statement, and at his desire a similar declaration was posted at the Market Cross. But she issued a declaration of her own, taking from him all practical share in public affairs; he was to lose all authority previously given him—even the privilege of sitting beside her in Council and at public places—and his name would no longer appear with hers on treaties and other documents.

The Council members then turned their attention to the conspirators; Morton, Lindsay, and Ruthven were proclaimed outlaws along with Kerr of Fawndonside, who had held his dag on Mary during the murder. James and Argyll were officially pardoned and their titles restored, but they were still forbidden the Court. Lethington was to remain in the Highlands in disgrace.

Within a week Mary was settled in Edinburgh Castle. The rooms were smaller and far drearier than Holyrood, but she preferred them to the memories of her apartments at the palace. Bothwell was at her side constantly; she made no decisions without first consulting him and leaned heavily upon him for advice. For himself, though her trust flattered him, he found this closeness unbearable.

He felt torn between the desire to leave Edinburgh and the

longing to be with her whenever he could. His nights were haunted by the memory of the hours spent with her as they walked the castle ramparts and pored over Border maps in her apartments, their heads so close that the scent of her hair teased his senses. She was always so near he need only reach out to her. But he could not, and she might have been worlds away.

Restraint had always been unknown to Bothwell; he had taken what he wanted without a thought to the consequences. He had indulged freely in all pleasures, denying himself nothing—women least of all. Now he exercised restraint—denying himself the thing he wanted most.

But he could not take her as he had others; he could never take her carelessly—it was more than mere lust that he felt for her. And realizing this, he knew that he would likely never have her at all.

Only the business of punishment distracted Bothwell, and he was thankful for it. As though perjury were not enough, Darnley became overzealous in his efforts to help the Council. Townsmen, some innocent, some with only a tinge of guilt, were hauled off to the Tolbooth for questioning about the conspiracy. Everyone, including Mary, knew these men were being offered up by Darnley as a sacrifice to the altar of his guilt.

The rack was a favorite with the Tolbooth's masters of torture, and they used it well. Bothwell frowned on this method, not so much for its inhumanity as for its unreliability. Despite its widespread use, he had little faith in the evidence extracted by it, for he knew such extreme pressures would wring a confession to anything for the sake of respite. But he was a member of the Council and sheriff of Edinburgh; therefore he was obliged to attend these grisly sessions.

Now he watched as Jeremy Weir, a saddlemaker, was dragged in by two brutish guards who supported him under the armpits.

From Weir's bruised and weakened condition, Bothwell surmised this was not his first day there.

The chief warden nodded, and Weir was stripped bare and laid across the rack. The room was in total darkness, except where the flames of the open braziers stretched toward the ceiling. Shadows of the deadly instruments employed here danced on the walls. The saddlemaker was bound hand and foot, and with another nod from the warden the wheels were set in motion with a hideous grind. A mixture of terror and agony sprang into Weir's eyes; he sweated profusely, and his temples swelled—another quarter-turn of the wheel was indicated.

Weir moaned softly; his head jerked convulsively from side to side. Blood trickled from his wrists, and his muscles throbbed and quivered.

The warden asked, "Do you still refuse to confess?"

Weir had fainted. He was revived by a dousing from a bucket of cold water. His eyelids flickered and parted, and he gazed at the warden dully.

"Now will you confess?" the warden repeated.

Weakly, the saddlemaker murmured, "I've done nothing."

"Still obdurate? Another stretch."

Bothwell glanced at Darnley. He knew him for all his faults; he was an arrogant, brutal, power-mad boy who lacked even the meanest scruples. Yet he couldn't believe that even Darnley would allow an innocent to be tortured so—someone he had wrongly accused. Surely there was a conscience lurking somewhere in that empty head so innocently topped with blond curls. But there were no protests from Darnley; he sat looking on with detachment, his face immobile. Plainly, he felt no compassion for Weir's misery.

The wheel turned again; there was a crackle of bones as they slid from their joints.

Bothwell could stomach no more. He bolted to his feet and shouted, "Enough! Cut the poor wretch down."

The warden stared incredulously. "But, my lord, we have yet to extract a confession from him."

"He's half out of his head with pain now—another turn of the wheel and he will confess to the murder of God," Bothwell said.

"Then how shall we determine his guilt?" the warden protested. "He is charged with a crime that demands his death."

"Hang him if you must—but for God's sake, let him go to his death a whole man."

Bothwell shot a contemptuous glance at Darnley and spat viciously. Then he snatched up his cloak and stalked out.

"How long will you permit your husband to wantonly haul innocents off to the torture chambers, madam?" Bothwell demanded.

He was still furious when he confronted Mary with the injustice an hour later.

Wearily, she asked, "Whom has he accused now?"

"Who is not as important as how many. Scarcely a day passes that he does not add at least two more names to the already staggering list of accessories to Rizzio's murder."

"But you yourself advised that we make an example of the guilty parties."

"Aye, Madam. You mind I said the *guilty*—not the innocents. God knows I am not squeamish, but I cannot sit another day and watch the bodies of men being torn apart. If they are guilty, give them the dignity of going to their deaths in one piece."

"You will not have to watch it again. I shall order an immediate end to it. Why did you not tell me sooner?"

"Because I thought it would be over by now—and because I wanted to spare you the worry."

She looked at him strangely. "And I have spared you so little in the past."

"The past is done with—let it go."

"Some things can never be forgotten. Davie's murder taught me how to hate. Tears brew a salt which hardens when dry—as my heart has hardened since that night. And I have finally learned to place my trust where it will not be betrayed—in you, my lord. In my mother's time you were promised the command of Dunbar Castle, along with the lands and rents of Haddington Abbey. You shall have them."

"Take care, lest your enemies misinterpret your gratitude."

"Let them. I care nothing for their opinions."

She took a letter from the table and tapped it against the arm of her chair thoughtfully. "James has written me," she said. "He asks permission to return to Court."

"How will you answer him?"

"Frankly, I am not certain that I want him back. I can never prove it, but I know he had a part in the conspiracy. Yet he is my brother, and I cannot despise him."

"Then by all means allow him to return. What harm can he do alone? With my men to keep an eye on him, he is safer here than at home, where he is beyond watching."

"That too had occurred to me. But I am inclined to believe that he will not be troublesome now. His pardon and the restoration of his lands should go a long way to content him."

"For a while, perhaps, but his acquisitiveness will not let him rest for long. If I were you I'd not trust him too much."

She reached across to touch his hand. "I've already told you my trust lies where it should, now."

Her delicately pale hand lay so lightly on his sun-bronzed fingers. How fragile her slender hand looked compared to the greatness of his own. Then she withdrew it abruptly; he wondered: Had her hand trembled when it touched his? Had she let it linger there deliberately? Preposterous, he told himself; wishful thinking caused him to read meaning into an innocent gesture. He had become such a love-sick fool that now he imagined she felt more than mere gratitude for him.

"How soon will James arrive?" he asked.

"His letter indicates he will leave the moment he has my answer." Then, hesitantly: "I have decided to give a banquet on his return."

"To celebrate his homecoming?"

"Of course not! Argyll too will be allowed the Court—I want to see both you and Huntly reconciled to them before my accouchement."

"I doubt breaking bread together will accomplish that miracle."

"I ask only that you be civil to one another. Later, we may hope for more."

"Never more, madam. I've had a taste of your brother's friendship—which very nearly resulted in my ruin. He stands for everything I despise in men. His methods reek of dishonor; he is incapable of loyalty—except to his own greed. And even if I were willing to forgive the past, he could not. I've thwarted him too often."

"You admit that James is powerless without his allies. Then why not agree to a meeting with him?" She looked pleadingly at him. "If only for my sake."

He sighed. He would do everything in his power to protect her from her enemies; but how could he protect her from herself? And yet, he loved her more for her trust and generosity. In any case, what would he not do for her sake?

"Very well," he said, "have your banquet. I will attend."

She rewarded him with a grateful smile.

2

April rains drenched the streets. The snow-capped peak of Arthur's Seat melted from shades of brown to green. Patches of new spring grass shot up overnight, and the tamed morning winds carried a scent of spring.

The heavily booted tread of moss-troopers was still heard on the castle walks, for Bothwell had not relaxed his vigil despite the prevailing quiet. James returned to Court, seemingly humble and eager to please. He was given apartments in the castle, where his movements were closely watched.

"You see," Mary said, taking Bothwell aside after the banquet supper, "it was not so difficult after all."

"Was it not, madam? Your brother's company is scarcely my idea of a pleasant evening. My only consolation is that by tomorrow he and I shall be miles apart."

"Did James say he was going away?"

"No, I am leaving."

"But why? Where are you going?"

"To Crichton."

"Because of James?"

"You do me an injustice. What have I to fear from him? It's Jean. I've been away from her too long already."

He could not tell her his real reason for going—that he wanted her so desperately that he could no longer trust himself near her. He had been able to restrain himself thus far, but if he remained . . .

"I had forgotten Jean," she said. "You have neglected her horribly—and all for me. Why not write and ask her to join you here?"

He shook his head. "I'd stay if I thought you needed me, but you are well protected here. James may be trusted to keep your husband in check, while my men keep on eye on James."

He had left her no avenue of escape; she had no reason to ask him to remain.

"I wouldn't blame Jean if she despised me for robbing her of you this long."

"On the contrary, she likely blesses you for it."

"Then she is a fool," she snapped.

Her anger surprised him. He had intended the remark as a jest, but she had taken him seriously.

Crichton had undergone some remarkable changes since Bothwell had been there last. The orchards were well tended, the rooms were aired and sweet-smelling, and the servants performed their chores with an efficiency and skill that he had never had from them. Even his bedchamber had been decorated with new draperies and bed-curtains. Without doubt, Jean had accomplished miracles in the last four months, and he would compliment her on them—among other things he wanted to discuss with her.

Now he could sympathize with Jean's feelings for Alex of Boyne—now he knew what it was to love someone he could not have. But they could not continue as they had; an understanding would have to be reached between them.

Yet, despite Jean's coolness, she seemed genuinely glad to have him home. She had ordered his favorite wine at supper and had taken pains to see that he had the outside cut of meat, seared and crisp the way he liked it. After supper she sent a servant for brandywine and started to leave.

Bothwell pushed the decanter aside and rose. "Will you join me in my study?" he asked.

Puzzled, Jean nodded and followed him across the hall to the oak-paneled room where a fire burned in the hearth. Two armchairs flanked either side of the fireplace. He waited for her to settle herself in one.

She sat prim and still, her hands folded in her lap, and he found himself comparing her to Mary. It was unfair, he knew, for Jean could never hope to compete with Mary's charms. Not that he imagined comparison would matter to Jean, for she did nothing to improve her shortcomings; a little color might do wonders—a touch of lip paint, a dab of kohl on her eyelids. . . .

He said, "You've done right well in the time you have been

at Crichton. I've no doubt the other of my estates will prosper as well in your hands."

"I am glad you are pleased, but I deserve no special thanks. It is a wife's duty to manage her husband's households."

"Aye, but not all wives are so dedicated. It's said that a loveless match breeds a careless wife. Would it not have pleasured you more to do this for Alex of Boyne?"

"It would have been a labor of love. But I have no regrets."

"And yet, because you could not wed him you mourn the loss."

"I mourn only the loss of his love. Given my choice, I would still have wed you, my lord."

"Why? If actions count for anything, yours speak plainly. Surely you will not pretend fondness for me."

"No, I shall not perjure myself. But a woman must be practical in choosing a husband. Your property holdings are vast, and you are the most powerful noble in Scotland. Alex has none of your prominence."

"You are content to exchange love for such things?"

"Property is wealth. With good care one may make from a lean purse a heavy coffer."

He laughed loudly. "Spoken like a canny merchant, my lady."

She bristled. "Does it shock you to find a woman with more than curls under her coif?"

Still laughing, he shook his head. "It would take a deal more than that to shock me—but you are welcome to try."

Inadvertently, she had supplied him with an ideal solution to the problem of their marriage. Admittedly, their honeymoon had infuriated him; no woman had ever rejected him before. Her behavior had wounded his pride a little; now he was thankful for the way it had turned out. In time, he might have learned to care for Jean, but now that was impossible; he was too full of Mary.

Jean started to rise. "It was not my intention to amuse you—"

He said, "Please remain, I've something more to say."

She sat down again.

He began, "It occurs to me that since neither of us is a sentimentalist an understanding may be reached which will enable us to live together in peace."

A look of shrewdness came into her eyes. "What do you propose?"

"That you continue in the good office as mistress of my estates. For the rest"—he shrugged—"we shall both be free to pursue our own pleasures. Are you agreed?"

"Am I to understand that you are willing to waive your rights as my husband?"

He may have gone too far; no woman appreciated the fact that her husband could resist her so easily. But it was too late to repair the damage, for he had already made that quite clear.

"Aye," he said. "Have you any objections?"

Biting her lip, she said dully, "None."

"Excellent. Then we may consider the matter settled." Then gently he said, "I regret that you could not have made a more joyous union for yourself, Jean."

This was the first time he had used her Christian name, and it sounded strange to his ear.

"I might have done worse—and I am relieved to learn that you are not the man gossip reputes you to be."

"Had you expected to find me a beast?"

She nodded shyly. "On our honeymoon I bolted my door every night, for fear you would force me to submit."

He laughed harshly. "You needn't have. I leave rape for those who cannot have it otherwise."

She colored and looked away. "I would as soon we do not speak of such things—it is too intimate."

"Come now, my lady, there is no harm in frankness. I know

what folk say; they call me a ravisher of women—but the women I have known always seemed grateful for their so-called ravishment."

She rose clumsily. "You will excuse me, my lord—a headache—"

He was left alone with a mixture of perplexity and sadness for her. Jean's prim little mind could not bear honesty, and he pitied her. He was sorry that she would likely never experience the pleasure of love—if not for Mary, he might have taught her.

Jean's embarrassment lingered. At the midday meal the next day, her conversation was strained and she was careful to avoid his eyes.

Groping to fill the silence, she said, "I have made a wonderful purchase on bolts of lawn and cambric—enough to make several shirts for you."

He nodded.

"I shall send my seamstress to your apartments; she can use one of your old shirts as a sample."

He nodded again; why trouble him about such dull woman's business? She had created her own embarrassment and could damn well work it out for herself.

Bothwell was alone when Jean's seamstress came for the shirt, and once he saw Bessie Crawford the shirts were quickly forgotten. She was a perky little thing with a saucy red mouth and a turned-up nose that gave her face an elfin quality. He liked the curves of her figure that bordered on plumpness, and he especially liked the way she invited his open appraisal of her.

So, partly out of boredom and partly out of frustration, he looked into her mischievous black-button eyes and decided to explore Bessie's charms. But it was Bessie who made the advances by flaunting herself before him every chance she had.

Bothwell accepted the inevitable when he happened upon her one day as she swam nude in the brook that ran by the ravine.

3

Bothwell's days were filled with Border affairs, keeping the area both at home and in England peaceful during Mary's last weeks of confinement. But he dreaded the nights for the fears that plagued him until dawn. Time was passing swiftly; Mary's time to be delivered was near. Childbirth at best was dangerous, and after the terror Mary had endured, he was sick with worry for her. She was still such a child herself and so delicate—too delicate, perhaps, for childbearing.

He was afraid that she might not survive the ordeal and hated Darnley for endangering her so, and Scotland for demanding an heir. He hated the unborn child she carried—and envied it its closeness to her.

Thankfully, he had Haddington Abbey to distract him. Jean had accompanied him there, happy by the prospect of restoring another of his estates. But she had gone mad with spending, and he was forced to put a clamp on the purse strings.

He called Jean into the library and pointed out the window. "Those are pear trees you see, my lady," he said, as though he were addressing a dull child. "They yield only fruit—not money."

Unruffled by his scorn, she said, "I cannot restore the abbey if you will not allow me sufficient funds."

"Then hang the restoration. You've spent more than I can afford already."

Her impassiveness made him rage the more—if only she would lose her temper, shout back at him, or cry as other women did. But he couldn't seem to penetrate the wall of ice she had built between them.

"Investing in property is good business," she said. "Present costs are nothing if you consider the returns they will bring."

"Your obsession with property is maddening. If you had lived your life on the Border as I have, you would have learned early that a house and land today may be charred ruins tomorrow. Do you imagine the abbey fell into its present state by neglect? Haddington lay in the path of English invaders—"

"We are at peace with England now."

"At peace or not, we have gone far afield of the matter at hand. There will be no more spending. Is that clear?"

"Perfectly, my lord."

There was no hint of anger in her voice or manner when she left. Her icy chill lingered long after she had gone, defeating the warm June sun that flooded in.

He forgot Jean and took a letter from his desk that had come that morning. It was from Anna Throndsen; she had returned to Scotland, prepared to resume their relationship of four years ago, and possessive creature that she was, he could not have wanted anything less. But she was already firmly entrenched in his peel tower at Calder and there she meant to stay.

Wishing to avoid Jean's company that night, Bothwell took supper at a tavern and chose the long way back to the abbey on foot. The streets were pleasantly quiet; he passed the boot-maker's shop and the apothecary, stopping to glance at the wares they displayed. Then from over the blacksmith shop he heard someone call, "My lord." It was no more than a hissing sound with a note of furtive secrecy. He looked up and saw Bessie Crawford leaning out of an upper-story window.

"Please wait, my lord," she whispered.

He nodded, and she disappeared inside.

She came running out and dropped a respectful curtsy. "Good evening, my lord."

He smiled. "Good evening, Bessie."

"I wanted to say good-bye."

"Are you going somewhere?"

"Then Your Lordship doesn't know—"

"Know what?"

"That my lady Bothwell dismissed me from service."

"Likely you gave her good cause."

"She found no fault with my work. Someone told her of that day we met at the brook."

"Who do you suppose did that?"

"Agnes from the scullery—because I told her. She told cook, who told my lady."

"Then you have only yourself to blame—you should have been more discreet."

Ruefully, she said, "Aye, my lord. My father says there is nothing worse than a woman with a loose tongue in her head."

He chuckled. "Your father is a wise man, Bessie."

She hung her head. "I am fair ashamed, my lord. It is a heavy price I've paid for my boasting. Now I am without employment and unable to serve you."

She looked so appealing, her brazen button eyes gazing into his provocatively, and he was slightly irritated by Jean's meddling.

"You may still serve me, Bessie," he said. "Meet me in the Abbey Tower tomorrow at noon, and I will show you how."

"I will be there, my lord."

He nodded and walked on. So Jean had shown herself a woman after all. She might not want him for herself, yet she resented any other woman's having him.

Bothwell met Bessie in the tower and forgot her the moment he left her—Mary alone dominated his thoughts now. The sound of hoofbeats in the courtyard sent him flying to the window, thinking it might be someone with news from Edinburgh. The child was due any day now, and it was a hellish time for him.

He was like a man haunted, waking in the night to her imagined screams of pain. Sometimes he would turn suddenly, thinking he had heard her call. The previous night a bitch had howled until dawn and a black crow had flown in through the kitchen window. The servants said that together they were omens of death. He had always been contemptuous of these so-called omens, but he was vulnerable these days.

4

Bothwell heard the bell announcing the midday meal, and mechanically he went to the dining hall. Jean was already seated at the table and waiting for him. Gimlet-eyed, she watched the servants lay out the food. When they had gone she speared a slice of cold meat and brought it to her place, but she made no attempt to eat. Instead, she leaned back, folded her hands in her lap, and looked at him.

"There is a matter I feel compelled to discuss with you, my lord."

"Now?" he asked irritably.

"It cannot wait."

"Then pray be brief, my lady, for I've no mind to fash myself with petty problems."

He waited, expecting to hear of another household crisis.

"This is not petty, my lord. It concerns your recent conduct, which has caused me great hurt and distress."

Scornfully, he asked, "Have I trampled your geraniums again?"

"Would that it were so minor an offense. I refer to your unfortunate affair with Bessie Crawford."

He smiled. "There was nothing unfortunate about it. I found

it rather pleasant—though I'd not lend it the dignity of calling it an affair. Rather, it was a tumble."

"Then you do not deny it?"

He shrugged. "Frankly, you surprise me. I had not thought you would stoop to spying on me."

"It was not I who saw you leaving the tower. In your flagrant disregard for the opinion of others, you might have thought how this would reflect on me. This makes twice I have heard of your indiscretions from servants—and with my own seamstress, which is most degrading of all."

"Forgive me, my lady, I am not the snob you are. Seamstress or no, Bessie is more woman than you may ever hope to be."

She stood, scraping her chair back, her face flaming red. "How dare you," she stammered. "You not only compare me to that—that slut, you make light of my humiliation as well. Indeed, you may ask my pardon."

Her voice had turned shrill; she sounded like a fishwife, but he had had the satisfaction of having roused her ire at last. He preferred even this to her insipid dourness. But he had no patience to deal with her now.

"I have not asked your pardon," he rasped, "nor do I intend to."

"I demand that you make amends for the hurt—"

Softly, in that deadly tone his men had learned to fear most, he asked, "You demand?"

She faltered. "Something to console me—the pain you have caused me."

He smiled, but there was no humor in him. "Would it pain you less if you held the deed to Castle Hailes?"

Her sudden calm was amazing, but he had expected it.

Her voice sounded like a kitten's purr. "Castle Hailes."

"Aye."

She sat down again. "Naturally, my hurt is still acute, but

with the added responsibility to occupy me—it may be easier to forget."

"I thought you might find it so."

"How can I thank you?"

"No need." He reached for the brandywine and poured some into his goblet. "Hereafter, my lady, I suggest that you look to your own affairs and leave me to mine. We have an agreement, you and I, and I expect you to honor it."

If Jean had more to say it was lost to the commotion that came from the hall. Bothwell went to the door and opened it; servants had gathered on the threshold, whispering excitedly. A courier came in, paused to undo a scroll, and held it at arm's length.

"I have joyous news to report, my lord," he said. "At nine of the clock, this nineteenth of June, in the year 1566, the Queen of Scots was delivered of a fair son."

A deafening cheer went up from the servants. Here was the news that Bothwell had been waiting for, but somehow he could not share in the joy. His throat felt hot and dry; the excited talk and laughter droned in his ears unpleasantly, like the crashing of cymbals.

His voice came in a hoarse whisper. "The Queen, is she well?"

The courier had not heard. ". . . a fine laddie, I am told, my lady," he said to Jean. "Kicking and screaming scarce an hour after he was born."

The women cooed. But Bothwell cared nothing about a squalling brat; he wanted to know about Mary.

He spun the courier about sharply. "Speak, man," he shouted. "For the love of God, tell me of the Queen."

An abrupt silence fell on the room; everyone stared at him.

The courier pulled free and stepped back. "Her Majesty is well enough, my lord," he answered. "It has been a sore time for her, but she came through it with royal patience and endurance."

An embarrassed silence followed. Bothwell was painfully aware of their probing glances. Jean in particular studied him with an odd scrutiny, her mouth twisting in a smirk.

Bringing himself up short, he said, "Wine for everyone. A toast to the future King."

They raised their cups and drank. Bothwell drank too, but to a private toast—he thanked God that Mary's life had been spared.

CHAPTER X

1

Mary lay propped up in bed on pillows, watching him. "Well, what do you think of him?" she asked.

Bothwell glanced at the sleeping infant in Lady Rere's arms, pretending to admire him. The mere sight of Darnley's child stabbed at him. Yet he knew the hope of Scotland lay in that frail body; Mary's fondest dream was that one day this babe would wear the joint crowns of England and Scotland.

The night before, the people of Haddington had thronged the streets to celebrate the royal birth; there had been dancing and singing in every close and wynd. This morning, on his way to Edinburgh, Bothwell had seen the same expression of joy everywhere he passed. Chapel bells had rung the happy news throughout the night; bonfires still lighted the hills, carrying the tidings north.

But he could take no joy until he had seen for himself that Mary had come through it safely. Now he stood at the foot of her bed, looking at the infant, when he had eyes only for her. She looked so tired, so worn and pale. . . .

He glanced away from the child. "A fine lad, madam," he said.

She laughed. "You've scarcely looked at him."

"Enough to see a deal of his father in him."

Her smile vanished. "I pray God he will be nothing like Harry."

Reres clucked her tongue at Bothwell. "Can you say nothing cheering to Her Majesty? He's a bonnie lad, and well you know it." She slipped the blanket from the baby's head. "Look at his hair, gold as new wheat—and his eyes, bluer than a summer sky."

"Your artistic sense amazes me, my lady," Bothwell teased.

They were old friends, Bothwell and Reres; she was Janet Beaton's younger sister, but they were not at all alike. Where Janet had light, honey-colored hair and was slender, Reres was dark and plump. Nor did she have Janet's education, or beauty, though she seemed not to mind the lack of either, for she was always merry as a cricket, chirping away about this nonsense or that.

Having recently given birth to a daughter, Reres had been made the Prince's wet nurse. She adored gossip, and Bothwell surmised that in the weeks to come, Mary would know everyone's secrets. It would be good for her to have a gay magpie like Reres about, to ease the strain of her ordeal and worries.

Reres turned to Mary. "Pay him no mind, madam. Were you to show him a horse, I've no doubt he would examine it so fine, down to the last hair on the tail."

Judiciously, he said, "When purchasing a horse, the tail should receive no less consideration than the head."

Mary laughed. "You are a better brew for me than the most potent medicines, my lord."

He made her a sweeping bow. "How next shall I amuse you, madam? I can turn cartwheels, hang from the chandelier—"

Still laughing, she shook her head. "Nothing so arduous. Just bring a stool close and we will talk."

Reres took the baby back to his nursery.

"What shall we talk about, madam?" Bothwell asked.

She thought a moment. "Tell me what you have been doing since you left Edinburgh."

"You've had my letters on Border affairs—for the rest, it can scarce be of interest to you."

"Yes, I've had your letters—but they were so brief. A line here concerning the disquiet in Liddesdale, a line there about Morton—but nothing more."

"What more was there to say?"

What more indeed? That I love you desperately and longed to be with you? That even now I must sit here making small talk, for the words I want to speak may not be said?

"Something of a more personal nature, concerning yourself." She paused and looked at him strangely. "About your homecoming—your reunion with Jean after your long absence."

He shrugged. "We live friendly and quietly together. Better than some couples, no worse than others."

"Friendly and quiet—not exactly an idyllic relationship."

"It has its advantages, madam. I enjoy the comforts of a well-ordered house—and the freedom to pursue my own pleasures. Jean has position and property to content her. Thus, we have a perfect arrangement."

Smiling, she rearranged the coverlet. "Except where Jean's former seamstress is concerned."

He threw his head back and bellowed with laughter. "I marvel how quickly she gathers her gossip."

"Who?"

"Reres, of course. Only she could have told you that. Her spy system would make Elizabeth envious."

Mary smiled guiltily. "She *is* a veritable wealth of information. However, that does not disguise the fact that you are the rogue folk say. To consort with your wife's seamstress—and right under her nose."

"More's the shame that it cost me a fair bit of land to buy my peace for it. Now I can take ten seamstresses, for all Jean cares."

"Does she value property more than her husband's affection?"

"Aye, madam. But she'll have no more from me. Hailes was the first and last of such gifts."

"I fear we have neither of us chosen our mates well."

"Perhaps, then, we should take solace in each other, madam."

She leaned back against the pillows wearily as though suddenly wilted. Her skin had a sickly pallor against the heavy red and gold hangings.

He stood. "Forgive me, madam, my visit has been overlong. You should take some rest now."

She offered her hand. "We will talk again when I am stronger."

He took her limp hand in his and brought it to his lips. "When you are stronger, we may find an occupation more strenuous than talk."

2

Bothwell needn't have left Edinburgh so soon. He could have stayed on a week at least, but he could not trust himself in Mary's company too often. Neither did he intend to return to Haddington. Jean's chilling aloofness drove him away; there was a certain ghostlike quality about her. When she was near, his awareness of her came only from the swish of a skirt or the sound of something moved. She seemed to merge with the gray stone walls and seemed less than a shadow.

He decided to take a brief holiday and thought of Anna Throndsen. Despite her tiresome complaints she knew how to please a man. Her gay, passionate nature might be just what he needed. With Anna he might even forget Mary for a while.

Anna looked even more striking than he remembered; her

long black hair, unbound and wind-blown, framed her face, and her dark eyes lighted with pleasure at the sight of him. Bothwell held his arms open to her, and she ran into them laughing.

She clung to him, murmuring, "It is so good to be in your arms again. How I've longed for you."

He pressed his lips to her throat. "Were there no others to still the longing?"

"Others, yes—but none who could stir me as you do."

He laughed. "I've never asked you for steadfastness."

He was suddenly hungry for the first time in days. He had been with her only a few minutes, and he was nearly his old self again.

He set her down. "I am ravenous," he said. "Feed me."

Pouting, she snapped her fingers at him. "That for your male sentiment. We are reunited after four years and all you can think of is food."

"Would you deny a starving man the hospitality of your house?"

She stuck her tongue out at him. "Fill your belly then—till you burst, for all I care."

He watched her go to the door; she still had the same provocative walk, her thin cotton skirt clinging to the outline of her long legs, her low-cut bodice leaving little to the imagination. Despite her affected airs of a high-born lady, there was much of a slut in Anna, and he had always been charmed by it. She reminded him of a predatory cat, ever stalking its prey. Her sensual mouth held unspoken promises; her dark, intense eyes laid bare her passion. And, conversely, there was much in her that had earned his dislike, for he knew her to be a greedy, vindictive creature.

Anna returned with a servant who laid out food. He started to eat immediately, no whit disturbed by her catlike stare. Then, abruptly, she snatched the half-eaten lamb shank from his hand and gnawed at it hungrily.

Between bites, she said, "You have been back in Scotland nearly a year. Why did you not send for me?"

He wiped his greasy fingers on a cloth. "I had no time to think of you."

"But time enough to take a wife."

"I'm not getting any younger; the time was right for it."

"I had always cherished the hope that you would eventually wed me. You appear, however, to prefer that drab little creature to a real woman."

He wondered if Anna and Jean had ever met.

She read his thoughts. "Oh, I have made it my business to see the noble Countess Bothwell—the sight of her near put me in a faint. To think you could have had any woman you desired—instead, you chose that—that—"

"You are not to speak of my wife in that tone, Anna."

"I meant no harm, only that you deserve better."

He cut a slice of cheese. "Meaning yourself, no doubt."

She got up and came around to his back. "I've no wish to quarrel after having been parted from you so long," she said, leaning down to embrace him.

He reached back and pulled her face to his; her lips tasted of lamb. Her tongue slipped between his lips, and she snatched the cheese from his mouth and ate it.

"This is much better than quarreling. Come here where I can make proper love to you," he said, patting his lap.

She obeyed willingly and snuggled close. His hand slipped into the bodice of her dress and he felt the coolness of her flesh.

"We will be more comfortable upstairs," she whispered.

Bothwell lay back, watching her approach the bed with slow, deliberate steps. Then she broke into a little run and threw herself on top of him. He half-turned to avert the impact, and she bit his ear savagely. Muttering an oath, he gave her a resounding smack on her bare buttocks and she sank back into the pillows laughing.

His lips stifled her laughter and she dug her nails into his arms, making little animal noises of delight under his caresses. On his part, Bothwell felt nothing. Fiercely, cruelly, he kissed her again, and deep inside he felt only coldness—it seemed a wall of ice had numbed his senses.

His own intense need impelled him on; in desperation, he pulled her to him brutally. She clung to him convulsively, writhing, moaning, clawing, whispering obscenities—then she went limp in his arms.

Sighing contentedly, she nuzzled her head in the curve of his neck. She said, "We are so wondrously matched—only you can stir me so."

He glanced at her coldly, wishing she hadn't spoken. He moved away and saw her bewilderment. She moved closer, urging his hands to her body again, but he could not make even that small gesture.

He sat up; it was always the same for him now when he was with other women—he saw only Mary's face, heard only her voice. Violently he shook his head, trying to push the image away. He didn't want to admit the truth, but it soared through him like quicksilver; she had spoiled him for other women.

The sultry days of summer turned the Border to a rolling carpet of green, patched with delicate pastels of wild blooms. Furtive hoofbeats were heard through the Border; couriers traveled between England and Scotland, carrying word from Morton to James and back again. Despite his watchfulness, Bothwell knew that Morton himself made hurried rides into Scotland, crossing back into Newcastle again before he could be intercepted.

Then Bothwell had news that brought him to Edinburgh again. In exchange for his pardon, George Douglas was willing to name those involved in the Rizzio conspiracy, starting with James and working his way down. Confronted with the proof of James' guilt, Mary would be forced to punish him. But Bothwell knew this would not be an easy pardon to obtain, for George Douglas had been the first to plunge his dagger into Rizzio, and Mary had vowed never to forget that. It was then Bothwell recalled that Rizzio had told him of the seer's warning about a bastard's treachery—Douglas was a bastard.

Now Bothwell stood in Mary's audience chamber, listening to her protests.

"No, I cannot pardon the man who dealt the first blow to Davie," she said.

"First or last, he was only a tool for the others—a mere twig on the tree."

"Granted, but his dagger passed my shoulder to loose the first spurt of blood—the man is a butcher."

"What of it? You have the chance to use him to your advantage," Bothwell argued.

She shook her head. "It is over, let it be. I want no more turmoil."

Scornfully, he asked, "Who is it you wish to protect—your brother? You found it easy enough to pardon him, though you knew his complicity."

"You agreed with me—we had no proof against him."

"Aye, he has a knack for casting the stench of his deeds onto other shoulders. Deny it though you will, given his way you would be dead now, or spending your days in a dungeon."

She winced as though he had struck her—his outspoken truthfulness was always hurting her.

She shook her head. "The others perhaps—but not James. I grant you his ambition, but he is my brother—he would never seek my death."

"Need I remind you that he sees you as his only obstacle to the throne?"

"He knows his illegitimacy prevents that."

"Aye, he's too practical to dream of the impossible—there is the Regency and he wants that. He was nursed on the milk of discontent since birth. I could almost pity him that luckless chance were it not for the danger he constitutes to you and the Realm."

"You speak of him as though he were a deadly plague."

"Is he not, madam? I wager he could be more so, reunited with Lethington and Knox."

"Lethington is still in the north, and Knox appears to prefer the safety of Ayrshire."

Bothwell got up and started for the door. He turned. "Remember, madam, your brother is responsible for two seditions already; a third could follow, and it may not be so easy to put down."

His hand was on the knob when she called him back.

"Bothwell, I know you mean this for my own good, but you move so swiftly. I must have time to think."

"How much time have they ever given you? You miss the point entirely; the time to strike is now, before they can prevent it."

Her voice came very low. "I cannot."

"Very well, then, go to Alloa with James. Believe his lies, let him pet and console you—you have always preferred that to the truth."

"I thought you would accompany me to Alloa."

"Not unless you command me to. The company I must keep there would put too great a strain on me. My captains are able seamen; they can sail their ships without me."

"No," she said, "I'll not command you."

3

Mary remained at Alloa for three weeks and returned to Edinburgh in mid-August. But a restlessness had her traveling again within a week. This time it was a hunting expedition in the game-rich Ettrick Forest. Bothwell joined her party at Glenarton, where they had ridden from Megotland hoping to find better sport.

The first day there they rode in a party to the forest's edge, then separated in twos, taking off in different directions. Mary and Bothwell rode east together, the barking hounds running before them.

They trailed a stag for nearly a mile, but the hounds lost his scent. Suddenly the sky blackened and the forest turned dark. There was a single roll of thunder and they were in the midst of a heavy downpour. Lightning threatened to split the sky; their horses reared up in fright.

Bothwell looked about for shelter; he knew the area well and remembered the ruins of an old Roman peel tower nearby.

He turned to Mary. "Can you ride?"

"Yes, I think so."

They wove their way through the trees until the forest slipped behind them and they were racing across the slippery moor into a blinding rain. Mary's thin silk cloak lay plastered against her wet back. The feather on her tiny velvet hat had broken and lay to one side of her dripping curls, but she smiled gaily.

Her smile faded when a crack of lightning burst down.

"We are nearly there," he shouted over the pounding rain.

She nodded, and though she tried to hide it, he sensed her fright as lightning shot flames through an evergreen.

At the entrance, Bothwell dismounted and led the horses into the roofless structure. He helped Mary down, and she ran to an area sheltered by the partially remaining floor of an upper story. He tethered the horses in a dry spot and went to her.

She huddled close to him, trembling in the chilling wet. Pieces of stone from above crumbled at their feet. She pressed closer, burying her face in his chest. He held her stiffly, glancing about for shelter. Then he saw a flight of steps leading down.

"Wait here," he said. "I'll see where that staircase leads."

"Don't leave me." Her voice was like a child's in fright.

"There may be nothing but an abyss at the bottom," he said, disengaging himself.

Only a dim ray of light showed the floor beneath the last step; from there he groped his way along the narrow passage. He found an opening along the wall and turned in. The floor felt soft underfoot, and bending down, he touched the thick blades of grass that grew between the stones. He retraced his steps and returned to Mary.

"I've found a vaulted room below," he told her. "We can keep well out of the storm there."

She followed him down, holding his hand tightly.

"There are patches of grass to sit on," he said.

"You have provided me with the luxuries of a palace, my lord."

She seemed more at ease now.

He chuckled softly and sat down beside her. "A mere trifle, madam."

The room was saturated with the musty smells of age and the sweetness of greens. Slowly, his eyes became accustomed to the dark and he could see her silhouetted against space. A rustling noise startled her, and she drew closer, clutching his arm.

"What was that?" she whispered.

"A field mouse, no doubt."

She shivered, and he took off his doublet, placing it over her shoulders.

"I am behaving very badly," she said. "As a child I saw a man struck dead by lightning; I can never forget his charred body."

"You are safe enough from the storm here—but there are dangers you may not have considered."

"What do you mean?"

"Are you not afraid to be alone and unprotected with a man of my sinister reputation?"

She laughed. "But you are my protection. Your person alone is worth an army to me."

Deliberately casual, he said, "There are women who deem it an insult if a man does not make at least one advance."

"May not a man and woman be friends without putting stress on the physical aspect of their relationship?"

She had said something like that when he had warned her about Rizzio's familiarity. The comparison stung him; did she think him a mere vassal, an unfeeling, inanimate thing—a convenience to serve her?

He concealed his hurt with cynicism. "Men provide me with all the friendship I want—women serve another need."

Her voice held amusement. "I think you rather enjoy the scandalous tales reputed to you. I wonder if they are not somewhat exaggerated."

Her closeness was maddening; he fell into a broody silence. She turned, brushing his cheek with her hair, and he smelled its fragrance mingled with the wet. Was she deliberately taunting him?

Though her face was hidden in darkness it was clear to him in memory. In his mind, he traced a finger over her long, slanted eyelids, the smoothness of her cheek, her soft lips. Then he no longer trusted to memory. He paused, waiting for her protest—but none came.

Tossing restraint aside, he crushed her to him; he kissed her deeply, fiercely, attempting to appease the hunger that tore at him. He thought she would pull away, but she lay quietly in his arms, her lips open to his. The months of wanting her rushed at him with a savage thrust.

He fumbled with her gown like a gawky with his first woman, pressing his lips to her throat, to her breasts. Sightlessly, he explored her body: the swell of her breasts, the gentle curve of her hips, her thighs, cursing the dark for robbing him of the sight of her. He felt an upsurge of passion in her; her body quivered in the shock of his violence, then she was still.

There had been no tender embraces, no gentle kisses, no words of love—only a physical need to satisfy his craving. Now he wanted her to know that lust alone had not driven him, but he could not summon words adequate enough.

Gently, he found her lips and tasted the salt of tears.

"God forgive me," he murmured. "I've hurt you."

"No."

"Then why do you weep?"

"Because my soul has just passed through the gates of hell."

He kissed away her tears. "We are a long way from heaven or hell—time enough to fear them when we must."

He held her close, silencing her fears. Slowly, she responded to his touch, shyly at first, then deeply, gladly. Her rapture heightened his joy in her; her delight in his caresses aroused his senses. She gave herself willingly, generously, and he was filled with an awed humbleness.

She cuddled close, her body molded to the contour of his. He treasured her hand to his lips as though it were made of fragile glass. He had held countless women in his arms—but none like her.

In loving her, she had plumbed unknown depths in him. She had awakened in him a geyser of feeling, and he was humbly grateful. In his cynicism, he had never suspected that he could feel so deeply about a woman—but Mary was not like the others. This had been no brutal encounter. It was more like a long, loving caress that left a feeling of ecstatic pleasure and spiritual peace in its wake. This delicate, fragile creature, who in love matched his own desire and passion, would always be a part of him now. He was prepared to be in love, and love her forever. He had found the love Janet Beaton had spoken of so long ago, and he thanked God that it had not come too late for him.

The patter of rain had ceased long ago. He knew they should go, but he had not the heart to disturb her. He wanted this moment to last—to keep her for himself. Now that she had given herself to him, he wanted to possess her wholly; he could never share her with anyone.

She stirred and he kissed her hand. "We must go," she murmured.

"Aye, they will be searching for us."

She moved closer. "Hold me a moment more—then never again."

Her words penetrated his brain dully. *Never again!* Did she think he had taken her so casually? His grip on her tightened as though he would fuse their bodies, merge their hearts, until they shared the same heartbeat.

How could he make her understand? His glib tongue had uttered the phrases of love so heedlessly before; he had used them so wantonly, they seemed time-worn and meaningless now.

"Help me," she pleaded.

"When have I not?"

"I need your strength—help me forget you."

"I would sooner you ask me to part with my life."

"I must—"

"It's too late. I am selfish enough to keep you at all costs now."

"It would be a sordid kind of love—we could never hope for more."

"God knows how often I've told myself that. You deserve better, but there is no cure for it now. Can you blot today out of your mind?"

"No, it is something I will cherish forever—and I shall always bear the grief of what might have been." She sighed heavily. "I thought love came more happily."

"Happiness is a stolen moment, a fleeting thing."

"If there were only ourselves to consider—but there is Scotland. How often have you reminded me of my responsibilities? Now you ask me to forget them."

"If the past has taught me nothing else, I have learned to take what happiness there is while I may. Who knows what tomorrow may bring for either of us?"

"Tomorrow may bring Elizabeth's signature to a document naming my son her heir. Shall I deny him that? The slightest stain to my honor could jeopardize his future."

He could not deny her good sense. Darnley had already placed the Prince's legitimacy in doubt. For her sake he wished this day had never dawned. Where could it lead, what could he bring her but hurt and dishonor? There was no future for them, only clandestine meetings, elaborate schemes to hide the truth from others. He didn't want that for her, nor did he relish it for himself. It was not in his nature to skulk in the dark, to hide his deeds.

Yet, despite her resolve, he knew he could bring her to his will. More lovemaking, more arguments, and she would weaken. But he loved her too well to use such tricks. He wanted her to come to him of her own accord, not because passion betrayed her.

He rose and pulled her to her feet. She clung to him; dry sobs caught in her throat. He let his hands fall loosely to his sides; he could not trust himself to touch her again.

"We had best hurry," he said. "The others will be wondering where we are."

They found their way back along the passageway and climbed the stairs hand in hand. In the courtyard, she paused to fix her hair and straighten her gown while he went for the horses.

He lifted her to the saddle, his hands lingering on her waist. "You will never forget me," he said.

Tears shimmered in her eyes as she gazed at him, heartbreak on her face. "No, I will always remember your arms, the touch of your hands, the feel of your lips on mine—and this day."

4

"We grew concerned for your safety, madam," James said later.

"You needn't have. Lord Bothwell kept me from harm's way."

Argyll's smile implied lewdness. "Wedded life has mellowed you, my lord." He clucked his tongue in mock distress. "I fear your indifference has offended Her Majesty. See, she has not touched a morsel of this delicious food."

Argyll was right; Mary's plate lay untouched. Bothwell too had no appetite; he sat morosely opposite her, thrusting his dagger viciously into his meat. Despite the confidence of his last words to Mary, he had a sense of great loss.

James glared at Argyll. "Need I remind you that Her Majesty's position renders her inviolable, my lord?"

Flustered, Argyll half-rose and bowed to Mary. "Your pardon, madam, I meant no offense—only a jest, only a jest," he murmured.

In his haste, Argyll overturned his wine. It ran down the table into Bothwell's boot as a hound ran to lap it up from the floor.

Bothwell bolted to his feet and clamped a hand on Argyll's shoulder. "Sit down, you fool, ere your senseless jest cause more damage." He turned to Mary. "With your permission, madam, I will retire to my chambers."

Mary nodded stiffly.

The spilled wine had given him an excuse to leave—had he

stayed, he might have made a fool of himself. Wanting her, having her so close, yet not daring to touch her drove him nearly wild.

The morning dawned gray with thick rain clouds hovering overhead and a cool, wet breeze blowing in from the sea. Bothwell woke to the sound of voices below his windows. Looking out, he saw Mary and Darnley talking in the garden. He dressed hurriedly, hoping for a few words alone with her.

As he came out through the back door, he saw Darnley walking toward the stables. Mary was still there, watching him go.

Bothwell came up behind her. "May I speak with you, madam?"

Startled, she turned. "You tread on cat's paws, my lord."

"An old habit, learned long ago."

Tiny lines of stress around her eyes told him that she too had spent a restless night.

She glanced up at the leaden sky. "There will be no hunt today," she said.

"None for me in any case. I ride for Crichton shortly."

She nodded. "Just as well that you do. Harry and I return to Edinburgh tomorrow."

Unreasonable jealousy seized him. It infuriated him to know that for all his weaknesses and depravity, Darnley still had a husband's claim on her.

He blurted, "To share the same bed?"

She avoided his glance. "We are reconciled. He promises to curb his drink and swears he will never betray me again."

"And you believe him?"

"I must—for the sake of our child—and Scotland."

"If that is your wish—"

She touched his arm. "You have Jean—surely something can be salvaged from your marriage."

"Does it please you to think so?"

"No. I am not without jealousy, but I haven't the right to begrudge you what happiness you can find with her."

"I love you. I don't care a damn that Darnley is your husband, or that he has a right to you."

Her eyes implored him. "Please, no more. My decision is made; help me to abide by it." She worried the gold crucifix that hung in the hollow of her neck. "I shall always be grateful for yesterday—we have had that much at least."

Wordlessly, he put her hand to his lips, then he turned and walked away.

CHAPTER XI

1

Jean had changed from the dull, drab creature that Bothwell had left nearly a month ago. She was still a long way from being beautiful, but there was an improvement. She had cast off the dull grays and powder blues that he had grown so used to seeing; now she gowned herself in bright colors. More amazing, she had discovered the art of painting her face.

Even her attitude toward Bothwell had changed; she went about smiling now, solicitous of his needs, clucking over a loose button on his doublet or cross with the cook for not preparing his food just the way he liked it. But he knew that her smiles were not for him; they were secretive and self-satisfied, which both confounded and amused him. Evidently Jean had a secret, but she was confiding in no one.

Nevertheless, after months of wrangling with himself emotionally, he was grateful for the peace he now found at Crichton. He was no happier than before, but the atmosphere of ease and comfort, created by Jean's expert management, did much to restore his peace of mind. Then Ormiston came with disturbing news.

"The Queen has recalled Lethington," he told Bothwell. "He is expected to return to Court within the week."

It didn't take much imagination to know who was responsible for that decision; James had likely badgered Mary until she had finally relented. But why? She had been warned about the danger of allowing Lethington to ally himself with James again.

She couldn't fully realize what she was doing, and Bothwell hoped he could still prevent it. She was at the Exchequer House now to study finances for the Prince's christening; he would go there and try to reason with her.

"Has the King taken residence there with her?" Bothwell asked.

Ormiston snorted. "Not likely. He is more apt to be found at the nearest brothel these days."

"When last I heard they were reconciled."

"If anything, matters are worse between them now. He vagabonds his nights in taverns and brothels, and voices his grievances against her to anyone who will listen."

"What grievances has he?"

"The usual—but the nature of them is the true ignominy." Ormiston paused to pour himself some wine. "He complains that she is cold to his lovemaking and that he would find more pleasure in a dried-up old spinster."

"The puking tosspot. He dares drag her name through the muck."

"There is more."

"I have heard enough, spare me the rest."

"With Lethington's return he has even more to complain of."

"Aye, well he may. Banded together with James, Lethington will surely seek his ruin."

Despite his outrage for Mary, Bothwell took satisfaction in the knowledge that she could not bear Darnley's lovemaking. The reconciliation had been a failure, and he hoped it was because of that afternoon in the Roman peel tower.

Mary Seton admitted Bothwell into the small anteroom of the Exchequer House.

"Her Majesty is at supper, my lord," she told him.

"Tell her I am here."

"But, my lord—"

Mary's voice called from the next room. "Who is it, Seton?"

"My lord Bothwell, madam."

She came to the doorway. "Let him come in."

Seton followed him in.

He said, "I must speak to you in private, madam."

Mary glanced at him uneasily. "Leave us," she said to Seton.

When they were alone, Bothwell said, "Is it true that you have recalled Lethington?"

She avoided his eyes. "Yes."

"Why? You were warned against this. What changed your mind?"

"He is the only one capable of negotiating with Elizabeth on the Prince's succession."

"A point made very clear by James, no doubt."

She nodded. "With the Prince's christening only three months away, Lethington's talents may be put to good use. He may succeed where others have failed."

"And for that you are willing to risk his joining forces with your brother again?"

"It is a risk I must take. Besides, James will not defy me; he has given his word."

"How can you be so naïve? Do you also believe that Elizabeth loves you, and that your husband is not a depraved, wine-sodden ass? Perhaps you are too fond of self-deceit to see the truth."

She turned on him, her eyes blazing anger. "You forget your place, my lord—even *you* can go too far."

He laughed harshly. "What is my place? Shall I stand ready for you to shake out of your pockets when trouble arises? You've used me in the past—but I'll not allow the past to repeat itself."

Her anger had subsided. "Why do you oppose everything I attempt? You have my trust—my love—I care nothing for the others. I know their treacheries and I despise them for it, but I also need them. When will you learn to compromise?"

"What compromise is there with unprincipled cowards?"

"Must I beg?"

He knew that he would yield, as he always had. Instinctively, he knew her decision was wrong, but he could not stop her—and more, he would stand by her despite the consequences.

He said, "Though I am certain you invite fresh grief in restoring Lethington, I will not oppose you."

She smiled. "And will you agree to do something more for me?"

"What more can you ask?"

"When Lethington returns I want you to meet with him. Since your duties will bring you into frequent contact with each other, attempt a truce. As enemies neither of you can work for the good of the Realm."

"The final irony! Have you forgotten that it was Lethington who plotted my murder while I was in Paris by bribing my servants?"

"Would you do less to him if the opportunity presented itself?"

He grinned. "Do you think it was lack of opportunity that prevented me from doing away with him thus far? Murder, however, is not among my vices. But were I so disposed to rid myself of an enemy, my methods would be quite different. I do not hire assassins to do my work." Then, sighing, he said, "Very well—you shall have your truce."

She squeezed his hand gratefully. "I promise you will not regret it."

He already did, but when he saw her hopefulness he had not the heart to tell her so.

2

His peace made with Lethington, Bothwell prepared to leave for the Border in the morning. Mary would be joining him there a week later, after he had rounded up the outlaws for Justice Court.

The Border, deep in autumn, was a patchwork of color; the hills, purpled with heather and bracken, streaked with orange and russet reeds; spindle trees dotted the hedgerows with coral-pink seed heads; crisping leaves of gold and bronze rustled and swirled on sharp October winds.

There were signs of early frost in the air as Bothwell started on his first day of rounding up outlaws. Behind him Hermitage glowed blood red in a sunrise that spilled over the moors and into the streams with an effect of flowing gold. He rode for Liddesdale at the head of three hundred horsemen. On a hilltop he sighted the Armstrong peel towers pushing their roofs skyward from marshy burns. He sounded the battle cry, *"A Hepburn!"* and bounded down the steep slope with his men close behind. His methods were swift and clean; smoke the offenders out of their homes before they knew what was about them, then secure them fast for safekeeping.

He led the raid from one peel tower to the next, until his prisoners numbered more than a hundred, then he gave the order to return to Hermitage. For himself, Bothwell could have gone on for hours more; his days spent at Court had stored in him a boundless energy. But he planned on taking the Elliots tomorrow and wanted his men fresh for the chase.

Morning dawned wet and gloomy. Bothwell rode out with his troopers, clattering over the planked moat. They turned in the direction of Witterhope Burn, bypassing the peel tower of Robert Elliot of the Shaws, whose peace-loving ways troubled no one. On they rode to where the burn joined Liddel Water and came to a halt at the peel of Jock o' the Park, an Elliot of treacherous reputation.

Coming up the narrow approach, Bothwell spotted a rider on horseback making for Kershope Burn. He spurred his horse in pursuit, leaving his men to follow in the distance. He raced past the peels of Whithaugh and Mangerton, Elliots he had already routed into Hermitage's prison. By now he knew that his prey was Jock o' the Park and dug into his horse's sides, urging the tired beast on.

Jock's horse was fresh and took the road with ease. For a while it looked as though Jock would make good his escape, but Bothwell's horse began to gain on him and they met head-on at the junction of Liddel Water and Kershope Burn. Jock looked about desperately for an avenue of escape, but Bothwell's dag was trained on him an instant later.

Jock called out, "If I surrender, will you spare my life?"

Bothwell would as soon have taken him dead as alive; his grudge against the Elliots went back to the Chaseabout Raid, when they had refused to give him their allegiance and had gone over to the English instead. But Justice Court would send him to the hanging tree soon enough.

"Agreed," Bothwell said, "but you've the Queen's justice to meet as well as mine."

Jock made as if to come forward, but he bolted from his horse to get away on foot. Bothwell shot twice, wounding him in the thigh. Jock stumbled forward, and rather than risk his horse's bogging in the marsh, Bothwell dismounted. He dropped his pistol and started toward the wounded man. In the distance he heard the thundering hoofbeats of his troopers.

He was only a few feet from Jock when he stumbled on a hidden tree stump; his head struck a rock, and for an instant he lay there, stunned. Jock saw his chance and lunged forward with his two-handed sword, thrusting it deep into Bothwell's hip.

The heavy blade tore through flesh and bone. Pain slashed through Bothwell, but he fought off the sensation of blacking out and reached for his whinger, driving it twice at Jock's chest. Jock retaliated with his sword, a blow to Bothwell's head and another to his arm.

The trees above trembled and swirled; the ground on which he lay spun beneath him. Blood gushed from Bothwell's head and ran down his face, merging with another trail of blood that stained his white leather jack. His left side screamed in agony; he tried to rise, but fell back, sinking into a black whirlpool.

Bothwell woke to a bumping, jarring motion. Rain fell on him; his eyes trained upward on a slate-gray sky. There were voices all about him; he recognized Dalgleish's deep throaty tones. Someone called, "Mind the ruts, don't jog him more than you need." His eyes closed and he sank back into unconsciousness. . . .

Waking again, he heard shouting, angry voices, distant and unreal. Pain seared through him; he was cold and wet. Violent clashes of steel mingled with the whinneying of horses, unbearably piercing in his ears. He opened his mouth to speak and tasted blood. . . .

3

Cool hands stroked his forehead. A woman's voice filtered through the haze. "Fetch more blankets," she said. "The fever makes him shiver."

Rough hands held his head and forced a bitter liquid down his throat; he retched and spit it out. He was unable to open his eyes, and he thought he was blind. He tried to rise, but strong hands restrained him—he was too weak to resist. The same bitter brew was forced through his lips again; swallowing, he drifted back into unconsciousness.

Slowly he emerged from a black pit. He could not speak; his tongue seemed stuck to the roof of his mouth.

Dimly he heard the woman's voice again. "No more purgatives; they rob him of what little strength he has left."

A man replied sharply. "Were it not for me, he might not be alive now."

Her voice rose in anger. "If he lives at all, it will be despite you, drowning him as you have in those evil brews."

"So say you, my lady. These are tried remedies, known to cure."

"By the grace of God, perhaps—not by your ministering."

A door slammed. Bothwell moaned. His head throbbed; he felt dizzy and light-headed. Again he tried to rise; the exertion brought a queasiness to the pit of his stomach.

He tried to bring his thoughts into focus—there had been a skirmish, he had been wounded. He recalled the paralyzing effect of Jock's blow to his hip and panic seized him. He had lost his leg. He struggled to free himself, groaned, and fell back exhausted.

The woman said, "You must not move."

"My leg, I can't feel my leg," he moaned. "They've cut it off."

"Easy now," she murmured. "Sleep."

He slept fitfully, shouting wild, incoherent orders. He cursed, rolled uncontrollably on his pillow, chills shot through him, and he wondered vaguely why no one had lighted a fire to warm him. Wild, distorted visions floated through his dreams and mingled with his pain in torturous agony. Then he finally slipped into a restful sleep, and when he woke again, the restraining ropes were gone.

His throat felt dry and cracked; he called for water and drank in long, thirsty gulps.

"Drink slowly, my lord."

That was Paris' voice; he would speak French to him.

"My eyes," he said. "Am I blind?"

"The bandages, my lord."

"Remove them."

"I will call the physician."

"Wait," Bothwell called. "Tell me where I am."

"At Hermitage, my lord."

Sleep threatened to overtake him again, but he willed himself to stay awake. He heard returning footsteps, and the bandages were lifted from his eyes. He blinked and saw only a blur of movement; then, gradually, the haze lifted and Janet Beaton stood at his bedside.

"Thank God you are still among us," she said. "We had about despaired of your life."

He tried to smile—his fever-cracked lips split and bled. "How did you get here?" he asked.

"How else but on a horse? I heard of your mishap and came immediately."

"How long have I been here?"

"Five days, and nearer death than life all that time."

He was suddenly aware of a peculiar odor. He sniffed and made a wry face. "What is that stench?"

The physician came forward. "A healing ointment for Your Lordship's wounds—a mixture of egg yolks, rose oil, and turpentine."

"I marvel you can stand it," he said to Janet.

She laughed. "If the stench has not entirely murdered your appetite perhaps you will take some broth."

"He must be bled first, to cleanse his system," the physician said.

Janet turned on him angrily. "Has he not bled enough without your taking more of him?"

The physician appealed to Bothwell. "My lord, I have tolerated as much interference as I will. My Lady of Buccleugh has thwarted me at every turn. I must ask Your Lordship to decide who is to have charge here."

Bothwell knew Dr. Gubbins from past experience; he had been summoned to Hermitage on other occasions to care for the wounded brought back from raids. He recalled now that he had questioned Gubbins' methods of cauterizing gunshot wounds by pouring boiling elder oil into them. He had watched his men roar with pain and had listened to their groans long after the treatment had ceased, until they either fell asleep from exhaustion or lost consciousness.

He said, "You have had your will of me—my Lady of Buccleugh will take charge now."

Gubbins accepted his dismissal with martyred forbearance. "As you wish, my lord. I shall leave those remedies already prepared in your servants' care."

Janet sighed in relief. "Now for your broth," she said.

She sent Paris to fetch it from the kitchen and returned to Bothwell. "Another day of Master Gubbins' ministering would have you in your grave." She paused to adjust his quilt, then ticked off on her fingers in singsong voice, "Hellibore to stimulate your heart, aloe to purge your system, barleywater to soothe you, yarrow to stanch your bleeding, and mandrake root to make you sleep."

He grimaced. "The man is a bungling fool. Had I had my wits about me, he would not have been allowed near me."

Paris returned with the broth, and Janet fed it to Bothwell slowly. He took only a few spoonfuls, refusing the rest. Weariness enveloped him; he wanted desperately to sleep. The weakness he felt embarrassed him, and he disguised it with anger.

He growled at Janet, "Let me be; you'd reduce me to the state of infancy if you could."

She smiled; her eyes told him that she understood. He had never been able to deceive Janet; she knew him too well.

When he opened his eyes again, burning rushlights threw the room into shadowy softness and a fire blazed brightly opposite his bed. He tried to raise himself on his uninjured arm, but a sharp pain in his hip forced him back. His groan brought Janet to his bedside.

He said, "I thought you had deserted me."

"You'll not be rid of me that easily."

"I am hungry."

"A good sign," she said, plumping his pillows. "I will send for more broth."

"No more of that weak, stinking brew—I want meat."

"A fine thing to say when I took the trouble to fix it myself. You will take broth or nothing."

"Meat," he said stubbornly.

"Very well, glut yourself to death for all I care."

She left and returned shortly with a tray.

"From your pigheadedness, I judge that you are well enough to feed yourself," she said, thrusting a small pewter dish at him.

"What is it?"

"Gruel."

"Take it away. I'll not eat that swill."

"Nor will I have all my good nursing go to naught to satisfy your whim."

"You have no heart, browbeating me as you do in my weakened condition."

She snapped her fingers at him. "That for your condition! You are weak as an ox."

She urged a spoonful at him, but he clamped his mouth shut.

"I'll not be fed," he snarled. "Prop me up. I'll help myself."

She sighed. "Some folk snatched from the jaws of death have been known to reform—in your case it has made you even more evil-tempered."

He dug the spoon into the gruel murderously and brought it to his mouth. The taste was sickening; he swallowed quickly to force it down. When he had eaten all he could, he sent for Ormiston.

Janet had told him that Ormiston had trotted his hulking form past the sickbed more than a dozen times daily. When he was not in the bedchamber, getting in everyone's way, he badgered them constantly for reassurance that Bothwell would live.

Ormiston approached the bed grinning. "Now that I see for myself, I can tell the men you are truly on the mend," he said.

There was no need to say more; the friendship they shared made it unnecessary.

Bothwell said, "Tell me about my encounter with Jock. Did he escape?"

"He's one Elliot that did not—we found him dead in the muck, half a mile from where you lay."

"What of the others?"

"Those we had imprisoned here managed somehow to work themselves loose from their cells. When we returned with you wounded, we found them in revolt, our entrance barred. It was Robert Elliot of the Shaws who brought the matter to an end by exchanging the outlaws' freedom for the keys to the castle."

"Was there no other way?"

"None. There was no time to give battle; you were too near the grave, and sore in need of care."

"No matter, you did your best. More's the pity, though, for the gap it will leave in Justice Court."

"Aye, the Queen will have few punishments to pronounce."

Bothwell remembered to ask, "What day is this?"

"Saturday, the twelfth of October."

He was to have met Mary in Jedburgh on the tenth.

"Does the Queen know of my injuries?"

"Aye. Immediately after you were settled I dispatched Paris with the news. He caught up with her party a few hours after they had left Borthwick. We despaired of your life then, and Paris told her so."

"How did she take the news?"

"Paris said there were tears in her eyes. To keep her informed, she sends a messenger from Jedburgh daily for news of your progress."

"Send word to her at once. Tell her that I am recovering."

"Aye, my lord. Shall I also send word to my lady Bothwell, telling her to come?"

"No, say only that I am on the mend and there is no longer cause for concern. Hermitage has no accommodations for women."

"The Lady of Buccleugh seems not to mind the inconveniences."

"My Lady of Buccleugh is unlike other women," he said.

4

Paris returned from Jedburgh on the fourteenth with news that threw the entire garrison into chaos; Mary was coming to Hermitage the following day. Although the promise of seeing her delighted Bothwell, he was concerned for her safety in undertaking so arduous a journey. The treacherous roads she would travel—what there were of them—were a mass of steep braes, peat bogs, and flooded burns, made more dangerous by bands of roving outlaws. It would take her hours to cover the twenty-five miles to Hermitage, and because there were no accommodations for her to spend the night, she would have to return all in the same day.

Bothwell heard the commotion of Mary's arrival and waited impatiently for the sight of her. Though his strapped hip and arm prevented him from rising to meet her, he was in a half-sitting position, for he had insisted on being moved to the study, where he could lie on a couch. He smiled, picturing the sight he must make, swathed in bandages and covered with furred robes—but at least he looked less of an invalid here than he did in bed.

At last the door opened and Mary rushed in. She was accompanied by Huntly and James. Bothwell leaned forward in greeting, but pain forced him back.

Mary hurried to him. "You've had me worried half to death, my lord," she said.

"You needn't have fashed yourself, madam. Only the good die young."

"We heard fearful reports of you at Jedburgh. First you were dying, then rallying, then dying again. No one knew what to expect, until Paris brought news of your recovery."

"Truly, you've had a narrow escape with death, my lord," James said.

Bothwell shot him a fierce look. "To my enemies' delight, no doubt. I am almost sorry to disappoint them."

Huntly approached the couch. "Rumor had you already dead. At least Jock o' the Park paid for his sins; his head makes a grisly decoration for the Tolbooth at Jedburgh."

"Aye, but thanks to my clumsiness, most of his kinsmen got clear away."

Mary said, "More thanks to your Jock that his sword did not have greater thrust."

He adored the sight of her and wondered if her russet riding dress were warm enough. His thoughts were so full of her that it

was difficult for him to follow what the others said. Some curls
had fallen from under her toque, threatening to fall to her
shoulder; it was only with the greatest effort that he did not
reach out to toy with them. Then fearing his face might betray
him, he shouted for Paris and ordered food.

Mary fussed with his pillow, filled a plate for him, and
half-fed it to him. He let her have her way, knowing the delight
she took in doing it. At last the meal was over and Huntly took
James on a tour of the castle.

When they were alone, Bothwell said, "You should not have
come. I dread the thought of your ride back."

She bent close and took his hand in hers. "I had to see for
myself that you were recovering. I've been living a nightmare
since the news reached me. If I had lost you—"

"But you didn't. I'll be hale and hearty in a week or two."

She sat down on the edge of his couch. "It took this fright
to make me realize how much you really mean to me. I lit a
candle at mass every day and prayed for you."

He pulled her to him and kissed her.

"When you are well enough to travel, come to me at
Jedburgh. You can convalesce there," she said.

He glanced up at the iron coronal that hung from the ceiling;
gusty, chill winds flicked through the open casement, flapping
the bearskin hangings. The coronal swung on its chains, casting
strange flashes from its flaming rushlights.

"No," he said, "I will convalesce here and join you when I
am able."

"But why? I have rented a house there; you may have the
comforts that are not available to you here."

"I'll not be tortured by your nearness."

"Have you forgotten your promise so soon?"

"What do you mean?"

"That you would wait for me—until I came to you of my
own accord."

"And have you?"

She stood. "Am I not here? Why do you think I came?"

"To pay your respects to a subject wounded in your service—and to discuss Border affairs."

She shook her head.

"Why, then?"

She turned away from him. "I could have sent Huntly and James in my place. They would have carried my message to you—if it were only that."

He knew what she was trying to say, but he wanted to hear it from her nevertheless.

"Say it then."

Her shoulders quivered, as though on a sob. "You leave me no pride. Why must I tell you what you already know?"

"Say it."

"I love you—I cannot forget you. The thought of losing you nearly drove me out of my mind. I told you that I prayed for you, but more, I prayed to know the feel of your lips again—to be in your arms. I marvel that God did not take you from me for such blasphemy."

"Come here," he said gently.

She turned and knelt beside the couch.

He caressed her cheek. "Forgive me for taunting you so, but you trouble your conscience needlessly. If there is any sin, let it be mine. I'll not have you punish yourself—it was I who forced myself on you."

"And I welcomed you, despite my vows to God. How could I have hoped to deceive God? I think He knew what I felt for you in my heart even before I did—He knew that I loved you even before that afternoon. I thought seeing you wed would cure me of my love for you, but it did not. Your mishap with Jock—it may be God's warning—"

"What kind of God is it that begrudges love?"

"Give me time," she pleaded. "You ask me to cast aside the teaching of a lifetime."

He softened. "If it's only time you need, then take it. But remember, even a lifetime can be painfully short."

Mary had returned to the armchair when James and Huntly came back.

James said, "You keep a well-ordered castle, my lord. A bit stark and ominous for my taste, but then I suppose it serves its purpose as a grim warning."

"Hermitage was not designed for beauty," Bothwell said.

"To be sure. The exterior speaks for itself."

Huntly said, "Your secretary was kind enough to show us some of your papers, my lord. Their content will give Her Majesty full understanding of Border affairs."

James went to the casement. "It has begun to rain, madam; our way back will be that much more difficult now. If we start soon we may make Jedburgh before nightfall."

Mary rose. "Order the horses, and we shall be on our way."

James crossed to the couch. "A speedy recovery, my lord. We hope to see you up and about soon."

Bothwell hid his amusement. "Your good wishes have strengthened me already, my lord."

Huntly's farewell was brief. "Take care not to exert yourself, lest you have a relapse," he said.

Bothwell was alone with Mary again. He took her hand and put it to his lips. "It seems only minutes ago that you arrived—now you must go."

"Would that I could stay here with you forever. There is so much I want to know about you, but there is never any time."

"There will be time aplenty, later—we've a lifetime ahead."

"How long is a lifetime?"

"Who knows? A day, a month, a year—sometimes there is

more endurance in brevity." Then, abruptly, he said, "Go now, I'll not rest until I know you are safely back at Jedburgh."

She bent to kiss him and hurried to the door. She was gone in a moment, and he felt an unbearable loneliness deep inside. Her scent lingered on his pillow where she had bent down to him; her voice was still in his ear, her kiss still on his lips. He pictured her riding over the moors and longed to be with her. Then he heard the rain and worried for the miles she had yet to cover.

The next day Mary sent a mass of writing to Bothwell. He guessed the content: evidence for the Court of Oyer and Terminer that he was to hold at Hermitage. But the instant he was alone he searched for a personal note from her. He found it between two affidavits of grievances against a criminal. She had composed a sonnet in French.

Her graceful verse told him all that she felt, her grief in nearly losing him, the hazards she would endure for him; and she closed with calling him "love of my heart." He read it twice, treasuring every word, then, folding it, he slipped it under his pillow.

5

Although he was still confined to bed, Bothwell improved rapidly. By the end of the second week his pain had lessened, but there was still the danger of his wounds opening. He knew himself to be the worst patient; he had never borne idleness easily and such imposed inactivity served to make him more irritable.

Three days after Mary's visit, another messenger came from Jedburgh, and unexplainably, Bothwell had an immediate sense of something wrong. His instinct was confirmed when he saw Ormiston's tight-lipped silence and the wary-eyed look he gave him.

"What's happened?" Bothwell asked.

The messenger said, "The Queen is dangerously ill and feared dying."

Bothwell bolted upright to a sitting position. The motion sent a hot flash of pain through him, and he toppled backward violently.

Ormiston rushed to help him. "My lord, take care," he said.

Recovering, Bothwell gasped, "How did it happen?"

"Following Her Majesty's visit to Your Lordship, she complained of a pain in her side. Her condition worsened; there were frequent spasms of vomiting blood, and she had lost consciousness when I left Jedburgh."

Bothwell lay back cursing himself for the injuries that had brought her to his bedside. Why had she endangered herself? The hazards of that ride had been too strenuous. He blamed himself for permitting her to leave; conveniences or not, he should have insisted that she stay the night. Her russet riding dress was so thin; how quickly the rain would have penetrated it.

He said to Ormiston, "Prepare a litter for me."

"No, my lord. The ride would kill you."

Grimly he said, "I gave an order."

"Aye, my lord, but I'll not obey it."

It seemed incredible that Ormiston of all men should be guilty of such flagrant disobedience. He knew they both shared the same violent nature, but they had never clashed before.

"Think well, my lord," Ormiston pleaded. "What good will you do her, if you arrive dead on her doorstep? In a few days, perhaps, when you are stronger—"

Reason had left Bothwell. He shouted, "You dare oppose me?"

Ormiston nodded and stood arms akimbo in a show of obstinacy. "Aye, when I know it is in your own best interest."

Wide-eyed, the messenger glanced from one to the other.

His voice dangerously quiet, Bothwell said, "I am at your mercy now, but not for long, then you'd be wise to keep out of my sight."

"You will thank me for this, my lord."

Bothwell rasped, "Get out."

Ormiston turned and left with the messenger close at his heels.

Left to himself, Bothwell began to plot how he could get away without Ormiston's help. Dalgleish? No, he would side with Ormiston. Paris! Aye, he'd not dare oppose him, but how could they get past the guards, whom Ormiston had probably alerted by now?

Frustrated by his immobility, furious at being crossed, he thought of several ways in which to repay Ormiston. A quick death was too good for the faithless traitor; he would have him skinned alive, or hanged, brought down alive, then drawn and quartered . . .

His thoughts suddenly sickened him; his concern for Mary had unhinged him. Ormiston was right; he was in no condition to travel. But Mary had come to him when he had needed her most. Her visit had done him more good than all the remedies they had poured into him. Her love had lifted him to the skies; he counted it as his most precious possession. But if he must pay for it with her life, then he would glady reject it. He would give anything to make her live—even if it meant giving her up.

The days passed slowly, agonizingly. The news from Jedburgh told him they despaired of her life. Bothwell lay on his couch staring into the flames, his mind on Mary. Prayer did not come easily to him, but he prayed for her; imploring, demanding, then reverently, humbly asking God to spare her life.

Then, nearly a week later, Dalgleish came into his study to tell him that a litter was waiting for him in the courtyard. Two husky troopers carried him down the narrow turnpike stairs and placed him on a pile of bearskins, covering him from neck to toes with a furred robe. Ormiston shouted orders to the men and checked the ropes that held the litter, then he left and returned with another robe for Bothwell.

His hands were gentle as a woman's as he smoothed it out and tucked it under Bothwell. They had not spoken a word to each other since their argument; both were too stubborn to take the first step in making amends. Now their eyes met for an instant and Bothwell winked. Ormiston's solemn mouth parted in a grotesque grin that revealed his brown-stained teeth.

It was a grueling journey. The men steering the litter horses kept them at a steady, slow walk, but even with care, the jogging motion started up the throbbing in Bothwell's head. The rhythmic beat of the horses' hooves pounded relentlessly. They stopped occasionally to give him wine, or to readjust his covers, then they were on the move again.

Ormiston rode beside the litter, alternating between anxious glances at the sky that threatened rain and calling out to "mind the ruts." He kept a sharp eye trained to the road, and when they came to a steep decline he dismounted to help steady the litter.

Bothwell counted the pain and discomfort as nothing, for each jolt brought him closer to Mary. He could only hope that he was not too late; it seemed that he was engaged in a race with death. If he could reach her in time, he knew he could make her live.

It was late afternoon when Ormiston sighted the spired roof of Ferniehirst Castle; they were less than two miles out of Jedburgh now. With the journey's end so close, Bothwell's impatience mounted. Every part of him ached with weariness; he felt a sticky wetness under his bandaged arm and knew it was blood. Lifting the sling, he saw the telltale stain on the white linen—the wound, scarcely healed, had opened again. Then he saw the high-arched structure of the town port overhead.

Huntly came out to greet them. He looked at Bothwell and smiled grimly. "I never thought to see you reduced to this mode of travel," he said.

"How is she?" Bothwell asked.

"There is little hope, I fear. She lost consciousness again today, and her eyes and voice have failed."

"Take me to her."

"To what purpose? She will not know you."

"I must see her."

"You should rest." Huntly turned to Ormiston. "Get him to bed; his face is the color of death."

Bothwell shook his head. "I haven't come all this way to be put to bed. I want to see her *now.*"

They carried him, litter and all, up the tower stairs to Mary's bedchamber and set him down beside her bed. She lay very still, her breathing barely perceptible. Her face was like white stone bleached in the sun. He touched her hand; it felt cold and lifeless.

Arnault, her physician, forced heated wine between her lips. James stood at the window looking out, then he crossed to her bed and glanced down at her. His face was a mask of coldness, his eyes bright with intent—he had the look of a vulture contemplating carrion flesh.

Arnault massaged Mary's hands vigorously, then he lifted the covers and rubbed her feet. There was no response; he turned away.

Bothwell gripped his arm. "Is that all you mean to do?"

"I have done everything humanly possible, my lord."

"You will exceed the impossible, until you have restored life to her body."

James said, "If God, in His wisdom, sees fit to call her away, she must go."

Bothwell glared at him. "And the sooner the better, to enable you to get on with your plans, eh, my lord?"

Arnault shushed them. "You forget yourselves, my lords. Brawling has no place here."

Daylight faded to dusk, then the black of night, and the tree outside Mary's window was lost to view. Despite Huntly and Ormiston urging him to rest, Bothwell remained at her bedside. He had studied the wall tapestry, depicting the meeting of Jacob and Esau, for so many hours that it seemed the figures had moved.

Gradually the tedious hours passed and Mary's breathing deepened. He touched her hand for the hundredth time and felt some warmth. It was only a slight improvement, but he was thankful for it. Suddenly he was acutely aware of his own weakness; the day's arduous journey, his long vigil at her bedside, took hold of him.

Ormiston must have sensed his fatigue, for he looked pleadingly at him. "Will you take some rest now, my lord?" he asked.

Bothwell nodded wearily and permitted himself to be carried to the chamber below Mary's where a bed had been prepared for him.

He woke to the news that Mary had recovered sufficiently to summon her nobles to her bedside. She had regained a little of her color, and her speech had returned. In a weak, halting voice, she begged them to keep "love, unity, and charity among themselves." Then, after a long pause, she recommended the Prince to their care, and looking at James, she urged that they press no man to their faith. She turned to Bothwell, and their glances met—her eyes spoke a message that only he could understand.

Later Bothwell met with the Privy Council to discuss emergency measures in the event of her death. Darnley's name was conspicuously absent, but he was very much on everyone's mind. Bothwell had heard that Darnley had been advised of Mary's serious illness days ago, but devoted husband that he was, he had seen no reason to cut short his hunting trip to be with her.

The next day Mary was worse again. By Thursday, late afternoon, she was in a deep coma. Bothwell had been at her bedside since morning, helplessly watching the life ebb out of her. Her Maries knelt at her oratory praying and weeping. Huntly sat in a chair near the fireplace, his legs sprawled out before him, his eyes fixed in a glassy stare on the bedposts. And James, too practical for tears or exhortations, took inventory of her jewels and silver.

By midnight there was no hope of recovery; her face had the yellowish-white pallor of death, her mouth clamped tight, her arms and legs stiffened. Seton, thinking Mary was already dead, opened the window to let her spirit depart. The blustery winds coursed through the room with chilling rawness, and Bothwell ordered the window shut—he could not give up so easily.

He shouted to Arnault, "Heat some wine, work on her."

"But, my lord—"

"Work on her, I say."

Arnault pried open her mouth and poured wine down her throat. Binding cords were placed about her shacklebones, knees, and toes. Aided by servants, Arnault massaged and pulled at her limbs with unceasing effort. But there was no response— he looked at Bothwell.

Grimly, Bothwell said, "Keep working."

They worked on Mary for three hours; when one tired,

another took his place, until her mouth and eyes opened. Great beads of sweat formed on her forehead, her breathing seemed less shallow, and a touch of warmth had returned to her hands.

Exhausted, Arnault left her bedside and went to sit down. "She is sleeping now," he said.

Bothwell reached for her hand and warmed it in his. He leaned forward as best he could and whispered, "You *will* live."

A hideous fear had taken hold of him these last hours: that she might not want to live. He recalled her words at Hermitage, that God would punish her for loving him. Was her religious dogma so powerful and unyielding that it made her prefer death to adultery? Was she afraid to live and love him?

He lay back on his litter, still holding her hand as though he meant to let his life flow into her. Night shrouded the window with velvety blackness, then gradually it changed to gray and the branches of the pear tree were visible again.

He felt her fingers move and she turned her head toward him. She saw him, and her lips moved, forming his name soundlessly.

CHAPTER XII

1

Nine days she was ill and so near dying that it filled him with horror to think of it. But she had passed the crisis and had awakened to speak his name. He marveled at the endless depths to which she could stir him—before Jedburgh he had loved and adored her; now, after nearly losing her, she had become even more precious to him.

By the end of the first week of convalescence, Bothwell was able to limp about on his own; he had even managed to climb the stairs to her chambers without assistance. His hip was still troublesome, his arm still in a sling, but his head wound was finally healing and he could dispense with the bandage.

He was in an armchair at Mary's bedside, amusing her with some outrageous stories about his Borderers, when Darnley appeared and her laughter suddenly died.

"It appears the invalids keep each other in high spirits," Darnley said good-humoredly.

Mary glared at him with distaste. "Is that all you can say, after your long delay in coming here?"

"You have others enough to hold your hand, my dear. I doubt you needed me at all. Besides, it was your own incontinence that brought this down on your head."

"What are you implying?"

"Simply that you might have exercised better judgment than to fly away in such haste to the bedside of your wounded gladiator. Frankly, I cannot but wonder if you would show me the same concern."

"Since it is unlikely that you will ever risk your life for the Realm, there is little cause to wonder," she said contemptuously.

Darnley shrugged and turned to survey the prominent scar over Bothwell's left eye. "Perhaps now you will intrigue the ladies less, scarred as you are, my lord."

Bothwell smiled. "I have never claimed a pretty face among my assets, sire."

It was obvious that Darnley's courage lay in his drunkenness, and Bothwell kept his temper rather than upset Mary any more.

"It would do you good to be a little daggered like my lord Bothwell," Mary told him.

The malicious smirk left Darnley's face. He turned mottled, which accentuated his bloatedness and dissipation. Blustering, he shook his fist at her. "You will live to regret that, madam," he said, staggering out.

Mary lay back exhausted.

Bothwell looked at her anxiously. "If his visit results in your relapse, I'll—"

"No, it's nothing. I am only tired."

"I'd still like to whip the arrogant hide off him."

"Let him go—to the devil—or to whomsoever else he consorts with these days."

"Wherever he goes, I warrant he'll not be troubling you again—not for a while, at least."

Bothwell's prediction was confirmed when Darnley left for Linlithgow the next day without even saying good-bye to Mary.

By the ninth of November, Mary was well enough to resume the Border progress. Although Bothwell's wounds still had him hobbling about, he was able to ride. They set out with a guard of one thousand horses, commanded by Lord Home. They rode to Berwick, then to Eyemouth and Coldingham, and on to Dunbar, where the progress ended.

Bothwell had supervised the refurbishing of Dunbar when he and Mary had planned the progress two months ago. Mary's apartments had been redecorated with a canopied bed from Crichton, some tapestries and a needlepoint love seat from Hailes, and what other comforts he could think of for her. The fortress itself had been given a thorough going-over, which made it seem less bleak now.

Her many hours spent in the saddle left Mary exhausted, and she rested two nights at Dunbar instead of the one originally planned. But Bothwell suspected it was more the news that caught up with her there. Though it was only a rumor, Mary had word of a design by Darnley and his father to seize the Prince, imprison her, then set up a regency in Darnley's name. This, with the christening only a month away, was enough to plunge her into a deep depression.

"You can no longer afford to ignore him," Bothwell told her. "To do so makes him more desperate and his schemes more dangerous."

"There is no dealing with him—I have tried every way I know how. At times I think that if I am not free of him I will be driven to take my own life."

Her misery tore at him. She looked so ill; her eyes reflected her despair. He had always loved her fighting spirit in times of adversity—even that seemed gone now, as had her will to live. During her illness he had blamed himself and their love; now he realized it was Darnley and the hopelessness of her marriage. Somehow he had to restore her spirit.

"Better to die, is it?" he said contemptuously. "Well, why not, if that is your wish? Give it to him—all of it—your son, your Realm, your crown. Let him tear down in a day what it has taken you six years to build. Aye, death would be a simple means of ending your misery. I'll not lift a finger to stop you, for I'll not wait around to see it."

Where there had been hopelessness, he now saw alarm. He might have wished for more, but at least she responded. "Pay me no heed," she said quickly. "He drives me to such extremes; he discredits me everywhere—Rome, Spain . . . " She went to the table, picked up a letter, and handed it to him. "Even now I am obliged to answer to charges he has made against me to the Pope. He accuses me of being dubious in my faith. What am I to say, how can I ask financial aid of Rome, when he writes such lies?"

Bothwell knew there was more to this rift with the Pope and Spain than she cared to admit—they had quarreled over it. The papal nuncio, Bishop Laureo, had offered Mary a solution to end Scotland's internal strife, but she had refused it. Laureo's plan had included the execution of her six leading Protestants; James, of course, headed the list. Even Bothwell approved it, for there had been two seditions headed by James and his allies already, and he feared a third. But Laureo had not taken Mary's refusal as final; he was prepared to find someone else less squeamish to support him.

Bothwell let the Bishop's proposal go for the moment. "Protest his charges in the strongest terms," he said. "As for dealing with your husband, James offered a possible solution only this morning."

"What, short of putting him in his grave, will put an end to his scheming?"

"We must wait, of course, until after the christening, since it is imperative that he attend."

"For God's sake, don't keep me in suspense," she said impatiently. "Tell me what it is."

"Pardon your rebels—Morton, his Douglases—the lot."

"How can you even suggest it?" she asked.

"It may be your only answer."

"It would reunite them with James—something you have warned me against repeatedly."

"Aye, but Darnley knows the exiles have a score to settle with him. Once they are back, you are his only protection—he'd not dare scheme against you."

"What of you? Their daggers are sharpened for you as well. They have you to thank for the collapse of their conspiracy."

"I am inclined to think they would be better to have here than in England. Despite my lookouts, Morton crosses the border regularly—he is in constant touch with your brother, Lethington, and God knows who else besides. I can tell you from experience that exile makes men desperate and hungry. If your rebels are pardoned and restored to their lands, their bitterness may be assuaged. Morton may have learned his lesson from the Rizzio conspiracy; he may be more disposed toward peace now. In any case, he and his Douglases should serve as useful tools for keeping Darnley in line."

She shuddered. "I must have time to think."

"I warn you, the longer you wait, the more mischief Darnley will create."

2

From Dunbar they went to Craigmillar Castle. It was only two miles from Edinburgh, but the high ground on which it was built seemed more healthful for Mary. Yet nothing seemed to do her good, for she had no peace. Too often Bothwell found her sprawled across her bed in tears; she complained of the pain in her side again, but he knew that Darnley was the real cause of her grief.

Darnley had written from Glasgow that he had no intention of attending the christening, and he renewed his vile accusations about the baby's legitimacy. His absence would furnish Elizabeth with the excuse she needed to refuse to ratify the infant's succession to her throne. Mary would be shamed before a host of ambassadors sent by the world's powers. Aye, Bothwell thought, *she has every reason to be ill,* and he feared that she would fall into a state of collapse if matters did not soon improve.

Of late, she had become so deeply depressed that he feared she would drift even beyond his reach. Desperately he fought to prevent it; he cajoled and forced her out for walks in the garden, taunted her to anger—he even played a buffoon just to see her smile. But there were no opportunities to be with her as he wished, no time to stir her, to awaken her senses, for they were always under the watchful eyes of James and Lethington.

Nor was Bothwell the only one concerned with Mary's state of mind. Although their concern was for different reasons, James, Lethington, Argyll, and Huntly were each of the opinion that something had to be done about Darnley. Bothwell sat in conference with them daily. They discussed divorce, on the grounds of adultery—Darnley had furnished them with sufficient cause there. But adultery was a Protestant issue, not Catholic.

James had suggested the divorce and Bothwell suspected his reasons were twofold, yet it would provide a swift end to Mary's grief. But knowing James, he realized that Mary would have to give something in return. He could hazard a guess at the terms—Darnley's removal for the exiles' pardon.

"A divorce may solve nothing," Bothwell said. "Even if he retires to another country, he can still slander the Queen and do mischief."

"I have in mind a more permanent means." James smiled. "His past treacheries provide us with sufficient grounds to indict him for treason. After they are divorced, the Privy Council will issue a warrant for his arrest."

"To which he will undoubtedly offer resistance," Argyll suggested. "Prisoners are often killed in such scuffles."

Bothwell glanced at James, who sat contemplating his fingertips. "A convenient method for disposing of an inconvenient prisoner," he said. "That way you eliminate the danger of any embarrassing evidence he might give at his trial." Darnley could implicate even James in the Rizzio conspiracy.

"But regicide would have serious repercussions," Huntly murmured.

"You miss the point, my lord," Lethington said. "We shall take no action until they are divorced—when he is no longer king. Therefore, his killing cannot then be termed regicide!"

"And why not?" Bothwell said to Mary later. "It will be well worth it to rid yourself of Darnley."

"James stands to gain the most with Morton and Lindsay returned," she argued. "He will have the support of his allies again."

Bothwell shrugged. "It was already on your mind; now you have an added incentive."

"How can you ask me to pardon the men who murdered Davie—and would have done the same to me?"

"Would you rather burden your son with the stigma of bastardy? I need hardly remind you that if Darnley absents himself from the christening he will accomplish just that. With the rebels pardoned he will do anything to please you."

She covered her face with her hands; tears splashed to her yellow satin skirt. He watched the spreading circles on the fabric with morbid fascination. He could do nothing more for her now; there was no immediate comfort for her unhappiness.

Actually, Bothwell didn't relish the prospect of having Morton and the others back in Scotland. They were a murderous lot and would need constant watching. But he could deal with them if he must, whereas Darnley was still beyond his jurisdiction; his rank prevented anyone from taking overt action against him. But it was James' second reason for eliminating

Darnley that plagued Bothwell most. Despite his recent good behavior, Bothwell knew that James' ambition would never be sated with less than the regency. Elizabeth and Cecil worked unceasingly toward that goal, for it would give them a strong ally in Scotland. With Darnley out of the way, Mary was their only obstacle . . .

The others came to Mary that evening; she found fault with divorce because her church would not recognize the grounds. Argyll suggested an annulment on a plea of consanguinity, but she opposed that too, for fear it would render the Prince illegitimate.

"Not at all, madam," Bothwell said. "There is my own case to prove otherwise. You mind my parents' marriage was annulled, which neither jeopardized my legitimacy nor hindered my succession."

"Rest assured, madam," Lethington soothed, "we of your Council shall find the means that Your Majesty shall be quit of him without prejudice to your son."

Mary was still not convinced. "I will that you do nothing that may stain my honor," she said.

This was typical of Mary, and it made Bothwell smile. She was desperate to be rid of Darnley, but she refused to commit herself for fear of dishonoring her name. She preferred to pretend ignorance and let the blame fall to others if anything should go wrong. That was the privilege of royalty, and they used it whenever they had need, he thought.

Bothwell knew where Lethington's guidance would lead— they had already discussed reestablishing the Ecclesiastic Court. The Protestant Kirk would set up a hue and cry, but James could be depended upon there—he knew how to silence them with conciliations. Lethington assured Mary that although James was as faithful a Protestant as she was a Catholic, he would "look through his fingers" at whatever means they employed.

Another meeting was held before they left Craigmillar—this time without Mary. Darnley had become so detestable to everyone that hatred had united them. Whereas in the past Bothwell had never given his allegiance or support to any faction, he did now. With Argyll, Huntly, Lethington, and James, he put his name to a bond that swore them to proscribe Darnley.

A responsibility that should have gone to Darnley fell to Bothwell. Mary put the success of the christening into his hands, giving him full charge of the reception and entertainment. It was a task that gave him malicious amusement, for he knew how the other lords would resent it.

"Keep me informed of your progress," Mary said as Bothwell took leave of her for Stirling.

"Leave everything to me," he assured her. "You've enough to worry you just getting Darnley to attend. Use any means you must—but see that he is there."

She nodded. "You have less than three weeks. Can you manage?"

"Aye, you will be well pleased." He smiled. "I have a few surprises of my own in mind for it."

"Write to me."

"I will send Paris with word of how it goes."

3

Mary's entrance into Stirling was a royal occasion that Scotland had not seen since her father's time. She rode at the head of gorgeously attired attendants and silver-helmeted halberdiers, up the twisting approach to the castle. Her prancing palfrey, caparisoned in gold and silver, carried her upward as she laughed and waved to the cheering crowd. No one seeing her would have guessed that only a week ago she had been so ill and despairing.

Bothwell waited at the moat to welcome her; the spectacle she made filled him with pride. Their glances met briefly and spoke a message their lips could not, then he turned his horse abreast of hers and rode the rest of the way with her.

The seventeenth of December dawned white with wintry brilliance; a light snow had fallen all night, continuing into the day, coating the ground and houses with a fairy-tale touch. The castle rose in tiers above the town, perched as an eagle on its mountain crest. Wind-flapped banners decorated the ramparts that commanded a view of the Ochil Hills, the Firth of Forth, and the Highlands.

Inside, tapers burned from early morning; smells of roasting meats and fowl permeated the castle. Servants hurried to the Great Hall for last-minute touches on the newly woven tapestries hung there, beneath which a table displayed the christening gifts.

On a red velvet cover lay the great jeweled fan from the Duc de Savoy, from France a diamond chain and pendant, from Elizabeth a massive gold font, encrusted with precious gems. Countless other gifts lay beside these: gold and silver plate, jeweled goblets, pearl rings, gold chains, and a vast assortment of hand-embroidered baby clothes.

Outside, the wooden drawbridge shook with the weight of horsemen riding to and from the castle. Below, the town bulged with retainers and burghers from all over Scotland. Stirling was a town packed and brimming over with merrymakers who had thronged there to see the event.

In the Great Hall, dressed in deep-blue satin and velvet—a color chosen "to symbolize loyalty," Mary had told him—Bothwell welcomed the guests. He glanced back at Mary, who was seated on a raised dais between two oriel windows, receiving the ambassadors and nobles. She was magnificent in regal beauty; her gown in cloth of silver was encrusted with tiny sparks of rubies to match the wide lace ruff that fanned out from her shoulders; a tiara of diamonds and rubies crowned her silver-white wig, piled high with curls. She was like a splash of stardust on the crimson velvet cloth of state.

Having received the last guest, Bothwell gave the signal for the huge oak doors to swing shut. He turned to view the hall. He had scarcely set foot out of the castle in three weeks; now he took satisfaction in the result.

His glance fell on Jean; she was also gowned in blue, a shade lighter than his, with white satin inserts at the skirt and deep cuffs of ermine on her extra wide sleeves. She stood at the great hooded fireplace talking with Fleming. Even with her face painted, Jean made a poor contrast to the voluptuous Fleming. Near them stood James, dressed in a suit of green, and Argyll in red. Mary had chosen the colors for all her nobles and had presented them with the materials for their outfits.

One person was conspicuously absent—Darnley. Although he was in the castle, he had sent word earlier that he would not attend the baptism. Bothwell had a mental picture of him drunk and slobbering; better that he stayed away, enough the guests knew he was there.

A blare of trumpets, the tap of drums, announced the ceremony about to begin. The French ambassador, Du Croc, carried the Prince from his nursery to the Chapel Royal between two rows of barons and gentlemen who lined the way with lighted wax candles. Following him, the Catholic nobility walked in solemn procession, bearing the great serge, the salt, the cude cloth, the basin and ewer. Bothwell led Mary from her dais to the chapel door and there he left her.

They had argued about that earlier; he had finally convinced her to let it go. As always, he remained adamant in avoiding the Popish rituals, but he watched the ceremony from the doorway with James, Huntly, and the Earl of Bedford. He saw the

Archbishop of St. Andrews take the baby from Du Croc, who was a proxy godfather for the French King. The Countess Argyll, proxy godmother for Queen Elizabeth, held the baby over the golden font. He heard the Prince named Charles for the French King and James for Mary's father. Then the heralds sounded their trumpets again, and the baby's names and titles were proclaimed three times before the assembly.

Musicians on the gallery struck up a stately march, and the Prince was carried back through the crimson-and-gold-draped passageway to his nursery. The guests marched from the chapel to the Great Hall, where tables had been set for supper. Darnley still refused to show himself, and Bothwell took his place at the table with Mary and the French and English ambassadors.

"I shall report a most delightful evening to my Queen, madam," Bedford said to Mary.

Mary smiled. "You may thank Lord Bothwell for that; everything was arranged by him. A pity your mistress could not have torn herself away from the pressing duties of state to attend."

"Her Majesty is a stern taskmaster—she is no less hard on herself than others. But there is another whose absence can scarcely go unnoticed. The King—"

"Is in his apartments, ill," Bothwell said.

Bedford met his glance. "Of course, my lord. Why else would he not attend the christening of his own son?"

Bothwell had seen Mary tense and her look of relief at his answer. It had been inevitable; someone had to raise the question of Darnley's absence. Now it was official; Darnley was ill and unable to attend. He knew no one would really believe that excuse, yet he was equally certain that no one would dare suggest otherwise.

After supper there was dancing. Bothwell led Mary to the floor in a galliard. "Do my arrangements please you?" he asked.

"So well in fact that I have discovered a new side to you."

"Then I am not entirely the crude ruffian folk say?" he teased.

"I never thought you were."

Paris edged his way through the dancers, motioning for Bothwell's attention. "My lord," he whispered. "Can you come?"

Bothwell danced Mary off the floor and left her with Du Croc. He followed Paris out through the passage to the lions' den that separated Mary's apartments from Darnley's.

"What's happened?" he asked.

"It is the King. He is roaring drunk and threatens to attend the reception."

"His servants have had their instructions. Why didn't they stop him?"

"They cannot restrain him—he is past reason."

There were sounds of a scuffle at the other end of the tunneled passageway. A high-pitched voice rose above the others: Darnley's. Bothwell rushed forward to come upon a fierce struggle. Anthony Standen vainly attempted to raise Darnley's sluggish body from the cobbled walk while his valet, Taylor, and another man held his flailing arms.

Darnley's insults rang through the hollow passage. "Let me go, you swine," he screamed. "Unhand me this instant."

Bothwell looked on with disgust; he had to act quickly, before Darnley burst into the Great Hall. He could imagine Mary's horror and shame; sober, Darnley was difficult enough; drunk, he was revolting.

"How dare you lay hands on the King's person?" Bothwell said angrily. He pushed the servants aside and helped Darnley to his feet. "Are you hurt, sire?"

Darnley's confusion showed in the half-light of a torch. "These sniveling dogs could not have felled me without the advantage of number," he slurred. "I'll teach them to attack their master." He lunged forward to pounce on Standen.

Bothwell caught him by the arm. "Why stoop to soil your hands on varlets, sire? Leave them to me. I'll see they are punished."

"But, my lord," Taylor protested.

"Silence!" Bothwell shot him a fierce look. "Help me get the King to his apartments."

"I will not be hidden away—escort me to the Great Hall," Darnley demanded.

"By all means, sire," Bothwell said. "But surely not in those garments. Shall foreign ambassadors see the King of Scotland in such mean attire?"

"I had ordered a suit in cloth of gold," Darnley said, almost in tears. "But the tailors have not completed it."

Bothwell nodded sympathetically and steered him toward the garde hall. "Come, sire, we will choose another outfit from your wardrobe." Once they were in Darnley's bedchamber, Bothwell managed to ease him into a chair. "A drink for His Majesty," he commanded.

Taylor put a goblet of brandywine in Darnley's limp hand; he raised it in salute to Bothwell and drank.

"Now we shall select an outfit for His Majesty," Bothwell said. "Does Your Majesty favor maroon, green, purple perhaps, or—"

The goblet clanked to the floor; Darnley had fallen into a drunken stupor.

"Put him to bed," Bothwell said, eyeing him with disgust.

He returned to the lions' den, but not the Great Hall—he went to stand on the parapets. His shirt beneath his doublet felt clammy, stuck to his skin. Despite his outward calm, the scene with Darnley had left him tense, on the verge of panic.

Panic for fear he would not be able to avert that near-disaster of Darnley's entrance into the hall. Leaning against the guardwall, he looked down at the sheer drop of cliff. The wind pierced his doublet, chilling him through. Below there was only the white expanse of fields and hills, lonely and remote.

The passageway was deadly quiet now; thank God he had been able to prevent that near-catastrophe—but the danger, he knew, was not over; it had merely been postponed. There were still two days remaining before the guests departed. Darnley would have to be watched closely—in the meantime it would be like walking a tightrope.

Refreshed, Bothwell returned to the Great Hall, wondering if Darnley's shouts had been heard above the music and noise. If any of the ambassadors' servants had witnessed the scene they would surely report it to their masters. Mary motioned him toward the oriel windows where no one could overhear them.

"You were gone so long. What is amiss?" she whispered.

"Nothing that need concern you."

"What are you hiding? It was Harry, wasn't it?"

"What good does it do you to know? He has been put to bed."

"He has spoiled so much already—if he spoils this too . . . "

"Leave him to me."

Later that night Bothwell lounged on the bed as Jean sat brushing her hair at the dressing table. He had seen the last guest to his chambers and could finally relax.

Jean set the hairbrush down abruptly. "Why did you bring me here?" she asked. "You have neglected me all day."

"You knew my duties would keep me occupied," he said drowsily.

"And I must sit patiently by, waiting for you to notice me. Will there never be an end to your duties?"

"Why this sudden craving?" he asked. "You've never shown any particular inclination for my company before."

"Because your indifference humiliates me. My place should have been beside you at the supper table, but I am sent to the ladies' gallery instead. You are the first noble in Scotland, yet your wife is given no more honor than the wives of lesser-ranking men."

"Now we come to the crux of the matter; it's not my company but the honors my rank provides that you crave."

"Have I not the right? Why should I not enjoy the honors of your position?"

"Be quiet," he murmured, pinching out the candle. He turned away from her and slid down under the covers.

4

Bothwell had a wild bull hunt planned for the following day in the park below the castle. The guests returned half-frozen and ravenous to an enormous supper laid out in the Great Hall.

On Thursday, the last day of celebrations, Mary gave a banquet and masque. The Latin tutor, George Buchanan, and Sebastien Pagez collaborated on a unique method of serving the food. The first course was served on a platform decorated with laurel and pulled into the hall by twelve satyrs with lighted torches. In the background nymphs sang Mary's praise in verse written by Buchanan. After each course the platform disappeared to serve the next in a different guise; once a rocky hill, then a fountain, lastly a globe out of which a child emerged to symbolize the infant Prince.

Later Bothwell directed the company outdoors to watch a spectacle that he had personally prepared. A sham fortress had been erected in the courtyard, and after the guests had assembled, a regiment of centaurs and Moors, demons and Highlanders, began an assault. The defenders retaliated with shots of fireballs and fire spears, and the spectators took sides, cheering the warriors on, amid the clamor of music and cannon blasts. Night turned to day in a flash of red, orange, and white; the fort was blown to pieces with fireworks and gunpowder. This was the surprise Bothwell had promised Mary.

Hot possets awaited the guests when they returned indoors. Mary drank a farewell toast to those who were leaving in the morning to spend Christmas in their own countries. Despite her gaiety, Bothwell saw the strain beneath her dazzling smile. When the last guest had finally gone upstairs she seemed ready to collapse with fatigue.

They were alone in the Great Hall except for the servants, who were clearing away empty goblets or extinguishing tapers. She looked like a weary child, and he had a wild desire to carry her off to bed, to stay the night with her cuddled in his arms. He knew she needed rest, yet he could not let her go.

The hall was in darkness now, save for the firelight where flames dimmed and blazed again in a stubborn refusal to die. "It's selfish of me, I know," he said, "but stay awhile. I've not had you to myself in days."

They went to the fireplace. She sat down in an armchair; he settled himself on a bearskin rug at her feet. He stretched one leg to poke at the smoldering log with his boot. The burning embers danced up into flames, then steadied.

"Will Jean not wonder where you are?" she asked.

"Like as not she is asleep by now, scarcely aware that I am not beside her."

"I would never have thought her to be the cold creature she is."

He shrugged. "Doubtless she would be otherwise with someone else. She would have made a warm, loving wife, wed to Alex of Boyne."

"How can she prefer that clout to you?"

"You, my love, are prejudiced and in no position to judge." He grinned. "You may even agree with her a year from now—sooner perhaps."

"Do you take my love so lightly? I shall love you forever as much as I do now."

"Love may not have been intended to withstand the test of time."

"It must—if it is genuine."

"You romanticize. At the start a flame flares to brilliance, then slowly diminishes, lacking the luster and fire of before. Gradually it dulls—then it is gone. This may also be true of love."

She shook her head. "No, not dull, steady perhaps, but everlasting."

"Experience has taught me that the secret of love is brevity."

"You speak from a cynicism grown out of the past. I doubt if any of your countless affairs ever really touched you." She leaned forward to look deeply into his eyes. "There must be constancy in love."

One affair had touched him, for he had loved Janet Beaton, but that had been a prelude to the love he had for Mary. She had changed him so that even he could believe a love like theirs would be everlasting. "Pay me no heed," he said. "You are all I shall ever want."

Later that night, Bothwell jerked awake to the sound of thundering hooves. Sleep still fogged his brain; for a moment he could not tell if the horsemen were approaching or leaving the castle. Seconds later, he heard the groaning wheels of the drawbridge lowered. Reaching for his robe, he went to the window to peer out. A white half-moon illuminated the sky to silver black, and he could make out the silhouette of men on horses.

Jean roused and drew aside the bed-curtains. "What is it?" she asked.

"I don't know. A company of horsemen just rode out."

"At this hour?"

"Aye, something is wrong," he said, lighting a candle.

"Surely whatever it is will keep till morning," she said.

He was already halfway out in the corridor. "I'll find out now," he murmured. "Go back to sleep."

He went down the corridor silently on slippered feet, listening briefly outside each chamber door; everything seemed quiet. He went downstairs to the royal apartments, into Mary's guard hall.

"Who rode out?" Bothwell asked the sentry.

"The King and his retinue, my lord."

"Has the Queen retired yet?"

"I think not, my lord. There are lights in her presence chamber."

Bothwell crossed to the door and knocked. Mary called to enter. The room was in semidarkness with only the fireplace and a single taper burning for light. She ran to him. "I am glad you are here."

"What has happened?"

She clung to him; he took her icy hands in his to warm them. He cradled her head in the curve of his neck, stroking her hair. Again he asked, "What's happened to unnerve you so?"

"Harry," she said, "it is always Harry. Oh, God, will I never be free of him?"

"What has he done this time?"

"He came to my bedchamber after midnight, demanding his rights."

"And you refused him?"

"Naturally! The mere sight of him sickens me. I tried to put him off, but he would not leave. I threatened to have the guards remove him, but he only laughed at me."

"Doubtless he was sodden with drink."

She nodded. "I was desperate; think of my humiliation if I

had been forced to involve the guards. To frighten him, I told him that I was pardoning the exiles."

"How did he react?"

"As you may expect. His eyes turned wild with terror, then he ran."

"Aye, he has cause to run. Someone no doubt alerted him to his danger—he knows about our conference at Craigmillar last month. Do you know where he's gone?"

"To the devil, I hope."

He grinned. "Even the devil is selective in the company he keeps."

"How can you jest? God knows what new troubles Harry may brew once he is out of my watching."

"Perhaps not. Pardoning his fellow conspirators may frighten him enough to put a clamp on his plotting."

"Do you really believe that?"

"It depends upon what carries the greater force with him. I've seen him cower in fright at the mere mention of his enemies—yet his drive for power is so strong that it's near unhinged his mind."

"In any case, I am relieved to be rid of him—although I wish it had been under different circumstances."

"Why? Your messenger reached Newcastle two days ago. For all we know, the exiles are already on their way back. Better that he learns it from you before they arrive. At least he is warned."

He heard the changing of the guard; in an hour the sky would light with dawn. He glanced at Mary; she seemed calm now. "It's time you were in bed," he said.

"Stay awhile longer. I don't want to be alone."

"You need rest."

"And you will return to Jean—to sleep beside her."

"She is my wife. Where else shall I sleep?"

"While I am the usurper."

"Of all the women I have ever known, Jean is the least of your rivals." He took her in his arms. "Why trouble yourself over her?"

"Because she *is* your wife, which gives her more right to you than I."

"She has the right to expect certain considerations. But it is you I love. What more assurance do you need?"

"Forgive me," she murmured, pulling his mouth down to hers. "I am always so afraid of losing you."

"Play the shrew and you have found the one sure way of doing just that," he warned.

5

Two days later Mary left Stirling with Bothwell, Huntly, and Jean. They journeyed to Drummond Castle in Perth, where they remained a week for hunting and welcomed in the New Year of 1567. Formalities had been set aside for the holidays; by day they hunted in the snow-covered woods; at night they sat around the fire in Lord Drummond's cozy common room, talking, playing games. The change it brought in Mary was remarkable, for her old vitality was returning.

Only Jean's sour disposition dampened the atmosphere. Her boredom was manifest and embarrassing to Bothwell. She either retired earlier than anyone else or cast a gloom on everything with her dourness. Bothwell knew her well enough to guess that something was brewing in her mind. Toward the end of that week her actions confirmed his suspicions.

He came into their bedchamber one night, expecting to find Jean asleep as usual. She had said good night two hours ago, but instead of a darkened room, he found her sitting up in bed waiting for him.

She watched him undress and waited for him to get into bed

beside her. "I am weary of so much travel," she said. "I want to return to Edinburgh."

"Why this sudden desire to be in Edinburgh?"

"It is my mother. She is growing old; I see so little of her."

"The Queen returns to town in two weeks. You can be with your mother then—or you may invite her to Crichton."

"I want to go now."

"I cannot take you there and be back here by the day after tomorrow to accompany the Queen to Tullibardine."

"It is not my intention that you should."

"Nor will I have you make the journey with only a handful of servants."

"My brother will escort me."

"Huntly made no mention of returning to town."

"We discussed it only awhile ago in his chambers. Like you, he is duped by a woman's helplessness—in this case, his sister's. Since Her Majesty insists that you accompany her on her travels, he has offered to be my escort."

"If you are of a mind to go, I shan't stop you."

"You could try." She moved closer. The crispness was gone from her voice; it came through the dark, soft and husky. "If I thought you wanted me to remain—"

He felt her warm breath on his face; their bodies touched. Puzzled, he lay motionless. The lacy nightdress she wore instead of her usual stiff damasks, her hair curled and beribboned in place of the long braid, the exciting scent she now used. . . . Suddenly he realized that Jean was trying to seduce him.

Why this change of heart after nearly a year of coldness? Could it be the small compliments he had paid her? Of late he found her more attractive and had told her so. Surely that wouldn't account for this change. But whatever the cause, he knew he didn't want her. He despised himself for what he was about to do; he didn't want to hurt her—but there was no kindness in rejection.

"When do you wish to leave?" he asked, moving away.

"Tomorrow," she said stiffly.

Jean was up before him; he suspected that she had lain awake long after he had finally dozed off last night. She was already dressed in her riding outfit; her small leather trunk stood strapped and ready at the door. She neither glanced at him nor spoke while he dressed.

"Shall I call a servant to take your trunk down?" he asked.

"I have seen to that."

Her eyes were red-rimmed. Guilt compelled him to speak, but he could think of nothing to say. His refusal had shamed her, yet he could not have done otherwise.

Paris came in to take her trunk. She followed him out. Bothwell went down to the courtyard with them. He lifted Jean into the saddle and threw a furred robe over her legs. "A safe journey, my lady," he said.

She nodded, her pale, pinched face a mask of silent reproach. Huntly waved a farewell, and they rode off. Bothwell watched them until they were out of sight, then he turned and went inside.

He searched for something to read in Drummond's sparse library. Finding a copy of Rabelais in the original French, he sat down with it in front of the fire. It was here that Paris found him an hour later.

"A messenger has come from Glasgow, my lord," Paris told him. "He brings news of the King."

"Has the Queen seen him?"

"No, my lord. Her Majesty will receive him here."

Mary came in a few minutes later with the messenger. Blue with cold, he told them, "The King lies ill at his father's house in Glasgow, madam."

"What ails him?"

"The pox."

"Have you seen him?" Bothwell asked.

"Aye, my lord. It was His Majesty who sent me."

"What are his symptoms?"

"He is a mass of pustules and scabs, my lord. He complains of a violent itching and pain. There is such a foul stench in his chambers one may not take a breath when passing his door."

"Has he been fumigated?" Mary asked coldly.

"Aye, madam, and treated with quicksilver ointment."

"Return to the King after you have rested. Tell him that I will send my own physicians from Edinburgh, and anything else he needs," Mary said, dismissing the messenger.

"The pox indeed!" Bothwell chuckled. "More likely the French evil, caught in some brothel."

"How do you know?"

"I've seen enough of it here and abroad to recognize the symptoms. It's like the pox, yet different—more virulent. Thank God you denied him your bed, or you would be sharing his misery."

Mary shuddered. "He grows more loathsome each day. Likely he already had it when he left Stirling. I doubt he knew, or he would not have asked to bed with me."

"You think not? He would contaminate you and the world if it suited him."

She left her chair and went to the window. He thought: *She is thinking of Darnley; perhaps she is sorry for him. His illness may soften her heart toward him.*

"Did Jean and Huntly get a good start?" Mary asked abruptly.

"You knew they were leaving?"

"Jean came to my chambers early this morning to make her farewells."

Then it was Jean she had been thinking about, not Darnley. He asked, "Have you noticed a change in Jean of late?"

"How do you mean?"

"Her gowns are more daring, she paints her face, she might even be called attractive—compared to the Jean of before. But it is last night's behavior that puzzles me most."

"I saw nothing strange. She appeared quiet and reserved as usual."

"No, it's something that happened later in our chambers. She was waiting up for me, prinked out in her loveliest nightdress, the room filled with her scent . . . "

"I had not imagined Jean capable of such artfulness," Mary said thoughtfully. "Were you taken in by her snare?"

"Need you ask? But to be frank, her sudden affection puzzles me."

She turned and smiled in a way that infuriated him. It was a smile used by women to imply their exclusive knowledge and wisdom. "Do you think her affection genuine?" she asked. "Is Jean so lacking in guile that you imagine she is sincere?"

"She has always been honest with me. Why should I mistrust her now?"

"She may fear losing you. She takes pride in being the Countess Bothwell—you have said so yourself."

"I've given her no cause to think she may lose her cherished position."

"Your indifference, your long absences—they are reasons enough. Also, she may suspect there is more between us than affairs of state. Who knows, Jean may have correctly interpreted our feeling for each other. She may sense something; women are wise in such things."

"Feminine intuition, eh?" He laughed. "A mystic notion invented by women to excuse their lack of logic."

Bristling, she said, "Think what you like then. It was not my intention to amuse you."

He went to her, drew her away from the window. "Pay no heed to my teasing, but you are always so vulnerable," he said, kissing her.

"I cannot bear to be mocked by you—even in jest."

"Then I shan't do it again. In any case, Jean needn't fret; she may keep her honors—you will always have my love."

They left Drummond Castle for Tullibardine, then on to Callander House, and from there back to Stirling. These weeks with Mary had brought to Bothwell a contentment he had never before known. In the past, his restlessness had driven him from one diversion to another, from one woman to another. With Mary he could take joy in the simple pleasure of being with her—she was no less happy with him. They guarded their time jealously, realizing that it could not last, yet hoping it might.

It did not last, for there was always Darnley. Healthy or ill, he made himself felt by stirring up fresh trouble. Ominous rumors came out of Glasgow; they heard of a plot devised by Lennox, Glencairn, and other fanatics to depose Mary. There were rumors of a ship lying in the Clyde, outfitted and ready to sail. One version had Darnley going to a rendezvous at Flanders with Philip of Spain, another had him conveying the Prince out of Scotland on it.

Once again Mary was thrown into despair; the vitality and calm left her, and she was flung into a state of nervousness far worse than the days following her illness at Jedburgh. She jumped at the slightest noise, wept without provocation, scarcely slept. She sat up late into the night talking with Bothwell, trying to think of ways to stop Darnley.

"First remove the source," Bothwell told her. "Take the Prince away from Stirling. Bring him to Edinburgh, to be close to you."

She agreed. "Then I must find a way to remove Harry from Glasgow. He must be taken away from his father's influence."

"I doubt he will come willingly. He is suspicious and not likely to leave his father's stronghold to go into the thick of his enemies."

"Somehow, I will find a way."

"What will you do with him after that?"

"Watch him, permit no one who may advance his mad schemes near him."

"Is that all?"

"What more can I do? My hands are tied until we are divorced."

"I know the terms we agreed upon for Morton's pardon; now I wonder if they really ever intended to keep their word. Somehow I find it difficult to trust them."

"Why must you always be so suspicious?" she said angrily.

"Because I know them well enough—and if you were not blinded by a misguided sense of kinship and mercy you would too."

"You are obsessed with dredging up the past. You were at Craigmillar when my divorce was discussed—everyone agreed to it. Even James promised his help."

"As always, James will help only himself."

Exasperated, she flung a cushion at him. "You are intolerable."

He ducked; the cushion sailed past him. He grinned. "Aye," he said with infuriating humor, "the truth often is."

CHAPTER XIII

1

Mary returned to Holyrood with the Prince and placed him under heavy guard. Bothwell learned from Huntly that Jean had gone to Crichton after spending only a few days in Edinburgh. Their parting at Drummond had affected him strangely, and he was relieved to find her gone. The hurt he had seen in her eyes continued to haunt him—her indifference had been far easier to live with.

Neither of them had ever had any romantic illusions about their marriage; each had taken from it what he wanted. Or had they? It occurred to Bothwell that Jean might have got more of the bargain. Until now she had denied him the one thing he might have wanted from her—a legitimate heir. Why else would he have wed? But loving Mary had changed his outlook on so many things that he wasn't even certain about wanting another woman's children now.

Jean had set the pattern for their marriage; it was too late for him to change now. If Mary had guessed correctly about Jean's sudden show of affection, he could reassure her. Jean's fears were groundless, for she was in no danger of losing her precious position.

Morton had returned from exile and was staying at the Douglas home in Whittinghame. Despite his pardon, he was still forbidden the Court. Mary still hoped the Council would find a way to secure her divorce from Darnley, and she asked Bothwell to test Morton's support. To humor her, he sent for Archie Douglas, Morton's kinsman, to feel him out on the subject.

They met in the privacy of a back room in a tavern on the Cowgate.

Bothwell waited for their ale to be served. He said, "I trust the Earl of Morton is well."

"Aye, my lord, he finds great relief in being home again."

Douglas had a way of examining his hands to avoid looking at anyone directly. Except for his carrot-red hair, he bore little resemblance to Morton; whereas Morton was short and chunky, Archie Douglas was slender and of medium height. His long, beaky nose and deep-socketed eyes gave him a hatchet-faced look, and in contrast to his title, Parson of St. Mungos, there was an aura of evil about him.

"Then he is content with his present state?" Bothwell asked.

"He would be more so, my lord, if he were permitted the Court."

"All in due time. Her Majesty cannot easily forgive his part in the Rizzio slaying."

"An unfortunate mishap, my lord—one the Earl has had good cause to regret. But, like the Queen, he too was betrayed. You mind, he acted on the King's bidding, or the Earl would never have ventured it at all."

Bothwell took particular notice of the murderous look in Douglas' eyes when he spoke of Darnley.

"A point well made," Bothwell said. "Which now brings me round to why we are here. Doubtless you know it was not a simple task to procure pardons for the exiles. Had it not been for the unwavering persistence of certain lords, Her Majesty would have remained inexorable."

"My lord Morton is truly grateful to them, especially to you, my lord, for he is acquainted with your travails in his behalf. Without Your Lordship's persuasions it might never have come to pass, for he well knows there is no one at present whose word carries more weight with the Queen."

Was there some hidden meaning behind Douglas' seemingly ingratiating words? Bothwell dismissed the thought. He and Mary had been too discreet; not even her closest confidants, her Maries, suspected anything. "It is my earnest hope that the Earl will be content to forget past enmities and live at peace with everyone."

"Enmities are one thing, my lord, betrayals another. There are offenses that demand revenge. The King enticed the Earl with false pledges and assurances, then betrayed him, casting the blame on his shoulders."

"Aye," Bothwell said, "but a man cannot be lured to murder unless he already has it in his heart."

"Being a near kinsman to the King, the Earl naturally sympathized with his complaints about the Queen's unseemly conduct with Rizzio."

"Well you know there was never any truth to that filthy rumor. Rizzio was a trusted servant and nothing more!"

"Being a Papist, he toadied to Rome and worked unceasingly to ruin the Protestant cause."

"Are we to use the time-worn excuse of religion again?" Bothwell asked irritably. "We both know the murder was designed to promote the ambition of certain men—the King because he wanted the crown matrimonial; the Bastard and his followers to return from exile and avoid forfeiture; Morton, Lindsay, and Ruthven for certain rich promises made to them in exchange for their help. They aimed at the Queen's life as well, and though they did treason, she is willing to forgive them. Why then can the Earl of Morton not do the same? The Council will deal with the King; we have already discussed measures, but we must proceed lawfully. Will the Earl lend his support to Her Majesty's divorce?"

"Aye. But he is impatient of the results. Why trouble over

lawful means? If the nobility and the Council are in concert, there is no point in delaying. We can make a swift end to him. The christening is over; he has acknowledged the babe as his. Of what further use is he?"

"Of no use, I grant you. Nevertheless, I urge you to be prudent. Let the Council take care of the King—regicide is too dangerous an undertaking."

2

Mary paled when Bothwell told her of his conversation with Douglas. "No," she gasped. "I cannot be party to Harry's murder."

"Don't upset yourself, love," Bothwell soothed. "Haven't you learned by now that it's a Douglas trait to think first of murder?"

"God knows how I loathe Harry, but I can't seek his life."

"If the eye offends . . ." He shrugged. "Besides, it would be more justice than murder—the wretch deserves it. But you needn't fret; neither James nor Lethington would contemplate such means. It would bring the wrath of the world down on their heads. I doubt they plan any immediate action for a while, so put it from your mind."

"Forgetfulness comes only in your arms."

"There's a matter easily remedied." He smiled, tracing a finger along her throat, down into her bodice.

"It is unthinkable. Even if you were able to slip past the guards, there is always one of my women asleep on the trundle bed."

"Dismiss her; say that you wish to sleep alone."

"There is still the servant who sleeps across my threshold. His dismissal would arouse suspicion."

"Complain that he snores too loudly. You are in a highly nervous state and cannot sleep with such clamor."

"Another would take his place."

"Aye, but one of my own choosing. The blackamoor who tends the gardens. He will not snore—nor will he betray us."

"How can you be certain?"

"Because he cannot speak—he is a deaf mute."

"And such an enormous brute. He terrifies me."

"You will find he is meek as a lamb, and devoted to me since I gave him the head of a boar I chased. It is a pagan omen of good luck—I'm told he keeps it buried at the foot of Arthur's Seat."

She grimaced. "And you wish to put that heathen outside my door?"

"Trust me. I will come to you later tonight."

"Take care that no one sees you."

"They shan't. I'll come by way of your private passage to the abbey."

"A delicious piece of irony." She laughed. "You must pass through a Catholic church, when you have always been so careful to avoid one."

"A mere expediency, my love. No need yet to inform the Pope that you've found him a convert."

It was after midnight when Bothwell left his apartments to take the back stairway that led to the abbey. A wintry wind tore through the shattered roof, weaving its way among the blackened columns. He glanced at the starless sky, red with snow clouds, and turned swiftly into the passage.

The thought of someone finding him in the abbey made him chuckle; tongues would flutter that the Earl of Bothwell had finally found religion—but the wrong one. His slippered feet trod noiselessly along the stone floor; passing the kitchen wing, he stopped to listen—there were no sounds. Farther along he came to the newel stairs that led to Mary's bedchamber. They were narrow and chipped with age, and he felt his way up carefully in the dark.

He rapped lightly on Mary's door; the bolt slipped from place, and light flooded the stairway. Mary stood before him in a night robe of gossamer silver lace. She came toward him with outstretched arms.

The tiny French clock on the mantelpiece chimed the half hour past midnight. Her bedchamber looked oddly different to him; the red and gold bed hangings had been drawn aside, its matching spread turned down. Above them, the gilt crowned initials of James V and Mary of Guise glittered against the dark oak ceiling.

"Is the blackamoor outside?" he asked.

She nodded. "The change was simple. If anyone thought it odd, they refrained from saying so."

"I knew you had no cause to worry." He kissed the tip of her nose while he undid the satin ribbons on her night robe, his lips traveling to her bared shoulders as he caressed her body hungrily. Her robe fell to the floor in a shimmery heap; he lifted her into his arms and carried her to bed.

She reached for the furred coverlet, but he pushed it aside. "You will be warm enough without it," he said.

He stood at the bedside gazing at her; her body was pearlescent against the rose-tinted silk sheet. Countless other women had lain like this before his eyes—but he had never seen them as he did her. She was so exquisitely lovely he could scarcely believe she was real. He bent to her; she thrust herself upward to meet his embrace.

Lying awake, Bothwell listened to the elements battling against the casements while she slept. Outside, the wind howled through the gardens and courtyard, a hound bayed its lament to the biting frost, hail and sleet rapped a metallic tattoo against the panes. The clock struck half past the hour of four—it was nearly time for him to go.

He kissed her awake and eased himself from her.

She murmured a protest and snuggled closer. "Not yet," she pleaded.

"I must. The kitchen help will be awake soon."

Reluctantly she let him go. He threw the covers aside; the chill air came as a shock after the warmth of bed. Shivering, he ran to the fire to rebuild it.

When he turned, he saw that she was sitting up and watching him. "Why are you smiling?" he asked.

"Because I love you—and because you are magnificent standing there in the firelight."

He snorted.

"Is it so strange that I should admire you? I love your body, its hardness, its strength, its grace—and your hands, they excite me just to look at them."

He came to sit beside her on the bed. "Please, no more, or you will embarrass me."

She leaned forward to kiss him; her fingers toyed with the crisp waves of his hair. "Beech leaves," she murmured.

"What?"

"Your hair. It is the red-brown color of beech leaves in autumn, then turns coppery in the sun."

"Flatterer. Plainly it is my virtue you seek with such fair words."

"Virtue indeed! When have *you* ever possessed virtue?"

Laughing, he pulled her out of bed and slapped her bottom. "Now fetch something to cover your nakedness," he said, "lest you corrupt me entirely."

She ran squealing to her wardrobe for a dressing gown. When she returned he was ready to go. He kissed her briefly, then started down.

They found brief happiness in those stolen hours they had together. Bothwell came to her as often as he felt it was safe.

They lay awake one night, cuddling, content in each other's closeness, but his thoughts were at odds with him and had been all day. Several times since entering her chambers, he had been on the verge of broaching the subject, but Mary had stopped him. She was in a lighthearted mood; he hated to disturb her peace—yet he must.

"How much longer will you allow Darnley to remain in Glasgow?" he asked abruptly.

She tensed in his arms. "These hours we have together are too precious to waste," she said. "I cannot think of him now."

"You must. The longer you wait, the more supporters he gains. You must bring him here before the month is out."

She sat up. "Must, must—always that I must do this or that. This week has been the happiest of my life. I live for these nights with you. My days count as nothing but hours to pass until I can be in your arms again."

"Do you think I take joy in reminding you? He is a threat to your very existence—it's not safe to let him remain where he is. Every day the desperate and disgruntled ride into Glasgow to join forces with him. I cannot rest for worry. There is a plot forming—God only knows what he is brewing now."

He got out of bed and threw on his clothes. Aye, he had a strange sense of foreboding; her safety had become a constant source of worry to him. Without her knowledge, he had ordered Lord Traquair to have her guard increased; he had even placed some of his own Borderers in key sentry posts around the palace.

She followed him, wrapping herself in a warm robe. "You said there was still time—Morton hasn't committed himself yet."

"Forget about Morton. You must go to Glasgow to bring Darnley here. Before you go, I'll stop off to see Morton to probe his mind—on my way to Crichton."

He had been dreading having to tell her that he was going to see Jean.

"Crichton! Why are you going there?"

"To make certain that Jean is well. I've had no word from her since Drummond."

"Do you expect she is pining away for lack of your love?"

"Surely you don't begrudge the little attention I pay her. I cannot entirely neglect my duty to her."

"She deserves your neglect. Was it Jean who wept with grief when you lay wounded at Hermitage? More likely she was too preoccupied with counting the inheritance that widowhood would bring her."

"You go too far," he warned.

"How quickly you jump to her defense, while I, a mere mistress—"

He caught her by the wrists, shook her violently. "Stop it. What is it you fear? I've told you, Jean is no threat to you."

She fell against him sobbing; he took her in his arms, sat down, and pulled her onto his lap. "Why do you torture yourself so needlessly? Jealousy ill becomes you."

"God knows I have tried to overcome it. I know how it angers you, yet I cannot control it. I have never told you of those nights at Stirling and Drummond when I lay awake trying not to think of you sharing the same bed, wondering if you made love to her—wishing myself in her place."

"Will you believe me if I give my word on something?"

"Yes."

"Then listen and believe me; I will never lay hands on Jean as long as our love endures. Does that satisfy you?"

She nodded. "Perhaps Jean will release you after I am divorced."

"What on earth for?"

"So we may be wed. I want to be yours wholly, in the eyes of God—and the world."

"And you think a few words said in church will do that? We are as much a part of each other now as we will ever be."

"But we cannot be so publicly. If we were wed—"

"Good Lord! Is that your measure of love? Has it never occurred to you that being with you as I am now is a far greater tribute to my love for you? I return to you each night because I want to—not because I am bound to you by legal ties. What better proof can you ask?"

"I seek respectability, not proof."

"And I wish it were mine to give you—but it is impossible. If we ignore all the other obstacles, one would still remain. Your nobles would never accept me as king; their hatred for me goes too deep."

"You could win their friendship."

"Not likely. But no matter. I care little for their love—enough that they fear me."

The clock reminded them of the hour; it was time for him to go.

"When do you leave for Crichton?" she asked, haltingly.

"This morning."

"So soon?"

"Aye. I'll see Morton first, then spend the night at Crichton. I should return the following day. Can you be ready to leave for Glasgow on the twenty-first?"

"That is scarce three days away."

"I wish I could spare you this, but there is no other way."

"I will be ready to leave."

3

Morton's greeting was very cordial; he insisted that Bothwell stay to take the midday meal with him. Lethington, too, was visiting Whittinghame that day and joined them later in the garden, where Morton led them to talk in private. They gathered under a gnarled old yew tree with overhanging branches which stood on sloping ground.

Time was passing rapidly. Bothwell had hoped to be gone by now, but he waited, for Morton had said nothing of importance as yet. They seated themselves on a circular bench, and he wondered why Morton had chosen this inconvenient place to talk. These melodramatics were ridiculous; surely they could have found privacy inside, rather than stay outdoors and freeze.

"Doubtless you know the purpose of my coming," Bothwell said.

"Aye, my lord." Morton looked furtively at Lethington. "But frankly, I am at a loss what to make of it."

"What confuses you?" Bothwell asked.

Morton scratched his red whiskers. "The means, my lord. What means do you propose?"

"My lord Moray and the Laird of Lethington here were the ones to propose the plan at Craigmillar. I expect they have acquainted you with it."

Morton glanced again at Lethington, who nodded imperceptibly. "Aye, the divorce. But it seems too uncertain, for I doubt Her Majesty's church will allow it. However, there are other ways of dealing with the traitor." Morton's little piglike eyes glittered darkly. "With certain assurances, I would gladly undertake the deed."

Bothwell's earlier suspicions were confirmed; the proposed divorce had been only bait for the exiles' pardons. And yet he felt strongly that among James' reasons for wanting Morton reinstated was the disposal of Darnley. Bothwell would make no objections there, for Darnley was a treacherous fool, a disgrace to Scotland, and a constant source of grief to Mary. He was willing to give his consent to have Darnley eliminated—but they had to proceed warily.

"However you decide to deal with the proud young fool," Bothwell said, "I strongly urge legitimate measures."

"He can be impeached, then indicted for his crimes," Lethington offered.

"Will the Queen agree to that?" Morton asked.

"Aye, she will agree to anything reasonable," Bothwell said.

Morton chipped at the tree trunk with his nail. "Will she give her consent in writing?"

"Never." Bothwell would not allow Mary to become implicated in this. Should anything go wrong, she could be named as an accomplice.

"Perhaps, if I spoke to her, she would make her will known to me."

Bothwell shook his head. "Nor will she hear any speech on it."

"Then I see no reason to do the deed. Should any harm befall the King, I would be the prime suspect. It is common knowledge that he betrayed me. They would say I did away with him to settle the score."

"It would be no lie, for you've sworn to take revenge on him often enough." Bothwell smiled. "I hear he works as diligently to make an end to you. Doubtless you know he is embroiled in a Catholic plot to destroy the leaders of the Protestant party—and you are among them."

"You are also Protestant, my lord, and in as much danger as the rest of us."

"Not really. For unlike you, I have a long history of loyalty to the Crown. In my case, it would not be in the Realm's best interest to eliminate me—you might say I am too valuable to the Queen."

Morton's mouth clamped shut; the point was well taken.

"Why quarrel among yourselves, my lords?" Lethington soothed. "We are all one in the matter. Rest assured, a solution will be found to satisfy every quarter."

Bothwell drew on his gloves. "Whatever you decide, I pray it is wise."

He left them in the garden to discuss their plans, but he had a fair guess at the outcome. Douglas vengeance always left a bloody trail; because Darnley was their kinsman, and had betrayed them, so much the worse for him.

It was past the supper hour when Bothwell arrived at Crichton. Jean's delight at seeing him made him immediately regret coming. Eagerly she followed him to his apartments, where he changed from his wet clothes to a robe. He stretched lazily before the blazing fire, taking sensual pleasure in its penetrating warmth.

Jean seated herself opposite him. She asked, "How long may you stay?"

"Only for tonight. I return to Edinburgh in the morning."

"I marvel that you made the journey at all."

"I have had no word from you in nearly a month. I thought you might be ill."

"Your concern is touching. I would not have imagined that you thought of me at all."

Oddly, there was no sarcasm in her voice, only sadness.

"As your husband, I am naturally concerned with your well-being."

"Nevertheless, you surprise me. I share your name, your house—the little we are together—but I think of myself as more your housekeeper. Someone you employ to maintain order on your estates."

"It was my understanding that you preferred it that way."

"Circumstances change—so do people. I wish to be more to you now."

He was not taken in by her sudden passion for him, yet he could not entirely accept Mary's theory. Jean had already humbled herself to him; he had refused her—now he must do so again. She forced him into a position he loathed.

His answer was delayed by Paris, who brought him a hot

posset and something to eat. Bothwell sipped the drink slowly, watching Jean's irritation at the interruption. When Paris had gone, he said, "Our present arrangement contents me."

"May not your contentment increase with an heir? Even *she* cannot give you that."

He glanced up sharply. "What are you implying?"

"That you have made the Queen your mistress." The corners of her mouth turned up in a half-smile. "I have always suspected that you felt more than mere loyalty for her—you betrayed yourself after Rizzio's murder. It was not, however, until the christening that I knew she shared your feelings. I admit you were both very discreet, I doubt anyone else surmised—but I knew. The way you look at her, the manner in which you hold her while dancing, how she hangs on your every word . . ."

He regarded Mary's love as an honor and would shout it for the world to know—but for her sake it had to be concealed. Now he wondered: If Jean had guessed, who else had?

"Have you spoken of this to anyone?" he asked.

"No, not even my brother—although I think he knows." She studied him closely. "Since you do not deny it, it must be true."

"Aye, it's true."

She leaned back complacently and folded her hands in her lap. "I will never divorce you."

"I have not asked you to."

"Not yet, but I expect you will. You think she loves you, but she does not. She will use you as she has in the past, and when she has wearied of the affair, she will discard you without a thought. Look at the lives she has ruined already—Chastelard, Rizzio. She is like a Siren, beckoning from the shore."

He flew out of his chair; only the barest thread of control kept him from striking her. He sensed her terror, for she quailed as he came close.

"How dare you deride her?" he rasped. "What do you know of love? Even a dullard like Alex of Boyne sensed your coldness. Think of him as you like, your knight on a white steed, mourn him, romanticize him, too, if that pleases you—but make no mistake, my lady, he jilted you. You are cold as death; appropriately, your heart is entombed in marble and steel. Yet you presume to measure the worth of another's love."

"If only you looked at me once the way you look at her," she murmured, tears sliding down her cheeks.

He turned away in disgust. "I cannot bear the sight of you."

He was angrier with her now than on their honeymoon. Her vicious attack on Mary was intolerable; in stooping to that level, she had earned his loathing, driving him even further from her. What had she hoped to gain by it? Possibly she thought he would buy peace again, as he had with Bessie Crawford. Whatever her motive, whether greed or affection, it wouldn't work with him.

Bothwell returned to Edinburgh the following morning. He went to Mary that night.

"Never leave me again," she said, throwing herself into his arms.

"It is you who must leave me now. Is everything arranged?"

"Yes, though I wish it could be avoided. The thought of being in the same room with Harry makes me ill."

"I loathe having to send you. I'd go in your place if I could."

She silenced him with her lips. "Forgive me for burdening you with my silly fears."

He seized her roughly. "Promise you will always burden me with everything that concerns you. As for your fears, I'll take no proper rest until I see you safely returned to me."

"I will be well protected. Traquair tells me you have ordered a strong guard to accompany me. But I would sooner have the assurance of you beside me than a thousand armed men."

He smiled and tweaked her chin. "You exaggerate—five hundred perhaps." Then, seriously: "I will go with you as far as Callander House, and there I must leave you. Alone, you will learn more."

"Much as I want you with me, I know that is best. I received Harry's answer to my proposed visit this morning. He is suspicious of everyone."

"Aye, likely he suffers the prick of a guilty conscience. What does he say?"

"Among other things, he wished that 'Glasgow might be Hermitage, that he might be you as you lay there,' then he has no doubt that I will be with him quickly."

He frowned. Did Darnley suspect anything? A scandal would ruin Mary with Catholics and Protestants alike. How often he cursed himself for placing her in this dangerous position. Every time he came to her he vowed it would be the last, but when he broached it to her, she flew into panic and swore she cared nothing for the risk as long as they could be together. And he knew that even if she were to agree to part, he could never let her go.

"Has he spoken jealously of me before?" he asked.

"No more so than others. He is jealous of everyone."

"No matter; to be on the safe side, speak ill of me should he bring my name up again. Despite his insults, do not defend me. Above all, you must gain his confidence so he will reveal his plans to you."

"I doubt he trusts even me now."

"Then restore his trust in you. Flatter him, promise him anything he asks."

"You know what he wants most. He is mad with lust."

"Tell him he may have that too—but only when he is completely cured. Under no circumstance let him kiss you, lest he contaminate you."

"I cannot do it," she sobbed. "You ask me to dissemble, to give my word falsely. It is a role I have never played."

"Nor have I—intrigue is not among my favored pastimes."

Contrite, she said, "I know this is not of your choosing. It has been thrust upon you for my sake—and I repay you with cowardice."

"You a coward! Nothing could be further from the truth. One of the things I love best about you is your bravery. You've faced danger before and come through it valiantly—you will again now."

The fire sputtered, then died; he saw her in the light of a single candle that burned on the night table. She lay close, almost a part of him, her pale skin a sharp contrast to his own tanned body. His lips brushed her temple; she opened her eyes and smiled.

"You are not asleep?" he asked.

"No, for I want to be conscious of your nearness. There will be too many long nights ahead without you."

"Only for a while—I will be here waiting for you to return."

"If I am successful, Harry will return with me."

"Aye, but he goes to Craigmillar first. He must not be permitted to leave there until he is thoroughly cured."

"And afterward—what then?"

"I don't know yet."

"The thought of having to give myself to him—to have his hands on me . . . "

"I promise you, it will never come to that."

He felt her go rigid in his arms; his lips soothed her until she quieted. She knew Morton's intent; Bothwell had told her what they discussed at Whittinghame. Although she had offered no real protest, she had refused to talk about it, even to Bothwell. It was as though she could pretend ignorance through silence. And for once Bothwell was thankful for her ability to deceive herself.

4

Bothwell was already mounted and had been waiting for Mary half an hour. He glanced up at her windows, wondering at the delay. Had she changed her mind about going? Her fears might have overwhelmed her. The palace doors swung open, and he looked toward them hopefully; Captain Erskine came out with more instructions for his men.

"What can be keeping her?" Huntly asked coming abreast of Bothwell. "We should have been away from here an hour ago."

Bothwell shrugged. His horse stamped about on the snow-packed ground impatiently, snorting and exhaling puffs of blue vapor. Again, Bothwell glanced up at Mary's windows, his irritation growing. If she had decided against the journey, let her have the courage to say so.

She came out at last, and his anger melted at the sight of her. Her face showed signs of strain; her anguish was written on it. He slid down from his mount and went to help her.

"Smile," he whispered. "You look more as though you were going to a burial than a reunion with your hsuband."

He felt her gloved fingers tighten on his arm as he lifted her to the saddle. Her lips trembled, then parted in a stiff smile.

They stayed the night, midway between Glasgow and Edinburgh, at Lord Livingston's house. At supper they sat opposite each other, but there was no opportunity for them to be alone. Her eyes told him what she might have said in private: *I am afraid—do not send me there. I love you* . . .

He sensed her need and hoped she saw his reassurances. Then he looked away abruptly, avoiding her glance. He recalled Jean's remarks: *The looks that pass between you . . . how she hangs on your every word.* . . . He could not take the risk of others recognizing those looks. And later, when Mary retired to her chambers, he said good night with more formality than he had ever used toward her before.

"Remember, trust no one," Bothwell warned. "Learn all you can from Darnley; let nothing, however small, escape your memory."

He had been up since dawn, waiting for the chance to speak with her in private, and had drawn her aside into the empty library the moment he saw her bright gold cloak on the stairway.

"So many instructions." She shook her head in bewilderment. "I can scarce remember what you told me only seconds ago."

"Then remember only this," he said, cradling her in his arms, kissing her.

"Where will you be tonight?" she asked. "I want to imagine myself there with you."

"In Edinburgh; then two days hence, I leave for the Border. The Armstrongs and Elliots are at it again, disturbing the peace." He grinned. "It will take a few broken pates to bring them to quiet."

"Take care, love. I'd not want to live if anything happened to you."

"This is routine business—there is nothing to fear."

"Still, I wish you were not going. Is there no one who can go in your place?"

"Shall I idle my days away at court till I grow fat and lazy?"

She wouldn't smile—not even for him. A layer of tears veiled her eyes, threatening to spill over. "I love you," she whispered. "Even if it condemns me to an eternity of hell, I love you."

He held her close. "Your escort is waiting," he said.

"Come out with me."

"No, I'll wait here till you've gone, or I'll not be able to let you go at all." He kissed her again and she hurried out.

5

Paris found him at Melrose on the twenty-fifth of January. No matter that Paris was half frozen and near dead with fatigue; he could rest later—after he had delivered Mary's message.

Bothwell pulled him into the room. "The Queen," he asked, "how did you leave her? Was she well? Has she seen Darnley? Did she learn anything from him?"

Paris nodded in rapid succession. Shivering, he eyed the bottle of brandywine on the night table longingly.

Bothwell followed his gaze. "You shall have all you want—later. The answers first," he said.

Paris undid the strings of his cloak and reached into his doublet. He handed Bothwell a letter and a bracelet woven of gold and silver thread. "From the Queen, my lord. She is well and told me to say she misses you sorely—she sends her love."

"What of the King—does she lodge in his house?"

"No. She stays at a merchant's house a short distance away and visits the King daily. Few people have seen him; only his physicians and servants are permitted to enter the sickroom. I am told he wears a silk mask to hide the blemishes of his illness."

"Aye, the so-called pockmarks. More an advertisement of his depravity. Is he truly as ill as he makes out?"

"No one is certain. He refuses to let the Queen's physicians see him—only his father's physicians attend him."

"To hide the true nature of his malady. But no matter, I am more concerned with what he has declared to the Queen."

"He admits little and denies much—the bulk of which you will see in the Queen's letter. But she has been able to extract his promise to return to Edinburgh with her. They will begin the journey in two days, though it will go slowly, for he travels by litter."

"Didn't Lennox even attempt to keep him in Glasgow?"

"The Earl has not shown himself since the Queen's arrival. He pleads poor health and keeps to his chambers."

"Poor health, is it? More likely a guilty conscience sickens him. Is there more?"

Paris stifled a yawn. "No, my lord, the letter will tell you the rest."

"Then get some sleep and hold yourself ready to return to the Queen in the morning."

Paris shuffled his feet a few steps, but he made no attempt to go. Hesitantly, he said, "The brandywine, my lord — you promised."

Bothwell glanced at the bottle; it was half full. "Take it all," he said, "you've earned it."

Paris snatched up the bottle and left.

Bothwell lighted some candles and sat down in front of the fireplace to read Mary's letter. He tore off the seal and a thick packet of papers tumbled out.

It began:

> *My lord. Being gone from the place where I left my heart, you may easily imagine what kind of countenance I had, considering what the body is without a heart. . . .*
>
> *. . . Yesterday he [Darnley] summoned my servant, Joachin, and asked why I did not lodge near to him, adding that, if I did, he would rise sooner. . . .*
>
> *. . . He told me how ill he was and said . . . I am young. You will say that you have often forgiven me, and that I repeat my offenses. May not a man my age, lacking in good counsel, fall twice or thrice and fail in his promises, and afterwards repent his faults and chasten himself by experience? If I can win forgiveness, I promise not to offend hereafter. I will ask for nothing except that we may be at bed and board together as husband and wife; if you do not consent to that I shall never rise from this bed again. . . .*

Knowing how Mary felt, Bothwell could imagine her revulsion in having to make that promise.

> . . . *I asked him why he had considered going away on that English ship. This he denied under oath, but admitted that he had talked with the English. . . . In the end he desired much that I would lodge in his house. I have refused and told him that he must be disinfected and that this could not be done here. He said that he had heard that I had brought a litter. . . . I believe he feared that I might take him prisoner. I answered that I would carry him away with me to Craigmillar, where the physicians and I could look after him without my being too far away from my son. He replied that he was ready to go wherever I wished, provided that I would assure him of what he required of me.*
>
> . . . *I have never known him to speak more mildly or to behave so well; and if I had not learned by experience that his will is weak as wax, and that mine is hard as a diamond, which no arrow could pierce unless it were shot by your hand, it might well have chanced that I should have pitied him.*

Squinting, Bothwell held the letter closer to the light. Her writing was smaller now and cramped, which made it difficult to read. He frowned; if she wavered out of pity now it would be disastrous for her—he was certain of the danger.

He resumed reading.

> . . . *Forgive my bad writing—you must guess at half of it. I cannot amend it because I am not easy. Nevertheless, I have great joy in writing to you while the others are asleep, since for my part I cannot sleep as they do, nor as I wish, that is to sleep in your arms, my dearest, for whom I pray God to protect from every evil and bring you good fortune . . . I am*

*worried and sleepy, and yet I cannot forbear scribbling so
long as there is paper. Cursed be this pocky lad who troubles
me so, for were it not for him I should have fairer subjects to
talk of. . . .*

    *. . . Shortly then, he will not come with me unless I
undertake to make bed and board with him as heretofore,
and will leave him no more. If I will so promise, he will do
whatever I wish and will follow me. But he begged me to
wait another two days. . . . And in order that he should have
confidence in me I had to pretend to give way a little, and so
when he prayed that I would promise that as soon as he was
cured we should make our bed together, I told him I would
accord him what he desired. . . . Alas, I never deceived any-
body, but I submit to your will in all things.*

    *Let me know what I am to do, and whatever befalls, I
will obey you. . . . In a word, so far as I can make out, he is
very suspicious, although he puts great trust in my words
and yet not so much but that he is keeping things back.
However, I will get everything out of him. . . .*

Bothwell found it difficult to share Mary's confidence. There
were plots afoot that Darnley would never reveal to her.

    *. . . I have not seen him tonight because I am finishing
your bracelet, but I can find no clasps for it and that is what
renders it imperfect, and yet I fear lest it may bring you
some harm or be recognized if by any chance you should be
wounded. He gets furious when I mention Lethington or you
or my brother. As for the Earl of Argyll I am afraid to hear
him talk about him. . . . His father still keeps to his own
rooms; I have not seen him.*

    *. . . If I learn anything more I will make a note of it each
night. Paris will tell you the cause of my sojourn. . . . Pay no
attention to your wife, whose feigned tears ought to have*

*less influence with you than the genuine suffering which I
endure in order that I may deserve her place. . . . May God
forgive me and accord you, my one friend, all the success
and happiness that I, your humble and faithful lover, wish
for you, and who hopes to be something more unto you as a
reward for my grievous toil.*

*It is late, and yet I want never to stop writing to you.
Still, having kissed your hands, I will put an end to this
letter. Excuse my bad writing and read it again. . . . Keep me
in remembrance and write to me. . . . Love me as I love you.
Marie R.*

He put the letter down and sat staring into the fire. A vision
of Mary came to him in the dancing flames; he saw her sitting
alone in her chamber, writing to him. Her anguish was apparent
in every word. Some of it made no sense at all; her thoughts
seemed jumbled.

He picked up the letter and read it through again, but the
parts that had seemed garbled before were no clearer now. She
repeated herself, then contradicted herself; she pitied Darnley
and then she deceived him. And for that she blamed Bothwell,
as though placing the guilt on him eased her conscience. *Let
her,* he thought. *Anything to make her odious task more bear-
able.*

He marveled that in the midst of her despair she thought of
Jean. Despite her troubled heart, jealousy still controlled her—
even his own assurances could not set her at ease. But he could
allow her that too, and he could understand why she regarded
Jean as her rival. What troubled him most was that her pity for
Darnley might cause her to forget his offenses.

She had asked him to write; what could he say now that he
had not already said to her a hundred times? She needed courage; mere words could not give her that. There would be no

letter—Paris could tell her what he wanted to say. For the rest, it would wait until they were together.

His eyes felt heavy for lack of sleep. He pinched out the candle and went to bed—tomorrow's raid needed a cool head.

Bothwell sent for Paris before dawn.

"Tell the Queen that you left me as I was about to ride herd on her outlaws," he told him. "And say that I shall return to Edinburgh when my business here is finished. Tell her also to take care that none shall beguile her, and that she should remember those who are not her friends."

"Is there no written word, my lord?"

"None, only what I tell you now." He thought of all the things he might say if Mary were here—but they would have to wait. "Of the bracelet, say that I am honored and that I shall wear it proudly and treasure it as a token of the sender's love."

"Is that all, my lord?"

"Aye, now go and return to the Queen with all speed."

He watched Paris go, wishing that he could go in his place. Then he called out, "Wait, there is more." He said softly, "Tell the Queen that I would send her my heart—if it were not already in her possession."

CHAPTER XIV

1

Bothwell had been back in Edinburgh only a day when a rider came ahead to announce that Mary and her party were approaching town. With the Earls of Huntly and Argyll, he rode out to meet her. They had gone only a short distance when the royal standard-bearer came into sight, and a moment later Bothwell saw Mary.

Although she had left him only ten days ago, it seemed an eternity. Her white palfrey stood out sharply against the other black and brown mounts. She saw him at the same time and made as if to spur ahead, then, checking her eagerness, she reined in and her horse pulled up with a jerk. Following her, Bothwell saw the litter that bore Darnley, its silver and gold curtains swaying with the jogging motion.

Bothwell trotted his horse forward and fell into line, abreast of Mary. Lord Livingston hung back to make room for him.

"I trust you've had a pleasant journey, madam," he said.

She nodded, and the plume on her toque bobbed merrily. "As pleasant as journeys go, my lord, though our progress is slow for the King's sake."

"It is nearly at an end, madam. The road to Craigmillar lies just ahead."

"We will not be going to Craigmillar. The King chooses to reside in Edinburgh."

Surprised, he glanced at her. Her lips were held tight in a

thin line of determination, but her expression revealed nothing. He recalled her letter; it had very definitely said Craigmillar. He wondered why she had changed plans.

"Surely not the palace, madam. There is still the danger of infection."

She shook her head. "Last night on our halt at Linlithgow, the King decided on a more convenient location—a house belonging to Balfour's brother. It is being prepared for him now."

Bothwell knew the house; it was a modest dwelling off Blackfriar's Wynd. "Kirk o' Field?" he asked.

"Yes."

"Unless I am mistaken, it has been in disuse for several years."

She shrugged. "The King himself chose it, and Balfour assures him it is in good repair."

He fell to silence. There was no logical explanation for Darnley's decision. Usually he demanded the most luxurious accommodations; now he was suddenly willing to reside in these meager lodgings.

They had passed the Potterrow Port and had turned into Blackfriar's Wynd, which led to the precincts of Kirk o' Field. There, those on horse dismounted to walk up the short flight of steps to the kirkyard, while Darnley's litter was carried to the front door.

Only a few in the retinue went inside with Mary and Darnley to wait in the reception room.

Balfour approached Bothwell. "You seem skeptical, my lord," he said. "Are you concerned lest these quarters may not be worthy of royalty?"

Bothwell turned to eye the smiling face. He had never trusted Balfour; he felt that distrust more keenly now. He knew Balfour as a plotter too clever to leave a trail—one who kept a foot in both Protestant and Catholic camps. He could be bought, but his loyalty went to no one.

"Royalty may reside on a dung heap and turn it to a palace," Bothwell said, "but it can work the other way as well."

Balfour frowned. "I presume you wish to make a point, my lord."

"No point, merely an observation. If I were the King, convalescing as he is, I would sooner lodge at Craigmillar."

"Perhaps. But you cannot deny this house is highly situated, pleasant and in good air, environed with gardens, removed from noise, and suited to the King's purpose."

"Purpose? What purpose can he have, other than to regain his health?"

Bothwell had the sudden sensation of a curtain dropped between himself and Balfour. He thought he had seen a sneer on Balfour's face, but it was gone before he could be certain.

"No other, of course, my lord." Then, bowing, Balfour said, "You will pardon me, my lord, I must go to the King. Doubtless he will have instructions for me."

Mary was still in Darnley's bedchamber, and while he waited to escort her to Holyrood, Bothwell took the opportunity to explore the house. His investigation was short, for there were only two stories: the one which held Darnley's reception room and bedchamber and another just like it on the floor below. The basement ran at different levels to allow for the sloping ground on which the house had been built. There quarters were provided for the servants, kitchens, and storage vaults. Modest lodgings, Bothwell thought, scarcely adequate to house a king—especially a king who set such store by his comforts.

"Why did he suddenly decide in favor of Kirk o' Field?"

"I don't know," Mary said later as she sat with Bothwell in her audience chamber. "This morning was the first I had heard of it. He was determined, and I let him have his way. It seemed not to matter where he convalesced."

"It doesn't really. But I've a notion that Balfour is somehow back of this," Bothwell said.

"You may be right. One of my servants told me that he saw Balfour and certain lords go to Harry's chambers last night. That may have been when he decided against Craigmillar."

For some unaccountable reason, the thought of Darnley at Kirk o' Field made Bothwell uneasy. Balfour's remark that it was *suitable for the King's purpose* had a sinister ring to it, and Bothwell was certain it had not been an idle remark. That enigmatic phrase sounded over and over in his mind; what purpose could be better served at Kirk o' Field than at Craigmillar?

Absentmindedly, he put her hand to his lips. "I'll leave you to your rest now," he said.

"Will you come to me later?"

"No, it's too risky with so many people about."

He saw her look of disappointment and took her in his arms. "Be patient, dearest," he said. "We must be careful."

Mary visited Darnley the following day and stayed through the evening to take supper with him before returning to the palace. Sunday and Monday she followed the same routine. She took only a small retinue with her on these visits and often went on foot along the back wall of the Cannongate, through St. Mary's Port, past the gardens of the Black Friars' monastery, which brought her to the east garden of the house. In this way she could come and go without attracting too much attention.

She did not see Darnley on Tuesday; in the morning she gave audience to the Savoyard ambassador, Moretta, and she set the afternoon aside for a fitting on a gown she was having made for Carnival Sunday, less than a week away. It was that same Tuesday that Jean came to Edinburgh.

2

Morton had moved from Whittinghame to St. Andrews, and Bothwell had gone to see him again about Darnley. But Morton proved uncommunicative, refusing to commit himself. He said that Archie Douglas and other kinsmen had taken residence in Edinburgh to represent him—and Bothwell wondered why anyone need represent him, and for what.

When he returned to Holyrood, he found Jean already settled in his apartments.

She laughed and came toward him. "You seem surprised to see me, my lord," she said. "Is it not a wife's privilege to be with her husband when she wishes?"

There was nothing in her manner to indicate that she remembered their violent quarrel at Crichton.

"You gave me no warning," he said warily.

"A strange word, warning. It implies attack, rather than an innocent visit. Perhaps you regard my being here more as an invasion."

This was odd behavior for Jean; she had come unbidden and seemed determined to stay. She had apparently decided to fight Mary for him.

"You are welcome here, of course," he said indifferently.

"For a moment, I thought you might send me away."

He drew off his gloves and sat down. "Now that I have assured you a roof over your head, perhaps you will be good enough to tell me why you have come."

"Why else, but to be with you?"

He shook his head. "If there has been nothing else between us, we have at least had honesty. It's not likely that you would travel bad roads—and in such weather—for the mere pleasure of my company."

"You do yourself an injustice, my lord. I find your company

most pleasurable of late." She paused. "Perhaps your long absences make it so."

His patience was nearing an end. The brittleness of his tone held a warning. "You've had your sport, my lady. Now, if you please, we have sparred enough. Why have you come?"

"Good news travels swiftly. Since the Queen is reconciled to her husband, I thought your madness had passed and that we too might be reconciled."

"My madness?"

"You object to that term? Then call it what you will—infatuation, fascination—it is all the same. You imagine yourself to be in love, but I know its true worth. You were dazzled by her rank; all men are—until they know her better. Now that it is over, however, I am prepared to forgive you. We need never speak of it again."

"You are too generous. But I fear you have made this journey for naught. Nothing has changed. I am as much in love with her as ever."

She started. "But her reconciliation with the King—"

"A political expediency, which you, and others like you, have interpreted as renewed love."

"Then you refuse to return to me?"

"I have never left you. We simply go our separate ways—an arrangement you seemed to prefer, until recently."

Jean's answer was lost to the sound of knocking. It was Mary's page with a message for Bothwell to come to her apartments.

Bothwell nodded. "I will be there shortly," he said. Then, turning to Jean, he said, "My apologies, my lady, we will continue this later."

She glared at him. "By all means, run to her. No wonder she keeps you; you are like clay in her hands. Virtue means nothing to you—whores are more to your liking."

Livid with rage, he clamped her arm cruelly. "For your sake, my lady," he snarled, "I hope you are calmed when I return."

When he entered her audience chamber, Mary was surrounded by her ladies. They were chattering all at once, and he was reminded of a nest of chirping fledglings. She saw him and clapped for silence.

"You may go," she told her ladies.

They gathered up pieces of fur and lengths of pale-blue brocade that lay scattered on the love seat.

"Leave it," Mary said.

When they had gone, she picked up the brocade to drape over her shoulder. "Do you like it?" she asked.

"Aye."

"I will wear it Sunday, for Carnival night. Naturally, it is still unfinished." She waltzed around, modeling it for him. "The shoulders will be bared and trimmed with ermine—"

"Is this why you summoned me?" His quarrel with Jean still irritated him; he wanted to be off somewhere alone. Instead, he was expected to cater to female vanity by admiring a new gown.

"No," she said.

"Then why?"

"You seem agitated." She frowned.

"A personal matter."

She hesitated, then tossed the gown on a chair. "Why is Jean here?" she demanded. "Did you send for her?"

"Good God!" he shouted. "Am I to be forever bedeviled by two jealous women?"

"Lower your voice; the guards will hear you." She glanced nervously toward the door.

"Let them, let everyone hear; then we will have done with it. I have only moments ago left one shrew, now I am with another."

"You quarreled with her?"

"Aye."

"Over me?"

"Aye, over you," he said dully. Softly now: "Jean had the mistaken notion that you and Darnley were reconciled. She took it for granted that you and I had parted."

She crossed to where he stood. "How dare she take anything for granted? She relinquished her right to you on your honeymoon. She has always preferred Alex of Boyne—now suddenly she cannot live without you. Her change of heart is touching, but it smacks of insincerity."

He put his hands to his ears. "Will this never end? Neither of you can speak of the other without disparagement."

"What did she say of me?"

"Let it suffice that you share the same opinion of each other." He went to the door.

"Where are you going?"

"To find some peace."

"Promise me—"

He turned and waited, knowing what she would say.

"—that you will not bed with her."

"Shall I sleep in the servants' hall, or in the garden perhaps, under your window, where you can watch me?"

She stared at him, mute with misery. He could have gone to her, kissed away her doubts—he could have told her what she wanted to hear again. But he had been badgered enough for one day; he could bear no more. Without a word he turned and left her.

He felt as though he were being strangled; they were tearing him apart. Mary pulled at him from one side, Jean from the other. In all fairness he could not entirely blame either of them, for each threatened the other's security. Mary, he knew, was driven by love and a desperate need for assurance that he loved her. But, God, need she doubt him? He was too full of her to so much as look at another woman.

As for Jean, he couldn't be quite sure of her motives. She had been content to let matters stand as they were until she had learned that he cared deeply for someone else. Her pride could not stand the blow. It was likely pride that made her fight for him—that and her fear of losing her high estate.

And he stood in the middle, committed to both women. He was bound to Jean in marriage, and for that she had every right to claim his loyalty and protection. Yet he knew that he belonged entirely to Mary, for she was in his soul—she was part of him, mind and body, blood and bone.

It was an insoluble problem. Once Mary was free of Darnley, she could take another husband. He would gladly divorce Jean to wed her; he wanted the right to be with her always, but her nobles—possibly Scotland itself—would never accept him as king. He knew that Mary would stand beside him in the face of any opposition, but she had borne enough grief; he would not be the one to bring her more. His marriage to Jean gave Mary the only protection she had against herself.

3

Darnley's period of convalescence was nearly at an end. He had taken residence at Kirk o' Field eight days ago, and still nothing had been resolved in the matter of Mary's divorce. Morton vacillated between taking Darnley into ward and vague hints of using more sinister means. Lethington spoke of divorce and retiring Darnley abroad, while James continued to *look through his fingers*. Alone, Bothwell could do nothing—the danger was too great.

Mary continued to visit Darnley and bring with her special foods prepared by her French chefs. Wednesday and Friday, she slept at Kirk o' Field; on Saturday Darnley's bed was returned to Holyrood and a lesser one brought in its place. Darnley insisted on having his velvet bed fumigated for Monday, when he would return to Holyrood to share it with Mary.

She was almost in tears when she told Bothwell of Darnley's plans. She looked forward to the coming Monday with the same dread that a condemned man awaits the headsman's ax—while Darnley regarded it as a triumph and meant to make the most of it. The day preceding his return was Carnival Sunday; he made his arrangements accordingly.

In the morning Mary would attend the wedding ceremony of her servants Christina Hogg and Sebastien Pagez, which was to be followed by a midday dinner in their honor. In the evening she would attend a farewell dinner for Moretta, the Savoyard ambassador. Following that, she would ride to Kirk o' Field with her nobles to spend the evening with Darnley and sleep the night there. Early Monday morning the nobles would return to escort Mary and Darnley to Holyrood in great procession.

It was before noon on Friday that Mary sent an urgent message to Bothwell and James, summoning them to Kirk o' Field. A violent quarrel had broken out between Darnley and Mary's other half brother, Lord Robert.

At the house, they came upon a strange scene. Lord Robert stood near a window shaking his fist at Darnley in impotent rage. Darnley half-stood in bed, brandishing a sword, while two servants vainly attempted to subdue him. His face flamed the color of the scabs that still clung to his forehead; he screamed hysterically.

Mary saw Bothwell and James and rushed to them. "Stop them," she pleaded, "or they will surely kill each other."

James went to restrain his brother, while Bothwell helped the servants with Darnley.

"Calm yourself, sire," Bothwell said. "This exertion will cause a relapse."

Darnley flung him off, but he quieted a little. He sat back

against the pillows. "Little you or anyone else would care," he snapped.

The sword clattered to the floor. Bothwell picked it up and placed it on a table out of Darnley's reach. Mary dismissed the servants and sank wearily into a chair.

"What happened?" James demanded.

He had addressed himself to Lord Robert, but Darnley answered. He pointed unsteadily at Lord Robert. "This son of a whore has the audacity to accuse me of plotting against my wife."

James started; the tiny veins at his temples were suddenly prominent. "May I remind you, sire, Lord Robert and I are graced with the same mother."

"I am well aware of that. You are two of a kind—whore-suckled bastards, both of you."

Mary gripped the arms of her chair. "This is outrageous, sire."

James held up a hand to silence her; he was going to let the insult pass. Bothwell wondered why—he would take a horse-whip to any man who spoke so disrespectfully of his mother. No one he knew would let an insult of that kind pass without seeking immediate satisfaction. He glanced quickly at James; he was his imperious self again. James' supreme hatred for Darnley had flicked only briefly across his face; now it lay hidden in those long-lidded Stuart eyes. Aye, James could afford to be patient, for he knew he would be shortly avenged by another means.

"We are not here to deal in personal issues, madam," James said. "If the King speaks correctly, my brother has made a grave charge."

"He is not entirely correct," Mary said. "Lord Robert did make mention of a plot, but it was terribly vague."

"He accuses me of authoring this imaginary plot," Darnley said.

"I have accused you of nothing, sire." Lord Robert turned to Mary for confirmation. "Her Majesty questioned me; I merely suggested the King might know better of it."

Darnley pounded his quilt. "There, you both heard it. Is that not an accusation?"

"I meant no harm, sire. My only intention is to warn the Queen."

"How did you come by this information?" Bothwell asked.

"From a stranger last night in a tavern. He was fresh from Glasgow and on his way to Berwick. He said Glasgow was thick with rumor, and he believed the Queen was in danger. Therefore, I thought the King, coming lately out of that town, might know more of it."

"He lies. I swear by my honor, he is lying," Darnley shrieked. "How could I hear any of it from a sickbed? He has made it all up to undermine me with the Queen. Therein lie the difficulties between my wife and me—enemies reporting ill of me when I cannot defend myself."

Mary went to him. "Sire, I beg of you, do not upset yourself needlessly. Lord Robert meant that you may have heard something."

"Then you believe that I know nothing?"

"Of course. You have sworn you do not. You would not falsify your word."

He moistened his lips and glanced about suspiciously. "Certainly not," he said.

Mary turned to the others. "Wait for me outside; I will return to the palace with you."

It was snowing again; enough had fallen to cover the sooty old snow with a fresh white layer.

James turned to his brother. "Are you content with the tempest you have created?"

"I thought it my duty to warn the Queen."

James sneered. "In the last month there have been more

than a dozen different rumors to come out of Glasgow—not one has been traced to the source. Did you think you could succeed where better men have failed?"

Bothwell said, "We may be certain of this much: the majority of those rumors are based somewhat on fact. I've no doubt but the King knows a deal more than he is willing to admit."

James nodded. "Granted, but there is no way of forcing him to reveal what he knows. This is a delicate situation, one that must be treated with the utmost caution. Of course, if the Queen would give her consent in writing to have him taken in ward. . . . "

"Well you know she will not do that." Bothwell had cautioned her against giving them anything in writing which they could later hold over her head.

James paused to examine a loose thread on his gloves. "Morton is of the opinion that she lacks zeal in dealing with her husband—her gentle nature poses a difficult problem."

"It is that same gentle nature you and Morton may thank for being alive today," Bothwell snapped.

He knew that James needed no reminders of the papal commission; it was still a useful barb.

Their talk ceased, for Mary came out and they started for Holyrood.

4

"A slight alteration on the shoulders and the doublet will fit perfectly, my lord."

Bothwell grunted his approval; his mind was on more weighty matters than his outfit for tomorrow's festivities. The tailor had him turn to the right and left, making a dart here, smoothing it there.

"Black is too somber," Jean said critically. "A brighter shade would lend more gaiety to the occasion."

He ignored her remark. Nevertheless, after glancing at himself in the mirror, Bothwell had to admit that it was a magnificent outfit; he would be dressed entirely in black from his Spanish leather boots to his velvet doublet, richly embroidered in silver. Despite Jean's criticism, he thought black very becoming. As the tailor had pointed out, it drew attention to the hard, lean lines of his body and made him seem even taller.

The tailor said, "If my lord will remove the garments now, I will go to my work."

Bothwell went to his dressing room to change and was back quickly. "Mind they are finished in time," he said.

"Aye, my lord, they will be here waiting for you before noon."

The tailor went out and collided with Paris, who nearly fell into the room.

"What are you up to, skulking outside my door?" Bothwell growled.

"I was about to knock when the door opened, my lord."

Glaring, the tailor pushed Paris aside and hurried out.

Bothwell waited for Paris to state his business, but he said nothing. Finally, Bothwell asked, "Well, have you come here just to gaze at me?" When there was still no answer, he shouted, "Are you daft? Say what you've come for, then go."

Paris went through some strange contortions with his eyes, indicating Jean as his reason for not speaking. Bothwell caught his signal and pushed him roughly through the study door.

To Jean he said, "It may take a few whacks on the head to learn what he's about—a sight better removed from your view, my lady." He closed the door and turned to Paris. "Now out with it, and be quick. Your actions have aroused more suspicion than anything you may have said."

"My lord, there is a man, Sandy Durham by name, lying drunk in the stables. I found him sobbing and pleading for refuge. He raves of a disaster so terrible that I am afraid to hear him speak of it."

"Who is Sandy Durham?"

"A servant of the King, who until this evening lodged with him."

Bothwell felt a creeping sensation travel up his back; it was an all too familiar feeling these days. Darnley's servant, frightened out of his wits and seeking refuge—he dreaded to guess what it meant.

"Take me to him," he said.

He followed Paris out, down the back stairway, out into the freezing night. The wind pounded at their backs with a force that hurried them along. Paris led the way into the stables, through a partition where a man lay huddled on a pile of straw.

"This is Sandy Durham, my lord," Paris said.

"Why have you left the King?" Bothwell demanded, pulling the man to his feet.

Durham struggled to free himself. "Please, Your Lordship, don't send me back—everyone in that house is doomed."

"What house is this?"

Durham looked up at him, his eyes wide with terror. He seemed like a man just awakened, fearful of what he may have blurted. "I beg Your Lordship to pay me no heed. It is the wine talking."

"Tell me," Bothwell said, tightening his grip, "or I'll send you back to the King to let him deal with you."

"No, my lord, don't send me back there."

"Then answer me."

"They will surely kill me if I do."

"And *I* will surely kill you if you don't." He exerted more pressure. "Tell me and I will see you are not harmed."

Durham considered this for a moment. He said, "Do I have Your Lordship's promise to keep me hidden if I reveal what I know?"

"Aye. Now make up your mind, which is it to be?"

"I will speak," he said quickly. The words gushed from him. "The house is a deathtrap, the vaults are mined with gunpowder. It is a conspiracy to kill the Queen and her nobles. I could not sleep there another night knowing the danger."

Bothwell had been suspicious and edgy since the day he learned of Darnley's decision to lodge at Kirk o' Field; his reliable extra sense had warned him of something.

"Who are 'they'?" he asked. "Who is planning to kill the Queen?"

Durham hesitated. He had sobered; a sly look came into his eyes. Doubtless he was thinking of being paid for his information.

"Very well," Bothwell said, "you needn't tell me any more. I will take you to the Queen and have you charged with treason. You will be sent to the Tolbooth—they are experts in extracting information. There is the thumbscrew, the boot, the rack—in your case they will likely use all three if you prove stubborn."

Beads of sweat formed on Durham's forehead; his eyes glazed with fear. "The King, his father, and the majority of his followers—Sir James Balfour comes often to speak privately with the King. There is a Jesuit priest, fresh from Paris, Father Edmund Hay."

Lennox, of course! He would encourage Darnley's dream of power. Father Hay was no stranger to Bothwell; he was one of the Papal emissaries sent from Rome, and he had been suspicious of Balfour from the start.

"When is this to take place?"

"It is planned for the moment when the Queen and her escort of nobles are assembled in the house."

Bothwell went over Darnley's plans in his mind. Mary was to sleep at Kirk o' Field tomorrow night. Early Monday morning all those nobles who were in Edinburgh would attend her there to escort Darnley back to Holyrood—the highest ranking among them would surely enter the house. It would be a master coup, everyone who had ever stood in Darnley's way eliminated in one stroke.

But Darnley's allies in this were Mary's coreligionists. How would her death benefit Catholic interests? Father Hay offered a clue, for he was the one who had proposed Bishop Laureo's plan to Mary. He surmised that Laureo's plan to execute her Protestant leaders lay at the bottom of this, but now it seemed they had added another victim to their list—Mary.

Bothwell started to leave, but Durham caught him by the sleeve. "My lord, you promised to protect me."

"You are safe enough; no will will look for you here. Find an unused stall and stay there. Paris will bring you food and blankets."

Bothwell's first impulse was to reveal everything to Mary, then he decided against it. She might not believe him; earlier that day she had told him of a letter Darnley had written to his father in which he spoke of his improving health and the joy he took in Mary's renewed love. He had played the part so convincingly that she believed he was sincerely repentant. Because she was so trusting, Bothwell decided to wait on the chance that she might confront Darnley with the plot to prove it false, and in so doing would warn him.

In any case, Bothwell still had to check out Durham's story. Walking back to his apartments, he heard the town crier call the hour of eleven—it was too late to investigate now. However impatient he was to see those mined vaults, he had to wait.

5

Carnival Sunday dawned cloudy with raw winds and a promise of more snow. Bothwell was at breakfast when the abbey bells sounded the first call to prayers. The Cannongate

Kirk followed suit, then the deep-throated chimes of St. Giles. He thought of the would-be murderers and doubted that any of them would miss church today. Perhaps they were even telling themselves it was God's work they were doing.

After escorting Jean to the Cannongate Kirk, Bothwell went to see the Douglases. Their house was on Blackfriar's Wynd, close enough to have seen any unusual activity at Darnley's lodging. He arrived just as they were leaving for St. Giles.

"Come with us, my lord," Archie Douglas said. "Master Craig will rejoice to see one of his flock returned."

"Another time. I have come on an urgent matter."

Douglas removed his cloak and took Bothwell into the library. "How may I be of service to you, my lord?"

"By telling me if you have heard of any new design against the Queen—rumors that may have come out of the King's lodging."

Douglas showed no surprise; there was only a look of cunning that sprang quickly into his eyes. "Can you be more specific, my lord?"

"No, except that the King may have allied himself with certain Catholics to the Queen's disfavor."

"Frankly, I cannot conceive of anything Catholic that would be to Her Majesty's disfavor."

Douglas was being wary and deliberately evasive, which gave Bothwell the feeling that he knew something. "Nor can I," Bothwell said to throw him off. "But there have been so many rumors of late, it seemed best to investigate this one before dismissing it entirely." Then, changing the subject abruptly, he asked, "What news have you from the Earl of Morton? Did he confide his plans for the King to you?"

By now Bothwell felt that Archie Douglas' hurried ride to see Morton at St. Andrews yesterday had been prompted by what he had learned only late last night from Sandy Durham. It was also suddenly clear why James had minimized Friday's incident between Darnley and Lord Robert—James knew the secret of Kirk o' Field and had sent Archie Douglas to alert Morton.

"The King returns to Holyrood tomorrow, does he not?" Douglas asked.

"Aye, it's a well-known fact, for he's spoken of little else all week."

"Just yesterday, the Earl of Morton remarked on His Majesty's marvelous swift recovery. I reminded him there is always the danger of a relapse—which can sometimes be fatal."

"The time for vague hints and sinister threats has passed," Bothwell said impatiently. "What position has the Earl decided to take regarding the King? He has yet to sign the bond proscribing him. Will he support the Council on the King's arrest?"

"Since the Queen refuses to sign the warrant of arrest, the Earl is reluctant to commit himself. You mind, Your Lordship advised that we proceed lawfully—therefore we are somewhat limited."

Bothwell nodded. "I can understand where legalities would constrain the Earl, seeing he's never fashed himself with them before." He gathered up his cloak and gloves. "I have kept you overlong from God already," he said. "I'll not have it on my conscience to detain you further."

Douglas walked with him to the front door. "Have a little more patience, my lord," he said as they stepped out into Blackfriar's Wynd together. "We will shortly find the means to deal with the King to everyone's profit."

Bothwell mounted his stallion. "My sole concern is how well the Realm profits."

There was no doubt in Bothwell's mind now that Mary could expect no help from the Moray-Lethington-Morton combine. If they rid her of Darnley it would be strictly for their benefit, not hers. He had thought that Morton would be a useful tool to use against Darnley, but it didn't seem to be working out.

Since leaving Archie Douglas, Bothwell had been trying all afternoon to see Mary alone. One thing after another prevented him; the midday dinner for the wedding couple, and later there were a score of lords and ladies surrounding her. Then when it seemed he might have the chance, James had taken her aside to say that he was leaving for St. Andrews because his wife was ill. That piece of news confirmed Bothwell's suspicions, for James always absented himself when some evil was brewing.

At last, Bothwell found the chance when Mary went to her apartments to rest before dressing for the evening. She had dismissed her ladies; there was no one to interrupt them.

She looked up from examining a pair of sapphire earrings. "One more night," she said. "What difference can it make?"

"Call it a whim, anything you like, but sleep here tonight."

"I believe you are jealous." She smiled. "My lord Bothwell may sleep every night with his wife, but I may not sleep one night with my husband—a floor removed from him at that."

"I've sworn that I would not touch Jean."

"Then why haven't you sent her away?"

"Because it would mean another scene—something I would prefer to avoid. Now, give me your word you will not sleep there tonight."

"I have already promised Harry that I would."

"Break your promise."

"He has been like a child planning this for a week. I haven't the heart to refuse him."

Aye, planning your destruction. "Will you not do this for me?" He went to her. "Is it so much to ask?"

She came into his arms. "If it is that important to you, then

I cannot refuse. But you must go now to let me dress—I want to dazzle you tonight."

He smiled. "You always do."

Bothwell sat opposite Mary at the dinner table; she was truly dazzling. She wore the pale-blue brocade he had seen before it was even finished; the ermine-trimmed neckline dipped low, blending into the creamy softness of her shoulders. Deep-blue sapphires twinkled from her ears and in the mesh snood that held her hair; they looked like stars in a winter sky. She was exquisite beyond belief; he could not take his eyes from her. Her beauty stabbed at him with a mixture of pain and fury, for he thought of Darnley and how he would destroy her to satisfy his ambition.

She laughed, turning to Ambassador Moretta, who sat on her left. The Bishop of Argyll, who hosted the dinner, surveyed the table and saw to his guests' needs; he ordered the glasses filled and proposed a toast to Mary.

She whispered something to Moretta; he chuckled. Mary's charm lay in her familiar manner with those inferior to her in rank; her flirtations and coquettishness melted the hardest armor. Earlier Moretta had complained of James' sudden departure, and although he was in town, Lethington, too, had made his excuses for not attending. It seemed the Earls of Huntly, Cassilus, and Bothwell could not compensate Moretta for the absence of those two. But Mary's graciousness had smoothed things over, and Moretta's humor improved.

After dinner, Mary and her company rode in a torchlight procession up the Cannongate, through the Netherbow Port, onto the High Street. At Blackfriar's Wynd they left the turmoil and crowds of revelers for the quiet precincts of Kirk o' Field. The Tolbooth clock struck the half hour past eight o'clock as they drew rein in front of the house.

The snow had turned to an ugly brown slush. Bothwell

dismounted, lifted Mary from the saddle, and carried her into the house, setting her down on the narrow stairway. She paused to let her ermine-lined hood fall back, then she started up to Darnley's bedchamber.

Even with the great violet bed gone and a smaller one in its place, there was still an overcrowding and closeness in the room. Only Huntly, Cassilus, and Bothwell went in with Mary. The others filled the reception rooms on the first and second floors, while their attendants, pages, and grooms stayed outdoors.

Huntly brought a high-backed upholstered chair close to Darnley's bed for Mary, then he joined Bothwell and Cassilus at dice. Bothwell found himself scarcely able to concentrate on the game; he was too fascinated by Darnley's behavior. He marveled that he could laugh and speak to Mary as he did, holding her hand, leaning forward to stroke her cheek, whispering little phrases of affection into her ear. He was a perfect study of innocence.

That and the knowledge that Paris was nosing about somewhere below distracted him. If Paris found the gunpowder, as Bothwell thought he would, they were enclosed in a veritable deathtrap.

Servants came in bearing wine and cakes. Mary took some wine diluted with water; Darnley asked for cake, insisting that she feed it to him with her own hands. Bothwell felt his dinner rising up in his throat; suddenly the room turned to haze, rage burned hot in his brain . . . .

Cassilus touched his wrist. "Your throw, my lord."

Huntly followed Bothwell's glance. He said, "Perhaps my lord Bothwell has wearied of the game." He reached across the green velvet cloth to remove the dice.

Bothwell took the dice and threw them. "No, no, I like it fine," he murmured.

Thank God they had diverted him. The seconds ticked on; ten minutes, an hour, more than two had passed. Still Mary

showed no sign of going. It was eleven o'clock, time they were
away. He rose and went to Mary. "The wedding masque,
madam," he said. "Have you forgotten?"

Mary glanced up. "Is it that late already?"

Darnley bolted upright, overturning the platter of cakes on
his quilt. "You promised to spend the night here with me."

"That was before I remembered my promise to Christina and
Sebastien. They will be heartbroken if I do not at least show
myself."

"Am I not more important to you than they?" Darnley
asked, clutching her hand.

She tried to smile. His violent protests were embarrassing.
She said, "There will be other nights, Harry. Tomorrow you will
be at the palace—we can be together then."

Darnley turned the shade of his plum satin robe. "No! I
want you to stay with me tonight. You gave your word; now
you withdraw it in favor of menials. I counted on your sleeping
here. Why can't you return after the masque?"

"Perhaps I may," she said.

She wrenched free of his grasp; the ring from her small finger
came loose in his hand. She stood watching him, obviously
undecided whether she should leave him. Bothwell saw that she
was beginning to weaken.

He placed her cloak over her shoulders. "We must go,
madam."

She turned to Darnley. "If not tonight, then I will be here
first thing in the morning."

"Go to your masque," he snarled, "the lot of you—dance
and make merry while I lie here and rot."

Bothwell took Mary by the arm and led her to the door. She
repeated, "If not tonight, then in the morning."

Darnley was suddenly calm. "Let it be tonight, dearest.
However, should you decide not to please me, then be here

early—remember, early. I will hold your ring as a pledge of your return."

She nodded.

He blew her a kiss. "With all the nobility—I want them *all* here to escort me to the palace."

"Yes, they will be here, too."

Bothwell hurried her out and down the stairway. "To horse," he called to the others.

The torchbearers came up to light the way. He carried Mary to her horse, then mounted his own.

Paris came running out from the cellar door. His face and clothes were black with soot. He made for Bothwell's horse, pretending to adjust the saddle strap. "My lord," he whispered, "Durham spoke the truth."

"Jésu, how begrimed you are, Paris," she said, laughing at his dishevelment.

"Get away, you'll soil the trappings with those hands," Bothwell said angrily, prodding him with his boot.

6

The party started off, retracing their route back to Holyrood. Mary fell into a preoccupied silence, but her mood changed when she entered the masque. She laughed, jested, and danced with the groom, and when the musicians struck up a galliard, she chose Bothwell to lead it with her.

"You look splendidly sinister all in black," she whispered.

"Perhaps, but not half so dangerous as you."

"How am I dangerous?"

He tightened his hold on her waist. "By enchanting me with your beauty."

She threw her head back and laughed, gracefully following him in the gay, intricate little steps. The dance ended; he released her. He saw Jean standing off to a side alone, watching them forlornly. Mary followed his glance. He bowed to her as Argyll came up to them. "I leave you in good hands, madam," Bothwell said.

She turned her back to him as he crossed to Jean. "Will you do me the honor, my lady?" he said, extending his arm.

Stunned, Jean followed him. She was stiff in his arms, lacking Mary's grace. They danced in silence, and when it was over he brought her some wine.

Mary joined them at the refreshment table. "I have decided to sleep at Kirk o' Field, after all," she said.

Bothwell turned sharply; this was how she meant to punish him for dancing with Jean. He glared at her. "Earlier you said you would not, madam."

She glared back at him defiantly. "I have changed my mind, a privilege often used by women—by some men, too, when it suits them."

He saw by the stubborn set of her chin that she would not be swayed. He could have slapped her for her willfulness, but he had to stop her from taking the risk of returning to that house. "Very well, madam," he said, "if you are so determined. But I must have a word with you before you go."

"It is late, my lord. Will tomorrow not do as well?"

"It will not. I must insist that it be now. I shall not keep you long—then you may go where you wish."

Mary said good night to the others, while Bothwell sent for Lord Traquair to join him in Mary's chambers.

"Now," Mary said, closing the door to her apartments, "perhaps you will be good enough to tell me why I am detained."

"With good cause, I assure you."

"Which will also excuse your outrageous behavior, I hope. I do not appreciate being ordered about by you before others."

"My apologies, madam." He made her an ironic bow. "It was not my intention to embarrass you. But when you have heard me out, you may consider that a small price to pay."

"I will be the judge of that." She flung herself into a chair.

He bent close; his voice held the chill of steel and the deadliness of its thrust. "I have had quite enough of your pettishness," he said. "We have quarreled this entire week, all because of Jean. It must cease. I cannot"—he paused—"no, I *will* not be held accountable to you for performing my obligations as I see fit. Tonight, simply because I took pity on Jean and danced with her once, you are about to spite me by placing your life in danger."

"My life?"

"Aye. Rather a costly exchange for a moment of willfulness, I'd say." Someone knocked. "That will be Traquair," he said, going to the door.

Admitting him, Bothwell said, "I have reason to believe the Queen is in some danger. See that extra guards are placed at every access to these chambers, and double the guard around the Prince. Allow no one but Her Majesty's women to enter these chambers."

"Aye, my lord."

Dismissed, Traquair bowed to Mary and left.

Bewildered, Mary asked, "What is happening?"

"A plot, my love, hatched by your own coreligionists and your husband. They mean to destroy you and your nobles. Kirk o' Field was intended as your grave; the vaults are mined with gunpowder."

"It cannot be true." She shook her head slowly, seemingly unable to grasp his meaning. "This is a nightmare—some hideous dream."

"This is no dream." He pulled her to her feet. "I am giving you cold, hard facts."

"No. You must be mistaken. I grant you Harry's faults; he is weak, he lusts for power, but he would not be party to my murder."

"Would he not? Have you forgotten the Rizzio conspiracy? He aimed at your life then, too."

"James and Morton goaded him into it—they promised him the crown matrimonial."

"Just as I imagine others are promising him the regency now."

"He has sworn his affection for me."

"He would swear to anything to gain his ends."

Her eyes had a dazed expression. He seized her out of desperation to make her understand and shook her violently. Her jeweled snood worked loose from her hair and fell to the floor.

"Listen to me," he shouted. "Your husband has betrayed you. He is power-mad. Only you stand in the way of his ambition."

"How could he have kept it so well hidden? Harry is like a child with secrets; he blurts them to everyone. Surely we would have heard rumors."

"There have been rumors aplenty for months, but nothing came even close to the truth. You mind he kept the secret of the Rizzio consipracy well enough—we had no warning of that either."

"When—does he plan to carry it out?"

"Tomorrow morning, I think, when we are all gathered in the house. Now I know why he took on so when you left to attend the wedding masque. He wanted you to sleep at Kirk o' Field to be sure of your whereabouts. Once everyone was safely inside, he could escape and leave us to our prepared fate."

"How do you know all this?" Horror had turned her skin ashen against the white ermine.

"From Darnley's servant. Some of it I learned late last night; the rest Paris had from him this morning."

"Why did you wait until now to tell me?"

"I've been here near an hour trying to convince you, yet you still doubt me. If you knew earlier you might have betrayed yourself while you were with him. Also, I needed time to gather proof."

"You have that proof now?"

"All I need. Do you recall remarking on Paris' begrimed state? He got that way examining the vaults at Kirk o' Field. Durham spoke the truth," he said grimly.

"What will you do with Harry?"

He had primed himself for that question. Doubtless she would argue against it, and though he hoped for her consent, he was prepared to go ahead without it. "He will be taken in ward. This time he will not escape punishment for his treacheries, for even you cannot save him now."

"He will not go without a struggle."

"That occurred to me."

"Is there no other way?"

"None. He brought this upon himself. You gave him every chance to reform, but he would not—rather, I think he could not. It's as though there is a devil inside of him that compels him to do these things."

"These last days he spoke so sincerely, I believed he might change." Her voice caught on a dry sob. "God knows I want to be rid of him—" She looked at him; a faint glimmer of hope remained. "You may still be mistaken. Perhaps, like myself, he too is an intended victim."

"Deceive yourself awhile longer, if you must. Shortly, you and all of Edinburgh will have proof of what he is."

He went to the door.

"Wait," she called. "What of your own danger? You might

be killed. I would sooner let them have their way with me than lose you."

She ran into his outstretched arms. He kissed her deeply, held her for a moment. "Don't worry about me," he murmured. "I'll be back, hale and scart, with Darnley trussed up and ready for the hangman."

CHAPTER XV

1

Bothwell hurried to his apartments to change clothes. Thankfully, Jean was asleep; there would be no need to make excuses for going out. He threw a heavy wool cloak over his leather jack and went across the hall to collect his men. Dalgleish, Powrie, and Wilson came out first, and the others followed. Paris walked at Bothwell's side, puffed with pride for the confidence they shared.

The palace guard challenged them, then passed them through when they told him, "Friends of my lord Bothwell." They proceeded up the Cannongate, where they were challenged again; the same answer opened the gates. They walked a space up the High Street, then turned in at Blackfriar's Wynd to call for Ormiston. At the monastery gate, Bothwell whistled a signal. Hepburn and Hay, the lookouts he had posted there earlier, stepped out of the dark.

"Have you anything to report?" Bothwell asked.

Hay moved closer to the torchbearer to warm his hands. "Aye, my lord. Archie Douglas and some men came this way more than half an hour ago. They are still about on the south side of the house, beyond the postern gate."

Bothwell nodded. That seemed to prove that Douglas had sure knowledge of the conspiracy.

"Over a score of the King's men are hidden in the surrounding cottages," Hepburn said. "Will the torches not give us away?"

"We've no cause for secrecy," Bothwell told him.

They resumed walking but had gone only a few feet when Bothwell's sharp ears caught the sound of scurrying footsteps. He signaled to Hepburn and Powrie, who moved to cut off the single exit. Bothwell closed in, caught the prowler by the strings of his silk cloak, then drew him out where he could see his face.

"Balfour!" he muttered. "Why are you abroad at this hour?"

Balfour struggled to free himself, but Bothwell's grip tightened. Seeing no way out, Balfour said, "I am on the King's business, my lord."

"Doubtless you are," Bothwell commented dryly. "What manner of business can it be that you must conduct it at two hours after midnight?"

"A private matter, my lord, which I am not at liberty to disclose."

"I think you had better, for I have a suspicious mind and will likely think the worst if you do not. Come," Bothwell urged amiably, "the King's secrets are safe with me."

"No, I cannot betray His Majesty's confidence."

"Not even if I press you?" Bothwell asked, casually toying with the hilt of his dirk.

Balfour was no match for Bothwell alone, much less for the fifteen men who accompanied him. Having been caught here, a few feet from Kirk o' Field, under suspicious circumstances, he was obliged to answer for himself. Still evasive, he said, "It appears that Your Lordship reads some sinister meaning into my being here. Yet I find it equally strange seeing you here with this strong guard."

They could stand here all night havering without Balfour's revealing a thing. To force the issue, Bothwell said, "I am on my way to investigate a rumor concerning the King's lodgings."

"Surely it is not Your Lordship's intention to wake the

household. As you can see, the house is dark—the King and Queen are likely asleep."

Obviously, Balfour had not been told of Mary's last-minute decision to sleep at the palace.

"I assure you the Queen is very much awake, for I have just left her—at Holyrood. As for the King, I'd be no whit surprised to learn that sleep eludes him tonight. Doubtless he is already feeling the scepter's weight in his hands."

Balfour's shoulders sagged on a deep sigh. "How much do you know?" he asked.

"Enough to have prevented the Queen from coming here to sleep. I know it is a Catholic plot with the King as its figurehead." Then, in genuine consternation: "Why should the Queen's coreligionists aim at her life?"

"Rome orders it. Bishop Laureo directs everything from Paris. The King has convinced Rome and Spain that as long as Queen Mary reigns there will be no Catholic revival in Scotland. Laureo's instructions were explicit; dispose of the Queen and the principal of her nobility in one stroke." Balfour shrugged. "Gunpowder seemed the best means. The King set me to watch here to see that nothing would go wrong. In the morning, when the Queen and her nobles were assembled in the house, the King would give the signal to light the fuse, then escape to his waiting horses. The rest you may guess for yourself."

Bothwell listened to Balfour with remarkable calm. "I've known gunpowder to be unreliable. How could you be certain it would have the desired effect?"

"The vaults are heavily mined—there is enough powder stored in them to demolish several houses."

"Since the house belongs to your brother, I presume you have the keys to it."

Balfour nodded, reached into his cloak, and withdrew a ring with several large keys attached to it. He held them out to Bothwell.

Bothwell refused them. "We will need only the basement key, which you will find for us."

"What need to go there now, my lord? I have told you everything."

"I want to see for myself this trap you've laid."

"Believe me, the powder is there. Our coming will be mistaken for the prearranged signal—they will light the fuse."

"Let them. Since the King has his heart set on an explosion, I will oblige him with one."

Bothwell prodded Balfour forward. They walked a short space and came into the east garden of Kirk o' Field. It was too dark to see in through the window that faced the garden. "The key," Bothwell said to Balfour. "Find it and unlock the basement door."

Bothwell was nearly at the door when Hepburn lunged forward to pull him back roughly. There was a deafening roar, thunder shattered the night, the earth trembled, then stilled. A blinding flash illuminated the sky, and Darnley's house splintered into the air, raining a shower of stones and debris to the ground. The wind blew gusts of smoke and dust into their faces; their eyes teared with the pungent sting of gunpowder.

Nothing of the house was left standing; only a pile of rubble lay scattered about. Had it not been for Hepburn's alertness, Bothwell would now be lying buried under it. No one seemed able to move; Bothwell and his men stood frozen in their tracks. Bothwell had been somewhat prepared for the explosion, but his men had had no warning. He was familiar with the effects of gunpowder, yet, like them, he stood paralyzed, unable to grasp what he saw.

Had Sandy Durham not taken fright, Mary would be at the bottom of that ruin, her body blackened, mangled beyond recognition. He too would have been caught in the blast, for he would have been in her escort. All at once he was enraged and depressed: rage for the pitiless youth who would have made this pile of rubble Mary's grave; depression for Mary, who would learn the truth about her husband tonight.

Abruptly, Bothwell came out of his reverie; surely the entire town was awake by now—the deepest slumberer could not ignore that loud report. No one had come out yet, but he knew it was only a matter of seconds before someone did. Suddenly he realized his folly in coming here with only his handpicked retainers. Neither he nor his men could take the risk of being found here; their presence would be certain to arouse suspicion among the townsfolk who saw them. Glancing about, he saw there were lights already showing in nearby cottages.

Then he thought of Darnley; there was not a sign of him anywhere. Had he been caught in the explosion, or had he made good his escape? He remembered the Douglases in the south garden; they could have taken Darnley in hand. He looked around for Balfour and saw that he had taken flight. He and his men had best do the same.

"Come away, quickly," Bothwell said, slapping Dalgleish and Powrie on their backs to rouse them.

The sound of his voice snapped the others into motion. They followed him through the Black Friars' gardens, over a break in the town wall, on to Holyrood by the Back o' the Cannongate. As though on signal, lights came from houses; voices made strange by fear and wonder could be heard coming from all directions. Noise shrilled the air with a frenzied pitch; children wailed, hounds bayed, men shouted, horses stomped and snorted, all in one great conglomeration of sound—it was a night thrown into chaos.

Luckily Bothwell's hastily chosen route kept them out of everyone's path. They heard the clamor but saw none of it, and by the same good luck, no one saw them. Their luck held at the palace too; they found disorder there as in the streets; sentries had deserted their posts to seek an explanation for what must have seemed the firing of a thousand cannons. This too must have crossed the conspirators' minds, Bothwell thought as he ran to his apartments. With the guards and the palace thrown into confusion, they could have taken the Prince from his nursery before anyone knew it.

2

Paris seized a robe and slippers from the wardrobe and handed them to Bothwell. Shouting drifted up from the palace grounds; hoofbeats thundered by.

Bothwell belted his robe and stepped into his slippers. "Fetch me a drink," he said.

Suddenly there was a pounding at his outer door. Paris started forward, but Bothwell pulled him back. "The drink," he said. "I will see who it is."

He let another minute go by; then, tousling his hair, he went to the door and opened it. A very pale and badly shaken Huntly stood before him. Bothwell pulled him in by the sleeve of his robe.

Huntly stared blankly at him. He stammered, "The noise— you heard?"

"Aye."

"Then Durham's story was true."

Bothwell nodded impatiently.

"I have just come from the guard hall where the Laird of Traquair had it from a rider sent to investigate. The house is in ruins—the King likely with it."

"I fear you may be right, for we never saw a sign of him from the time we arrived to the time we left—unless Archie Douglas has him."

"Was Douglas there, too?"

"Aye, my men saw him."

Huntly seemed utterly shocked and bewildered; Bothwell

had told him everything he knew earlier, yet he acted as though he had been taken by surprise.

"Has anyone told the Queen?" Bothwell asked.

Huntly shook his head. "I am on my way to her now."

Jean came out of the bedchamber. Seeing her brother, she closed her robe modestly. Her voice still drowsy with sleep, she asked, "What is amiss, my lords? There are men and horses abroad in the gardens, and you deep in talk at such an hour."

Bothwell turned. "It is the King, my lady; he is feared to be dead. His house has been blown to the sky by some mysterious means." Jean was a sound sleeper, their bedchamber faced the back of the palace, and the explosion may not have awakened her.

She gasped. "What of the Queen? She declared her intention to sleep there tonight."

"She is here in the palace, safe and sound—by the grace of God."

"A miracle," Huntly murmured. "Only a miracle saved her."

Bothwell took Huntly's arm roughly. "Come, my lord, we must go to Her Majesty." To Jean he said, "Keep to your chambers, my lady; there may still be some danger."

They hurried to Mary's apartments. Huntly prattled on about whether it would be wiser to wait for morning on the chance that Mary was asleep. Bothwell only half-listened; he knew that Mary was not only awake but awaiting his return with taut nerves. Aye, waiting and still hoping that he had been mistaken. For her sake he too had half-hoped to find that Durham had lied. He despised the grim task that had fallen to him—better it had been someone else to bring her this proof.

They walked through the torchlit inner quadrangle, heavily guarded by Traquair's men. Armed sentries guarded the entrance to the royal apartments. Bothwell and Huntly climbed the broad stairway hurriedly. At Mary's door the guards saluted Bothwell; they were Borderers, his men.

Margaret Carwood, Mary's tiring woman, admitted them. She curtsied. "Thank God you have come, my lords," she said. "The Queen behaves so strangely. She would not permit her ladies to prepare her for bed. She knelt there"—Carwood pointed to the small oratory between two stained-glass windows—"praying, until we heard that terrible report—it was like the wrath of God crashing down on us. I looked at the Queen; her body was rigid with fright. She tried to rise and would have fallen had I not caught her in time."

Huntly clucked his tongue. "Did you send for her physician?"

"Her Majesty forbade me."

"Where is she now?" Bothwell asked.

"In her bedchamber, my lord. I will announce you."

"No," Bothwell said. "You may go, but stay near, for you will be needed again."

She curtsied again and left.

Bothwell crossed to Mary's bedchamber door, knocked, then went in. Still in her ball gown, Mary lay sprawled across the bed. She had not answered his knock; she hadn't even looked up when he came in.

He sat down on the bed and touched her lightly. "Mary," he said softly.

She jerked herself up to a sitting position and fell into his arms. "Thank God you are safe," she said, burying her face against him.

Her fingers twisted the quilted lapels of his robe. He soothed her, stroking her hair. "Hush," he murmured, "you've nothing to fear now."

"It was all true," she said dully. "I prayed you were mistaken, that it would prove a hideous lie. Can you ever forgive me for doubting you?"

"There is nothing to forgive, dearest. Who would have

dreamed he was so desperate, far less that the Papists would be his accomplices?"

"To think that I let his fair words and false promises move me to pity. How you must despise me for my gullibility."

He tilted her face up to his. "I adore you for your gentleness."

She shook her head. "I thought Davie's murder had made me hard; it merely taught me to hate—and that for only a while. I forgave Harry in the past, but I will not forgive him again—he will have the punishment he deserves."

"That decision may no longer rest with you."

"What do you mean?"

"If my suspicions prove correct, he fell victim to the trap he intended for you."

"You said he would be taken in ward. Where is he?"

"Lying at the bottom of a rubble heap, for all I know. He never showed himself to me or my men."

She looked at him in horrified disbelief and made the sign of the crucifix across her breast. Clinging to him, her body trembled with sobs. He held her, feeling himself torn between compassion and rage—the one because it was that same gentleness he loved that moved her to tears, the other because she wept for a worthless boy who would be laughing now were she lying in his place.

He pulled free of her grasp and brought her to her feet. Her eyes were dry; she looked at him blankly, and he shuddered—it was like looking into the eyes of the dead. He had mistaken her convulsive sobs for weeping. Now he regretted that she could not weep, for tears would give her the release she needed.

She was limp in his arms. He sat her down and went for wine. "Drink this," he said, forcing the cup between her lips.

She swallowed, then coughed. He had given it to her full strength, without water as she usually took it. She tried to push it away. "More," he said, "you need it."

She took two more sips; it brought some color back to her face. The wine had revived her, for she seemed more in her senses now.

Bothwell knelt at her feet, took her hands in his. "Listen to me," he said. "Pay close attention, for if you blunder it may prove your undoing. There will be others here soon; your first reaction is of the utmost importance. You are distraught with grief, your husband may be dead—no one is certain yet. Do you understand me?"

She nodded.

"You had no warning of tonight's tragedy, or some may wonder why you did nothing to prevent it. Order Huntly to accompany me to Kirk o' Field. A crime has been committed; as sheriff, it is my duty to investigate. After we have made a thorough search of the area, we will report our findings to you. Above all, say nothing of our talk earlier. When we have gone I want you to go to bed, try to rest, even if you can't sleep. Promise me you will at least try."

She nodded again.

"I will go out first; follow me in a few minutes."

He turned to go, then he went back to her. "Remember that I love you," he said, "and that you are not alone."

She grasped his hand, brought it to her lips. He bent to her, kissed the top of her head, and went out.

Traquair had joined Huntly in the audience chamber.

"You told her?" Huntly asked Bothwell.

"Aye."

"How did she take it?"

"She is sorrowful and quiet."

Huntly shook his head sadly. "Tragedy follows her like an evil star."

When Mary came out, Huntly rushed forward to offer his arm. She took it with a grateful nod and allowed him to lead her to a chair. She dabbed at her eyes with a handkerchief. "There is little I can say, my lords, except that this crime shall not go unavenged. Go to Kirk o' Field, find out what you can, then report back to me."

Vehemently, Huntly said, "We shall not rest until the culprits are brought to justice, madam."

"We have our orders, my lord," Bothwell said from the doorway.

On the stairway, Traquair said, "Thank God you were forewarned. Without that, Her Majesty too might be among the victims now."

"Forewarned, aye," Bothwell said, "but never of this. The precautions I had you take earlier were based solely upon rumor. I had no hint of this terrible tragedy."

3

Bothwell dressed again, gathered his men, met Huntly in the courtyard, then rode off to Kirk o' Field. Everywhere they looked, people with cloaks thrown hastily over their nightclothes stood in doorways and on corners talking. Remnants of Carnival Sunday cluttered the streets and clogged the drains with bits of streamers and discarded food.

The crowds were thicker at Blackfriar's Wynd. Bothwell called ahead to make way for his party. He heard his name whispered by the onlookers, then passed on to others along the way. The stench of gunpowder filled the narrow wynd, smarting the eyes. Huntly pulled a cloth from his sleeve and held it to his nose. They dismounted before coming upon the ruin and walked the rest of the way.

Huntly stopped abruptly. "There is nothing of the house left standing," he said.

"Only the gallery," Bothwell said, pointing to a structure that rested on the town wall.

Soldiers, sent from the palace, were extinguishing the last flames. They picked over rubble, tossing aside broken bits of furniture, stone, and singed tapestries, searching for bodies.

"Have you found anything?" Bothwell asked.

"Aye, my lord. We have the bodies of four men—though it is difficult to be certain, for they were blown to bits and scattered in all directions."

"Is the King among them?"

"No, my lord. We discovered him some distance away, lying dead in the south garden, his servant beside him."

Bothwell and Huntly went through the postern gate and into the garden, where more soldiers stood guard over the bodies of Darnley and Taylor. What they saw was more grisly by contrast than a dozen mangled corpses.

Darnley lay on his back in the snow, his arms at his sides, his nightshirt drawn up to his waist, looking as though he were in innocent sleep. Taylor lay close to him, face down in a kneeling position, wearing a nightshirt, cap, and a slipper on one foot.

Bothwell knelt over Darnley and ordered a torch brought near. He turned the face from side to side, then examined the body for any telltale marks of gunpowder or bruises. Finding none, he repeated the examination on Taylor, with similar results.

Huntly squatted down beside him, staring in puzzlement at Taylor's corpse. "What do you make of it?" he asked. "I judge this spot to be no less than eighty paces from the house, yet both were blown into the air to land here without a blemish. Can it be?"

Bothwell frowned. "It seems incredible—I don't know what to make of it."

He reenacted the scene in his mind as it had been when the house exploded. He and his men had been in the east garden, hidden by the house from the Douglases, who were in the south garden. If Darnley hadn't been caught in the explosion, then he would have had to make his escape through a door into the south garden. . . . Bothwell got to his feet and saw the questioning faces surrounding him, frightened, confused faces, looking to him for answers—he could not satisfy his own questions, let alone theirs.

"Who discovered the bodies?" he asked a soldier.

"I did, my lord." A small, whiskered man stepped out of the crowd. "I came this way from my house to see about the confusion."

"Did you disturb anything?"

"Nothing, my lord."

Bothwell addressed the soldier again. "Is everything just as you found it? Nothing has been touched?"

"Aye, my lord. Nothing."

Here was a mystery that defied solution; even if, by some miracle, Darnley and Taylor had been blown eighty feet in the air without suffering a scratch or blemish, their faces and clothes would have been singed or blackened. More strange were the robe and quilt neatly folded beside the chair. It was beyond all reason to imagine these objects could have landed in their present state. Bothwell had used gunpowder often enough to know its trickiness; sometimes it destroyed only a portion of the objective, leaving other parts completely intact—here destruction had been complete. Then he remembered Darnley's servants; only four bodies had been found. What of the others? There had been eight servants at least, not counting the cook, Bonkil, and his assistants, who usually slept in the basement.

"Were there no survivors?" Bothwell asked the soldiers.

"Aye, my lord," one told him. "Of the three who slept in the gallery next to the King's bedchamber, all were saved. They escaped with only minor injuries. We found them wandering about, dazed, and took them to a nearby cottage for treatment."

"Bring them here for questioning."

The soldier went off to his errand as Huntly came up with a woman in tow. "Tell His Lordship what you told me," he said.

She shrank back, pulling her woolen shawl more tightly about her nightdress.

"What evidence can you give us?" Bothwell asked, scowling.

She curtsied and took a deep breath to muster courage. "It was shortly before the explosion, Your Lordship. I heard a disturbance coming from this garden. My cottage is but a small distance away, and though I could see nothing for the dark, sound traveled clearly."

"What did you hear?"

"Strange sounds, my lord. Shuffling, grunting, a few muffled cries. A man's voice cried out, 'Pity me, kinsmen, for the love of God.' Then it was quiet again—until the explosion."

Kinsmen! That struck a familiar chord—the Douglases were kinsmen to Darnley on his mother's side.

"Did you recognize the voice?"

"No, my lord, but it was high-pitched, thin and very high. Somewhat like a woman's—yet that of a man."

Bothwell knew only one voice to fit that description—Darnley's. It had to be Darnley, just as it had to be the Douglases who had murdered him—smothered him with his own nightshirt from the look of it.

Bothwell addressed himself to the crowd. "Is there anyone else who has evidence to give?"

Another woman stepped forward. She was less timid than the first. "I, my lord. When I ran from the house to Blackfriar's Gate after the explosion I saw several men running from this direction. I caught one by his silk cloak, but he shook me off and ran after the others."

"Did you recognize anyone?"

"No, it was too dark, my lord. I could scarce find my own way."

By now the soldier had returned with the trio of survivors.

They were Symonds, Nelson, and the ill-fated Taylor's son. Their accounts of the hours before the explosion tallied in every detail. After Mary and her party had left, Darnley called for wine and sang a Psalm before going to sleep. Symonds said it was the Fifth Psalm; Nelson insisted that it was the Fifty-fifth.

Bothwell waved the dispute aside and they resumed. Afterward, Darnley had wished them all a good night, then gone to bed. Nelson recalled snuffing out the last candle as Taylor lay down on his trundle bed. They could recall nothing more until they had been awakened by the blast. They could report nothing unusual, nothing that had aroused their suspicion.

Convinced that he would learn nothing more from them, Bothwell dismissed them and went to the ruins where the house had stood. One of the searchers had found a powder barrel; it was designed to carry one hundred pounds of powder. Bothwell ordered that it be kept for evidence, then he gave instructions for Darnley's body to be carried to the new provost's house in the care of servants. That done, he started back to Holyrood with Huntly.

On the way, Bothwell showed Huntly a man's slipper which he had found in the garden not far from Darnley's corpse. It was of deep-blue velvet, ornamented with a buckle of solid gold.

"Have you ever seen it before?" Bothwell asked.

Huntly turned it over in his hands. "Dozens of times, no doubt, but then who takes note of another man's footgear?"

"Aye, it will be difficult to trace—and it's not likely the owner will be eager to come forward to claim it."

4

Bothwell waited until midmorning to make his report to Mary. Mounting the stairway to her apartments, he saw that everything had been draped in mourning cloth; even the windows of her audience chamber had been hung with black. He frowned on the morbidness, wishing that she could dispense with that ancient custom of shutting out the daylight—but doing so would lay her open to a charge of callousness.

Fleming told him that Mary had slept a little and that she was awake now, though still in bed. When she heard his voice, Mary peered out from the bed-curtains and dismissed her women.

When they were alone, Bothwell went to her and embraced her briefly.

"Why didn't you return to me last night?" she asked, settling back against the pillows.

"I did, but Carwood told me you were asleep—I thought you needed that more."

She touched the tiny lines of weariness around his eyes. "You look so tired."

He had taken no rest at all; the strain of last night's gory work showed on his face.

"What did you find at Kirk o' Field?"

"This first," he said, placing a tray with an egg and a cup of warm milk in her lap.

She ate, though it seemed an effort for her to swallow. Then he gave her the details. She listened without interruption, her fingers tightly clenched in the furred coverlet.

When he had finished, she said, "But you told me last night that Harry had been blown up with the house."

"So I thought when he failed to appear—until I saw his body and realized the Douglases had strangled him. Huntly and I mulled it over several times. We've reached the same conclusion; he had to have met his death by Douglas hands. My men saw them there; no one else could have done it."

"You are certain it was Archie Douglas?"

"Aye, and Darnley's cry of 'Pity me, kinsmen,' confirms it. Archie Douglas knew of the plot before I did—his lack of surprise when I visited him yesterday betrayed him. James knew too, which accounts for his sudden departure from town."

"Without first warning me?"

"Aye, but not without warning Lethington, who, if you recall, declined the invitation to Moretta's farewell supper rather than risk accompanying you to Kirk o' Field. If you doubt me, this may convince you: before leaving town yesterday, James was overheard to say that 'ere another day dawned, Darnley would be cured of all his troubles.' What other meaning can you attach to that remark? I am certain that James ordered Archie Douglas to Kirk o' Field last night."

Grief-stricken, her face revealed utter despair. It had taken this to finally make her see what James was. Despite his treacheries and betrayals, she had always protected him, and Bothwell suddenly understood the reason. The same blood ran in their veins; she had clung to James because he represented the father she had never known.

"You should have let me die at Kirk o' Field," she said.

He longed to cradle her in his arms, to give her the comfort she sorely needed, but he fought against it for fear she would break down completely.

"Aye, surrender to them," he said harshly. "I have seen men ride into battle with only their own two fists for weapons. They were not always victorious—but they fought, and well, too. You will not even make the effort; you accept defeat before the battle begins."

His scorn had roused her from inertia before; it did now again. Her despair turned to anger. "You speak of battlefields," she said. "I envy you the luxury of honest combat—there at least you may exchange blows with an enemy you can see. My enemies are not half as considerate; they creep about in stealth, nameless, shapeless, until they strike."

"I grant you it's been difficult; you've borne treachery and grief, but you can't let them beat you now. Outfox them and you can have the lot of them groveling at your feet."

"How, tell me how?"

"Start by getting out of that bed. Call your women, have them dress in dole weeds, order your Council to meet this afternoon. But first, you must see your husband's body."

She shrank back in horror. "No, you ask too much. I cannot see him; it would be my undoing."

"It will be your undoing if you do not. Think how your indifference will appear to others. Despite what he was, he was your husband, he fathered your child, you made him King. If you seem lacking in proper grief now, the people will take it as an admission of guilt. You could be blamed for his death."

"He sought my life, *I* was the intended victim."

"Granted, but you cannot prove it. His accomplices will not come forward to reveal themselves. There are, however, certain facts that can incriminate you. You pardoned his enemies, men who were sworn to avenge themselves on him. Nor can you bring Archie Douglas to justice for murdering him."

"Then Lennox, Balfour—all of them will go unpunished?"

"Aye, for once you remove the lid from this caldron, its stench will taint us all. Remember, last night you announced your intention to sleep at Kirk o' Field—it was I who talked you out of it. Traquair knows we anticipated some danger; he can testify to that. The obvious question: If you suspected something, why didn't you warn the King?"

"You present a damning case against me—so well, in fact, that I can scarce believe in my own innocence."

"Precisely. To protect yourself, you must also protect those who are guilty." He left her side and went to the foot of the bed. "I will send Fleming and Seton to you. They will help you dress."

Once again he had succeeded in spurring her into action; but for how long? She responded, but not for the right reasons—fear alone had worked where all else had failed. Fear that he would leave her; but when she finally realized he would never leave her—what then?

5

The death knell sounded from every church tower; it had begun at dawn, first the melancholy tolling of the abbey bells, the others following. It was a proper day for mourning. There was no sun, only gray, raw cold with a silent sky and knife-edged winds. The air carried a hint of something ominous, as though the world had suddenly stopped.

Bothwell glanced at the others who waited with him in the courtyard. Like him, they too were clad in mourning. No one spoke; Huntly stood nearest to Bothwell, looking off into the distance toward Arthur's Seat. Argyll intently watched the groom adjusting the black trappings on Mary's horse. Lethington, always ultrasensitive to the cold, drew his fur-lined cloak more tightly about himself and paced. Bothwell noted with wry amusement that he did even this with exacting precision; five paces up, two to turn, then five paces back without once varying it. And Melville was doubtless already rehearsing his version of Kirk o' Field for the English Court.

Bothwell's thoughts were of Mary. She had looked so ill, so lost, scarcely well enough to make a public appearance. He recalled another time, just three weeks ago, when he had waited for her in this same courtyard; he had been worried then, too. That had been the start of her journey to Glasgow. He had told her to smile, for she had looked as though she were going to a funeral. How significant and weird those words seemed now.

Traquair called his mounted bodyguard to attention, for Mary had finally come out. The wind flapped her black veil, giving it the appearance of a trail of charred smoke. She was dressed all in black with no ornaments except for the tiny gold crucifix that sat in the hollow of her neck. Melville offered his arm and helped her to mount.

She sat her horse stiffly, displaying none of her usual grace in the saddle. The procession rode at a solemn pace up the Cannongate, where people had gathered to watch them pass. They gazed at the riders through sullen eyes, no sound coming from their stern, tightly drawn mouths. It was impossible to tell what they were thinking, and Bothwell hoped that for the least they had not yet made up their minds.

At the new provost's house they dismounted, and Bothwell led Mary inside. Surgeons had already examined Darnley; they reported that no marks had been found on his body. Mary stood rigid, flanked by Huntly and Argyll. She glanced down at Darnley without emotion. She neither spoke nor moved; her face, ghostly white beneath her veil, was like a mask. Her eyes, in trancelike stare, held no tears.

Melville touched Bothwell's sleeve. "What is your opinion of this hideous affair, my lord? None whom I have approached seems able to shed any light on it."

Bothwell shrugged. "It is the strangest accident. Perhaps a thunderbolt came out of the sky to burn the King's house. But I find it even more strange that there is neither burn nor bruise on him."

"Aye, a fact noted and remarked on by those who have seen him." Melville paused thoughtfully, then shook his head. "But a thunderbolt," he said skeptically. "I cannot believe the elements caused such havoc."

Lethington came up and rescued Bothwell. Of course, no one would believe thunder had caused the explosion, Bothwell least of all. He had said it facetiously, and Melville, so dour and literal-minded, had taken him seriously.

"We must take the Queen away, my lord," Lethington said. "It does her ill to prolong this."

Indeed Mary was making a poor show of herself. Not that

Bothwell expected her to wail and beat her breast in grief, but the occasion demanded some show of emotion. Yesterday she had appeared the loving, devoted wife; today, in widowhood, she was coldly indifferent—a contrast sharp enough to make the dullest wit wonder. Too sharp, Bothwell thought, not to do her serious hurt.

He went to her. "Come away, madam," he said loudly. "The King is beyond all mortal help now."

She permitted herself to be led away. Bothwell lifted her to the saddle and put the reins into her limp hands. He glanced at the crowd, so intent on watching Mary. They were so close, too close for him to whisper a warning on the unholy spectacle she made.

She was no better when they sat in Council at the Tolbooth. Even their investigation could not hold her interest—not even when a letter arrived from Archbishop Beaton, her ambassador in Paris. Lethington took it from the courier and broke the seal, then he handed it down the table to Mary. She refused it.

Bothwell took it from her. "We will have it read aloud," he said.

She nodded, and he returned it to Lethington, Bothwell only half-listened himself; he was more concerned with Mary. The spark of life he had seen in her bedchamber had already waned. He had had no illusions that it would last, but for it to have gone this soon.... Then his attention was drawn to something he heard Lethington say.

Lethington's smooth voice read without halt. *"On the advice of the Spanish ambassador I beseech Your Majesty to take heed to yourself. I have heard some murmuring likewise by others that there be some surprise to be trafficked to your disfavor.... Further in this matter I have also sought out Queen Catherine, if she had heard any speech intending to your hurt or disadvantage, but to no avail, she thought there was nothing to*

*be feared. . . . Yet I urge Your Majesty to cause the captains of
your guard to be diligent in their office . . ."*

"An odd letter," Argyll said, when it was finished. "Full of
ominous portent, yet signifying nothing clearly."

Lethington tapped his fingers on the table thoughtfully. "If I
construe its cloudy meaning correctly, my lords, I find it more
than odd this letter should reach us exactly one day too late."

"What is the date on it?" Bothwell asked.

Lethington turned to the last page. "The twenty-seventh of
January." He paused. "It occurs to me this letter may serve a
useful purpose, my lords. What better proof than this that the
King's life was not the sole aim of this tragedy? Her Majesty's
life was sought as well."

The letter offered another kind of proof to Bothwell. He
knew that in recent months Darnley had maintained an intimate
correspondence with De Alva, the Spanish ambassador in Paris.
Balfour had told him that the plot had originated in Paris, and
De Alva doubtless knew the details of it. Aye, he had warned
Beaton, but too late.

The Council dealt first with sending an official account of
the murder to foreign courts. When it was drafted, Lethington
read it aloud: "The matter is horrible and so strange as we
believe the like was never heard of in any country. This night
past, being the ninth of February, a little after two hours after
midnight, the house where the King lodged was in an instant
blown in the air, he lying sleeping in his bed. . . . By whom or in
what manner it appears not as yet. But we doubt not that
according to the diligence of our Council, who have already
begun, the matter shall be learned shortly. . . so that we may
punish the perpetrators with such rigor as shall serve for
example of this cruelty to all ages to come. We assure ourselves
that whoever had taken this wicked enterprise in hand dressed it
as well for Her Majesty as for the King. . . . For she by some

chance tarried not all night there by reason of a masque at the palace ... "

Lethington dipped his quill into the inkpot and went to Mary. He indicated a place on the document; she signed without comment. Bothwell signed next and the others followed.

Bothwell proposed they begin an inquiry into the murder. He presented the testimonies of Barbara Martin, who had seen "several men running away from the scene," and May Crockit, who had heard someone cry, "Pity me, kinsmen." Then he told them of finding the slipper near Darnley's body.

Argyll leaned forward. "Can you describe it, my lord?"

Bothwell glanced up sharply. "Deep-blue velvet," he said, watching Argyll closely, "with a large gold buckle."

"Did you lose it, my lord?" Huntly asked.

"No, not I." Argyll smiled. "But I may know who did. Just this morning Archie Douglas told me of losing a slipper of that description in the gloaming last evening on his return from St. Giles. You mind, he lodges in Blackfriar's Wynd and would come that way."

"Then I will see it is returned to him," Bothwell said.

Everyone was playing his part so remarkably well. If Bothwell needed further proof that Archie Douglas was Darnley's assassin, he had it now. Not that it did him any good, for to protect Mary and himself, he had to keep silent. Now he realized that Argyll was also involved in the plot, and he wondered how many more.

"Does this conclude the evidence, my lord?" Argyll asked.

"One item more," Bothwell said. "A powder barrel was discovered near the ruins, but it has mysteriously disappeared before note could be taken of its mark—thus we know nothing of its origin."

Argyll nodded. "Then for the moment we must attribute the crime to unknown miscreants. A watch will be made at all ports and at the border to prevent their escape. A reward of two thousand pounds and a yearly rent will be offered for any information leading to the apprehension of the criminals. We will proclaim a period of national mourning for the King and announce our findings from the Market Cross this afternoon."

As Lord Justice, Argyll fixed his signature and seal to the proclamation, and the meeting was adjourned.

Mary rode back to Holyrood between Huntly and Argyll. The townsfolk were still in the streets, watching, standing ankle-deep in a gray mist that came swirling up from the Nor' Loch. Lethington rode abreast of Bothwell, muffled in his cloak, his eyes trained contemplatively on Mary's back. Bothwell wondered at his thoughts and those of the sea of hostile faces surrounding her.

The inimical mood of the people was overpowering. An unnatural stillness hovered in the air; where were the hawking merchants, the shrilling children, the bustling housewives? There was only the gathering resentment and the death knell.

Bothwell sensed that Mary's real source of danger lay in the chill of their resentment. If she lost the good will of her people, what had she left? Her strength lay in her popularity with them. She had turned the hatred fed them by Knox into love; now he feared that love; a thing so fragile, so delicately balanced, had exploded with Kirk o' Field.

These simple, unsophisticated folk craved the truth; nothing less would appease them. But the truth lay buried in rubble, in the twisting gullies of men's minds; it could never emerge over the layer of scum that covered it. And it suddenly struck Bothwell that Mary, rather than Darnley, could well be the real victim of this tragedy.

Silence greeted them at Holyrood, where more people stood and watched. The last of Mary's bodyguard entered the grounds, and the gates closed behind them. She was safely inside, away from the judicial eyes, the mounting suspicion. These same people who had showered her with cheers and praise and adulation after Rizzio's murder could destroy her now.

CHAPTER XVI

1

Mary remained in seclusion four days, shut away in her chambers behind mourning cloths. Only a few had access to her: Lethington, Argyll, Huntly, and Bothwell, and they all came to her, hoping to bring her out of her lethargy. But no one, not even Bothwell, could pull her from the engulfing apathy that possessed her.

Her Council worked day and night, drafting measures, protecting her relations with Catholic powers. They gave Melville instructions and sent him to the English Court. Letters, documents, and official statements were presented for her approval; she signed them without reading one. Physicians tended her daily, prescribing remedies, but none could touch the source of her illness.

Below her apartments, Darnley's body lay in state. An honor guard had borne his remains to Holyrood the day following his murder. Nobles and gentry came to view his body; Mary never entered the Great Hall.

On the fifth day, Darnley was buried in the abbey vault that held the remains of Mary's father and his first wife, Queen Magdelaine. In deference to his rank, custom demanded that Darnley's coffin be carried through the streets of Edinburgh, followed by his bereaved widow, her nobles, and gentry. Cannon blasts and royal salutes were in order, and the tolling of church bells, but, as Lethington had pointed out, Mary was scarcely in condition to withstand the ordeal.

The less her people saw of her now, the better; her indifference would enrage them. They would expect tears, something to show her sorrow. Her present state would serve only to justify their doubts, for they were already whispering that she had brought Darnley out of Glasgow for sinister purposes.

Therefore, Darnley was laid to rest at night; his body was carried to the abbey vaults in torchlight, followed by a small procession of nobles. Mary knelt in prayer during the brief mass read over him, and the troublesome boy, who was not quite twenty-one, was interred.

Later, while the others sat at the funeral supper, Bothwell went to Mary. He found her in her audience chamber with Seton, embroidering another of her endless altar cloths. He motioned to Seton, and she slipped out quietly.

He did not speak at first, but stood there, looking at Mary, frowning worriedly. Her fingers moved without halt, stitching, pulling the silk thread through the cloth, smoothing, all seemingly without consciousness. Her face was chalk white against her mourning robe; there were deep violet shadows under her eyes.

Mary broke the silence. "Each night I have dismissed my women, expecting you to come to me—but you never do."

He stared at her incredulously. "Are you mad? Would you risk my being seen coming here at such a time?"

"You need risk nothing to be with Jean. She is your wife, therefore entitled to your company without fear of scandal, while I, a mere mistress, lie here languishing for you."

Her jealousy did not anger him; he was too concerned for her state of mind. She seemed broken, beaten, lacking in the will to live. He had watched her retreat from life with a gnawing fear—she seemed to be suffering from a sickness of the soul.

Softly, he said, "Jean returned to Crichton three days ago. She complained of feeling ill, and I wanted her out of this broody atmosphere."

The needle flew more swiftly. "Then why are you still here? I marvel you are not there to hold her hand."

"My place is here with you."

"You may just as well be the other side of the world, for all I have seen of you."

Furiously, he ripped the cloth from her hands and tossed it into the fire. "That is your world," he said, pointing to the flaming fabric. "You want no other."

Stunned, she stared into the fireplace, watching the cloth curl and shrivel to ash. "You are my world," she said.

He rushed to her and drew her into his arms. "No," he said, "only a part of it. Scotland, its people, they are your world, too. Don't discard them," he pleaded.

"Why not? They only wish to destroy me. How often must they try before they succeed?"

"Continue as you are, and they will have no need, for you will have destroyed yourself."

"That might be best for everyone. Without me, the Protestant lords would govern in harmony, and you could live at peace with Jean."

"Knowing you has spoiled me for Jean—and all other women."

She looked deep into his eyes. "Then you do love me?"

"Have I ever given you cause to doubt it? Would I be here now if it were not for that?"

"What kind of love is it that keeps you away from me?"

"The kind that sees the necessity in restoring your reason first. If you will not think of yourself, then think of your son. What of his future? All these months of negotiating with Elizabeth gone to naught because you have suddenly decided to surrender."

"I can't," she sobbed. "My thoughts are in turmoil. You worsen them—hammering at me as you do."

His glance swept the room; the windows were shut tightly and heavily curtained in black, the candles glowed steadily without a flicker, and the tapestries hung against the walls, limp and still. Nothing stirred for lack of air. So had it been for a week; night and day, sunlight and air had been kept out. She was stifling, dying for want of air.

"Small wonder your brain is befogged; you've been cooped up in this stinking staleness too long." He went to the window, drew aside the draperies, and flung it open. "Come," he said, holding his hand out to her.

"I dare not. Someone might see me from the street."

"Who is to see you at this hour?"

She shook her head. "If the guards saw me there would be gossip."

"Gossip be damned," he said, dragging her to the window.

He stood behind her, pinning her body to the window seat, forcing her to lean forward. "Breathe," he ordered, "breathe deeply. Let the air into your lungs." He whipped off her veil and thrust her head forward. "This will clear your brain of the cobwebs that clog it."

He held her that way until she shivered with cold. Then he pulled her back, closed the window, and lowered the draperies. His arms enclosed her; he kissed her cold cheek and warmed her against himself.

"There," he said, "I'll make an apple-cheeked lass of you yet."

He felt her tears on his face; she leaned against him and wept, sobbing uncontrollably. Sobs that he knew would melt her heartache and bring her back to life.

At last she quieted and looked up at him, half-smiling with embarrassment. "Now you have seen me at my worst," she said. "Weeping is such an ugly sight."

"Aye," he teased gently, "you are a right awful mess, puffy-eyed, red-nosed, and ugly. You had best repair the damage immediately, or Seton will think I have been beating you."

She went to her dressing table. He followed and watched her apply powder to her nose and eyes.

When she had finished, he said, "Arnault approached me today. As your physician, he feels this seclusion is hurtful to you. He recommends a change of scenery. I agree."

"But I cannot leave now. How can I end my mourning after only a week?"

He ignored her protest. "Tomorrow I will present Arnault's recommendation to the Council. I have no doubt but they too will agree. A public announcement to the effect that your seclusion at Holyrood is endangering your health will satisfy the people."

"I'll not quarrel with leaving here for a while," she said. "There are too many ghosts that haunt these chambers. But you cannot leave; your duties keep you here, and I will not go without you."

"You'll go—you must for your own good. Choose a place where I can visit you often."

"Seton House—you can be there and back in the same day."

"Seton House it is then. I'll leave that for you to tell the Council."

He smiled and opened his arms to her. There was a touch of the old sparkle in her eyes; even her cheeks showed a bit of pink. He thought: *Awhile at Seton, and she will be good as new.* The strong sea air, relaxing among friends, away from the dour climate of Edinburgh, would work wonders for her. She always responded well to the outdoors.

She cuddled close and ran her fingers over his face caressingly. "What spell have you cast over me that I am brought to life by the touch of your hands and the sound of your voice?"

He made a sinister face. "Witchcraft, taught me on a craggy mountaintop by a wizened old hag."

"Janet Beaton is no hag—though she is fifty."

"Aye, she is still a handsome woman, a marvel for her age. But what brought Janet to mind?" He held her off and laughed. "Surely you don't believe that nonsense about her?"

"Folk say she is a sorceress and practices her black arts in her tower at Branxholm. Even Reres, her own sister, suspects it is true. They say that you learned witchcraft from her."

"What nonsense, what utter nonsense. Janet is no more a witch than you are. She's taught me many things, but never that." His eyes twinkled with amusement. "Though I will admit a bit of magic would come in handy now and then. Now, for example, if it were in my power, I'd cast a spell to transport us to a wee stone cottage hidden in a vale among the Cheviots. I would command the winds to howl, the rain to fall, with a crack of lightning—"

"Please," she said, "no lightning. I fear it so."

"Very well, then, no lightning. A pity though, since I owe it so much thanks." He paused to think of that afternoon in the old Roman peel tower. "Now, to get on with my spell—we would be completely alone, not a soul for miles around, only you and I with nothing to do but make love, day and night. Does that please you?"

She nodded and snuggled closer. "You make me sorry that you are not a sorcerer."

"Aye."

He too was caught up in the dream; he had painted the picture so vividly that it seemed almost real. What wouldn't he give to be there with her now? But he was too practical for dreams; the hostile world lay too close outside her door.

He felt her slump against him; she was exhausted. Arnault had told him that she had scarcely slept all that week. Nightmares disturbed her rest, memories haunted her days.

He released her. "Can you sleep now?"

She nodded. "Suddenly I am very weary."

"Good, then I will send for Seton."

2

He was glad to have her out of Edinburgh. Mary had left for Seton two days after Darnley's burial, and none too soon. A fever began to spread over the town, spawned in dark wynds and closes by whispers, fanned by jealous hatred. Dead only a week, Darnley had become the *poor slaughtered lamb*. The people were quick to forget their ridicule of him, and that his debaucheries had been sinful and offensive to them.

Now he was remembered as a fun-loving lad, much given to sports and harmless revelry. His nightly rounds of taverns and brothels—what of it? He was young, too young to accept the weighty responsibilities of his position. His treacheries? That too a condition of his youth. Everyone agreed that evil had great sway with a youthful mind; given time and proper counsel he would have changed.

And so it went. They clamored for arrests, but none were made. Will Blackadder and James Cullen were arrested on the night of the murder for being at the scene, but lack of evidence had them soon released. Someone claimed he had seen Sir James Balfour that night, skulking about Rapperlaw Close, a stone's throw from Darnley's house—but Balfour was missing from town since that night and hadn't been seen since.

There was a dark hint of three women being sought, women who lived in a house nearest the garden where Darnley was found. It was said they could testify to the presence of eight heavily armed men who hid in their house. And still another unnamed witness had seen a light go out in Hamilton House at the same instant Darnley's house was blown up.

There the Council had it: a trail of rumors and clues long

enough to lead them to oblivion and back. Had they wished, these same Council members could have shed considerable light on matters to solve the crime. But who among them could be accused of such folly?

Lethington? He was in the thick of it with James and Morton. He knew the purpose of Archie Douglas' mission that night—he may even have instigated the murder. Argyll? He too was deeply involved. Why else had he troubled over Archie Douglas' slipper? Huntly? He knew the truth and with it the need for silence. Bothwell? If he told all he knew, Mary and himself would be dragged down with their enemies. There were pitifully few of the nobility who were not involved. So, with brows knit in feigned consternation, they all kept silent.

The day following her departure, Bothwell was doubly glad that Mary had gone. The cause of his gratitude lay pinned to the Tolbooth door while he rode up the High Street early that morning. It was a placard naming him as Darnley's murderer, along with Balfour, Chalmers, and Mr. John Spens. But the worst of it came lower down: *the Queen assenting thereto.* Muttering an oath, he ripped the placard off and doubled back to Holyrood with it crumpled in his fist.

"It begins," he said, tossing the libelous sheet at Huntly. "They suspected the Bastard and Morton at first—but that was soon squelched."

"What do you intend doing about it?"

"Nothing for the present. It may be the work of a crackpot, then again not." He snatched the paper away, read it again. "This much I can tell you; the author is an educated man—he's made a fine job of the printing."

"This could be serious," Huntly said. "The people are angry; their mood grows uglier each day. They cry vengeance for the King's murder—someone to pay with his life to the deed."

Bothwell crumpled the placard and threw it into the fire. "Do you imagine I am not aware of the danger? I dread to think what might happen if—" He stopped himself. "It's too soon to panic. There is only the one, and that lies in ashes now. This may be the last of it."

"Do you suppose Lennox had a hand in it?"

"To what purpose? He has more to hide than any of us. Why do you suppose he refused the Queen's invitation to take part in the Council's inquiry? You mind, he was a scant eight miles away the night of the explosion. Aye, camped with his men at Linlithgow, awaiting word from Darnley, no doubt, that the Queen and her nobles had been well disposed of."

"He appears to have gathered courage since. There is his letter of two days ago, demanding a full Parliamentary inquiry. He seems dissatisfied with the Council's handling of it, and may have instigated the placard to stir matters up."

"I think not. If Lennox intends doing anything, he will wait to learn just how much we know, and how far he is implicated. He can't be certain yet how much the Queen knows, or what she will do. No, I think Lennox will remain in safety for the time being. And I too will wait, to see if our anonymous friend will strike again."

Two nights later the phantom libeler struck again. More names were added to the list: Mary's servants, Sebastien Pagez, and Rizzio's brother, Joseph. And the defamer broadened his range, for he had stuck his handiwork everywhere; on the salt Tron, the Market Cross, church doors, the city gates, even the palace gates.

Bothwell could not ignore the fact that he had become the victim of a full-scale libel campaign. Portraits of him with the line *"Here is the Murderer!"* were dropped in the streets. Someone roamed the wynds and closes at night, crying his name, shouting his guilt. At his command, soldiers were sent out to catch the billstickers red-handed. They peered into haar-shrouded wynds, rain-drenched closes, grappled with shadows, but caught no one. Each morning there appeared a fresh batch of posters.

"Perhaps if you left town for a while," Huntly suggested. "You could remain on the Border until this blows over."

"That would be the worst possible thing I could do. It would be taken as an admission of my guilt." Bothwell leaned against the mantelpiece while he spoke, one hand resting on his dagger hilt.

It was a habit he had taken to these days; indoors or out, whenever someone approached him, his hand flew instinctively to his dagger and rested there until the person had gone. His nerves were raw with tension; though he despised the need, a bodyguard of fifty armed men was always at his side—his unseen attackers were frustrating him.

It infuriated him to rely on the protection of others; he had always had sufficient confidence in himself and feared no man. But how could he fight a phantom? Where could he seek it out? How could he know where it would strike next?

He recalled Mary's words: *My enemies creep about in stealth, nameless and shapeless.* He hadn't fully realized her meaning—until now. The unseen dirk, ready to strike when least expected. He would sooner face the bloodiest battle without benefit of weapons than suffer this anguish.

He pounded his fist against the wall. "If he would just come out into the open. Let whoever it is accuse me to my face—I could deal with that. It's not knowing that drives me to distraction."

"What good does it do you to rant and rave?" Huntly said. "This is a time for clear thinking; you must remain calm, or these placards will have done their work. The author has only accused you thus far, but he has no proof with which to back up his claims."

"What proof does he need? Public opinion has already found me guilty. I've seen their looks, heard their murmurings—

they've already convicted me. They regard me with such loathing—as though I carried the plague in my pockets."

"Why let public sentiment affect you? Admittedly their feelings run high now, but like the sea, tides change, and with them the current. Besides, your power is so great now that none can touch you. You command the Realm's strongest fortresses—with that, and the superiority of Leith, you have nothing to fear."

Bothwell turned on him angrily. "Good Christ! Do you think it's concern for myself? Aye, there's fear in me, a sick, deadening fear—but not for myself. I've faced slander before and care nothing for public opinion."

As he spoke he called to mind the latest posters found only that morning. One on the palace gates showed the letters M.R. in very large print surmounting an arm brandishing a sword and, just as great, the letters L.B. over a mallet. Another on the Tolbooth door had depicted Mary as a mermaid and Bothwell as a hare.

"It's these threats against the Queen that trouble me," Bothwell said. "The people are beginning to believe in her complicity. They say she lured Darnley to Kirk o' Field so his enemies could make short work of him. Even the bed that was removed at Darnley's request—likely he treasured it too much to bear its destruction—is used against her. They say 'she spared her bed but not her husband.' I tell you she sits her throne precariously—and thrones, like men, may topple."

"Aye," Huntly murmured.

Bothwell turned to look at him; did he detect a note of malice in Huntly's tone? Something in Huntly's attitude seemed odd—it was not so much malicious as contemplative. Now that he recalled, Bothwell remembered another remark that Huntly had made a few days ago.

Argyll had observed that some of the tapestries destroyed in the explosion had once hung in the Great Hall at Corrichie.

They, like other treasures, had been confiscated by the Crown after the old Earl of Huntly had died. Huntly had said to Argyll, "Perhaps those tapestries were better burned than hanging in strange halls."

Now Bothwell wondered if Huntly still bore a resentment toward Mary for his family's ruin. It had all been James' doing, and Mary had unwittingly supported his acquisitiveness. She knew only what James had told her, that the elder Huntly had gone against her authority. Possibly Huntly had never forgiven her; he might still be brooding over the past.

Then he turned away, ashamed of his thoughts; his nerves were so on edge that he was even beginning to doubt his friends. Huntly was devoted to Mary; he had never been anything but loyal. He had proved his loyalty at Rizzio's murder, and more recently at Kirk o' Field.

Bothwell was suddenly aware of Huntly's steady gaze on his back. Doubtless Huntly wondered at the abrupt silence. How much time had passed since he had spoken? One minute, ten, twenty? How long did it take to crowd the mind with insane suspicions?

They passed Lethington on the way down, and he called to them. "Wait up, my lords." He caught up to them and fell into step. "I am told there were more placards found this morning."

Bothwell nodded curtly.

Huntly said, "There must be an end to them before matters are entirely out of hand. The Queen's good name is at stake, as well as my lord Bothwell's."

"I agree," Lethington said, turning to Bothwell. "Have you no clue to the author's identity?"

"If I had, do you think he would still be at large?"

"I marvel that you venture out after nightfall, my lord. Despite your bodyguard, a lesser man would have given way under the strain."

"I am not so easily intimidated."

"Admirable, most admirable. But never fear, the Council is investigating the matter. The billstickers will eventually be caught."

"Aye, and when they are, I will wash my hands in their blood."

3

Mary was at Seton a week when Bothwell and Huntly rode down to stay for a few days. The placards were foremost on everyone's mind, and they spoke of that first. Mary had learned of them two days ago and had instructed the Council to spare no effort in finding the authors.

There was at least one bright spot to the day; she showed a marked improvement in both her appearance and her state of mind. She was alive again; her eyes had lost their haunted look, but more, she could find reason to smile. This is what Bothwell had hoped for when he sent her away. Lord Seton and his daughter adored Mary; they could be depended upon to spoil and pamper her—she had to improve in that atmosphere.

As he watched Lord Seton host the midday meal, Bothwell felt a sense of envy; the slime of politics had not touched this man. Seton had managed to remain aloof from court intrigues; he lived in peace, tending his orchards and land and breeding horses. His simple, untroubled life seemed appealing for the moment, and Bothwell found himself wondering if he would ever know such tranquillity.

Later, Mary and Bothwell went for a walk on the beach. Mary Seton wrapped her precious charge in a heavy furred cloak, fussing over her as though she were a child.

"See that you don't stay out too long, lest Her Majesty take a chill," Lord Seton warned.

They walked along the sloping path to the beach in silence.

When they were out of view from the house, Bothwell pulled Mary into his arms and kissed her hungrily.

"I've missed you," he murmured.

Her velvet-gloved fingers caressed his face, lingered for a moment on his temples, and came to rest on his eyelids. He felt the dull, persistent headache that had been with him for days slowly ease away. Her closeness aroused a desperate need in him, and he was aware of a deeper, more agonizing ache.

"You look so weary," she said, touching the corners of his eyes. "These lines were not here a week ago."

"Ah, youth, how it mocks old age," he teased.

She laughed. "You old? Never!"

"Thirty, the end of next month. A man of seasoned vintage for a lass of twenty-four."

She frowned, feigning deep thought. "What shall I give this ancient wreck for his birthday? A shawl for his withered old shoulders, a crutch, a corset to slim his paunch?" She poked his flat, firm middle.

"You've already given me all I shall ever want—yourself. After this hellish week, you are a balm for my frayed nerves."

"If only we could lay hands on the billstickers. I would make an example of them never to be forgotten."

"We may yet."

"You know who they are?"

"I'm not entirely certain, but their latest effort may have betrayed them. It was discussed over the Council table yesterday—Argyll unwittingly gave me a clue. He remarked that there are few men adept in painting mermaids and hares. These placards are a French device, and there are two suspects who could have learned the art in Paris."

"Who?"

"Kirkcaldy of Grange and James Murray of Purdovis."

She nodded. "Kirkcaldy is a past master in slander, and Murray speaks only evil of you."

"Aye, Kirkcaldy's grudge against the Hepburns may be traced to my father's time."

"Have you told the Council of your suspicions?"

"I've told no one yet, except you and Huntly."

"They must be apprehended and brought to justice."

"I need more proof first."

"In the meantime, they will continue to print their placards."

"Let them. Now that I am on to them, I can be patient awhile."

They walked along the beach. The Forth was the color of silver, polished to brilliance by the sun. A flock of gulls, with greedy eyes trained on the shore, bathed their twiglike feet at the water's edge. Bothwell threw them a bit of driftwood; they pounced on it, a mass of squabbling wings and pecking beaks, thinking it was food.

"I have had another letter from Lennox," Mary said. "He demands an immediate inquiry into the murder, before Parliament assembles. He asks for the arrest of those named in the placards."

"His guilt-stricken conscience seems to have abated itself. For some unaccountable reason, he is suddenly overbold with courage—I wonder what bolsters him."

"I told him that such matters must follow a legal course, therefore I must wait for Parliament to convene. As for the placards, they accuse so many I scarcely know whom to arrest."

He chuckled. "A fit answer for the faithless scoundrel."

"There is something else I did yesterday," she said hesitantly. "Joseph Rizzio came to see me; he begged that I release him from service and send him out of Scotland."

"You refused, of course."

"How could I? People are saying that he murdered Darnley to avenge his brother."

"There are a host of others in his position—myself, even you.

Except for Balfour, who found it prudent to leave town, none of us have fled."

"If I thought you would go, I would send you away, too." He stopped abruptly. "What have you done?"

She looked out on the water, avoiding his glare. "I have arranged for Joseph, Basso, Sebastien, and his bride to be smuggled out."

He forced her to face him. "What folly of mind possessed you?"

"I had not the heart to refuse. If he remained, Joseph might have been slaughtered like Davie. Sebastien and Christina were wed but two weeks ago, and Basso—"

"Aye," he said grimly, "you had neither the heart nor the good sense to refuse. Do you realize how this will seem? You must recall them immediately, before anyone knows they've gone."

"I can't. They left last night for Berwick and are likely on a ship bound for the Continent by now. They deserved that much for their loyalty. I could not sacrifice them—not even to save myself."

"Elizabeth would not have hesitated to sacrifice twenty like them, for she has the heart and core of a man. Whereas you—" He paused and smiled at her. "I love you more for not being like her. Had you consulted me, I would have advised you against it, for that act of kindness may cost you dearly. Their escape will be taken as a sign of guilt—and that you ordered them to murder your husband."

"Whatever the consequences, I am glad they are safely gone."

"This tenderness of yours will be your undoing."

"You are no better." She smiled. "Though you pretend with a hardened exterior, your heart is as tender as mine. What of Hay and Hepburn? Do you deny having sent them to Hermitage and that you rewarded them each with a horse?"

"You mistake practicality for sentiment, love. I sent them away with good cause. Some of the palace guard saw them returning from Kirk o' Field that night. As for their rewards, they've earned it. They can bear witness to the fact that Archie Douglas and his men were there, and they heard Balfour's confession in Thraples Wynd."

She took his arm and started walking again. "You are as ashamed of your good deeds as other men are of their sins."

The next day was rare for February, deceptive with its warm sunshine and a promise of spring in the air. Where the Forth had been silvery, now it took color from the blue, cloudless sky. In the morning Mary and Bothwell went out on the links for golf; after the midday meal, they held an archery match; Mary and Bothwell took sides against Seton and Huntly, who lost to them. As a prize the victors were treated to a dinner in Tranent.

The day's sports put everyone in good humor. Problems of state were forgotten momentarily, but that same night Bothwell had an urgent message from Crichton. Despite the hour he went to tell Mary about it.

Seton answered his knock. "It is late, my lord," she told him. "Her Majesty is asleep."

"Then wake her. I must speak with her."

"She needs rest; today's exertions were too strenuous for her. Surely whatever it is can wait until morning.

"It cannot."

"But, my lord—"

"I assure you, my lady, Her Majesty will con you little thanks for your interference—well intentioned or not."

When Mary finally came out she was still drowsy with sleep, and he was struck again by her childlike quality. Her hair was pulled back with a white satin ribbon and fell to her shoulders in a tangle of curls. Her slenderness was accentuated by a red wool robe that buttoned tightly at the waist then flared and trailed to the floor.

He took a lighted candle from the hall table and led her to a small sitting room. "I hated to wake you," he said, "but this is important, and I will be gone before morning. I've had a message from Crichton. Jean is ill—it's feared she may be dying."

She was fully awake now. A mixture of anger and suspicion came into her eyes. "This may be a trick to get you there," she said. "What did they say ails her?"

"There was no mention of that, but I think her illness is genuine enough. Before Jean left Edinburgh she complained of feeling ill, but I've had no word from her since and thought she was well again."

"It may be the pox. Why risk exposing yourself to that danger?"

"I don't think it's that—but even if it were, I'd still feel it my duty to be with her."

"She felt no such sense of duty when you lay near death at Hermitage. She left the task of nursing you to a stranger rather than inconvenience herself by coming to you."

"Janet Beaton is no stranger to me. Besides, I'd sooner have Janet's capable hands tending me than a dozen well-meaning but fumbling relatives." He took her in his arms. "Please don't make this more difficult for me than it already is. In all honesty, you must admit that you would think less of me if I didn't go. Haven't I broken enough of my vows to Jean? I'm honor bound to do this much for her."

She pulled his face down and kissed him. "Forgive me," she said, "it is my old jealousy returning. I realize now that it's not Jean, but your honor, that is my rival. Of course, you must go to her. I can send you now with a light heart—and love you more for it."

In that instant they were bound together everlastingly; come what may, he knew that neither time nor distance—not even death—could separate them. They were knit one to the other, entwined in the depths of their minds, bodies, and souls. Inevitably, the fire of their passions would ebb, then cool, but something far greater would linger into infinity. He looked at her and saw that she knew it too.

4

Bothwell left Seton before dawn and reached Crichton in less than two hours. Jean was asleep when he arrived; her physician kept her heavily drugged to ease her pain.

"It is a strange malady, my lord," he told Bothwell. "I am unable to discover the source."

"What troubles her?"

"My lady is alternately seized with agonizing cramps and acute nausea. I doubt she can survive the ordeal much longer."

"Surely you have some clue. In your long experience you must have encountered similar cases."

"I have, my lord, but it is generally thought better the cause shall remain obscure."

"If you suspect something, tell me what it is."

The physician paused dramatically. Then, lowering his voice to a conspiratorial whisper, he said, "Poison, my lord."

Bothwell stared at him. "What nonsense are you concocting? Who would poison my wife? She hasn't an enemy in the world."

"I know nothing of that, my lord, only that the symptoms indicate poison. Perhaps the Countess Bothwell attempted to take her own life. It is not uncommon for women to choose such means."

Jean take her own life—never! She was not the type. Of course, she had been despondent when she left Edinburgh; she had pleaded with him to let her stay. But he had been adamant; the unrest following the murder had made him edgy and he didn't want her about. That, and the heavy weight of responsibility that had fallen to him in the aftermath, made him want her safely away at Crichton.

Jean had accused him of wanting her out of the way so he could be with Mary. Her suspicions had enraged him; he had ordered her trunks packed that night and had sent her off in the morning. She had fought so hard to keep him, but he had turned his back on her. *My God,* he thought, *if she did this because of me* . . .

Horrified, he dashed upstairs to her chambers and turned her startled serving women out into the hall. He went to her bedside and called her name softly. "Jean." His voice had a strange, alien sound, especially since he had used her given name.

Her eyelids fluttered open, then closed again. She blinked, trying to bring them into focus. At last he saw a flicker of recognition.

He reached for her hand and held the limp fingers in his. "Why didn't you send for me sooner?" he asked.

"You had troubles enough," she said weakly. "I didn't want to burden you with mine."

"Who else would you turn to?"

Her hand tightened. She stiffened convulsively; her other hand clutched at her stomach and her features contorted in agony. He wanted to call the physician, but she begged him to stay and gripped his hand more tightly.

The seizure finally passed; the cramping and hollow retching had ceased, and she lay back exhausted. He thought she would sleep, but her eyes remained open, gazing at him.

Her breathing seemed more relaxed, but the seizure had taken its toll. She was a little weaker than before; plainly, her strength was ebbing away—how much could she endure before it gave way completely? He knew that she should rest. but he had to question her. Seeing her suffer this way confirmed his doubts—Jean had been poisoned.

He had heard of the agonizing death poison victims suffered. Those who were lucky died quickly; others lingered in unbearable pain.

He said, "Your physician believes you have been poisoned. Have you?"

She nodded.

"Who—"

"There is no one to blame—only myself."

"But why? You have every reason to live."

"You misunderstand—it was an accident. I took more than I had intended."

"You took it deliberately, yet you call it an accident?"

She turned away. "What matter how or why; I have already said too much. Why trouble yourself? You will be free of me soon."

He sat down beside her and slipped his arm under her back, supporting her against his shoulder. "It matters greatly. I have never asked for my freedom—this way or any other."

She rested her head against him and smiled. "You haven't held me since our honeymoon."

"For reasons known to both of us. Tell me what you've done—all of it."

"No, let me be, I beg you."

"Not until I've had the truth."

"It is too shameful."

"There is nothing you need feel ashamed of with me. I will understand."

"Promise you will never tell a living soul—especially the Queen—she would gloat so."

"She is the last to gloat over anyone's unhappiness. But you have my word. Nothing you say will leave this room."

She sighed and breathed deeply, as though to muster strength. "Until a week ago, I was with child."

Her words stunned him, but he let her go on without interrupting.

"Had matters been otherwise between us, you need never have known it was not yours. I would have let you believe I carried your child. But such as they were, you would have known the truth immediately."

"How long have you known?"

"Since the close of December. I thought if I could seduce you—even for one night. . . . But you wouldn't have me. I was so ashamed afterward and could not face you for what I had tried to do. Later I became frantic; the horror of discovery outweighed all else."

"That was the reason for your sudden visit earlier this month."

She nodded. "I was desperate. I had to make one more attempt, and when that failed, I did the only thing left. Ergot is often used to rid women of unwanted children—my chambermaid purchased it from the apothecary. I took it, but without result."

"You were ill during your stay in Edinburgh. Had you taken it then?"

"No, not until I returned to Crichton. My illness then was due to natural causes—it is common in the early stages of childbearing. When the ergot showed no sign of working, I increased the dosage."

"And poisoned yourself in the process."

"It was the constant retching and cramping that finally caused me to miscarry."

"Had you come to me at the beginning, you needn't have suffered this."

"Well you know it is Scots law to punish adultery with

death. I feared your anger; revenge might have driven you to expose me."

"Aye, a law forced upon the people by Knox—it sets us back in time a thousand years," he said. "But under my protection you had nothing to fear. You could have had the child—I'd have given it my name."

"You would do that for me?"

"Aye. God's blood! Do you think me such an ogre as to seek your death?"

"I thought you despised me—your generosity is far greater than I have the right to expect."

"I've no wish to sit in judgment on the moral conduct of others—I leave that to a deity higher than men. As for despising you, never; we are merely unsuited to each other."

She groped for his hand. "My heart is light now I have told you. I shall never forget what you were willing to do."

"You will, the moment there is ill feeling between us again."

"No, I will remember. You haven't even rebuked me for betraying you, nor have you asked the man's name."

"Alex of Boyne, is it not?"

"Will you seek satisfaction from him?"

He shook his head. "I'll not accost him."

"I am glad of that. He is not entirely to blame—I encouraged him. I used him at first, to pay you in your own coin, then I knew that I still loved him."

"Apologies are not necessary. I knew you loved him when we were wed. A few words said in church cannot erase what is in the heart. You might say love is a sickness that creeps into the blood. Some burns out like fever; others remain, never to be dispelled."

He spoke more to himself than to her, for despite his concern for Jean, his thoughts were always of Mary. He saw her face, the little dimple that creased her cheek when she smiled, the fire highlighting her hair, the way it reflected tiny jewels in her eyes.

Aye, she was in his blood, and he prayed that he would never recover from that sickness.

He glanced at Jean; she had fallen asleep and he tiptoed out. It was difficult to imagine her the victim of her passions; she had always impressed him as being so level-headed. And Alex, a bumbling dullard to all who knew him—to all except Jean. These two wholly conventional people had dared what he would have thought improbable for them. Actually, were it not for the tragic result of their affair, he could find it amusing. Yet, he could not suppress a little smile when he thought that he, of all people, had been cuckolded.

By morning Jean showed a slight improvement. The physician took encouragement that there had been no seizures during the night, but he would offer no hope of recovery yet. Bothwell would have liked to remain, but he could not. Instinct warned him not to prolong his absence from town; feelings were running high among the townsfolk since the first placard—staying away too long might be interpreted as evidence of his guilt.

He left Crichton in the morning with a promise to return the next day, and he stopped off at Seton before going on to Edinburgh.

He found Mary embroidering in her chambers. The draperies had been drawn aside; sunlight fell on her hair, producing the effect of a red-gold halo. In the distance the rippling sea twinkled cold and blue, framed in a setting of snow-tipped hedgerows.

She let the embroidery slip from her hands and ran to him. He glanced about cautiously.

"We are alone," she said, reading his thoughts.

He unfastened his cloak and tossed it on a chest.

She reached for his hand and put it to her cheek. "How is Jean?"

"Gravely ill."

"What ails her?"

"Her physician thinks that she's been poisoned." That much he could tell her; gossip would reach her soon enough.

"But how?"

He turned and looked out on the beach to avert her glance. "There are numerous ways—rancid meat, a poisonous root—" He shrugged.

"Surely she would have detected the spoilage before consuming a deadly amount."

"Apparently not. But why dwell on such morbid topics? Let's talk of other things—I have only a little time, then I must leave you again."

He would never betray Jean's confidence—not even to Mary.

"You've so much on your mind, I dread having to burden you with more problems."

He smiled. "My shoulders are broad."

"I have had news from France. Queen Catherine does not accept my account of Harry's death—she accuses me openly of having part in it."

"What do you intend doing about it?" he asked.

"I shall not answer her charges. Let my former mother-in-law accuse me to her heart's content—I'll not demean myself to offer a defense."

"I admire your courage, love, but the friendship of France is not a thing lightly tossed aside. She rules in her son's name; her policies are the policies of France."

"I have always valued Scotland's alliance with France, but I will not humble myself for a merchant's daughter."

"Merchant's daughter or not, she is a formidable enemy—one who can do you great hurt if she's of a mind."

"I am vulnerable to the whim of anyone who wishes to do me harm, Elizabeth, Catherine, Philip—even the Pope. Perhaps it would be best if I retired. We could go away together and live in peace. Think of the bliss to wake each day without fear of new plots or crises."

"Would you leave it all to James, to appease his greedy passions?" He seized her roughly. "Never let me hear you speak of that again. You were born to rule Scotland—no one shall take it from you."

"I wonder if you love Scotland more than you do me."

"You are Scotland—I cannot love you less, for I cannot tell you apart," he said, reaching for his cloak.

"Are you going already?" she asked. "Stay and take the midday meal with me."

"I'll take it in Edinburgh. Let folk see that I am not afraid to show my face in broad daylight."

"When will I see you again?"

"In two days. I've given my word to return to Jean tomorrow night. I will stop off here again on my way to town."

"She has her physician and servants. What can you do for her?"

"My being there seems to give her comfort. Would you have it on your conscience to deny her that?"

"It's not selfishness that compels me—my thoughts were of you. So much riding will exhaust you."

"I've done that and more in the past; the exercise will do me good." He bent to kiss her. "Now, let me see you smile, for I am sick to death of gloomy faces."

5

News of Bothwell's return had apparently reached Holyrood, for Huntly was waiting for him in the courtyard.

"Have you come fresh from Crichton?" he asked.

"Aye, with a slight detour by way of Seton."

"What of Jean? Has she improved?"

"Somewhat, but I will have more definite word for you after tomorrow."

They walked through the inner quadrangle and started up the staircase to Bothwell's apartments.

Inside, Huntly seated himself in an armchair. A servant knelt at the hearth to build a fire. Bothwell's groom helped him off with his boots. The quiet felt good to his ears; it was a peaceful change from the street noises. A moment later Huntly gave voice to his musings.

He said, "A pity your affairs prevent you from remaining with Jean. In times of adversity, folk are often brought close— who knows but this may be the very thing to bridge the gap between you."

"You read more meaning into this than you ought. Neither Jean nor I have any such illusions."

"Yet, despite the inconvenience, you return to her tomorrow."

"Aye, and every day thereafter, until she ceases to need me."

"In God's name why? If you bear each other so little affection—"

"Because I can do no less for her."

"Frankly, such logic is beyond my ken. However, lest you think me a prying in-law, I let the matter drop here and now."

"Just as well that you do," Bothwell said, tamping coltsfoot weed into his pipe. "Is there nothing new you have to tell me?"

"Aye, news aplenty. Balfour is back. He skulked into town one night and has posted a heavy guard around his house. That was two days ago, and there's been no sign of him since. Folk say it's a guilty conscience that prompts his fear."

"His was the greatest part in the murder than any ten men I know."

"Doubtless it was his brain that conceived it, but if you were of a mind to prove it, you'd find it a deal troublesome to do."

"Given the choice, I would as soon let it rest where it is."

Huntly nodded. "But mark my words, this laying low is only temporary—he will make himself felt among us yet."

A log collapsed and fell to embers. Bothwell got up to poke at the fire; an icy blast slithered down the flue, shivering the flames. He turned and glanced at Huntly, who stared intently into the fire. What visions did he see in the flames? He hadn't noticed it before, but there was a strong resemblance between Huntly and Jean. They had the same lackluster eyes, light blue and opaque; their profiles were almost identical, long-nosed, solemn, expressionless faces.

He thought: *How strange Huntly has grown of late.* He seemed more stoop-shouldered and withdrawn than ever. Bothwell had seen him retreat like this before, appearing to slip away without leaving the room. He coughed loudly to bring Huntly back.

Slowly, Huntly returned. "Lethington has had word from James," he said, as though he were totally unaware of his long silence. "He is expected to return to Court this week."

"Doubtless he will ask for lodgings at Seton."

"No need of that, since Her Majesty must be here to receive Queen Elizabeth's emissary."

The firelight reflected a malicious gleam in Bothwell's eyes. "Odd that James should plan his return to coincide so well with this Englishman's arrival." He grinned humorlessly. "Like as not, coincidence has no part here."

"Aye, he still maintains a lively correspondence with England."

"My thoughts precisely. Who has the Tudor bitch sent to spy on us?"

"Master Henry Killigrew."

"A fit messenger, with little penchant for fair play."

"Have you his acquaintance?"

"I've not had the honor yet, but I know him by reputation,

and none of it to his credit. A talented fellow with a knack for sowing dissension."

"Then we must be on guard. This is scarce the time for new troubles among the nobility."

Bothwell laughed. "The gap stands so great now, a further breach would go unnoticed."

Bothwell found Jean much improved on his return to Crichton. She was sitting up, taking nourishment, and well on her way to recovery. He stayed the night and left the following day to escort Mary back to Edinburgh.

He saw Mary's pained expression as they passed the sullen-faced townsfolk. In days past, their cheers had followed her through the streets, they had blessed her and had thrown flowers in her path. Now they watched silently, searching her face, waiting . . .

Later, in her apartments, she turned to him in agony. "They despise me," she said. "The air is filled with their hatred. It's like death's icy breath on me. And you, they hate you even more. If only I could tell them the truth; they make a martyr of a traitor, and vilify you."

"It would take the whole truth—and you cannot give it to them without first revealing that those of your own faith betrayed you."

"Even God deserts me when I need Him most."

"You confuse Rome with God, my love. *He* has not deserted you."

6

Killigrew arrived on the sixth of March, the day following Mary's return, but she kept him waiting two days. James too had returned, and with him Morton. Mary received them coolly; despite her relief in having James gone, his absence had displeased her. Nor did he see fit to offer an explanation, although his attitude seemed strangely altered.

He was more humble than Bothwell had ever seen him; his only desire seemed to be that of pleasing Mary and the Council. He deplored public opinion that denounced Mary and Bothwell; naturally, he told them, Darnley's murder had been a great shock to him, and he heartily agreed the conspirators should be apprehended and punished.

Then, slyly, he asked about Jean's health; he had heard rumors of poison—not that he gave the least credit to that line of gossip. On the contrary, he had severely scolded the gossip-mongers, "especially for calumniating my Lord Bothwell." Nevertheless, he thanked God for the Countess Bothwell's recovery to "sooner still the vicious tongues."

Morton stood beside James nodding approval. For himself, Morton had very little to say. Although she now allowed him the Court, Mary still regarded him with scorn; she would never forgive him for Rizzio's murder. She found the sight of him offensive and often commented on his lack of fastidiousness, but Bothwell knew it was not Morton's grease-stained doublets, or his gray-tinged ruffs, or his bushy, ill-kempt red whiskers that disgusted her—she still saw Rizzio's blood on him.

On the eighth of March, Mary granted Killigrew an audience. He was admitted to a darkened chamber; heavy black draperies covered the French windows, and all the candles had been snuffed out. The fireplace provided the only light in the room, throwing dim shadows on the walls and Mary.

She sat at the far end of her audience chamber, clad in deep mourning, her face hidden behind a veil. Beside her, on a low stool, sat her faithful Lady Seton. Killigrew spent only a short time with her, conveying his sovereign's condolences and presenting her with a letter written in Elizabeth's own hand. The interview over, Killigrew went to a dinner given in his honor by

James and attended by Argyll, Morton, Atholl, Lethington, and Bothwell.

Later, Mary and Bothwell laughed at Killigrew's consternation on finding such amity among the Scottish lords. Yet, despite her amusement, Bothwell detected a certain hollowness to her laughter.

"Something is troubling you," he said. "What is it?"

"Tomorrow is time enough. I want tonight to be happy."

"Tell me now. It will rest easier with you, once you've unburdened it."

She smiled. "Two hearts so close you know when I am troubled."

"I wager it has something to do with Elizabeth's letter," he said. "Let me see it."

"I wish I could burn it," she said, handing it to him.

Elizabeth's fine hand sprawled across the page:

Madam, my ears have been so much shocked by my distress, and my heart appalled at hearing the horrible report of the abominable murder of your husband. . . . Although nature constrains me to lament his death . . . I should neither perform the office of a faithful, nor affectionate friend, if I studied rather to please your ears than to preserve your honor. . . . People for the most part say, 'That you will look through your fingers at the deed, instead of revenging it,' and that you have not cared to touch those who have done you this pleasure . . . I implore you to believe me that I myself would not for all the gold in the world cherish such a thought in my heart. . . . Therefore I exhort you, counsel and implore you, to take this affair so much to heart that you will not fear to wreak vengeance even on him who stands nearest to you, should he be guilty; and that no consideration whatever will withhold you from giving the world proof that you are as noble a ruler as you are a righteous woman . . .

Bothwell stared at the letter until the words became a blur. She had done everything but write his name *on him who stands nearest you*. But how could she have known he was the chief suspect? Only the placards had dared to accuse him thus far; her letter had been dated only two days after the first one had appeared. Word of that could not have reached her in time to write the letter—unless someone who knew their theme had told her well in advance of their appearance.

How often since that ill-fated night had he cursed the luck that brought him to Kirk o' Field? Balfour had warned him to go no farther for fear the fuse would be lighted. That had sent Darnley rushing out of the house into the arms of Archie Douglas.

Now, in retrospect, Bothwell was plagued with doubts of his own actions. He had thought himself calm and cool-headed in his moves to counteract the plot. Now it seemed that rage rather than reason had governed him. Who could accuse him of conspiring to murder Darnley if he had gone to Kirk o' Field in broad daylight, found the mined vaults, laid the plot to Darnley's charge, then arrested him for treason? From the start, Bothwell had advised the others to use legal means; why hadn't he followed his own advice? Instead he had followed a path which had led him to be branded a regicide.

Unfortunately, he had been unable to forget the Rizzio conspiracy—the outcome of that had guided him. Darnley had escaped punishment for his part in that—he might have done so again with the gunpowder plot.

Forgetting Mary, Bothwell put the letter down and went to the door.

"Where are you going?" she asked.

"It's time for a cleansing," he murmured, leaving her to stare after him in bewilderment.

CHAPTER XVII

1

Elizabeth's letter had reawakened Bothwell's fury; if the truth were told, countless heads would roll, but he had no share in their guilt. He would admit to having been as anxious as they to dispose of Darnley, but not by outright murder. He had consented in the first place because of the measures proposed at Craigmillar: divorce, indictment, arrest.... The conspiracy involving Darnley and the Catholics had changed everything; if Bothwell hadn't intervened, Mary would have been the victim; thus the trapper had been caught in his own snare.

There were others who knew of the conspiracy even before Bothwell; no one had so much as tried to warn Mary—not even her own brother. There was Archie Douglas, the actual murderer. No one accused him—only Bothwell had been singled out.

To his face, the Council members were Bothwell's friends, protesting the placards, but he was not deluded by their good will; only his power induced their friendship. Should that power suddenly diminish, he had no doubt that they would turn on him.

Bothwell was aware of something brewing; Killigrew had returned to London like a cream-filled cat. Lennox still kept his distance, but his cries for vengeance were growing louder. There were rumors of secret meetings at the Lennox stronghold.

"Many from great houses attended"; that was the only clue to their identities.

With his usual impulsiveness, Bothwell decided the strain of waiting was over. Jean had fully recovered; there was nothing to interfere with his taking the necessary steps to halt the slander. Time and patience had availed him nothing; if anything, his defamers had grown more bold.

More posters had appeared since Mary's return from Seton, but now he had something to go on. There were few people in Scotland able to paint the figures depicted on those posters; all evidence pointed to Kirkcaldy and James Murray of Purdovis. The Privy Council met on the fourteenth of March and ordered Murray's arrest, but he was forewarned and escaped capture. Murray wrote from his place of hiding, offering to bring six men, or more, to bear out his accusations, "armed or otherwise."

Bothwell shrugged and thought: *So much for Murray.* He might not have been apprehended and punished, but the placards had ceased. Now he could deal with his accusers, for Lennox had found the courage to charge him openly. He wrote to Mary, demanding that Bothwell, and the others named in the placards, be tried immediately.

Mary stamped her foot defiantly. "I will not comply with his demands. How dare he force the issue when his own conduct will not bear investigation?"

"You must," Bothwell said. "Lennox wouldn't take the tone he has if he were without supporters. Besides, I can no longer live in the shadow of suspicion. A trial by my peers will put an end to this, once and for all."

"Are you so certain they will acquit you?"

"Reasonably certain. Who will testify against me? James, Morton, Argyll—Archie Douglas? They are not in a position to give false evidence, without first implicating themselves."

"I cannot share your confidence; the risk is too great. I'll not put you at their mercy. What justice can you expect from them? How can you be sure they will not turn on you?"

He smiled. "You underestimate me, love. Do you imagine that I intend to appear before them in the meek robes of a penitent? On the contrary, I will make my own justice by preparing a defense that they cannot contest. Two years ago James taught me a valuable lesson—one that I have never forgotten. Do you recall my trial of May '65?"

She nodded. "You were summoned to court to answer the charge of breaking prison after the Arran kidnap plot—but you never appeared, your cousin came in your place."

"I would have been mad to do otherwise. James had the town packed with his supporters. There were thousands of them; what chance would I have had? I doubt it was his intention that I should escape with my life, much less give me a fair hearing. Now it's my turn to pack the town—with Hepburns. My billies will provide good assurance against foul play."

He watched the little frown lines around her mouth and eyes. The start of tears glistened in the corners of her eyes, but he was determined and had to convince her. He took her cold, trembling hands in his.

She pulled free and turned away. "I cannot regard this lightly as you do."

"Lightly! Is that what you think? Good God, am I not aware of the danger? Regicide is not a mean charge—even the worst fool knows what the consequences could be. Can you believe I do not care? But I am charged with a crime I did not commit. I must have the chance to clear myself—you haven't the right to deny me that."

Her shoulders sagged in defeat. "Very well, have your trial—and I pray that God does not desert you."

Reluctantly, Mary wrote to Lennox, promising that Both-well would stand trial. On the twenty-eighth of March, Bothwell presented his request, to underlie the trial according to the laws of the Realm. Scots law demanded fifteen days for preparation, and the hearing was fixed for Saturday, the twelfth of April. Heralds posted notices on the market crosses at Edinburgh, Glasgow, Dumbarton, and Perth in which Lennox was summon-ed to the Tolbooth to prosecute the accused.

Meanwhile, Bothwell made his own preparations. The past had given him good cause for certain reservations regarding the law; he knew that innocence did not necessarily constitute justice. And on that premise he called all Hepburns, retainers, and adherents to Edinburgh.

They came in droves, these shaggy Borderers, armed and provisioned to stay a month, or more, if need be. More rode into town every day; they came from the borders that tipped England and from the east and west, wherever there was a man who owed Bothwell allegiance. They thronged to Edinburgh, all with one purpose in mind: to stand behind their lord.

Mary occupied herself with other matters. It was Holy Week, and through some misguided notion, she felt compelled to pay homage to Darnley's memory. Rich fabrics were brought from her storerooms and made into a funeral bed for Darnley's remains—fabrics cut from abandoned pavilions of Edward II of England on the field of Bannockburn. Then, to add to Bothwell's disgust, she spent the night of Good Friday on her knees in prayer beside the memorial bed.

He marveled that she could find it in her heart to forgive that faithless traitor. But, later, she confessed that she hadn't acted out of forgiveness, or sentiment, but out of fear. Death had not softened her image of Darnley; the agonies and misery she had endured because of him were still fresh in her mind. But she was tortured by guilt for wishing him dead.

Somehow, she blamed herself and lived in dread lest Bothwell be punished for her sin. Those hours spent on her knees had been a self-imposed penance—her prayers had been for Bothwell, not Darnley.

2

With all Bothwell had to do until the trial, fifteen days seemed little enough time, but Lennox thought the time even shorter—especially when Bothwell aborted his plan to march into Edinburgh with three thousand men. News had reached him in Glasgow that Bothwell had amassed a following of more than four thousand Borderers, and Lennox intended to meet force with force. Mary stopped him at Linlithgow with orders to appear at Justice Court with only the prescribed number of six men.

Lennox then retreated to Stirling and asked for more time to prepare his case. Further, he demanded that Bothwell be placed under arrest and detained until a new date for trial could be fixed. Bothwell could well imagine Lennox's motive; likely he hoped that a long delay would disperse the Borderers to their homes. It may even have occurred to him that the jury would be made up of Hepburn partisans.

But Lennox had only to see a list of the jurors' names for reassurance; it needed only a true appraisal of the men chosen to judge. Of the four assessors—Robert Pitcairn, James MacGill, Lord Lindsay, and Henry Belnaves—all were Bothwell's professed enemies, dating back to the old troubles when they had worked for England and he for Mary of Guise. The Lord Justice, Argyll, was an adversary who supported James. As for the jurors, Rothes and Boyd were both of James' rebellion two years earlier, after Mary's marriage to Darnley. Lord Herries had once been a friend, but he had gone over to Bothwell's enemies since, Lord John Hamilton was Arran's brother and certainly not given to fond feelings for the defendant, Caithness was another of James' allies, Semphill and Forbes were no friends, and Alex of Boyne had strong personal reasons of his own to see Bothwell ruined. Of those remaining, one or two were perhaps favorable toward Bothwell; the rest were at least neutral. Yet Bothwell voiced no dissenting views on his judges—only Lennox found fault with the jury.

Mary, however, dismissed Lennox's protests and informed him the trial would proceed as scheduled, for it had been on his advice that she had employed haste. Once that was settled, Mary turned her attention to the Prince, for the atmosphere was charged with danger. Bothwell felt that with so many armed men of opposing factions in town, the chance of brawling was a serious threat. He knew that if the verdict went against him there would be violence, and he suggested that Mary send the Prince to Stirling Castle.

His reasons were twofold; for one, the guardianship of royal infants had for generations gone to the Earls of Mar. This would remedy at least one ticklish situation, for Mar was at present governor of Edinburgh Castle. Bothwell wanted him out of that strategic post, for his wife was James Murray's sister, and she dominated Lord Mar. That and her unquenchable ambition made poor companions for Mary's interests.

Bothwell wanted the castle with its strong artillery, stores of ordnance, and royal treasures in friendly hands. He fully appreciated its value and had arranged for Cockburn of Skirling, a man loyal to both Mary and himself, to replace Lord Mar. Mary saw the good sense in this and placed her son in Lord Mar's hands. She gave him command of Stirling Castle, the ancient nursery of Scotland's future kings.

Four days before the trial Mary summoned Bothwell to her audience chamber. James was with her, and it was evident they had been quarreling.

She appealed to Bothwell. "Perhaps you can dissuade him, my lord, for I have had no luck," she said. "My brother is taken with a sudden desire for travel. He would go to France at a time when I need him most."

James said, "I would be less than human if I took no pride in my apparent value to you, madam. But you have others to advise you, my lord Bothwell here not the least of them."

"When do you expect to leave?" Bothwell asked.

"Tomorrow at dawn. There is a ship leaving London on the seventeenth, bound for Calais, and I hope to sail with it."

"If you waited—a month perhaps—until Her Majesty is better able to see you go."

James shook his head. "A month would defeat the very purpose of my going. My health has been poor of late; the weather has worn me out. What with frosts and snows, I am scarce able to leave my bed."

Mary said, "It is already April; the astrologers promise a mild spring."

"None to compare with the Continent, madam. My physician strongly recommends the temperate climates of Italy and France."

"You appear healthy enough to me," she snapped. Then, coaxingly: "At least wait until we have the verdict of Bothwell's trial—a delay of only a few days."

"But a pointless delay, madam. I've no doubt my lord Bothwell will have anything but a favorable decision."

Bothwell laughed scornfully. "Your confidence overwhelms me. Can it be that you already have the verdict in your pocket?"

"You jest, of course. I speak from the knowledge that you are as innocent of those charges as I, my lord."

Bothwell nodded. "Even more so, perhaps. But to return to the matter at hand—are you still so determined to leave us?"

"I have already given my reasons. Of what use will Her Majesty find me if I am ill?"

Bothwell turned to Mary. "There is aught you may do, madam, but wish your brother a good journey."

Her eyes blazed cold fury. "Let me remind you, my lord, you have begged favors of me in the past, and I have granted them. But there is a future too—when you return, your position in this Realm may well be somewhat altered."

James shrugged. "That is a risk I must take, madam."

He left them with Mary close to tears and Bothwell with a feeling all too familiar—that of a chill cold as death.

"He has some new scheme in mind," Mary said. "When James is taken with a sudden need for travel, it is always a warning for his enemies to beware."

"Aye, this feeling of something in the wind has plagued me for weeks. It's like waiting for the first clap of thunder before a summer storm begins."

She paled. "What are you thinking? There is a look in your eyes that frightens me." Her expression changed to horror; she ran to Bothwell. "James spoke of your trial—they will find you guilty. They have already decided, he knows. I will order a postponement."

He shook his head. "I grant you it's their fondest wish to dispose of me legally, but they dare not, for I know too much. If I go to the gallows, I will take every last one of them with me. No, love, you haven't hit on their scheme—I fear it's a deal more intricate and torturous."

3

A thick veil of mist preceded the dawn on the twelfth of April, then the sun came out and Holyrood's drenched gardens, patched with young blooms, sparkled in jewel-like brilliance.

Burly, sheepskin-clad Borderers filled the puddled courtyard, their number spilling out over the moat and onto the street, past the open gates. The abbey's morning bells harmonized with shrill peals from the Cannongate Kirk and the dour tones of St. Giles.

The town crier wound his way up the Cannongate, chanting the hour of seven as a west wind coaxed ribbons of smoke from chimneys toward the palace. Black-shawled housewives hurried to the din and clatter of the marketplace while stray hounds sniffed and pawed through rubbish heaps for their breakfast. It was Saturday; the town had awakened and come alive.

Bothwell stood at his bedchamber window looking out on the sun-dappled slopes of Arthur's Seat. He watched the slow progress of a shepherd leading his flock to graze on the grassy hillside. A stableboy passed his window, trailed by a string of horses on their way to the watering trough.

He had passed the night restlessly, dozing in semisleep, then waking and dropping off again. Some time before dawn he had got out of bed and had gone to his study. Selecting a book from the shelf at random, he had attempted to read, but the words flashed before his eyes meaninglessly; his thoughts whirled.

The night before, Mary had sobbed in his arms; the trial and its outcome filled her with terror. Nothing he could say reassured her—he could still feel her tears on his face. A letter written in Jean's hand lay open on his desk; he glanced at it and frowned. She had written to wish him well at the trial and, to his surprise, blamed herself in part for his troubles.

> *... Had I been a better wife, you would not have come to this travail. I cannot but reproach myself for the coldness and indifference I have shown you, thereby causing you to seek another's affection. But alas! She has used you badly. She will never love you, nor put your welfare above her own selfish desires. Humbly, I beg you to abandon her, for she*

*can only bring you to further shame and grief. She seeks to
rob me of my honorable estate, scorning both the law and
God who joined us together. You are under the spell of an
enchantress, whose guilefulness causes you to confuse love
for lust. I hold you in my prayers constantly that you may
soon recover from this sickness. I await your return. . . .*

It was artfully written, unlike anything he would have
expected from Jean. Unfortunately, he had received it yesterday in Mary's presence. His first inclination had been to slip it
into his doublet to read later, but Mary had insisted on his
reading it then. She had even pretended disinterest by returning
to her embroidery. He had scanned it carelessly to save further
argument, folded it, and started to put it away.

"What does she say?" Mary asked, attempting to sound
casual.

"She wishes me well for tomorrow."

"Is that all? It seems rather a long letter for just that."

"She speaks of other matters, too."

"Matters you would prefer to keep from me." She yanked
the needle violently and broke the thread. "Do you think me a
simpleton that I cannot guess what she is up to? Doubtless she
uses this occasion to turn you against me. It is not difficult to
imagine how she reviles me every chance she has. She is my
enemy, yet you protect her. Perhaps you care more for her than
you do for me."

Exasperated, he tossed the letter into her lap and went to
the window while she read it. Torches lighted the courtyard
below; steel-helmeted sentries stood at the gates and paraded
back and forth. Without turning, he knew she had finished
reading, and he sensed her justifiable anger.

When she spoke, her voice reminded him of a viper's hiss.
"She dares to call me an enchantress—that cold, bloodless
creature. What does she know of love?"

"Would you behave differently in her place?"

"Surely you don't think she is sincere! These words were not conceived by her, they are too astute. This eloquence is not hers, but rather the toil of another, more talented pen."

"Jean would not stoop to that form of deceit."

She laughed triumphantly. "There, you see, you *have* been taken in by her lamentations of false grief. You hold her words to be true, whereas mine are less than nothing." Then, her anger suddenly gone, she rushed to him. "Forgive me, dearest," she said, "I stand here quarreling with you when tomorrow may separate us forever. But if I seem a jealous shrew, it is because I live in constant fear of losing you."

He held her close, but with restraint, for fear of crushing her in his fierce need.

"Remember this always," he murmured. "Yours is the only love I shall ever want."

At dawn, Paris had come into the study, rudely jerking Bothwell's thoughts back to the present. Paris started a fire in the hearth, then drew aside the heavy green draperies and peered out.

"What will Your Lordship wear?" he asked.

"The blue stamped with gold."

Paris hesitated. "The occasion is somber, my lord. Would not black be more suitable?"

"I've no wish to appear somber."

It was past the hour of nine when Bothwell left his chambers. He had taken infinite care in dressing; from his appearance, he might have been going to a banquet rather than to hear a charge of regicide read against him.

His tall, lean frame did justice to Dalgleish's tailoring; his doublet of peacock blue, stamped with gold fleurs-de-lis, complimented his broad shoulders, as did the short, flared matching cape that he wore thrown back to reveal its gold satin lining. His long legs were hosed in a deeper shade of blue and booted in black Spanish kid. A white-plumed toque sat to one side of his reddish-brown hair, and inside his doublet Mary's note lay pressed against his heart.

She had sent it an hour ago; he knew the words without having to read them again: *My love, I dare not breathe, nor let my heart beat until you are safely returned to me.*

He met Lethington, clothed as always in black, at the inner quadrangle.

Lethington's greeting was jovial. "Will you take a cup of wine with me, my lord?" he asked.

"It grows late; we should be starting."

"There is plenty of time—we've half an hour, or better."

Bothwell glanced at the door leading to Mary's apartments. He would sooner have spent the remaining time with her; instead he nodded and followed Lethington across the quadrangle.

"I have just come from Her Majesty," Lethington said. "Her prayers go with you today, for she believes utterly in your innocence."

"And my judges, do they also believe in my innocence?"

"They must, of course, hear the evidence before deciding."

"There is no evidence—unless it is fabricated."

Lethington smiled blandly. "Who would dare in the face of that?" He pointed to the courtyard packed with Bothwell's men.

Morton came in, followed by Cockburn of Skirling.

Skirling approached Bothwell. "My lord," he said, "there is a messenger at the gates, demanding audience with the Queen."

"What does he want?"

"He has been roaming the streets since six this morning in hope of delivering a letter to Her Majesty from the English Queen."

"The devil he will."

Bothwell had no doubt the letter held a request for postponing trial. He knew Lennox had appealed to Elizabeth for help, imploring her to intercede on his behalf. A month ago, Lennox had pressed for immediate action; now he was cowed by Bothwell's show of strength. *Let him wail all he likes,* Bothwell thought. The trial would proceed as scheduled—nor would he trouble Mary further until it was over.

"Go out and tell him the Queen is still asleep, and that for his own good, it were best he does not loiter about the palace grounds," Bothwell said. "Later will be time enough to deliver his letter."

"Wait," Lethington said, "do you know if this letter is from the Council or the Queen of England herself?"

"He says it is written in the Queen's own hand," Cockburn said.

Lethington turned to Bothwell. "This would seem to call for a measure of diplomacy, my lord. I will go out to the man."

Lethington had been all too genial of late. His sudden willingness to accommodate aroused Bothwell's suspicions. He had no illusions about this friendship, but it was more to his advantage to keep Lethington as an ally for the moment. It was certainly better than having him wander off where he could not be watched.

Bothwell said, "I will go with you."

The courtyard sprang suddenly to life. Bothwell's jack-booted Borderers shouted a lusty cheer and climbed to their mounts. Ormiston came forward with Bothwell's high-prancing stallion, caparisoned in blue with gold fringe. Bothwell waved to them, and another cheer chorused up, then he gave the order to dismount and followed Cockburn to the gates, where the Englishman waited with Thomas and Willie Hepburn.

Lethington addressed himself to the man, who introduced

himself as John Selby, provost marshal of Berwick. "What business have you with the Queen?"

Selby answered, "I have a letter for the Queen of Scots from my mistress, the Queen of England."

Scowling, Bothwell said, "You've picked a damned inconvenient time to deliver it."

Lethington anticipated Selby's query. "The Earl of Bothwell," he said.

From the way Selby started, Bothwell knew his surmise had been correct. The letter had been sent in connection with his trial.

Lethington said, "If you give the letter to me, I will see it is delivered, though I cannot say when, for the Queen is still asleep."

Selby surrendered the letter reluctantly and watched Bothwell and Lethington return to the palace.

Lethington tried to convince Bothwell to show the letter to Mary. What harm could it do? He argued that despite Elizabeth's exhortations, the letter had come too late for postponement. Further, he doubted whether that had really been her motive. Why else would she wait until the eleventh hour, if it were not merely a token protest to satisfy Lennox? So, why not show it to Mary now? She would ignore it in any case, as well she ought. Finally Bothwell agreed.

Mary was very much awake, and had been since daybreak. She told Lethington to read the letter aloud. She listened, growing pale, then angry.

"... It is of extreme importance that matters should not be obscured, as they very well might be, by secrecy and cunning. The father and friends of the deceased have humbly begged me to ask that you postpone the inquiry, because they have noticed that these scoundrelly persons are trying to achieve by force what they cannot achieve by law.... Were you yourself not *guiltless, this would be reason enough to rob you of your dignity as a princess and expose you to the contempt of the multitude. Rather than such a thing should happen to you, I should wish for you an honorable tomb, instead of a dishonorable life. . . ."*

Mary sat still as stone, her lips tightly compressed, as if striving to compose herself before speaking. Bothwell cursed himself silently. She was already overwrought with fear; why had he permitted Lethington to sway him? Later, when the trial was over and the outcome known, would have been time enough.

Finally, she said, "What right has she to meddle in the internal affairs of my Realm? This is a matter for me and my Council to decide. No one—not the Queen of England nor the Earl of Lennox—shall alter my decision. The trial will take place today."

Lethington smiled. "Precisely the decision I knew you would make."

"Let us be off then," Bothwell said impatiently.

He wanted to be doing something, anything, rather than stand here havering. He bowed to Mary, "Until later, madam, when I hope to come before you, free and cleansed."

Her glance clung to him desperately, as though she were trying to memorize every detail about him. He read her thoughts and promised silently that he would return to her.

For the second time, Bothwell and Lethington came out into the courtyard, this time accompanied by Morton. Once more, Bothwell's Borderers cheered him; they mounted as one and raised their spears in salute to him. In the saddle, he looked up at Mary's windows; she was standing beside Mary Fleming, and in full view of everyone, she nodded, then waved to him. Her outward show of support touched him deeply, and he felt an enormous rush of pride.

He marched out between Lethington and Morton to the thunder of hooves at his back. On the Cannongate, packed with townsfolk turned out for the spectacle, he turned to his men with a smile and called lustily, "A Hepburn!" Their answer rang through the streets: "A Hepburn, a Sinclair, ho for the Armstrongs and Elliots," and a dozen names more called out behind them.

4

Inside the dreary Tolbooth Bothwell faced his accusers and judges. Seated beside him were his cousins Will and Thomas Hepburn, with Ormiston on his right. He listened to the clerk read his titles and the charge: "The mighty and puissant Lord James Hepburn, Earl of Bothwell, Lord of Crichton, Hailes, and Liddesdale, Great Admiral of Scotland. . . . For art and part of the cruel, odious, treasonable and abominable slaughter of the late King's Grace, dearest spouse for the time to our sovereign lady, under the silence of night in his own lodging beside the Kirk o' Field . . . "

Bothwell's thoughts turned grim; he was transported back to that night at Kirk o' Field. He envisioned the pile of rubble that had been the house. More, he saw a body lying broken and mutilated in the ruin—Mary. But for the grace of God that gave him warning, she might have lain there, irrevocably lost to him. In that instant, he hated Darnley more viciously in death than he had in life. Unreasonable rage heated his blood, and he wished the charges were true. He begrudged the real murderer his pleasurable task.

He was suddenly aware of someone tugging at his sleeve. Impatiently he jerked his arm away, but the tugging persisted. Scowling, he glanced to his right and saw Ormiston looked worriedly at him.

"What is this that you look so dark and gloomy, my lord?"

Ormiston whispered. "Hold up your head, for God's sake, and look blithely."

Bothwell didn't answer, for he scarcely heard.

Ormiston moaned. "God save us, this tragedy will bring us all yet to mourn."

"Hold your tongue," Bothwell muttered. "The end is not in sight."

The clerk called, "Matthew, Earl of Lennox," but his servant Robert Cunningham stood in his place. He produced a paper from which he read: "My lord, I am come here, sent by my master to declare the cause of his absence. The shortness of time and that he is denied of his friends which should have accompanied him to his honor and surety of his life. I demand in my master's name a postponement of this trial for forty days. But should this court persist in the hearing of this case now, and find the accused innocent of the said crime, then they shall be guilty of willful error and not ignorance."

Bothwell's counsel protested Cunningham's request, on the grounds that Lennox himself had insisted on this date. The Lord Justice Argyll voted with the defense, and the trial continued. Bothwell stood and made a formal denial of the charges. No one came forward to challenge him, nor did they present evidence of his guilt. After a while the jury retired to deliberate their findings.

Light refreshments were served. It was already past three o'clock, and those present had missed their midday meal. Bothwell had no stomach for food, but he took the wine Paris brought him, gratefully. Time passed slowly, and he was constantly aware of the men who sat across from him and of those who were only a few doors away, deciding his fate.

There were Lethington, Argyll, and Morton, whispering; all three, he knew, were his bitter enemies. Of the jury, the few friendly faces he had seen were scarcely enough to cheer him. For the rest, though they pretended lack of bias, each man was his enemy for one reason or another. He laughed inwardly, recalling something Mary had told him last night. The scholarly Master George Buchanan had been heard to comment that "the jury had not been chosen to try, but rather they had been picked to acquit."

At seven o'clock, after a seclusion of nearly four hours, the jury finally returned. Caithness, their foreman, stood and delivered the verdict. He addressed himself to Argyll, "My Lord Justice, we the jury have unanimously voted the said Lord James, Earl of Bothwell, delivered free and acquitted of art and part of the said slaughter of the King."

A wild cheer rang out from Bothwell's men, who packed the back of the courtroom. Some ran to the windows and shouted the verdict to those outside. More cheers chorused up from the street, and the jury was dismissed with the court's thanks.

Argyll said to Bothwell, "We most humbly beg that my Lord Bothwell will not seek revenge with his accusers, but will be content to let the court's decision rest."

Bothwell nodded his agreement, and seconds later he was lost to view as his men clustered around him to give their congratulations. In a few moments Mary would know the verdict too, for he had sent Paris to Holyrood with the news.

For the first time since Darnley's murder, Bothwell felt at ease; relief flooded over him, sweeping the tension from his body with an effect of fetters suddenly cut loose. He had an uncontrollable urge to leap upon the table and shout. Instead, he contented himself with sending a crier through the town and struck bills sealed with his arms in key places, offering to defend his honor in open combat against anyone who would come forward to accuse him.

He left the Tolbooth in a very different mood than when he had entered. Catching sight of him on the steps, his men went wild with joy. They rushed to him: lairds and gentlemen and their retainers. Laughing, he pushed his way through the thick wall of men to his horse; then, mounted, he leaned over to Ormiston and told him to buy up all the wine he could, so that every man here could drink his fill.

Bothwell waited until midnight before going to Mary. It was a risky business, since the palace was filled with noblemen come to town for the opening of Parliament two days off, but tonight his recklessness knew no bounds.

Mary was expecting him and had left the door to her private passageway unlatched. He stopped to gaze at her from the doorway; she had discarded her mourning and wore a low-cut gown of white satin with trailing sleeves deeply cuffed in ermine. She had combed her hair the way he favored it, in long shimmering waves that fell to her shoulders.

She ran to him and threw herself into his arms. He held her tightly, inhaling her fragrance, relishing the luxury of her closeness.

She caressed his cheek with her lips and murmured, "Now we can be wed."

Incredulous, he released her and stepped back. "Are you daft?"

"Don't you want to marry me?"

He nodded. "More than anything, but I already have a wife."

"There is always divorce. You are totally unsuited to each other."

"Aye, but scarce reason enough to apply for divorce. Even if I were free, why in God's name now? Do you imagine that I consented to have Darnley put away in order to wed you? It may be possible in a year, when this scandal is forgotten—but certainly not now. How can you even consider rushing headlong into marriage with a man so recently cleansed of regicide?"

"And if a year is not enough?"

"Then we continue to wait. Be thankful there is Jean to

prevent you from doing anything so foolhardy. Besides, I doubt your nobles or the people will have me as their king. Have I not already had proof of how well they love me?"

"You were tried and found innocent."

"Do you imagine that today's verdict ended their suspicions?"

"What more can they ask?"

"I knew from the start it was never a question of my innocence or guilt—my enemies are not the actors they fancy themselves. Fear, not love of justice, prompted their decision—fear of my power, fear that I knew the truth and would reveal it should they vote against me."

"You knew, and yet you urged the trial as much as Lennox. Why?"

He shrugged. "For a matter of record. Now no one may malign me without risking arrest. Aye, I was relieved at the outcome, but I've had second thoughts since." He drew her into his arms again. "Now do you see why it is impossible for us to wed?"

"Impossible or not, we must be wed at once—I am with child."

He felt the blood rush from his brain. "Are you certain?"

"Yes," she said, smiling. "I've been certain for a month now."

"And you said nothing until now!"

"You had so much on your mind—Jean, the trial—I wanted to wait."

He had thought that once the trial was over he could find some respite from intrigue, but that didn't matter now—she could not bear an illegitimate child. He was already contemplating his next move.

In the morning, he would speak to Huntly. His marriage to Jean must be dissolved. Telling her would be difficult, for he had assured her countless times that he would not leave her—and he had meant to keep his word. The most difficult part would be getting the nobility to accept him—that would take special handling.

He glanced at Mary. She was smiling; her face was radiant, and despite the monumental problems that loomed ahead, he was smiling too. Her announcement had finally penetrated his brain; she was with child—and by him. *The loveliest princess in the world* was bearing his child. And for the second time that day, he felt swept away with pride.

He scooped her up into his arms. "You shall give me a son," he said.

She laughed. "What will you do if it is a daughter?"

He kissed the tip of her nose. "Drown her in the Nor' Loch—unless she is exactly like you."

"You are absurd."

"Am I? Our first shall be a son, then a daughter, if you wish, then another son, then—"

"Stop, I beg you. Would you keep me forever with child?"

"Aye, if only to keep you all to myself."

He set her down in a chair by the fire and settled himself on the hearth rug at her feet.

A tiny frown creased her forehead. "Are you really happy about the child?"

"Aye, though for practical reasons I could wish for a better time."

CHAPTER XVIII

1

Parliament met on Monday, the fourteenth of April, and Bothwell's acquittal was ratified. The entire assembly of nobility, bishops, abbots, and priors held a thorough review of the trial to determine its legalities. No one could find cause to dispute the court's decision, and once again, Bothwell heard himself declared free and discharged of all accusations. By order of Parliament, it was announced publicly that anyone calumniating him for the crime did so on pain of death.

On Wednesday, Mary made her first public appearance since Darnley's murder. She rode through the streets in black velvet robes of state, her face hidden behind a long, flowing mourning veil. People leaned from windows and galleries, more thronged into the streets to watch the procession, but there were no cheers or smiles—only their dismal, stony silence.

Passing the Netherbow Port, a woman's voice called, "God bless Your Majesty, if you be innocent." Bothwell, who rode closest to Mary, saw her jerk back as though in pain; her veil could not hide the heartbreak on her face. His first impulse was to order the hackbuteers, who replaced the usual escort of Edinburgh bailies, to silence the woman, but force or violence would accomplish nothing, he knew—and there had been too much of both already.

Mary's one salvation had been the love of her people; even

Knox had been unable to destroy that. But she had lost it and must somehow regain it if she was to survive. And Bothwell was doubly afraid for her when he thought of their coming marriage. He still didn't know how he would effect it, but whatever he did, Mary had to appear blameless.

The ride was over at last; he helped her dismount and went before her carrying the scepter. The return trip was less trying, for it was already dusk when they left the Tolbooth, and few people were out.

Later that night, Bothwell told Huntly his plans.

Appalled, Huntly gaped at him. "Divorce Jean! Why, on what grounds?"

"Consanguinity, that very ancient and convenient issue."

"There is the dispensation, obtained before you were wed."

"Aye, but it's worthless, and you know it. We applied for it to please your mother, though God knows I've always held it in suspicion. The legate's signature smacks of forgery—and if that were not enough, Jean and I ignored the terms required of us, which renders it invalid."

"How so?"

"If you had troubled to read it, you would know it clearly stipulates we were to be wed by a priest, in the old faith. You mind we were wed in the kirk, by a Protestant bishop."

"You made no mention of it at the time."

"What odds to me? The old canon laws have aught to do with the kirk. Our vows were binding enough for me—and I'd have stuck to them had matters been different."

"Have you told Jean?"

"Not yet. I am riding to Crichton on Sunday. I'll tell her then."

Huntly got slowly to his feet and started for the door. He looked very weary, years older than his age. "Very well," he said, "I will abide by whatever you and Jean decide. But I cannot for the life of me see how you will gain the lords' consent to marry the Queen."

"There I have a plan, though it's not entirely clear yet. Frankly I will admit that gaining their consent troubles me less than the haste with which we must proceed. If needed, will you help?"

"Aye."

Bothwell put his hand on Huntly's shoulder. "You've been a good friend," he said.

For the five days that Parliament was in session, Bothwell's rule was supreme. New laws proposed by him were passed by the assembly unopposed. He took particular satisfaction in one, for it abolished penalizing those who followed the Reformed Church and ordered all subjects to live in amity, despite religious differences.

2

The same night that Parliament adjourned, Bothwell gave a supper in his apartments at Holyrood. Twenty-eight guests were invited, twelve earls, eight bishops, and eight lords, all of whom had sat in Parliament. Bothwell officiated with an alert eye trained on the table, seeing that no one's plate or glass remained empty. He toasted them genially, jested, and joined in their ribald songs.

He watched them, too, and waited patiently for the right moment. The expense of this night's merrymaking had not been borne for the sake of ingratiating himself with these men—he had a very definite purpose in mind, and that they would all know shortly.

His glance swept the table again; very shortly indeed, he thought. With the exception of himself and Huntly, who already knew his intent, everyone there was well on the way to mellowing, and he chuckled to think of their heads the next morning.

A serving maid squealed and ran from the room, rubbing her buttocks. Glencairn, with a leering smile, attempted to follow her, but Caithness restrained him. Argyll and Cassilus put their heads together and sang a chorus of the "Ballad of Tam Lin," their thick-tongued voices, off-key and ear-shattering, pierced the laughter and shouts. Boyd turned to say something to Rothes and vomited into the rushes.

Bothwell decided the time to approach them would never be better; he stood and clanked his goblet for silence.

Shouting above the din, he said, "A word, my lords and gentlemen."

He reached into his doublet for a paper and waited for them to settle down. Slowly, their bleary eyes focused on him. Unrolling the paper, he held it close to the candelabrum. "I have here a document I would read," he said, "after which you would all greatly oblige me by setting your signatures to it."

There were two parts to the document; their boredom was manifest to the first, nor did he blame them, for they had already heard these words several times this week. But they listened again: "Having been calumniated by evil-willers, slandered and accused of the odious slaughter of the King, James, the Earl of Bothwell, had been tried by his peers in a court of law and had been found guiltless." Therefore, he asked them "as noblemen to answer unto God to take plain and upright part with him in his quarrel."

En masse, they agreed to sign. Glencairn was the first on his feet; he stumbled forward.

Bothwell put his hand up to stay him. "Wait," he said, "I have not finished."

Glencairn tramped noisily back to his seat.

Bothwell resumed. "Weighing and considering the time present, and how our Sovereign and Queen's Majesty is now destitute of a husband, in the which solitary state the commonweal of this Realm may not permit Her Highness to continue and endure"—he paused to see their reaction.

Morton came suddenly alert. He leaned forward, his beady little eyes narrowed, stroking his greasy red whiskers thoughtfully. Some of the others were also listening now.

Bothwell took up the paper and began to read again. "But at some time Her Highness may be inclined to yield unto a marriage, and therefore, in case the former affectionate and hearty service of the said James, the Earl of Bothwell, done to Her Majesty from time to time, may move Her Majesty so far to humble herself as preferring one of her native-born subjects to all foreign princes, to take to husband the said Earl, we every one of us, underscribing, upon our honors and fidelity, obliges us and promises not only to further, advance, and set forward the marriage but to hold its adversaries their enemies and spend life and goods in its defense. Failing to do so, we are never to have reputation or credit in any time hereafter, but to be accounted unworthy and faithless traitors."

Caithness gasped audibly. Sutherland made the sign of the crucifix across his breast. If nothing else, the document had a sobering effect.

Bothwell sent Paris for pen and ink and had it set before him. "Well," he asked, proffering the pen, "who will be the first to sign?"

Huntly rose, came forward, and signed, then Argyll, Cassilus, and Sutherland, then Glencairn. Caithness and Rothes were next; the rest followed suit, except for Eglinton, who left the table and slipped quietly out the door. Bothwell saw him go but made no move to stop him; he didn't want it said later that anyone had been coerced.

3

Early the next morning Bothwell was on the road to Crichton. From there he planned to ride to Seton to play a scene with Mary they had rehearsed two days ago. In his mind, he tried to frame his words to Jean. What could he say to ease the hurt? Poor Jean, she had suffered enough blows to her pride—now this.

How empty his promise of never abandoning her seemed now. He looked up. Crichton was suddenly before him, shining white in the sunlight, surrounded by gentle rolling hills of green. He wished for another ten miles to go before facing Jean. As he dismounted, he vowed that if nothing else, she would have complete honesty from him.

She must have spied him on the road, for she came running out to greet him. "I knew you would come," she said breathlessly. "My letter could not have failed to rouse you from that madness."

They were already off to a bad start; it hadn't occurred to him that she would interpret this visit as a wish for a reconciliation.

"I must speak to you," he said.

She followed him in. At the door to his study he stepped aside to let her enter. Aware of her questioning glance, he took his time removing his gloves and cloak. She sat down, folding her hands primly in her lap, and waited. He knew that as her favorite pose, and he disliked it intensely; it suggested reproach and self-righteousness.

As always, he was struck by her plainness and wondered why he had ever chosen this insipid creature. Likely he had known the reason all along—even at the time of their marriage he must have had some unconscious warning about Mary. Jean had respresented safety to him; she could never excite him, nor did she possess a shred of the warm, passionate nature he demanded in women. He had protected himself, eliminating the danger of becoming enamored of a wife, by choosing one who held no attraction for him. And knowing this, he felt doubly guilty.

Straightforwardness, to the point of bluntness, had always been his way, yet now he sought more subtle means. But there was nothing for it, except to blurt it out.

"I am applying to the court for a divorce," he said.

He heard her sharp intake of breath and the rustle of her skirt flicked by sudden motion. He didn't meet her glance.

Softly, without emotion, she said, "It is because of my conduct with Alex of Boyne. I knew you could never really forgive that."

"It has nothing to do with you—the Queen and I are to be wed."

Her voice edged with bitterness, she said, "So, it is not enough that she robs me of your affection and lays you open to the vilest suspicion of regicide—now she seeks to deprive me of my husband entirely. I had hoped it would not come to this—and yet, there was never really any doubt in my mind, despite your promises to the contrary. But she shall not have you. She has had two husbands—mine will not be her third."

Dispassionately, he said, "I shall apply for a divorce within the week. You will not contest it."

"My brother will never allow it."

"He has already agreed to it."

"It appears you have thought of everything—everything, that is, but my consent—and that you shall never have."

"You *will* consent to it—here and now."

"I find your self-assurance remarkable. Why should I comply with your demands when it is entirely to my disadvantage?"

"The Queen is with child by me."

She laughed scornfully. "Are you certain it is yours?"

Her insinuation flared his temper, but he held himself back. "It is mine," he said.

"She seemed willing enough to play at this game," she said, tossing her head defiantly. "Now let her bear the consequences."

He would sooner have cut out his tongue than say it, but he had to. "Have you forgotten your own plight so soon? You would have deceived me had you been able."

Tears sprang to her eyes. "I knew you could never let that pass."

"Only because you forced me to remind you. If you were desperate to avoid a scandal, think how much worse it is for her. A queen, scorned by her people and the world for adultery."

She stared past him, out to the garden budding with new spring blooms. Minutes passed in strained silence; he heard the bleat of sheep and glanced out at two strays nibbling grass in the garden. He recalled Jean's words during her illness: *I will never forget your generosity.* But he had known she would and had told her so.

At last she said, "Go to her; tell her she has won."

He felt drained and a little numb; there seemed nothing more to say. He picked up his gloves and cloak and left her still staring out the window.

Unexpectedly, Bothwell found Lethington at Seton; important papers requiring Mary's signature had been the occasion of his visit. This suited Bothwell perfectly, for Lethington would prove an ideal witness.

Lethington said, "Had I known you were coming here, we might have made the ride together."

Bothwell smiled. "You were still abed when I left town. I rode first to Crichton."

"How is the Countess Bothwell? Fully recovered from her recent illness, I trust."

"Aye, my lady is enjoying excellent health again."

Lethington gathered up his papers and prepared to leave.

"If you are in no particular hurry," Bothwell said, "I will accompany you back to town. My business here will be brief." He pulled the marriage bond out of his doublet and winked.

Lethington nodded. "I will wait for you in the garden, my lord. It is such a lovely day."

The garden, Bothwell knew, would make an ideal listening post, so convenient to see, and perhaps hear, in through the huge library window, where Mary was waiting for him now.

He crossed the Great Hall and knocked on the library door. Mary called to enter. Inside, he stood with his back to the closed door. He said softly, "Don't come to me; Lethington has us in view."

When he knelt and kissed her hand, Mary whispered, "Have you seen Jean?"

"Aye, she will not hinder us."

He felt Lethington's eyes boring in and nearly burst out laughing, imagining his frustration in being unable to hear. He paced the floor nervously, hoping he looked like a man treading shaky ground.

"Open the window," he said. "That way we'll not have to shout." Then, he began uncertainly, "Madam, your nobility is of the opinion that you cannot long continue in the state of widowhood."

"Indeed, my lord. And has it not occurred to them that it may be too soon for such matters? My late husband has been gone only a few short months."

"You have a duty to the Realm and your people, madam. However reluctant you are, you must leave the graveside."

She shook her head. "Later, perhaps—in a year's time—"

"It is the will of your people, madam."

"So, now you represent my people, my lord. They have chosen a persistent spokesman in you."

"I am somewhat more than a mere spokesman, madam." He

reached into his doublet and withdrew the bond. "This will explain more fully."

She took the bond and read it. Traces of anger formed around her mouth. "This is outrageous, my lord. You have had no encouragement from me—and you are a married man with one wife already."

"My wife has consented to a divorce. As for encouragement, my faithful service and Your Majesty's good favor can testify to that."

"You did what I would expect of any loyal subject. My hand in marriage, in exchange for those services, is not yours for reward."

"Is that your final word, madam?"

"It is. Return to your friends and say that despite your very tender and affectionate proposal, my answer is an unequivocable no. You may further say that I am willing to forget this insult, providing it is never mentioned again."

They heard a slight rustling sound just below the window; Lethington was still there.

Angrily, Bothwell snatched the bond from her hands, bowed, and left. He stormed out to the garden, where Lethington waited for him.

"We can go now," Bothwell growled. "The sooner I am away from here the better."

Lethington's eyes twinkled maliciously. "From the look of you, all did not go as you had anticipated, my lord."

Bothwell stalked ahead to the horses and mounted. He tugged viciously at the reins and spurred forward. They rode in silence for a while, with Bothwell plunged into a black mood.

Then Lethington said, "I take it you have had a flat refusal."

"Aye, you take it correctly," he muttered. "Too high and mighty to wed the likes of me."

"Was that the reason she gave you?"

"No, but I've no doubt that's why she refused. I'm good

enough to risk my life—as I've done countless times for her and her mother—but not good enough to be her husband."

Lethington leaned to a side and patted his shoulder. "Patience, my lord, she may come round yet. Women are coy; they like coaxing."

"That's not the case here."

"Frankly, after your many conquests over women, I would not have thought you to fail in this. However, it's a wise man who knows when he is beaten."

Bothwell glared at him. "Beaten you say, the devil I am. It's a wiser man still who knows when to change his tactics."

4

On Monday, the twenty-first of April, Mary left Seton for Stirling Castle. She was, as she told Lord Seton, taken with a sudden desire to see her son. Her company was unusually small for her accustomed mode of travel; she had as her escort only Huntly, Lethington, Sir James Melville, and thirty horsemen. But she called it an informal visit and chose to dispense with a large retinue.

Bothwell was also traveling that day, but toward Liddesdale on the business of rounding up thieves who had been raiding Biggar. He planned on amassing one thousand men to settle the outlaws' hides. Headquarters were set up at Calder with orders for his men to join him there, and if some thought the location odd, no one questioned it.

Late Tuesday, Bothwell was roused from sleep by a message from Mary. He had warned her against contacting him, but away from him her courage flagged. For that he could do nothing; it would be sheer folly to send her reassurance in writing now. But for her second concern, he had to do something and quickly.

Despite his long talk with Huntly, and the promises he had

from him, certain difficulties had arisen. In her letter, Mary referred to Huntly as "your faithless brother-in-law." She warned that he was opposed to their plan and had called it a "mad enterprise." Further, Huntly had other misgivings, being charged with treason not the least among them. He was worried about Lord Livingston and the Earl of Sutherland, who had joined Mary at Stirling, each accompanied by his retainers. This unexpected force alarmed Mary too, for she ended with: "For the love of God be accompanied by more, rather than less, for that is my principal care."

On Wednesday, Bothwell had another letter from Mary, written before she left Stirling:

> My Lord, as to the time and place I leave that to you and your brother-in-law. I will follow him and there shall be no blunder on my part. He finds many difficulties. . . . As for my part, I will act in accordance with what has been arranged.
>
> It seems to me that your long service and the high opinion the lords have of you ought to gain your forgiveness even if you should advance yourself beyond the status of a subject. You hazarded this venture not in order to ravish me and hold me captive but to be sure of a place near me. Nor can the arguments or remonstrances of others prevent me from consenting to that which you hope your service to me will enable you to secure. In a word, it is for you to make sure of the lords and to become free to marry; since for your own support you can after such loyal service, reasonably proffer this humble request joined to an importune action. Make your excuses therefore and persuade them as best you may that you are compelled to chase your enemies. . . .

Mary planned to spend that night at Linlithgow Palace. Given his choice, Bothwell would not have come within miles of it, but Huntly's sudden loss of heart made it imperative that they meet. He sent one of his men with instructions for Huntly to meet him on the beach at midnight.

Bothwell was there an hour early, pacing the deserted beach from one end to the other. At times, he stopped to face the palace, glowing white in the moonlight, cutting its pattern of crenellated parapets into the star-bright sky. But his glance always returned to the lighted windows in the northwest tower.

Those were Mary's apartments, and he wondered what she was doing at that moment. He pictured her in bed, reading, or at her dressing table, brushing her hair. Perhaps thoughts of tomorrow kept her from sleep. Once, he had the mad impulse to call to her; how she would love a walk along the beach on this mild April night. He longed to have her beside him, to talk to her of trifles, to blot out the memory and thoughts of the events that encompassed them.

He came alert suddenly to the sound of movement on his left. A tall, shadowy figure approached him; he recognized Huntly's shuffling step and hunched shoulders. Taking him by the arm, Bothwell led him down the beach to the archery butts where they could talk.

They halted on the edge, where the water came sloshing in on gentle laps. Bothwell went straight to the point. "What madness is this you are doing to plague the Queen?" he demanded.

"Then she has written you. I thought she might."

"Aye, not once, but twice, despite the danger. If you had any doubts why did you not bring them to me?"

"I thought she might listen and reconsider, but I knew once you had your mind set, nothing could sway you."

"The time to oppose me was last Sunday when I made my plans known to you. You were agreeable then; what happened to change you?"

"I have had more time to think on it. This is treason you are planning; if I help you I will become party to it. Should even the slightest thing go wrong, we would be completely ruined."

"Too much has been ventured to turn back now. I am resolved to either lose all in an hour or bring to pass this thing I have taken in hand. Even if you forget your promise to me, there is still the Queen. Will you desert her now, knowing she is with child?"

"Aye, and about to take a husband who already has a wife."

"Have you listened to nothing I've said?" Wearily he repeated that part of his plan. "In a few days I will apply for a dissolution of my marriage, on the grounds of consanguinity. Jean will, in turn, divorce me, using adultery as her excuse. That should prove the simplest part, since there are a score of witnesses to testify to my brief encounter with Bessie Crawford. When that is done, Jean and I will both be free to remarry."

"You make it sound so simple, and perhaps it is, but there is something even you did not foresee. What of Sutherland and Livingston? They have at least two hundred men and are not likely to be passive."

"With nine hundred troopers at my back they would be fools to interfere." He started back toward the palace. "Are you convinced now that your fears are groundless? Everything will go by rote; I've left nothing to chance."

"I pray God you are right."

"Then you are still with us?"

"Aye."

Bothwell expelled a sigh of relief. "Good. Now let's hear no more talk of failure or treason—and for God's sake don't upset the Queen."

Later in the afternoon of Thursday, the twenty-fourth, Bothwell marched his troopers from Calder. By now every man knew his purpose, and more, that he had taken it in hand with Mary's consent. Will Blackadder had overstepped his bounds by

telling them, but Bothwell thought it might be for the best, for
these men might not do treason, even for him.

They rode to a small village called Over Gogar; from there
Bothwell could watch both crossings—the Almond River and
the ferry route. Mary and her cavalcade had to come by one
of these routes to reach Edinburgh.

Taut with anticipation, Bothwell waited. The sky had begun
to darken in the east, and with the sun gone the air turned chill
and damp. He hoped that Mary had dressed warmly for the long
ride ahead. Huntly still disturbed him; perhaps he had shown
poor judgment in trusting him. There was always the chance
that Huntly would run scared and ruin everything at the last
minute.

Behind him, the men jested and laughed. The setting seemed
so natural, one that he had lived through dozens of times
before. They might have been out to round up outlaws or, as in
the old days, splash across the Tweed to do their worst to an
English village. But the risk here was far greater than any he had
ever taken before; should something go wrong, all would be
lost.

Hoofbeats thundered up from the west; from the sound,
Bothwell knew they were close. A few minutes more and they
would be in sight. He waited, ready to spring the instant he
knew their route. A signal from him and his troopers were in
the saddle. He saw the cavalcade, but they were still too far to
recognize anyone. Yet, his searching glance found Mary; he
would know her at any distance, for no other woman sat a
horse as she did.

He heard the stomping hoofs at his back and raised a hand to
quiet them. The cavalcade turned to the little Gogar Burn
Bridge. He saw the first riders; they were almost at the
bridge—there was Mary, riding between Huntly and Sutherland.

"Now," he shouted, and they raced forward in a body.

All stress had left him in the relief of motion; the chill air slapped at his face, invigorating him. Seconds later, his men had the cavalcade surrounded. He spurred forward and took Mary's horse by the bridle. Instantly, Sutherland and Livingston drew sword. The others started to follow suit, but Bothwell's men moved in, forming a tight ring around them.

Mary raised her hand. "Sheathe your swords," she said. "I will have no bloodshed on my account." Then, turning to Bothwell, she asked, "What is the meaning of this, my lord?"

"There is grave danger in Edinburgh, madam. The town is overrun with rebels, and I've come to take you to Dunbar for safety's sake."

Without waiting for her answer, Bothwell turned her horse around.

"One moment, my lord," she said. "Shouldn't we dispatch a rider to call the citizens to arms?"

"As you wish, madam."

She selected one of her escorts with instructions for the provost.

"If you please, madam," Bothwell urged, "we remain here at great risk."

They rode off with Bothwell slipping back to the rear. Some of his men rode between Mary and her escort; the rest kept an eye on the others.

Bothwell came abreast of Lethington and Huntly. He said loudly, "You've no cause for alarm; none of you are in danger."

Lethington asked, "Is the town really in the hands of rebels, my lord?"

Bothwell grinned. "Have you a better motive for this?"

Lethington smiled. "I might hazard a guess, my lord."

Bothwell glanced at Huntly, who sat in guilty silence, and cursed himself for entrusting him with so much. Then he spurred forward, but not before he heard Blackadder's remark to Melville.

"Blackadder," he barked, "come here." He waited for him

to come abreast and drew him out of earshot of the others. "Who gave you leave to tell Melville I have the Queen's consent?"

"His protests were the loudest, my lord. He has no faith in this supposed uprising and vows to see us all hanged for treason."

"Aye, not one of them believes this tale of rebels, but that's no reason to confide in them. Who else have you blabbed to?"

"No one else, my lord, I swear it."

"There's no need now. Melville's clacking tongue will do it for you."

"I thought only to quiet him, lest he strike fear in the men."

"Next time keep your thoughts to yourself."

They were passing Edinburgh now. It lay heaped above them less than a mile away. The castle guns were trained on them and firing, but they might as well have fired at the moon for all the good it did at this range against a moving target. Apparently the messenger Mary had sent hadn't accepted Bothwell's story either.

Bothwell joined the front ranks but kept his distance from Mary. Night had fallen; the sky changed from a flaming sunset to fast-moving black clouds. By the time they passed the outskirts of Musselburgh, it began to rain and the road turned to mud, splashing from one rider to another. Again Bothwell worried if Mary were warm enough; her thin velvet cloak would soak through in no time. He moved into position beside her, removed his rough wool cloak, and put it over her shoulders, then rode off before she could speak.

They reached Dunbar at midnight. Though still outwardly respectful, Bothwell's manner changed. He led Mary into the Great Hall, where a fire blazed in the hearth and the long dais table was set with food.

He said, "I have ordered a light supper, madam, though it

may scarce be compared to what your French chefs might prepare. But it will suffice to warm the insides."

She flung off his cloak as though it were filth and handed it back to him. Then she went to join Sutherland, Livingston, and Melville, who were warming themselves at the fire. Huntly and Lethington stood a little way off whispering—Huntly appeared agitated.

Smiling, Bothwell followed Mary. "Your manner indicates that you have already guessed there is no uprising, madam."

"I have, my lord. Perhaps now you will do me the courtesy of explaining why you have brought me here."

"Aye, madam. You may recall the humble proposal of marriage I made you last Sunday at Seton—a proposal you received with indignation."

"Was it humility that prompted you to overtake me on the road?"

At last Huntly rose to fulfill part of his role. He said, "You have one wife already, my lord. How do you propose to take another?"

Bothwell glared at him. He thought: *Damn this brother-in-law of mine for his bungling.* It was common knowledge that Huntly had signed the marriage bond with the others a week ago; why hadn't he thought of Jean then?

Employing a tone he would use to a dull child, Bothwell said, "You mind your sister and I are related in the fourth degree, my lord. I have merely to claim consanguinity to annul our marriage."

Blackadder's admission had apparently left Melville unconvinced, for he said, "This is treason, my lord. Set Her Majesty free at once, and I am certain she will grant you a pardon."

"My word on that," Mary said, "if I am permitted to leave now."

"You will be free to go, madam—once I have your promise of marriage."

"Never!"

Bothwell shrugged. "Then I pray you will be comfortable—
for here you shall stay until you have had a change of heart."
He turned, for servants were carrying platters of food to the
table. "Come, madam," he said, "this dispute needn't dull our
appetites."

Mary threw her head back haughtily. "I would prefer to eat
alone—if you will have a servant show me to my chambers."

He bowed. "Your pleasure is mine, madam." He snapped his
fingers and his steward came forward. "Show Her Majesty to
her chambers, and see that food and wine are brought to her
immediately."

She turned from him with royal fury and followed the
steward out.

From his position as host, Bothwell glanced about at the
group who joined him at the table. He wondered if there were
any truth to the maxim that good table companions made for
good digestion; if so he prepared himself for an uncomfortable
night.

Huntly sat morose and silent, gazing at nothing in that
far-off way of his. Sutherland and Livingston assumed the roles
of outraged fathers, whispering among themselves. Melville
shifted between fear and indignation, darting furtive looks at
Bothwell or muttering to himself. And Lethington nibbled at
his food delicately without bothering to conceal his cynical
amusement.

Only Bothwell ate with relish; the others scarcely touched
their food. He helped himself to a thick slice of beef and a
chicken leg, and washed them down with a few tankards of ale,
finishing the meal with a large, juicy pear. He called for the
water vessel and a towel, and proceeded to wash and dry his
hands with meticulous care.

Pushing his chair back, he rose and bowed. "And now, my
lords, I am off to press my suit with the Queen," he said.

"The long ride has likely wearied her," Livingston said. "Wait until morning at least and let her sleep."

"By morning the matter may be settled or, for the least, her heart somewhat softened toward me," Bothwell answered.

He started for the stairway, but Melville rushed after him. "My lord," he stammered, embarrassedly. "You would not—use force?"

Bothwell looked down at the short, round figure before him and realized that Melville's dour, literal brain had caught his meaning. He said, "I am prepared to use whatever means will prove most effective, for I *will* marry the Queen. Aye, whether she will or will not, with her consent or without it."

Melville flushed, compressed his lips in a tight, thin line, and walked away.

5

At Mary's door, Bothwell paused and knocked softly. He waited, then hammered at it furiously. He shouted, "Unlock this door at once, madam."

His voice rang through the bare stone corridor and down the stairs into the Great Hall. He jiggled the iron ring fiercely. "I warn you, madam, open the door, or I will break it in."

He stepped back and lunged forward, ramming his foot into the door. The rusty old lock gave way on the first try, and the door swung open. Mary screamed as he slammed it shut and waited for him with outstretched arms. He limped to her, his leg bruised from the impact.

She burst out laughing, and he stifled the sound with a kiss. "What if they should hear you?" he said. "You might find it difficult to explain, after claiming rape."

"Who can hear us behind these walls?"

He sat down and rubbed his leg ruefully, then he walked up and back to work out the kink.

She giggled softly. "You looked so ridiculous limping in."

"So, my pain amuses you, does it? See how you like this?" He threw her off balance and she screamed again. Then he tossed her on the bed, tickling her. She bit the pillow not to laugh, wiggling to avoid his relentless fingers. At last he let her go.

She sobered. "It went well," she said. "Everything fell so neatly into place, exactly as we planned."

"Aye, by rote. Of course, Lethington hasn't been taken in by any of it. And Huntly has gone completely to pieces. But the others will bear good witness to your ravishment."

"And you? To protect me, you are willing to invite the world's scorn."

"I've lived with their scorn nearly half my life—abducting you will merely confirm their opinion of me."

She looked at him adoringly. "Has any woman ever been paid so great a tribute?"

Her gratitude embarrassed him. Abruptly, he said, "Tomorrow I will let the others go and you will send word secretly to the provost of Dunbar to come to your rescue."

She moved close. "Tomorrow is still hours away—there is tonight."

Mary was asleep when Bothwell tiptoed out at dawn. A pair of sentries lounged at the far end of the corridor. He came toward them, and they stood at attention.

Bothwell asked, "Any incidents to report?"

"None, my lord; it has been quiet all night."

"Then our guests are still with us."

The sentry winked. "Where would they go, bolted in as they are?"

He nodded and passed on to his own quarters to change clothes. He relaxed in an armchair while his barber shaved him and he approved his valet's choice of a purple and black doublet. Despite what lay ahead, he felt curiously light-hearted and more at ease than he had in weeks. Everything had gone smoothly, and he even began to wonder if his doubts had been for naught. An hour later he left his apartments and went downstairs, out into the morning.

It was one of those rare mornings, clear and bright, with a fresh breeze blowing in from the sea. He climbed the steps to the seawall and looked down at the foaming waves crashing against the jagged rocks below. The sun had come up like a giant fireball and turned Dunbar blood red. Milky clouds edged in gold dripped along the sky, traveling over the Forth in majestic parade.

Strolling to the far end of the wall, he watched a row of small fishing boats anchored a quarter mile from shore, bobbing up and down weightlessly on gentle swells. Then he turned and went back indoors.

His guests had already come down and were waiting in the Great Hall. He greeted them pleasantly. "Good morning, gentlemen," he said. "I trust you have all had good rest."

"Your thoughtfulness exceeded itself, my lord, even to the point of placing guards at our doors," Lethington said wryly.

"A necessary measure, I assure you, since one of you may have become overzealous in your duty to the Queen."

Sutherland flushed. "If any harm has come to Her Majesty—"

"That you may judge for yourselves, my lords. I will ask Her Majesty to join us—after you have satisfied yourselves, you are free to go."

"Her Majesty, too?" Livingston asked.

"No, she will remain—until she has consented to our marriage."

"This form of persuasion will afford you nothing, my lord," Melville said. "Whatever promises you extract from her are worthless if obtained under duress."

"We shall see. Now I will fetch Her Majesty, for I know you are all eager to be on your way."

Mary was awake and dressed when Bothwell came for her. "What have you done to yourself?" he asked. "You look pale as death."

She laughed. "A little paint does wonders for the complexion. I thought it might be prudent to show the effects of my harrowing night."

He nodded admiringly. "A clever touch, dearest. You may bring the lot of them slobbering to your feet."

Livingston and Sutherland rushed to her and fell to their knees.

Livingston said, "We could not leave without seeing you, madam. Rest assured, this perfidy will not go unpunished."

She turned away, too overcome for words.

"I've no wish to hurry you, my lords, but you've a long journey ahead," Bothwell said.

They made their farewells and left. When it was Melville's turn, he said, "Be of good heart, madam, we will not suffer this indignity to you."

Mary choked back a sob. "It is too late for that."

As they left, Bothwell thought: *The sanctimonious cowards.* He would never leave her to the fate they imagined for her.

CHAPTER XIX

1

The tides rolled in and out; white-crowned waves washed over the reefs in never-ending sheets. The sun rose, showering its warmth on the hillside carpeted with wild flowers in shades of gold, blue, white, and pink. Rain fell and hit the water like coins, splashing from the washed red towers of Dunbar, drenching its walks and terraces. And inside the thick fortress walls, Mary and Bothwell passed the days and nights seemingly forgotten by the world.

No one had come to rescue her; some protests reached Bothwell through spies, but they were only suppressed oaths and muttered threats that he could not take seriously. Later he would concede that although his methods had been somewhat rough and high-handed, he had acted out of necessity. Who among the nobles would not agree that women adored mastery? More, who among them would not be willing to risk his all in view of that prize?

Her second day there, Mary gave her official consent to their marriage; now Bothwell could apply for his divorce. Jean presented herself before the commissioners of a Protestant court and charged him with adultery. To speed matters, Bothwell sent his own men to bear witness that he had been with Bessie Crawford on two separate occasions.

Jean's petition was granted, and she was declared to be "no

longer repute bone of his bone, nor flesh of his flesh." But if Jean was free to remarry, Bothwell still was not. For this he applied to the Catholic Consistorial Court. David Chalmers presented Bothwell's suit to the presiding archbishops; the marriage was declared annulled on the grounds of consanguinity. It was Catholic collusion, but Bothwell was free to remarry and Mary would not have to wed a divorced man.

Mary's so-called imprisonment was relaxed; Bothwell dismissed his moss-troopers and retained only a company of hackbuteers. Mary's ladies were permitted to attend her, and there were archery matches and riding for exercise. The business of government continued; the Privy Council met at Dunbar with Lethington presiding as secretary. And no one made an attempt to rescue Mary from her cruel ravisher.

"It goes well," Mary said. "Even better than I dared hope."

They were in her apartments having a late supper. She had been at Dunbar a week, and she was the happiest that Bothwell had ever seen her.

Bothwell sat at the table absentmindedly cutting designs into the cheese with his dirk. "Perhaps," he said, "but I've been to sea often enough to distrust such calms."

"You have been preoccupied since the Laird of Ormiston's visit last night. What did he tell you?"

"Rumors mainly, but there's a ring of truth to them. There is a gathering of the nobles at Stirling. Morton, Atholl, Glencairn, and Argyll are there, and the Earl of Mar has thrown in with them. That disturbs me most, because he has charge of the Prince."

"Mar has always been loyal and held himself aloof from the warring factions. Only last week he pledged his loyalty anew and promised to protect my son with his life."

"Aye, before he knew of your intended marriage with me. You forget the animosity he bears me."

He began to thrust his dirk into the cheese, leaving craters an inch deep.

She frowned. "This new coalition worries you."

"Some, though I'm not overly concerned by it. They would have marched on me a week ago, but my troops discouraged them. That much at least proves they are reluctant to test my strength—and I mean to increase it in the near future."

"How?"

"By keeping a small standing army about us. Another five hundred men, added to the two hundred hackbuteers we now have, and two hundred more on foot should suffice—later we can think of acquiring more."

"That will take money—much more than we can afford."

"That, my love, is still the insoluble ingredient here."

Suddenly she laughed delightedly. "I have it, the perfect solution. There is Elizabeth's hideous font, sent for the christening—the jewels and gold will bring a vast sum."

He grinned. "A wondrous touch of irony. For once English gold shall go to support the Scottish Crown, rather than finance its rebels. I'd like to see her face when she hears of it!"

Four days later, on the sixth of April, Bothwell was ready to take Mary back to Edinburgh. She had been away eleven days and was loath to leave when the time came.

"It has been like living in a world curtained in magic," she told him. "I've been reborn here; I am devoid of the memory of yesterday and ignorant of tomorrow. I am lost in your love—and in loving you."

He knew what she meant, for he felt it too. But he envied her the blessed forgetfulness; his practical side kept him too well aware of their precarious situation. Unlike her, he could not pretend; his prime concern now was how the people would receive her when she returned to Edinburgh. But he could not awaken her or refuse when she asked for one last stroll on the hillside.

On the way up she stopped to pick a small bouquet of daffodils and cowslips. Bunched together, they looked like a crown of gold in her black-gloved hands.

At the top, she stooped and picked one more daffodil. "For you," she said.

He took it and slipped it into his doublet. She turned to look out at the sea, her veil ballooned out like a trail of smoke.

"If we could have just one more day," she pleaded.

"And tomorrow, you would ask for another. We cannot dally here forever."

She glanced up. "How blue the sky is today—not a cloud anywhere."

Her eyes seemed almost yellow in the sun. Like her hair, they too changed color; they were gray sometimes, then hazel, then deep brown, depending upon the colors they reflected.

2

The violet shades of evening were descending over the town when they entered by the West Port. Unsure of the reception they would have, Bothwell had deliberately chosen the less conspicuous route to avoid riding the full length of the High Street. For that same reason he took her to the castle instead of Holyrood.

Bothwell dismounted at the Grassmarket, ordered his men to put away their spears, and led Mary's horse the rest of the way on foot. People watched from the street, behind windows, and on galleries with surly, unsmiling faces. Mary never once turned her head; she stared straight ahead at the castle, preferring the grim fortress to those hostile faces.

The ordeal was over at last and she was safely inside.

Bothwell took her to her apartments and posted sentries outside her door. He gave orders that no one was to have access to her without his permission.

"How long must we stay here?" Mary asked, removing her cloak and glancing about the bare audience chamber.

"Until I am assured you are in no danger."

"Danger from what?"

He stood with his back to her, looking down at the Grassmarket. "From the nobles—the people—God knows what. But here, at least, nothing can touch you. The town is mine as long as I hold the castle—and you are safe."

"I loathe it here in these tomblike chambers."

She came to stand beside him, and he sheltered her in his arms. "Aye, fortresses ill become you," he murmured. "Your setting should be a French chateau, bathed in gentle sunshine with gardens and lazy streams flowing past your doorstep."

"You paint a lovely scene, but it is incomplete. Where are you?"

"I have no place there; the serenity would drive me mad in a week."

"Then it is not for me, either. I cannot imagine myself anywhere on earth without you."

"You may feel differently after we are wed."

She laughed. "Are you trying to frighten me so I will release you from your promise?"

He scowled and affected a fierce look. "I wonder, do you really know me? I have a vile temper and shall likely beat you often." Then, with genuine fierceness, he said, "I am insanely jealous where you are concerned—I must possess you completely. I cannot bear to have other men so much as look at you. Given provocation, I think I would kill for that."

She drew back. "You really meant that."

"Aye."

"You will never have cause to doubt me."

He brought himself up short; there was still so much to do. "Tomorrow," he said, "we will send the Parson of Oldhamstocks to inform Master Craig that the marriage banns are to be published this Sunday."

"At St. Giles?"

"Aye, and thank your stars that it's not Knox, but his successor, with whom we must deal."

"But a Protestant minister! Why not my own priest, and at the abbey?"

"Did you think I would wed you with the mass?" he asked.

"Of course. Any other choice is impossible."

"Then our marriage is impossible, for I'll not be wed in any faith but my own."

"Why are you so unreasonable? I will lose the little standing I have left in the Catholic world. What could I say—how can I excuse it?"

"Tell them it is the will of your people. It will be no lie, for your religion is anathema to them."

"Is there nothing I can say to change your mind?"

"Nothing, for I'll not convert—not even for you."

Her shoulders slumped. "I have gone this far; I cannot turn back now," she said. "There is our unborn child to consider. I'll not burden it with the stigma of bastardy."

"Is that your only reason? If I thought it were—"

"No, I would sooner die than lose you."

He held her close, burying his lips in her hair. He wondered what he would have done if she had refused to give in. Could he have left her? She was so much a part of him—such a vital part.

Public opinion was divided; some believed that Mary had connived in her own abduction, others held that she was still Bothwell's prisoner. But they had no time to worry about that, for trouble arose elsewhere. John Craig, the minister of St. Giles, had refused to call the marriage banns. He demanded a signed statement from Mary, stating that she had been neither kidnapped nor kept a prisoner against her will. But even her compliance in that failed to satisfy him, and another day passed before he finally agreed—and then not fully. There was still the question of when the wedding could take place.

Craig wanted to publish the banns on three consecutive Sundays and had flatly refused to let them hold the wedding the following week. Further, he asked to be given audience with Mary and Bothwell in order to speak his mind. His request was granted that same afternoon.

Craig stood before the Council table in open defiance. To his own amazement, Bothwell found himself without a shred of rancor toward the minister; he felt, rather, a grudging admiration for his courage. There were not many men willing to endanger themselves for their convictions.

Bothwell addressed Craig. "Please explain your reasons for placing these obstacles in our way."

"Because I abhor and detest this marriage and do regard it as both odious and slanderous to the world, my lord."

Bothwell saw Mary stiffen. He warned, "Take care, Master Craig, lest you have occasion to regret your overbold language."

"I am without fear, my lord, for I speak the law of God. My cause is just. I lay to your charge the law of adultery, the ordinance of the Kirk, the law of ravishing, the suspicion of collusion between you and your wife, the sudden divorce and proclaiming within the space of four days of it—and last, the suspicion of the King's death, which this marriage will confirm."

Determined to remain calm, Bothwell said, "I grant you my methods seem strange and immoderate, but compelled as I was by love, and being of an impetuous nature, the matter was brought to a hasty conclusion. As for my divorce, you will find it quite within the law, for it was done to the satisfaction of the Kirk and the Archbishop's Court. Lastly, I have been tried and declared free and innocent of the King's murder. Therefore, it seems that in your zealousness you have passed the bounds of your commission."

Craig's broad-featured face reddened. "I think not, my lord. The bounds of my commission are the word of God, good laws, and natural reason, and I can prove whatever I have said. Aye, by your own consciences—"

Bothwell's patience was at an end. He brought his fist down on the table with a crash. It was futile to argue further; Craig's stubbornness was fortified by his self-righteousness.

"Enough of this havering," Bothwell said. Then, menacingly: "See the banns are called at St. Giles this coming Sunday."

3

The banns were called that Sunday, but with a scathing sermon from Craig. He denounced the marriage publicly and repeated everything he had said before the Council. But he could not be accused of inciting the people, for they had been whispering those same things before that.

"There is only one way to satisfy them," Mary said. "I will give you my official pardon. According to Scots law the guilt of rape may be absolved if the woman later acquiesces."

Bothwell had thought of that days ago, but he hesitated to make use of it, except as a last resort.

Mary rode to the Tolbooth and made her speech before an audience of lords, bishops, and various dignitaries. "My lords," she said, "I am informed that certain doubts exist in your minds. You may dismiss these scruples, for although I was angered by the conduct of my lord Bothwell, in the seizure of my person, I have decided to forgive his offense in consequence of his subsequent good behavior; and his excellent services in difficult times past merit further recognition; therefore it is my present intention to promote him to still greater honor."

When Mary and Bothwell returned to the castle later, she left him and went into St. Margaret's Chapel. He strolled about the courtyard and wandered up to the section called the Devil's Elbow.

It was a mild day with no wind, yet here the wind howled madly. He walked along the narrow, open passage; on his left was a row of prison cells—one of them had held him five years ago—on his right there was a waist-high wall with archers' cutouts and below a sheer drop of jagged rocks to the Grassmarket.

He stopped at the cell that had been his and thought of the strange twist of circumstances. He had been imprisoned here for allegedly plotting Mary's kidnapping—that had been a charge concocted in Arran's frenzied mind and used by his enemies to ruin him. Now, to all outward appearances, he had indeed kidnapped Mary, and he was about to marry her.

He glanced down over the side and recalled that desperate night when he had made his escape. Seeing the treacherous descent, he was again grateful for the darkness that had hidden it from him that night. It had been enough to know the dizzying height and those rocks; to see them would have been worse. Then he turned and went back to the courtyard.

Mary was just leaving the chapel when Balfour approached her. He swept her a low bow and said, "May I have a word with you, madam?"

"Later perhaps," she told him, taking Bothwell's arm.

"I beg Your Majesty's indulgence; it is of the utmost importance."

"Very well," she said. "Come to my apartments."

Bothwell had a sudden sense of uneasiness. Balfour seemed strangely insistent. He had already been lodged in the castle when Mary and Bothwell had arrived from Dunbar; the reason had never been made clear. Bothwell recalled now that Skirling had remarked on Balfour's high-handed manner and had resented his being there. But Bothwell had been too pre-occupied to pay it any mind.

Mary drew off her gloves and sat down. She glanced at Balfour. "You may begin, but please be brief."

"It is a simple matter, madam. I am here to ask the fulfillment of a promise made to me some months ago."

"I cannot recall having made you any promises, sir."

"Not you, madam. I refer to one made by the late King, wherein he spoke of rewarding me with the command of Edinburgh Castle—when a vacancy in that post permitted."

Balfour and Darnley had been thick enough in the Kirk o' Field plot, and Bothwell thought he likely spoke the truth. This would have been his reward for helping Darnley dispose of Mary and her nobles. "Have you this in writing?" Bothwell asked.

"No, my lord, only the King's promise by mouth."

"And since he cannot testify to the contrary," Mary said, "you expect me to take you at your word."

"Aye, madam. It is my hope that you will honor that promise."

Bothwell watched Mary closely; her fingers gripped the arms of her chair, but her voice remained calm. She said, "What you ask is both impossible and impractical. Even if I were of a mind to grant your request—and I can see no good reason why I should—that post is already filled."

"Only temporarily, madam. Skirling himself told me that he is to receive a higher appointment—someone must replace him here."

"Skirling's successor has already been selected," Bothwell said.

Balfour's expression changed; his thin mouth twisted in a sneer, and his eyes turned hard and cunning. "I had hoped it would not be necessary, but you leave me no alternative, madam. There are certain facts about the King's death which might prove embarrassing, if they be known."

Mary stiffened. "Such information should have been brought before the Council at the time of inquiry."

"I hesitated to do so, under the circumstances, madam."

"I can well understand your reluctance," Bothwell said, "since you were so deeply implicated in the events of that night."

"That would be difficult to prove, my lord. But not so, were I to seek proof of your activities that same night. There are witnesses who could place you at the scene when the explosion occurred."

Furious, Mary said, "If the entire truth were told, your guilt would be paramount."

"It occurs to me that had you wished the truth known, madam, it would have been made public long before this. Doubtless, and prudently too, you are as anxious to suppress matters as others may be."

Bothwell thought: If Balfour could be silenced until after the wedding, they could deal with him later. Somehow, he would find a way to ease him out of the castle. The Laird of Beanston, a Hepburn, had been promised the post, and he would have it. It was imperative to have the castle governed by a friend.

"We cannot ignore the merit of his argument, madam," Bothwell said. Then to Balfour: "You understand that if you are given this post, your loyalty must be to Her Majesty alone."

"As it has always been, my lord."

Mary had apparently perceived what Bothwell had in mind. She said, "The Laird of Skirling will relinquish his post to you."

When Balfour had gone, she turned to Bothwell. "Will there be no end to this? Everywhere we turn, someone is there to thwart us."

"I marvel there hasn't been more opposition," he said, "but the worst is nearly over. After the wedding I will find some pretext to replace him—another post—where he'll not have the opportunity to betray us."

"I shall not draw an easy breath until we are married. I fear that something more will happen to prevent it."

"Nothing will go wrong—tomorrow we will return to Holyrood and we will be wed as planned on the fifteenth."

4

Their first night back at the palace, Mary created Bothwell Duke of Orkney and Lord of Shetland. With her own hands she placed the ducal coronet on his bowed head; she had wanted more for him, but he would not allow it.

"I want nothing but what is rightfully mine," he told her. "My ancestors held these titles before me—now they are returned to their own."

"But I gave so much to Harry, and you, whom I love more than all else in the world, will let me give you nothing but a mere title."

"You give me yourself; what more could I want?"

The day before the wedding they signed a marriage contract. A special provision was made for a Protestant ceremony, and on Bothwell's insistence, a clause was added that all documents were to be signed jointly by himself and Mary, but none by him alone. Their signatures were witnessed by the Lords Fleming and Lindsay, the Earls of Crawford and Huntly, with Lethington's and Bellenden's names below theirs.

That night Mary and Bothwell supped apart. He sat at the table with Huntly and the others, eating, drinking, and jesting, but his thoughts were far removed from that room. The clock chimed nine; it was still hours away from the ceremony. For himself, Bothwell needed no laws or religious rites to know that

Mary belonged to him—he believed the tribute to love greater without the confines of marriage.

His thoughts were suddenly scattered by Melville's entrance. Rousing himself, Bothwell said, "We have here among us a great stranger. Come, sit down and sup with us."

"I have already supped, Your Grace."

"Then take a cup of wine with me." Frowning, he pretended to study Melville. He teased, "You look not at all well. I fear the zeal of the commonwealth weighs too heavily on your shoulders."

The jest was lost, for Melville answered, "Every little member must serve for some use, but the care of the commonwealth appertains most to Your Grace and the nobility, who should be as fathers to it."

Laughing, Bothwell prodded Huntly with his elbow. "I knew he would find a pin for every bore!"

The man was a dull, wearisome creature. He was adequate enough, sometimes even clever on diplomatic missions, but that was the best to be said for him. Bothwell thought of a way to hasten Melville's going. If he remained the celebration supper would die in an agony of boredom.

Looking down the table at Ormiston, Bothwell asked, "How is your wife's health?"

"Not good, Your Grace. She ails and complains and grows more crotchety every day."

"Perhaps if you gave the poor woman respite—she is never without the company of children. Each time I see her, there is one in her arms and another in her belly. How many have you now?"

"Ten, Your Grace—not counting the one she is bearing now," Ormiston said, grinning sheepishly.

Everyone laughed. Only Melville kept a long face; a trace of color began to creep up from his neck.

Bothwell appealed to the others. "He will not desist. Twelve years wed to this one—after his first wife died in childbed—and well you know the results. For her sake I am obliged to find him a wench—one who is stalwart enough to bear some of the burden, so to speak."

A great roar of laughter went up from the table, Ormiston the loudest among them.

Outraged, Melville said, "I will pay my respects to the Queen."

Bothwell raised his goblet in salute. "Doubtless she will take much satisfaction in your company."

Bothwell left his guests at midnight for a stroll in the garden. It was a warm, starlit, windless night; a full moon hung low over Arthur's Seat, bathing it in strange, eerie light. All at once he was light-headed and wanted to shout aloud to rouse the world. It might have been the wine, but he knew it was not.

He was brought to mind of his ancestors; some had been lovers of queens, his father had courted Mary of Guise, but he would be the first to marry one. And such a queen—he could scarcely believe in his good fortune.

The wedding guests assembled in the Banquet Hall; Huntly, Sutherland, Crawford, Boyd, Fleming, Livingston, Oliphant, and Glammis stood in a knot at the French windows. The Catholic Primate, John Hamilton, and the Bishops of Ross and Dunblane kept to themselves; that they were here at all was astonishing, for they had implored Mary to refuse this Reformed ceremony. But she had given her word and would not break it. Ross had shaken his head sadly and said, "Then I fear you are lost forever, madam."

Standing at the altar decorated with primroses and bluebells, the Protestant Bishop of Orkney and John Craig waited to perform the ceremony. Unlike Craig's disapproving silence, the

Bishop, resplendent in robes of crimson and gold, basked in the glory of officiating at a royal wedding. He fawned on his reflection in the window, adjusting his gold-fringed sash, smoothing his heavily embroidered sleeves.

Bothwell stood alone, watching for Mary and her ladies to come through the doorway. He was dressed magnificently in an outfit of gold silk and russet velvet, a topaz-hilted dress sword strapped to his side. Mary, he knew, would wear black, as she had for her wedding with Darnley. According to custom she would discard her dole weeds after the ceremony.

At last he heard the light tapping of heels on the stairway and the swish of silken skirts. A moment later he saw Mary and her ladies enter. Mary wore a black-figured gown that bared her throat, which was encircled in a black lace ruff. A tiny gold crucifix hung from her neck; in her hand she carried a small Bible bound in green velvet, one that he had often seen her reading from.

The beautifully hand-painted pages were a familiar sight to Bothwell, with their dazzling purple peacocks, lush pomegranates, exquisitely colored butterflies, and scenes from the Gospel. He knew why she carried it to the ceremony, and he felt a stab of guilt. She needed something of her own faith to bring her through the ordeal of a heretic ceremony.

Of all she had endured in the past, this, he surmised, was likely her greatest trial, for by giving in to him, she had sacrificed a lifetime of teaching and beliefs. Her love was far more selfless than his, and he felt suddenly humble and grateful; had they been alone, he would have gone on his knees to her.

His contempt for the superstition and corruption of the old faith had outweighed his consideration for her. If he had thought more deeply, he might have seen what this meant to her. Because of his stubbornness, he realized her anguish too late. He had hurt her not only personally, but politically as well, for this ceremony would alienate her from every Catholic power.

He glanced at her, saw her love and trust, and vowed that she would never have cause to regret this union—he would never betray her trust in him. She slipped a trembling hand into his, and he led her to the flowered altar. She looked to Hamilton and the Bishops of Ross and Dunblane for comfort, but found none there. Her glance left them and fell to the floor. Seeing that, Bothwell thought: *God forgive me!*

They faced the Bishop of Orkney and Craig. Mary still gripped Bothwell's hand—in desperation, he thought. The Bishop's voice droned an ironic sermon from the eighteenth verse, the second chapter, of Genesis: "And the Lord God said, 'It is not good that man should be alone, I will make him a help-meet.' " He looked at Bothwell meaningfully—if anyone had forgotten Bothwell's reputation with women, the Bishop was not likely to let them. The revelation of his sermon brought an occasional twitter from the guests—especially when they recalled that Bothwell had never been alone where women were concerned. Then to his surprise, Bothwell learned, through the Bishop, that he was "repentant for his past life, and had confessed himself to have been an evil-liver."

The ceremony was short, without organ music or choir. Mary had stumbled through it like a sleepwalker; they had exchanged vows, and rings, and were pronounced man and wife—then he kissed her, deeply, lingeringly.

They turned from the altar to mingle with the guests. Bothwell watched her from across the hall, where Huntly, Crawford, and Fleming had led him for a toast. Mary seemed almost herself again; she looked up suddenly and missed him, then seeing him, held out her hand, and he was with her in an instant.

He whispered, "I want you to myself for a while."

5

In her audience chamber, Mary went to her oratory and fell on her knees. Bothwell waited for her to finish; the minutes ticked on, five, ten, fifteen—she seemed to have forgotten him. His patience wearing thin, he began to pace. Still she made no sign of rising. He left her and went to the bedchamber, then to her dressing room.

A cool breeze drifted in from the open window. Glancing down at the courtyard, Bothwell saw a guard remove something from the palace gates; he looked at it, then showed it to another guard. They seemed puzzled, then one of them took it and came toward the palace.

"What have you there?" Bothwell called down.

"A placard, Your Grace, written in a foreign tongue."

"Bring it here," Bothwell ordered.

It was written in Latin, a line from Ovid:

Menses Malas Maio
Nubere Vulgus Ait

Translated, it read: *The people say, that wantons marry in the month of May.* He hadn't realized that Mary was looking at it over his shoulder, or he would have burned it.

"You took long enough to make your peace with God," he said, hoping to distract her.

She turned on him in unexpected fury. "Spare me your mockery. I have had all I can bear of your religious views for one day."

"By that I suppose you mean the ceremony."

"You call that sham a ceremony? A more fitting term would be a pagan rite, lacking in all spiritual comfort. God has never been furthest from me as He was then."

"I grant you it had none of the pomp and mummery of your

mass, but you will find it just as binding. God cares nothing for the religion you follow—only that you believe in Him."

"So say you, but *you* are not the final authority. I am lost, lost forever—doomed to an eternity of hell."

"You babble superstitious nonsense—a trick used by your priests to cow their flock into submission."

She clamped her hands over her ears and shook her head hysterically. "No more," she screamed. "You claim to love me, yet you could hurt me as you have. Why? Your faith never meant as much to you as mine does to me."

He had asked himself that same question, and her reproach was more than he could bear. A mixture of guilt and rage choked him; it was over and done with—why could she not let it rest?

"If this marriage is so abominable, then have it annulled," he snarled. "Most folk believe that I ravished you—tell them that I also forced you to wed me."

"Is nothing sacred to you?"

"What has that to do with it? I've no wish to hold you to anything you find so detestable."

"Oh, God," she shrieked, "I wish I were dead." Without warning she lunged at him and attempted to pull his dagger from his belt.

He slapped her hand away and pushed her onto the sofa. "Have you taken leave of your senses?"

She sobbed. "Give me your dagger, I want to kill myself."

Turning away from her in disgust, he flung open the door and went out. He came headlong into Melville and Erskine, and from the way they looked at him, he knew they had overheard the quarrel.

"We are on our way to see the Queen," Erskine said.

"Come back later," Bothwell told him. "She is not fit to receive visitors now."

He left the palace by a back entrance and walked toward

Arthur's Seat. The day was warm and damp, with a pale sun drifting in and out of murky clouds. He walked quickly, as though to burn his fury out in speed. His doublet felt suddenly unbearable; the heavy velvet sleeves clung to his arms uncomfortably, and his neck felt wet inside the close-fitting ruff. He removed his doublet, swung it over his shoulder, and walked on.

He was halfway up before realizing how far he had climbed. His anger was still at its peak; was this a preview of what he could expect? Did today set the pattern for a wedded life spent in quarreling? Better to end it now, before it destroyed them. Yet, he knew they could never part—not now or ever—they were too much a part of each other.

He stopped at St. Anthony's Chapel and sat down beside the spring. Slowly, his anger subsided; grudgingly he admitted that it had been sparked by a bad conscience. He was cynical, contemptuous, often vastly amused by the old faith, but rarely infuriated by it. He understood that the true source of his rage had been with himself, not with Mary or her religion. Yet, he could never set aside his own religious convictions—not even for her. To do so would compromise his personal integrity.

He leaned back, listened to a shepherd's horn, watched the birds fly in and out among the cliffs. A breeze rustled the grass; he closed his eyes and dozed. He woke to the feel of rain on his face; it fell in great, heavy splashes that drenched his cambric shirt. Lightning flashed the sky as he ran to the chapel for cover. It brought to mind the first time he had made love to Mary. She had tapped a well deep inside of him—she had reached his heart.

It was a brief shower; the sun came out again, warm and bright. He had no way of knowing how much time had passed; it seemed like hours since he had left her sobbing. Suddenly he had a desperate craving for her, to hear her voice, to hold her close . . .

He hurried down, his boots splashing in the wet, polished

grass. Overhead the sky was bright blue and cloudless. Below, the rooftops on the Cannongate glistened with the freshness that comes only of a summer rain. The world seemed newly born, innocent and beautiful. This was his wedding day—he had taken to wife the loveliest princess in the world.

Bothwell found Mary's audience chamber deserted, her bedchamber door closed. He knocked and went in; that too was empty. The gown she had worn for their wedding lay across the bed, her Bible beside it. The sun had gone from the courtyard, casting the room in chill shadow. No tapers had been lighted; dying embers glowed in the fireplace.

He turned to go when he heard voices from her dressing room. The door was slightly ajar. Glancing in, he saw Mary in an armchair, her foot resting on a stool as Fleming adjusted her shoe buckle from a kneeling position. Seton stood at her back, fastening a gold mesh snood in her hair.

Mary had discarded her mourning for a gown of yellow silk with a white taffeta bodice and a wide ruff of white lace.

She glanced up as Bothwell came in; her eyes revealed a mixture of surprise and relief. "You may go," she told her ladies.

"I thought you had gone—forever," she said, reaching for her other shoe.

He took the shoe from her hand, knelt, brought her stockinged foot to rest on his knee. Caressing her ankle, he bent to kiss her toes. She leaned forward, and he pulled her down beside him into the rushes.

CHAPTER XX

1

"I will discover you day by day," Mary said. "I want to know everything about you, your childhood, your days—how you were as a boy."

"A savage," he murmured, nibbling her ear. "Wild, beastly, and completely unmanageable."

"I can see you as you must have been, coppery-haired and freckled—"

"My hair was lighter then, but no freckles."

"None?"

"A few perhaps, across the bridge of my nose."

She traced a finger across his face. "It is a beautiful nose; the nostrils are a trifle wide, but it becomes you." She kissed his eyelids. "Open your eyes, I want to see them. They are wonderful eyes, so intense and fathomless. Did you know they change with your moods? At times they are soft and warm, as they are now, but I have seen them turn fierce and hard, like steel—that is when I am afraid of you."

"You, least of all, have cause to fear me."

She smiled and touched his hair. "The color of beech leaves in autumn," she said. "I shall order a wig for myself to match it."

It was the morning after their wedding day, and they had awakened to the luxury of finding the other still there. No need now for Bothwell to skulk off before dawn, to leave the warmth of bed before someone discovered him there. He had the right to her now—to sleep late into the morning with Mary in his arms, to take breakfast with her, to leave their apartments hand in hand for all the world to see.

Alone in their apartments they were happy; they quarreled, but briefly, once over her gift of a horse to Lord John Hamilton. As he had warned her before their marriage, Bothwell was jealous and he begrudged any man the sight of her—he wanted her only to himself. She gave him no reason to doubt her, yet he did. Inwardly, he knew it was himself that he really doubted, for she could have sought in higher places for her husband, but she had chosen him.

But even their happiness could not blind them to the mounting danger. To the people, Bothwell was a tyrannical dictator, imbued with insatiable ambition. They still regarded him as Darnley's murderer and thought Mary had been his accomplice. And from Stirling there were rumors that he intended taking possession of the Prince, "to murder the child, as he had the father."

Bothwell's tight security measures were another source of contention. Armed guards had been posted at Mary's door; when she went out, a company of two hundred hackbuteers were always in attendance. Nor did Bothwell allow anyone whom he did not trust to have access to her if he were not beside her; he could not forget that her life had been the object of two conspiracies already. This encouraged talk that his beastly jealousy kept her a prisoner and isolated her from the nobles.

Even the French ambassador, Du Croc, believed it, and when Mary denied it, he showed his doubt openly. For himself, Bothwell scorned public opinion; he was having a difficult enough time keeping the guards for lack of money. Elizabeth's font had been melted down and minted into new coin, but that would soon be gone and the treasury was dangerously low. But whatever the cost, he feared for Mary's safety and the guard stayed.

As for the Prince, he had a solution in mind. "Send him to France," he told the Privy Council at their next meeting. "He can follow his mother's example of having been brought up and educated there."

"The lords will never allow it," Crawford said.

"How dare they tell me what I may and may not do with my own child?" Mary demanded.

"He is your child, madam, but they hold Stirling, and the Prince is in their charge," Lethington said.

She turned on him angrily. "What treason is this?"

"No treason, madam. You may see the child whenever you wish—but only in their presence—and you may not remove him from Stirling without their permission."

Bothwell cursed himself for having ever allowed the child to be separated from her. He blamed himself for giving their enemies this rallying point; with the Prince in their possession they held the upper hand.

He stood and faced Lethington. "By what authority do you speak? Are you their representative?"

"I represent no one but Her Majesty, Your Grace. My knowledge is based on what I have heard—the lords at Stirling have sworn to defend the Prince with their lives."

"What dangers do they imagine for the child? Who threatens him?"

Lethington moved back in his chair, as though to ward off a blow. Of late, he had shown unreasonable fear of Bothwell. "Forgive me, Your Grace, the lords accuse you of having certain designs on the Prince's life."

Bothwell took a step closer. The air turned heavy with expectancy; he was aware of everyone's eyes on him. Likely, they thought he would attack Lethington. "I have never even attempted to see him," he said.

Lethington nodded.

"I was the one to suggest that he be sent to Stirling."

Again Lethington nodded.

"Have I ever, to your knowledge, made an attempt to remove him?"

"No, Your Grace."

His rage finally got the better of him. He thundered, "Then, in God's name, what grounds have they for those accusations?"

"Perhaps it were better not said, Your Grace."

"Say it, confound you. We have no secrets here."

Lethington looked about fearfully. "That you murdered the father and will dispose of the son in like manner."

More to himself than to anyone there, Bothwell murmured, "The trial, Parliament's ratification of my innocence—it was all for naught."

"Since it is Your Grace they mistrust," Boyd said testily, "it might be better if you separated from Her Majesty—at least until a better understanding may be reached with the nobility."

"Never," Mary said. "My husband's quarrels are my own. We shall bear them together. More, I intend to increase his powers by having Parliament grant him the crown matrimonial—he shall be King."

"Even if it ends on the battlefield, with your Crown at stake?"

"Yes, even then. I care not to lose England, France, and Scotland for the sake of my husband. If need be, I will follow him to the world's end in a white petticoat."

2

"We must try to regain France's support," Mary said.

They were alone in their bedchamber. Mary sat at her dressing table brushing her hair; Bothwell lay sprawled across the bed watching her. Times like these, they could pretend nothing was wrong, for they felt each other's closeness without the need to touch.

But with the passing days the pretense was more difficult to keep. They could not ignore the signs of impending war—they knew the contest would come soon. They tried to keep these solitary hours apart—a time reserved for them alone—but even that had become impossible. Mounting pressures, knowledge of the inevitable, lay wedged between them, invading their peace.

"A good notion," Bothwell said, propping himself up on one elbow. "How do you propose to do it?"

"The Bishop of Dunblane will take my excuses for our hasty marriage to the French Court. He will know how best to present our side."

"It's worth a try. Once we have France's backing, the Pope and Spain may follow."

She blew out the taper, crossed to the bed, and knelt in prayer on her little footstool. Finished, she climbed into bed beside him.

She cuddled close in his waiting arms. "I will begin to draft it tomorrow—will you help me?"

"Aye. It's a difficult task you've set Dunblane, but he's an able envoy and may bring it off." He sat up. "And while we're about it, we may be able to solve the problem of Balfour by sending him to the English Court with an official announcement of our marriage. While he's gone, I'll slip the Laird of Beanston in to fill his place."

Mary spent all that morning and most of the afternoon on her instructions to the Bishop. It was an arduous test of her early training, requiring the dignity of a Queen, with the added ingredient of humility, for it was also an apology to her family.

Only the most delicate handling would accomplish the desired effect, and when she had it finished, she gave it to Bothwell to read.

It was quite long but artfully phrased; she began at length with Bothwell's history, from his succession up to the present. She praised him lavishly for his years of service to her mother and herself. On touching the events of Rizzio's murder, she spoke of his rescuing her:

> *He not only delivered me out of the hands of those who held me captive . . . but also dissolved the whole company of conspirators, enabling me to recover my former authority. Indeed it must be confessed that service alone at that time to have been so acceptable that it could never be forgotten to this hour. He has so increased these outstanding services by his zeal and diligence that I could not have looked for greater attention or loyalty in anyone.*

Pausing, Bothwell looked up at her and smiled. "Praising me as you do all but brings a modest blush to my cheeks," he said.

Innocently wide-eyed, she asked, "This modesty you profess is very newly acquired, or is it that I have never noticed it before?" Then, seriously: "It's all true; your record speaks for itself."

He resumed reading; the ticklish part came next, for she spoke of the abduction. The wording seemed strangely familiar, and then he remembered that she had borrowed this portion from one of her own letters to him, written two days before the abduction. She elaborated a little more in Dunblane's instructions, but bits of that other letter flashed before Bothwell's eyes now:

> *Your long service . . . ought to gain you forgiveness even if you should advance yourself beyond the status of a*

subject. You hazarded this . . . to be sure of a place near me. . . . You can after such long service reasonably proffer this humble request joined to an importune action. . . . That you are compelled to chase your enemies . . .

Though he said nothing, Bothwell was slightly irritated; it rankled that she had made it seem as though he had married her to save his skin. She implied that only her rank could protect him:

At no time could he find himself in surety unless he were assured my favor would endure without alteration. This certainly could only be obtained in one way if he could persuade me to take him to husband . . .

Bothwell could shrug and remain indifferent when they called him ravisher, tyrant—even murderer—but he found it intolerable to have anyone think he needed her protection. He knew, of course, that she hoped to soften their opinion of him, and that it was necessary for her pride and her political future for the world to believe that she had really been abducted—and for that reason he kept silent.

The remaining pages dealt with her final acquiescence to him and his divorce from Jean. She excused her participation in the Protestant ceremony, promising never to leave her religion again, *not even for him,* and she asked them not to lay the blame for that to his charge. Then she said:

Now that he is my husband whom I will both love and honor, all who profess themselves my friends must profess the like friendship toward him. . . . Although in some points he has behaved recklessly . . . yet I desire the King, the Queen, my uncles and other friends to bear him no less good

will. And be assured that in all that they may require of him,
they will find him ready to do them honor and service . . .

When Bothwell had read it all, he said, "Those who tutored
you in statecraft may be proud, love. It's a masterpiece of
dissembling."

"Do you think they will accept it?"

He shrugged. "They well may, for it has a ring of sincerity."

That evening Bothwell sent for Balfour and offered him the
mission to England. But after thanking him for the honor,
Balfour refused, claiming ill health.

Bothwell swore after Balfour had gone. "The sly dog—he saw
through our scheme and squirmed out of it nicely." He paced
the length of the audience chamber. "He's been warned, I'll
swear to that."

"Who could have known?" Mary asked. "We told no one our
plan."

"It doesn't matter who—that he knows is enough. I've
underestimated him. He's too sharp to refuse outright—we
could have ordered him to go. What better excuse than to plead
ill health? He knew he had us there."

"Have you thought of removing him by force?"

"Aye, and dismissed it too. He's packed the castle with his
own men; they'd defend it for him against us. It also occurs to
me the town might take sides, and I'm not willing to test their
loyalty now."

"If only we had a larger army. We could pawn my jewels and
arrange for a loan to pay for soldiers."

He smiled. "It would still not be enough, love. We'd need a
strong force to invade the castle. Your mother and I held it
against the English with only a handful of men."

"It seems hopeless."

"No, not hopeless, never that. You mind the lords urged me
to make a Border progress at the last Council meeting?"

"Yes, but you put them off."

"Aye, but it seems a good idea now. What better excuse to raise an army—and with the Council's blessing. It's only a matter of time before we meet the rebels on the battlefield—I want to be ready to strike the first blow."

She shuddered. "Is there no way of avoiding bloodshed?"

"None that I can see."

3

On the first of June a proclamation was issued, summoning earls, lords, barons, freeholders, landed men, and substantial yeomen to "report with arms and provisions to the Queen and her dearest husband, at Melrose on the 15th of June." The supposed object of this mass mobilization was to put down the disorder in Liddesdale.

From Stirling more lies were poured into the already poisoned well of public opinion. The royal summons, they said, was not for Border discipline, but to subvert the Realm's laws and to take possession of the Prince by force. Mary answered these charges in a public denial: "As for my dearest son," she said, "of whom shall I be careful, if I neglect him? Without him I could not think myself in good estate and should be comfortless all the days of my life."

"It's no use," Bothwell told her. "The rebels have inflamed the people so against us that your assurances are lost on them." He laughed harshly. "I have always been so contemptuous of their methods, but their success must be admitted. Perhaps I should have scorned my enemies less and employed their ways more."

"You could never be like them—and I thank God for that."

The fierceness of her tone made him chuckle. He watched her flick the needle in and out of a piece of tapestry; firelight and candles played across her face, casting iridescent shadows on her wine-colored gown. He frowned, for she looked pale and a little worn.

Scarcely a morning passed now that he did not awaken to her retching. At the beginning he rushed from bed to help her, but she would shoe him away, preferring to be left alone. Later, when she felt better, she laughed and teased him that despite his experience, he was still a novice on the mysteries of childbearing.

Yet neither her minimizing nor her teasing could reassure him. He knew childbearing could be dangerous, and she seemed so fragile; it would be an ordeal for her. Stronger women succumbed to the hazards, and much as he wanted this child, he would never forgive himself if he lost her because of it.

The following morning they learned of Lethington's and Fleming's secret exit from the palace during the night. They had taken all their possessions with them, and Bothwell suspected that Lethington had gone to join the rebels. He had always warned Mary against trusting Lethington as she had, but she refused to listen because of some misguided sentiment she had for him.

While at supper that evening, Bothwell had a strange message brought to him by Paris. There was nothing on the plain seal to identify the sender, and from the paper's battered condition, it appeared to have been dispatched under frantic circumstances.

He tore it open and read the short note: *Grave danger awaits you, take heed of the Queen and yourself. At any moment your enemies may attack the palace.* It was signed simply: *A friend.*

Handing it to Mary, Bothwell asked Paris, "Where did you get this?"

"From a sentry at the gate, Your Grace. He told me a youth gave it to him and said it was for the Duke. Then the boy ran off."

"Whoever sent this, we appear to have a friend in the enemy camp."

"Then you think this warning genuine?" Mary asked.

He nodded. "Enough to realize that it's no longer safe to remain here."

"Then we will move to the castle. You said it is impregnable."

"Aye, but I'm damned if we'll go there now. For one, I mistrust Balfour, and we need men. I can rally them from the Borders, but I'll not leave you here while I do." He thought a minute. "Lord Borthwick maintains a good stronghold; he's a friend and loyal. You will be safe with him."

She started for the door. "I will order my trunks packed."

He nodded. "Pack lightly, for we'll not be gone long. Take only what you need and be ready to leave in the morning."

At the door she turned to him. "In the event of an attack, do you trust Balfour to hold the castle in our names?"

"I don't know, but if the past is any indication, he's never been in league with the Protestant lords. What little can be traced to him, he appears to favor the Catholic side. You mind the Douglases were out to hang him at the time of Rizzio's murder, but he escaped in time to save himself." He smiled ruefully. "There's one good turn we'd have had from the Douglases had they succeeded."

"We have his promise of loyalty."

"Aye, but I'll remind him of it tonight, in case he's forgotten."

4

"Let them come; we can stand them off forever here," Bothwell told Mary as they stood on Borthwick Tower.

The weeks of waiting were almost at an end, and he felt vital again. Since Darnley's murder he had been forced to play his enemies' game: plot and counterplot. Circumstances had swept him into the path of intrigue with a sickening feeling of helplessness. Despite his scorn for those methods, he had become one of the major participants. Now at least he could act, and it was like emerging from a stagnant, disease-ridden pool into a clean, swift river. He was in his own element again, standing with his face to the wind, taut with excitement and eager for the battle to begin.

He looked out over the fields and recalled another time he had stood here. The years rushed backward; he saw the black ribbons of smoke rising from Crichton again. He vowed, though his enemies had robbed him of his possessions and freedom in the past, they would not take what he had now. He looked at Mary; sooner than part with her, he would part with his life.

She touched his arm. "Where are you?"

Puzzled, he said, "Here, beside you."

"No, you were gone for a while—gone where I could not follow. Your eyes were so strange and distant, as though your spirit had disembodied itself to travel far away. Promise you will never leave me like that again."

"You have my word—henceforth, you shall accompany my spirit on all its travels. But don't bank on it, for disembodiment is a trick known only to the devil."

"Some say you *are* the devil."

He smiled. "Then beware, for it's said 'you can catch the devil, but you cannot keep him.' "

She threw herself into his arms. "Don't even jest about that. A few moments ago I had a taste of being without you—it was unbearable. You are my life—my sole reason for being—without you I'd not want to live."

"You would find it otherwise, if you had to. But remember, I'll never leave you—no matter where I may be—even in death, the part of me that matters most will be with you."

Quickly, she made the sign of the crucifix. "It is unlucky to speak of death with war so close."

"What superstitious nonsense is this? Every man talks of death on the eve of battle; it's something he has to face." Then, seeing her distress, he smiled. "You'll not be rid of me that soon—I've years to plague you yet. Now, let me see you smile, for I'm off to Melrose in an hour and I want to take that sight with me."

Bothwell was back in two days; it had been a wasted ride; the rebels had been there before him, spreading the lies that he kept Mary and the Prince prisoners and that it was their duty to rescue them. Disappointed, Bothwell left a company of fifty hackbuteers to wait for recruits, and he returned to Borthwick in an ugly temper.

Mary sensed his mood and made no attempt to draw him out, except to tell him that a few supporters had trickled in during his absence. But Lord Borthwick was not so perceptive. Glad of Bothwell's company, he kept up a stream of talk during supper. "I know him from his cradle days, madam," he said pointing his greasy dagger at Bothwell. "Aye, he may take on the fine ways of a duke, scowling into his plate, but I can recall a thing or two to take him down a peg. The many times he took refuge here to avoid his tutors. He ran them a merry chase, and it's one of God's miracles that he ever learned to read and write."

Mary laughed. She seemed never to have her fill of hearing about Bothwell's boyhood days. "Did his tutors come after him?"

"They did—and often too. But I never once betrayed the fugitive. Why should a man clutter his brain with books when all he need know is how to wield a sword against his enemies?"

Bothwell winked at Mary; his gloom was lifting. "What good are swords against account books and charters?"

"I have a man who sees to those—there is not a charter, deed, or paper that passes my hand without first having my mark on it."

"Aye, and that man you speak of is likely robbing you blind—and you too ignorant to catch him at it because you cannot read."

Borthwick brandished his fist. "Let me catch him once, and I'll lop off his arm to teach him a lesson."

Mary and Bothwell laughed. Borthwick was such an easy target, and Bothwell always knew how to touch a sore spot with him.

Paris burst in on them, and from his look their laughter died. Breathlessly, he said, "The castle is surrounded, Your Grace. There are armed men outside, clamoring to be let in."

Bothwell rushed from the table, with Mary and Borthwick following. Men were hammering at the barred iron gate from outside. He looked through a gun loop. Despite the darkness he recognized one of them; it was young Kerr of Cessford, a murderous scoundrel who had recently taken part in his own uncle's murder.

"What do you want here?" Bothwell called.

"For the love of God, let us in," someone answered. "The rebels are pursuing us; we will all be killed."

Bothwell turned to Mary. "They must be desperate to use such a timeworn trick. That ruse was old in Roman times."

She looked out. "They are only a handful; what could they hope to gain? We have at least twenty men to their one."

"That handful is only what they want us to see—I wager there's an army close behind. Doubtless they planned to rush in when the gate opened, and take us by surprise—if their little deception had worked." He called to them. "Try a change of tactics, something new perhaps, if your imaginations can stretch that far."

"Is that the Duke of Orkney?" someone asked jeeringly.

"Aye."

"It were better that you answer to the names of traitor, murderer, and butcher."

Bothwell's laughter filled the courtyard, but the sound held no humor; it was more like the crackle of gunfire and almost as deadly. "More likely, you will answer to me sooner," he shouted.

There was fresh activity outside. From the thud of hooves, Bothwell's trained ear had the number at several hundred, at least. His eyes, used to seeing in the dark, searched the area across the moat. It was rapidly filling with men. The moon sailed through a cloud and lighted their faces; Morton and Home stood at their head.

Morton dismounted and came forward. "Where is the Queen?" he shouted.

Mary clutched Bothwell's arm. "Here, beside my husband," she said.

"Send him out, madam, our quarrel is not with you. We are sworn to avenge the King and to bring his murderer to justice."

"My husband has been acquitted of that charge. You use it only to excuse your treason."

"Be sensible, madam, relinquish your husband. He is a coward, clinging to you for protection. Send him out and we will go away."

"Never! You are the cowards, not he. You were willing enough to endorse this marriage two months ago. You swore to defend his innocence with your lives."

"For the last time, madam, will you reconsider? Your position here is hopeless; I have a thousand men surrounding you."

She flung her head high. "I will stay with my husband at all costs."

Someone shouted, "Whore, Jezebel, you are both alike. Let him come out and fight like a man. He gave his pledge to meet

anyone in single combat who called him murderer—let him
honor that challenge now."

Insensate rage clutched at Bothwell. He tore himself from
Mary's grasp and made for the gates. She screamed, "Stop
him!"

Borthwick and two sentries grabbed him, pinning his arms
back.

Bothwell struggled fiercely. "Let me go, you fools," he
shouted.

Borthwick said, "Use your head; by going out you will be
playing into their hands. Their taunts could not arouse you for
yourself, so they touch the one closest to you—the Queen."

"I'll kill them for insulting her," he said, wrenching himself
free, and he dashed for the gates again.

Frantically, Mary called to him. "Bothwell!"

Her voice pierced his maddening fury. He turned, his hand
poised on the bolt, ready to release it.

She ran to him. "What chance would you have? They are so
many—you are only one. After they kill you, they will turn on
me."

Slowly, his calm returned. He moved away from the gates.
She had used the one appeal that would keep him inside; he had
to think of her.

"Well, madam, what is your answer?" Morton growled.

Bothwell answered for her. "That your head shall decorate
the Netherbow Port, Morton. For the rest of you—your
carcasses will rot for carrion."

Frustrated, the rebels fired a volley of futile shots at the
castle.

His arm around Mary, Bothwell led her back indoors. "Let
them fire away all night," he told her. "These walls are
impregnable." But inside, he dropped the mask of bravado. "I
must find a way to get out," he said.

Borthwick started. "How? For truth, we are completely surrounded."

"I am of no use here. Doubtless Morton's troops are only an advance guard; Atholl, Glencairn, and Mar will swell their ranks to three times that size."

On the verge of tears, Mary said, "They thirst for your blood; you will never escape alive."

He sat down opposite her. Taking her hands in his, he said, "I must go, love. Outside I can raise troops; here I can do nothing but sit and see our cause rot."

Resigned, she said, "I will go with you."

"No, it's too risky. Besides, I'll stand a better chance alone."

"Take me with you; I can ride as well as any man."

He shook his head. "The Laird of Crookston's son is all I need. When I've gone send word to Huntly and Hamilton in town, tell them to meet us at Dunbar with as many men as they can muster." He looked at her forlorn face. "It's only for a day—two at the most. Once they know I've gone, the rebels will have no excuse for remaining, then you can join me. Slip out tomorrow night; I will wait for you in the woods at midnight—a mile west of here."

"What if I am unable to come?"

"Then I'll wait for you the next night again—and the next—until you are there." To Borthwick, he said, "I'll need a disguise. What do you suggest?"

"Why not resort to old and tried measures? It worked for you once; it should again. Sandybed disguised you as a woman; so can I."

"Aye, but who can accommodate me? Women of my size are rare."

Borthwick chuckled. "Who else but my wife! She is twice your size in width, though not near as tall—but we'll make it do."

In their bedchamber, Mary stood at his back, gazing at him in the mirror. She smiled, despite her misery. He looked back at himself and shuddered in horror; he wore a bright green satin gown, slit to fit his shoulders, with a voluminous skirt that barely covered his knees. A silver wig clustered with curls covered his hair. He turned to the left, then to the right, pursing his red-painted lips, imitating a woman admiring herself.

Borthwick looked on with equal horror. "The mere sight of you is enough to cure a man of all women for the rest of his life."

Bothwell pouted and batted his eyelids. "I may lack beauty—but I can cook and sew."

Mary was no longer smiling when she brought him a hooded cloak. "Take care, love," she said.

He held out his arms to her. "Until tomorrow."

They embraced for only a moment, then he pulled away. To Borthwick he said, "Keep her here; don't let her come down with me."

His escape was bound to be difficult; only a miracle would get him past the rebels without being seen. Mary would be frantic if she heard gunfire; she might even rush out to help him. With her safe in her chambers, with Borthwick to watch her, he was at least free of that worry.

Young Crookston waited for him with their horses at the postern gate. Slowly, with painful care, Bothwell lifted the rusty bolt. The slight noise he made seemed magnified a hundred times to his ears.

Mounting, he said to Crookston, "If they see us, take the opposite direction from me. That way they won't know which of us to follow."

They galloped out and made only a few yards when Home's men spotted them.

"Now," Bothwell shouted and raced off to the west. He

turned once to see Crookston riding to the east with a company of men hot in pursuit of him. Passing only a breath away from more rebels, he heard the whack of arrows discharged from their crossbows. Crouching low in the saddle, he felt one pass less than an inch from his temple. Cruelly he dug his spurs deeper into the horse's sides and sped on.

His hood had slipped off, the wig hung askew on his head, and his skirt had climbed to his waist and ballooned out grotesquely over the horse's rump. At last he reached the wood and stopped to listen; there was no sound of pursuing horsemen behind him. He felt that he was out of danger now and hoped Crookston was too. Dismounting, he flung off Lady Borthwick's hideous garments and resumed his ride in comfort.

So near Crichton, he knew every tree, footpath, and bump in the road. He thought of Jean lying snug and untroubled in her bed. Did she still keep his bedchamber aired and smelling of cedar? A mental picture of that comfortable bed reminded him of how tired he was. He thought: Jean was likely glad to be rid of him and had ceased doing the things that would remind her of their strange marriage.

Since his marriage to Mary, it had been rumored that he preferred Jean. Some said he still thought of her as his wife and held Mary as his mistress. As proof, they cited his frequent letters to Jean. He did write to her, but only out of necessity. There were transfers of deeds and charters, accounts to be settled—business matters left unfinished by their swift divorce. To favor Jean over Mary would be like preferring base metal to gold.

It was still hours to dawn when he rode into Morham. He roused the gatehouse guard, who after a lengthy barrage of questions finally lowered the drawbridge to let him in. A sleep-dulled stableboy took his horse, and another servant, in nightcap and robe, let him into the house.

Bothwell asked for pen and ink, sent the man back to bed,

and went to the library. Inside, he lighted some candles and sat down to write. He calculated the men he could raise from his territories. The Border lairds could be counted on to follow him; men like Ormiston, Langton, Wedderburn, Waughton, and Bass, each with his own retainers, would make a good-sized army—but still not enough. There were also Seton, Yester, and Borthwick—he could be certain of them—but his greatest hope lay in Huntly and Hamilton with reinforcements from Fleming. For the rest, he could enlist supporters from nearby districts.

He wrote brief messages to Huntly and Hamilton, then went to the servants' quarters to send them with riders. Suddenly he was overcome with weariness; he had had almost no sleep in three days. Riding to Melrose, his futile efforts there, the ride back to Borthwick, and tonight's mad dash to Morham—all without rest— had caught up with him.

The need for action had equipped and sustained him with tremendous energy; now that he could only wait, his body demanded rest. Sleep tugged at his eyelids, his shoulders ached, and he longed to stretch out on something soft. He felt even too tired to climb the stairs, and he thought of the couch in his mother's sitting room across the hall. It was too short for him, but he curled up on it anyway and fell asleep.

He was still asleep when his mother found him in the morning. She stood with arms folded, looking down on him disapprovingly. "Are there not enough beds here that you must sleep tangled in a knot?" she asked.

Yawning, he stretched and grinned up at her sheepishly. He marveled that her scolding never ceased to make him feel like a small boy caught at the honeypot. "I arrived late and didn't wish to disturb the household," he said.

"You've come at odd hours before—have I ever complained?"

He got up and went to the window. His body felt stiff and

ached from the cramped position he had lain in all night. It was still early, but it was already oppressively hot. Unbuttoning his shirt, he glanced up at the blinding sun; he had never known mid-June to be this hot.

Irritably he said, "I needed sleep, not companionship."

"There is trouble." She didn't put it as a question but as a statement of fact.

"Aye, it's come to civil war."

"You knew it would. Months ago you sat in this very room and told me that you and she could never wed for just that reason. What changed your mind?"

"She is four months with child. If not for that, we would have waited a decent interval—until the people found me more acceptable."

"Then you merely did what had to be done."

He turned on her angrily. "No. You make it sound as though I were pushed into it unwillingly. I wanted her, I had to have her."

"Is she worth having, for all this?"

"If it's worth having the one thing that means more than life itself, aye, then she is worth having."

"I pray God she cares as much for you."

"She risks a kingdom for me."

He had no appetite, only an enormous thirst that he quenched with ale. A thousand thoughts nagged at him, and they were all of Mary. He worried that the rebels had consolidated forces outside Borthwick. Despite his confidence in those massive walls, anything could happen. If it came to open combat, there were not enough men to defend the castle against a strong attack. Should any harm come to Mary . . .

After an early supper, he started for Borthwick. From his mother's stables, he borrowed a cob and a man's saddle for Mary.

His mother held him in a long embrace. "God be with you—both of you," she said.

His son, Willie, clung to her skirts, tears in his eyes. Bothwell found the child's affection for him strange, for they scarcely knew each other. He promised himself to see more of the lad in the future, then he mounted, waved, and rode off.

The long summer daylight lingered; he knew it would stay with him throughout the ride. He rode slowly for the sake of the riderless horse that trailed behind on a rope. Mary came to his mind, and his spirits rose to think of her riding beside him on the trip back.

He would take her to Dunbar; his messages must have brought results by now. The courtyard at Dunbar was likely filling with men from all over the Border. Ormiston would surely rally the moss-troopers—he had more confidence in them than in an army three times their number. They were fierce fighters, the kind to have at your back in the thick of battle.

He came as far as the wood below Borthwick but dared go no farther. The horses tied to a tree, he sat down to wait for Mary. Dusk came quickly; the little light left in the sky was hidden by thick branches of leaves. Gossipy birds twittered overhead, a few rabbits flitted by, and a chipmunk watched him from a clump of bushes.

The interminable waiting frayed his nerves; he felt certain that something had gone wrong. She would be here by now unless . . . He shook his head, the thought was too awful to contemplate—yet it persisted.

With maddening haste, his mind jumped to a dozen possibilities; by some remote chance the rebels could have gained entry to the castle. They might have attempted to take Mary prisoner. She would resist and could have been killed in the struggle. He swore, if they harmed her—whatever happened, he couldn't bear another minute of not knowing. He jumped to his feet and started to run.

Breathless, sweating, his temples throbbing, he ran toward Borthwick blindly, oblivious to the dangers that might await him there. Not caring that his weapons lay back in the wood, he raced across the clearing.

"Bothwell."

He heard his name but did not stop; it was in his mind, he told himself. He had heard Mary call; she needed him.

"Bothwell, wait!"

He stopped sharply and turned. A lad stood before him, then he heard the sound of laughter; it was like tinkling crystal.

"Don't you know me, dearest?"

He stared into the moonlit dark; it was Mary dressed in breeches and doublet, with a man's toque on her head. Confused, nearly stumbling, he rushed to her, crushing her in his arms, kissing her hungrily.

"Thank God you are safe," he said. "I'll never let you out of my sight again. These past twenty-four hours have been hell."

"For me too. We heard the commotion last night. I thought you had been captured. Then we learned Crookston had been taken instead of you."

They walked back to the wood. "How did you get out?" he asked.

"Lord Borthwick lowered me out a window."

"What took you so long? I've been half out of my mind with worry."

"I took a wrong turn—I am not as familiar with this area as you."

He kissed her again and lifted her to the saddle. Surprised, she said, "A man's saddle! How did you know I would be wearing breeches?"

He smiled. "Two minds so close we share the same thoughts."

She reached over to touch his hand, and they galloped off toward Dunbar.

CHAPTER XXI

1

They arrived at Dunbar at three in the morning. Mary showed no sign of weariness; the ride seemed to invigorate rather than tire her. She asked for food and consumed a hearty meal. Bothwell listened with pride to her plans for their campaign against the rebels. Danger seemed only to intensify her courage; she was ready to dare anything.

She would have sat up the rest of the night with him, to pore over maps and plot their next move, but he wouldn't have it. "If you won't think of yourself, then think of our child," he said.

"Men," she scoffed, "you are all alike. Childbearing comes naturally to women, but you make it seem so mysterious—"

"Must I carry you upstairs like a spoiled infant—or will you go of your own accord?"

Stubbornly, she folded her arms and tossed her head.

"As you wish, madam," he said, gathering her up into his arms.

In their chambers he set her down on the bed. "Stay with me," she pleaded, settling back on the pillows.

Her voice fell soft and childlike on his ear; she looked so appealing. Reluctantly, he shook his head. "There is a deal to do and so little time."

"Please. It will be dawn soon," she said, extending her arms to him. "Stay until then."

He couldn't resist. "Only if you promise to sleep."

"I will—in your arms."

The courtyard began to fill with men; irregular contingents supplied by the Border lairds, retainers from the Lothians, and Bothwell's trusty moss-troopers. They were shabby, most of them, hardly the kind of army he would choose, but he needed manpower and they were that, at least.

A fresh summons had been issued throughout the area for all men between the ages of sixteen and sixty to rally to their support. They waited for the response and for the arrival of two hundred hackbuteers that Bothwell had left behind at Melrose and Borthwick.

Despite lack of sleep, Bothwell was a mass of energy; he was up at dawn and everywhere at once. He checked the storeroom for artillery, calculating how much he would need and the quantity of arms to be issued. The giant cannons were dislodged from their mountings and made ready for field use. Water barrels were prepared, for he knew their importance on a hot day in battle.

Toward afternoon, Paris came to the ramparts with word of a deputation of three burgesses who had arrived from Edinburgh. Grimy and sweat-soaked, Bothwell left the supervision of the cannon to Ormiston and went to his chambers. He didn't want these men to report the Duke of Orkney had been doing lackey's work.

Washed, and wearing fresh garments, Bothwell joined Mary in the Great Hall, where the deputation waited. The trio bowed to them.

"What news do you bring?" Bothwell asked.

"The Lords Morton and Home with divers more have entered the town, Your Grace. We heard their proclamation and request for support at the Market Cross." The spokesman turned to Mary. "We beg Your Majesties to excuse this, and believe that only a scant few townsfolk joined them."

"How strong would you say the rebels are?"

"Well over a thousand, Your Grace, with more said to be on the way."

"Did the castle give no resistance?"

"None, Your Grace. Not even one cannon shot was fired."

"What did their proclamation say?" Mary asked.

The man paused; he looked first at Bothwell, then to the floor.

"There's no need for squeamishness," Bothwell said impatiently.

"Your Grace's pardon, they claim to have undertaken this revolt to deliver the Queen from captivity, to punish the murder of the late King, and to protect the Prince."

Mary laughed scornfully. "For that they need only look among themselves."

"Are the Earl of Huntly and Archbishop Hamilton still in town?"

"Aye, Your Grace. They entered the castle yesterday."

Alone with Mary, Bothwell said, "With Huntly and Hamilton in the castle it seems strange they did not turn the guns on the rebels."

"Likely Balfour had something to do with that."

"Aye, but they would outnumber him."

"You were suspicious of Balfour from the start."

"It's more than that; something is not right. You sent word from Borthwick for Huntly and Hamilton to join us here."

She nodded. "The messenger may have been intercepted by Morton's men. He may never have reached them."

"I thought of that and sent another from Morham. They must have received one of our messages, yet they remain in town. Why?"

Something else was worrying him, but he hadn't told Mary. This morning he had learned that the rebels had been inflaming the Border against him. They had spread the lies that he held Mary prisoner and had designs against the Prince's life. Despite their loyalty to him, Borderers were simple, credulous folk, and communications were almost nonexistent in those remote areas. They were apt to believe what they heard and would hesitate to do treason—even for him. Some accepted the rebels' lies, while others who were still in doubt kept to their homes. This would leave a serious gap in the men he had hoped to amass.

They had more word from Edinburgh the following day. Balfour had sent Edmund Hay with urgent word that Bothwell should march on the town. The rebels, Balfour said, would retreat and disband if he turned the castle guns on them, but if Mary and Bothwell stayed at Dunbar, he would be forced to make terms with their enemies, for they outnumbered him.

The decision to march or stay rested with Bothwell alone. He paced the Great Hall's earthen floor, torn between the impulse to move and the prudence of staying at Dunbar until he had more men. If Balfour told the truth, he had to march or risk losing Edinburgh. On the other hand, if Balfour lied and he had already joined the rebels, his message was a trap. It could be a grave error to leave Dunbar with the scant troops they had.

The awaited hackbuteers had arrived late last night; there were sixty regular cavalrymen, the moss-troopers, and some infantrymen, that was all. Of course, they would pick more up along the way: Seton, Borthwick, and Yester with their detachments, Fleming and Lord Hamilton with their reinforcements—and he hoped for more volunteers.

He also had Mary to consider; early that morning she had been violently ill, vomiting and nearly fainting. These last few days had done her little good. He had ordered her to stay in bed all that day, and exhausted, she had given in without argument. He worried about her making another march and the risk of anything happening to her. But if they should lose the capital . . .

His shirt felt wet and stuck to his back; the Great Hall was stifling, heat-baked, and turned to an oven. He went out on the terrace, hoping to find a breeze there. A glaring sun beat down on the motionless water; sluggish waves lapped the reefs. The quay was deserted; no children played at the shore, no women waited for returning fishing boats. The world seemed hushed, clothed in a haze of relentless heat.

"I have decided to march," Bothwell told Mary. "We lose everything if Edinburgh falls to the rebels."

She sat up in bed. "When?"

"Tomorrow morning. I will send word to the others. They can meet us at Haddington."

She threw the covers off and started to get out of bed. The color had returned to her face; her eyes lighted with excitement.

"No," he said, easing her back against the pillows, "stay where you are. You'll need all your strength to carry you through tomorrow."

"You worry needlessly, dearest. I grant you I was ill this morning, but I am fine now."

"If you will not rest for your own sake, then do it for mine. I have enough on my mind without your adding to it."

His sharp tone kept her from protesting; obediently she lay back.

2

Frowning, Bothwell turned in the saddle to look back at Dunbar, burning red in the sunrise. Doubt still plagued him as he led their small army away from its protective walls. He thought: *God grant I have made the right decision.*

Mary rode beside him, looking more like a country lass than a queen. She had discarded her man's attire and had borrowed what she could from the women at the castle: a short red petticoat, sleeves tied in points, a cutting scarf from a moss-trooper, and a velvet toque.

Bothwell fastened his glance on the standard-bearer. The royal standard hung limp from its pole; even at a gallop there was no breeze to unfurl it, and the Red Lion rampant lay hidden in the folds of gold.

With each village they passed, more recruits fell into rank, and by the time they reached Haddington their number had risen to six hundred horses with infantry besides. On entering the town, they were joined by Seton, Borthwick, and Yester with more detachments. Mary took heart in their increase and expected even greater response along the way.

But Bothwell felt no such confidence; he could only look at their army and think: *Not enough.* Where were Fleming and Hamilton? They should have been at Haddington with the others; they had promised to meet him, yet no one knew their whereabouts. In any case, he couldn't wait for them—perhaps they intended to join him near Edinburgh. Turning, Bothwell gave the signal to resume the march.

They halted a mile farther on at Gladsmuir, to read Mary's answer to the rebel's proclamation. A herald read her statement: "The rebels lied; my husband has already been declared innocent, which the rebels have ratified in writing. As for my alleged captivity, my public marriage, endorsed by the same men who now oppose it, disproves that charge unalterably. And lastly, the Prince is in the rebels' care, and therefore in no danger from others."

Then she promised a reward to the men there if they fought well for her cause. The herald's voice intoned, "Forty pounds Scots to any man for slaying an earl, twenty pounds Scots for slaying a lord, ten pounds Scots for a baron and a piece of his property besides." The army listened, cheered loudly, and the march resumed again.

They halted at Prestonpans for the night, but Bothwell, remaining adamant that Mary have the comfort of a bed, took her to Seton. They arrived there weary and hot, but confident that the following night they would sleep at Holyrood. He insisted that she go to their chambers and take supper there, promising to join her soon. First, he had to talk with Seton and the others to brief them on his plans of attack.

He came in softly, thinking she might be asleep; instead he found her at the window looking out. She had bathed and changed into a thin pale-green robe. He went to her and kissed her forehead—it felt feverish to his lips. He touched her cheeks, her throat—they too felt hot.

"Were you ill again?" he asked.

She shook her head. "You worry about me, when it is you who needs rest more."

"I think it is because I love you too much."

"There can never be too much love."

He knelt at her feet, took her hands in his, and kissed her palms. "No, not the way you mean." He paused thoughtfully. He knew the feeling well enough, for he had lived with it since the day he knew he loved her—but it was so difficult to put into words.

He began, "In loving you too much, I live with the constant, gnawing fear of losing you. I told you once that even the look of another man would drive me to kill for you—now that you really belong to me, the danger in that is so much greater."

Then, more to himself than to her, "Aye, loving you has robbed me of an inner peace. I cannot rest for fear of something happening to you. It's a feeling new to me, and I'm in awe of it for your ability to do this to me."

Her eyes were aflame with pride and love. "I thought you had already paid me the greatest tribute—but this is more than I have the right to expect."

He rose, feeling a little strange for that long speech; only she could make him reach so deeply inside of himself, she alone had taught him to love. "Now see what you've done," he said gruffly. "Next you will have me spouting poetry from one of your books."

"Your own words are more beautiful than any found in books, for it came from your heart."

He pulled off his boots and shirt and lay down on the bed. She came to lie beside him. Weariness flooded over him; all at once he felt the effects of the past week. Physical exertion had nothing to do with it—he had done as much and more without feeling it—he knew it was worry that exhausted him.

He had fought battles with deadlier foes and had always been at ease on their eve. His only concern had been the outcome; the possibility of meeting death had mattered little. Basically, he was a soldier with a soldier's philosophy; without giving it much thought, he believed that if death came, let it—he could never imagine himself dying peacefully in bed. Given a choice, he would take a warrior's end—a swift, clean thrust of the sword.

But the past had been different; there had never been so much at stake, never so much to lose—and for the first time Bothwell experienced fear. It was a strange, gnawing terror, and he struggled with it awkwardly. It was not fear for himself, but for Mary.

What would happen to her if they lost tomorrow? She would be entirely alone if he were captured or killed. If she fell into rebel hands what would those greedy brutes do with her? With him gone there would be no one to lead her army, for in all humility he knew himself to be the only one she had capable of that. Seton, Borthwick, the others—they were brave and willing to fight, but they knew nothing of strategy. They could follow, but they could not lead.

He moved restlessly; despite the open casements there was no air, and the oppressive heat encompassed him. His pillow was soaked and clung to his neck uncomfortably; the sheet felt clammy and creased under his bared back. He lay wide awake, staring at the ceiling, intensely aware of Mary's closeness.

She turned to him and kissed his eyelids. Her fingers caressed his face, soothing his temples in short, gentle strokes.

He reached for her and drew her mouth to his. "Don't stop what you are doing," he murmured.

Slowly, he felt the tension ease away and drowsiness overtook him.

Daylight came as burnished gold; the sun glittered darkly through a lacy pattern of scorched leaves. Bothwell had been awake long before dawn, but he lay there watching her sleep. She had moved close to fit the contours of his body, her head rested on his shoulder, and he felt her warm, even breathing on his chest. A rush of tenderness swept over him; he longed to crush her to him, but he let her sleep—there would be other nights.

Toward dawn he heard someone tapping at the door and slipped from bed. Seeing Paris, he asked, "What now?"

"A rider is here with news of the rebels, Your Grace."

"Do you know what it is?" he asked, stepping out into the corridor.

"Aye, they marched out of Edinburgh at two o'clock this morning and are headed toward Musselburgh."

Bothwell swore. He had hoped to take them by surprise. The courier had said the rebel forces numbered about three thousand, for they had been joined by Highlanders. They had no artillery to speak of, but their cavalry was well trained.

He sorted the information in his mind: their armies were equal in size; he had the field guns from Dunbar, four great brass cannons; the rebels seemed to have none. But the difference lay in the caliber of their men, and Kirkcaldy of Grange, the only professional soldier on their side, led them.

Kirkcaldy would command the horse, made up of well-trained men, while Bothwell had only his moss-troopers and the hackbuteers to count on. For the rest, his was a rabble army, undisciplined and taken from the civilian populace.

Bothwell returned to his chambers. Mary was still alseep. He lighted a candle and looked at her little French clock; dawn was only an hour away—he must wake her soon.

He blew out the candle and went to the window. Usually these were the coolest hours, but no breeze came in from the sea now to rustle the leaves, no sounds at all on this heat-heavy night. There was no sign of rain in the sky; the moon had gone, and the last stars were fading with a promise of clear weather ahead. He was still at the window when the tawny light of day came. He went to the bed and kissed her awake.

She opened her eyes and smiled up at him. "Such a lovely way to begin the day," she murmured. "I shall expect the same every morning."

He bowed. "Your wish is my command, madam."

She reached out to him and pulled him down beside her. "We have something to celebrate today."

"Have we?"

She laughed. "Let me give you a hint. Something that took place just one month ago today."

"You will have to do better than that if I am to guess. Was it a great event, or small?"

"That would depend—seeing how you have forgotten already, perhaps our wedding was a small event in your eyes."

"Oh, that! I thought you meant something really important."

"You *had* forgotten."

"Look under your pillow," he said, chuckling.

She drew out a dark-blue velvet box; it contained the Hepburn ring. The emeralds bridling the horse's head glittered in her hand.

He smiled at her pleasure. "A small gift to commemorate a small event—our first month together as husband and wife."

"But I have no gift for you."

"I have you."

She read the engraved motto aloud: "Keep Faith." She put it on and held her finger to the light to admire it better. "I will wear it today for all to see."

"I'm glad you are so well pleased," he said. "But you had best dress now; we must be on our way soon."

She put his hand to her cheek and fondled it there. "You could not have chosen anything I would want more," she said. "I shall wear it always."

While she dressed, he told her of the message the courier had brought.

"Then we shall fight them in the field and bring their leaders prisoners to Edinburgh," she said.

Her optimism delighted him. "You have no doubt of the outcome?"

"None, for we have the greatest general on our side."

3

They rejoined the army at Prestonpans and began working their way south, toward Musselburgh. It was a slow, torturous march under a blazing sun. The huge cannons rolled on behind them, on platforms with wooden wheels that groaned with every turn. The men made several stops for water, until Bothwell ordered the barrels closed. He wanted to conserve their supply for later, when they would need it most.

By noon he had chosen his position on the high ground of Carberry Hill. The field guns were placed to command the slope, up which the enemy had to advance for an attack after first crossing the burn at the foot of the hill. As an added feature, Bothwell also had the advantage of the old entrenchments from the Battle of Pinkie, fought on those grounds twenty years before. He had assured himself an excellent defense from every aspect.

Defense was their only course for two reasons; for one, Mary could not bring herself to open fire on her own subjects, but more, Bothwell thought it made good military sense. The rebel troops were far superior to his own; despite his artillery, a charge into enemy ranks would be foolhardy. Better to fend off an attack than to initiate one and lose his vantage point.

His position set, Bothwell went to review his men. Again he was struck by their shabby, disheartening appearance. Then he discovered that only a few had brought provisions as ordered; the rest had come totally unprepared. They had not even thought to bring water—such a vital thing on a broiling day. Their only supplies were the barrels he had brought from Dunbar, scarcely enough to slake the thirst of so many.

Cursing them for dolt-headed fools, he returned to Mary. She smiled wanly and put her hand out to him, then she turned suddenly and ran. Following, he found her crouched over, vomiting into the grass. The heat had sickened her. He looked around for shade, but there was none, not even a shrub to protect her.

He left and returned with a light silk cloak and four long pikes. Driving the pikes into the ground, he tied a corner of the cloak to each of them and improvised a tent for her. At least now she had some shelter from the sun, and she went to sit down under it gratefully.

He brought her a jug of water. She took the cup he offered and drank quickly, then she held it out for more. Through her stiff, forced smile, he knew she was ill. The heat was too much for her—too much for everyone.

He glanced up at the sky for the hundredth time that day. "If only it would storm," he said. "God knows it's hot enough for it."

His glance searched the road, past the rebels' advancing army. He looked for a swirl of dust—some sign that Huntly was coming. Where was he? Where were Fleming and Hamilton? He had sent word to them last night again.

She read his thoughts. "What are our chances if Huntly and the others do not come?"

"Better with them, but we can manage without them if we must," he lied.

Without reinforcements, how long could these civilians last on such a day?

"They will come," she said.

He looked toward the men; they worked sluggishly, unloading carts of munitions, making the cannons ready for firing, passing out arms. He saw them stop to rest now and then, and to watch the rebels take up their position on a hillside just beyond the scope of his cannons.

"Go to your men," she said. "They take their courage from you."

His moss-troopers hailed him. In their lack of deference, they showed more reverence and respect than if they had bowed and scraped at his feet. He welcomed their intimacy more now, because it seemed to give the others heart. He knew most of the troopers by name and passed among them, asking about their families, jesting with them, lending his shoulder to an extra-heavy load they had to lift, encouraging them.

Dalgleish tapped his shoulder. "Look, Your Grace, a party on horse approaching. They carry a white banner of truce."

Bothwell judged their number at close to fifty. "They intend a parley, no doubt," he said and ordered thirty men to escort them to Mary.

He could make out the elegantly clad figure of the French ambassador, Du Croc. He knew Du Croc had been employed these last days in attempting to bring about a peaceful agreement between Mary and the rebels. That was likely his purpose in coming here now. Having little patience with the formalities observed by diplomats, Bothwell waited before joining them.

He came up in time to hear Mary say with royal indulgence, ". . . if, however, they are ready to ask my pardon, I will grant it."

Apparently Du Croc had given her the rebels' all too familiar peace terms. Bothwell knew what her answer had been without having to hear it—she would never leave him.

He stepped up to where the Frenchman stood, and they saluted each other. Bothwell asked loudly, "Am I the sole object of the rebels' hatred?"

"The lords profess themselves Her Majesty's obedient servants," Du Croc said. Then, lowering his voice: "But they are Your Grace's mortal enemies."

"So have they always been. But what harm have I done them? I have never troubled any of them since my marriage; they are under no threat from me." He glanced at Mary, pride in her filling his eyes. "Their words proceed from envy of my favor.

But Fortune is free to any man who can win her. There is not a man among them who does not wish himself in my place."

He knew this was breaking Mary's heart. She could not bear the thought of her subjects about to engage in fratricidal battle. And he knew that she was deathly afraid for him. If there were some way to prevent her suffering—to end her agony the sooner . . .

With his usual impulsiveness, Bothwell said, "Owing to the Queen's distress, I should like to spare her the sight of bloodshed. Will my enemies agree to single combat? I will gladly meet any man of equal birth—my cause is just, and God will be on my side."

"The lords have already proposed that," Du Croc said, "but I felt loath to suggest it. Now, however, since it is Your Grace's wish, I may speak frankly. They have offered to send twelve men to engage you—and as many more as it will take to beat you."

Mary's eyes widened in horror. "No, I will never allow it—it will be your murder." To Du Croc she said, "My husband's quarrel is my own; we will stand it together."

Du Croc shook his head sadly. "Is there nothing I can say to avert this tragedy?"

Bothwell started to argue against Mary's refusal; he knew himself to be a better swordsman than anyone the rebels had, and it was the one way to end needless bloodshed. But the protest died on his lips, for the rebels were beginning to ford the burn.

He turned to Du Croc. "The time for parleying is over. Will you imitate the man who tried to mediate a peace between the armies of Scipio and Hannibal, when, like us, they were ready to engage? Taking neither side, he stood in a position where he could see the bravest battle he had ever beheld. If you will do the same, I promise you will see a fight well fought."

Without waiting for Du Croc's answer, Bothwell mounted his black charger and rode to the front lines. But there was no battle; the rebels, about four hundred in number, took up a position at the bottom of the hill and came to a halt. Bothwell moved his advance guard to the foot of the hill, hoping to force matters. The rebels moved toward them but made no attempt to attack.

Held high, and supported on two poles, the rebel banner glared in the sun. They had chosen a standard to substantiate their charges. On a large expanse of white cloth had been painted a green tree under which Darnley lay. Beside him knelt the Prince, out of whose mouth the words came: "Judge and revenge my cause, O Lord."

Disappointed, Bothwell thought: *We wait again*. In an hour his troops would be looking into the shifting sun, and he could no longer hold out the hope of rain. He glanced again at the far-off hills; no longer the hope of Huntly, Fleming, or Hamilton coming. They would be here now if they were coming at all. His army was slowly depleting; of the bulk of his troops, a few hundred had already deserted, and the rest were swiftly demoralizing.

He knew that half of them believed the rebels' charges and that Mary stayed with him out of shame of his having ravished her but would otherwise be glad to leave him. Some even thought she was secretly on the rebels' side. Yet he could bear them no grudge.

Like his Borderers, these were simple folk, and his enemies had done an excellent job of circulating their propaganda. Why should they suddenly believe him now, merely because he asked them to?

Below, the rebel cavalry looked appallingly good to him; his moss-troopers were no match in an uphill charge against those well-trained men. More to break the monotony than to hit anything, he ordered a round of cannon fire. Listlessly, the gunners fired the fuses. As he knew it would, nothing happened; the rebels were just beyond the cannons' scope.

The sun's concentrated heat increased. Spirits flagged. Small groups of men slipped out of rank before Bothwell's eyes and disappeared downhill toward the rebel camp. Swiftly, he spurred forward into the troops, cursing, threatening, even pleading with them to stay—but it was no use. They were tired, heat-sickened, and hungry. They had no food but knew where they could get some, for the rebels had plenty.

Somehow he had to keep those who remained. By now he knew the rebels' game. They had never intended to fight; they were waiting for his troops to deteriorate, then they would attack. But it would be carnage by then, not a battle.

His conscience could never allow that. Desperately he tried to think of a way to restore his troops' morale. He could see only one solution—single combat. But first he had to convince Mary. He went to Seton and Borthwick to enlist their help.

"You will never come out of it alive," Seton said. "They have no regard for honor. It's their intention to wear you down, then kill you."

Borthwick agreed. "Aye. They prate of justice, but they care nothing for it. Power, greed, that is their prime concern, and they will seize it any way they can—only you stand in their way."

Bothwell sighed and gave them all the arguments he had given himself. He ended with, "Are you willing to see these men massacred? It will surely come to that, unless I do something to prevent it."

Grudgingly, they shook their heads.

"Then for God's sake, help me. She must be made to see the necessity."

4

Mary's voice bordered on hysteria. "No, never! Whatever the outcome, I cannot let you do it."

"You have no right to condemn these men to certain death for the sake of one," Bothwell said. He appealed to Seton: "Tell her that I am right."

"Aye, madam, it's true. Your army is no longer in condition to fight. Their blood will turn this hillside red if there is battle now."

Borthwick said, "We are as much against this, madam, but it is our only chance."

"Leave us," she said, "I want to talk to my husband alone." She waited for them to go, then faced Bothwell. "You are asking me to condemn you to death to save them." Her hand swept out toward the troops. "If God can read what is in my heart, He knows that I would stop at nothing to prevent their bloodshed—but not at the cost of your life. Don't ask that of me."

"We cannot think only of ourselves; there is the Realm. You cannot toss it into the laps of such men."

"What good are kingdoms—or the world—if you are not here to share them with me? I would sooner lose it all than part with you."

"We are not here to defend love, but your Crown. Our personal feelings must be set aside to decide a far greater issue—who shall rule Scotland. That must be your prime concern." His tone softened. "Do you think I want to die when there is a lifetime to be lived with you? Believe me, I've racked my brain, there is no other way."

She put his hand to her lips and kissed it. He felt her tears slip down his fingers. "God protect you," she murmured.

He had no words of comfort for her; his own agony in

leaving her, knowing that he might never see her again, tore at his insides. Yet he guessed that her ordeal was worse; she must stay behind to wait, imagining the worst, praying for a miracle that would bring him back.

He left her for a moment to send his challenge to the rebels. The first to accept was James Murray. Bothwell smiled; nothing would give him more pleasure than to kill the author of those defamatory placards. He called for his armor, but a grumbling arose from his Borderers.

Ormiston acted as their spokesman. "Your Grace cannot cross swords with an inferior," he said. "We will not suffer that degradation."

Mary joined in his protests. "You are my husband, King Consort of Scotland. I will not have you fight a man of lesser birth and a traitor besides."

A mixture of vanity, pride, and resentment churned in Bothwell. His hand closed on the hilt of his sword. He longed to fight; this accursed inaction was nerve-fraying. How much longer could he stand this unending impasse? He felt a savage desperation to fight, yet Ormiston, his Borderers, Mary, they were right—he should not accept a man of lesser degree.

The rebels had proposed a series of champions for him to fight; their intent was plain—they would not honor the duel. Yet, unprincipled though he knew them to be, he could not believe that even they would dishonor the sacred field of combat—chivalry could not be that much in the past. The field of honor had always been so dear to his heart; was he the only man left who believed that God fought on the side of right? If he won the combat honestly, would they betray that trust, turn on him in a body, and hack him to pieces?

He glanced at Mary and saw her pain, but he could not allow her suffering to sway him. It was good sense that won out at last; he would take their advice and refuse Murray. If his enemies intended more than one opponent, then he had to start with the highest and work his way down. He would have to destroy their leaders first.

Bothwell went to the front lines and shouted across, "The Duke of Orkney rejects Murray as unworthy. I name Morton as the first to fight me."

Morton accepted, chose the broadsword, then delegated it to Lindsay.

Bothwell chuckled. "Likely Morton's belly quivers at the thought of facing me," he said. Lindsay suited him as well; he had never forgiven his threat to *cut Mary to collups* after Rizzio's murder.

Once again there were arguments: Lindsay was not a fit opponent; neither his rank nor his ancestry matched Bothwell's. But this time he would not be swayed; he had to start somewhere, and he accepted.

Lindsay sent word back: "I will fight the Duke what way he pleases, on horse or on foot, doublet alone or in armor, man for man, or six for six, or twelve for twelve. If the murder be not avenged by me, God will revenge it." Then he removed his armor and made a great show of kneeling in prayer.

His voice was deliberately raised for the benefit of both sides: "O Lord, I beg Your mercy to preserve the innocent, and in Your justice, to overthrow the vicious murderer of the innocent blood of the King." On and on he went, intoning everything that served his memory.

Losing patience, Bothwell shouted, "Lindsay, is your tongue to be your weapon? If God were with you, there'd be no need to implore Him now."

Finally Lindsay rose and put on his armor again. Twenty men from either side fixed the conditions of combat. There was more delay, more interminable waiting. Bothwell glanced at his troops anxiously; others had deserted. Their position looked hopeless; no one expected him to come out of the duel alive. He could guess at their thoughts; why bother to wait around when the end seemed inevitable?

He wondered how many hours had passed since they had come here. It was already evening, though the sky was still bright as day. How many hours in the heat? Awhile ago, he had heard someone remark that it was nearly eight, and still the heat gave no respite. His armor was already hot to the touch; he felt seared and worn in its confines. Armor had never been to his liking; the heavy, two-handed sword he held felt heavier for his sleeves of mail, and he longed for his light rapier.

They were ready at last, but the most difficult part was still before him. While waiting, he had avoided meeting Mary's glance, afraid for the anguish he would see in her eyes.

He stepped up to her and embraced her. The words he might have said stuck in his throat.

She clung to him, murmuring, "Come back to me, please come back." Then she removed the small gold crucifix from her neck and held it out to him. "This will protect you," she said. Seeing him about to refuse, she added, "Lay your prejudices aside this once, for my sake."

He took it, wound it through his sword belt, and turned from her. Mounting his charger, he called his men to follow and rode off to the appointed place.

He waited for Lindsay; an hour had passed, but there was no sign of him. Two, nearly three, hours had gone by, and still no one showed himself—he had been duped. Lindsay never intended to fight the duel; like all their devices, it had been another of the rebels' tricks—another means of delay.

Bothwell was seized suddenly with fear; even now the rebels might be launching an attack. Without him the Royalist army was leaderless. Mary could be killed. Alarmed, he ran to his horse, mounted, and rode back.

Galloping into camp, he saw that he had guessed correctly. The rebel army was advancing, carrying their vicious banner before them. Kirkcaldy, with two hundred horses, had begun a flanking movement.

Black with rage, Bothwell shouted, "The sniveling cowards! Time will· show them for the faithless traitors they are." He laughed bitterly. "The field of honor—dishonor they mean." He turned to his troops. "Fight, damn you, take up your arms, or you'll be massacred where you stand."

The men moved back in frightened disorder. Bothwell dashed in among them, forcing guns, pikes, battle-axes into their hands, which they let fall. Kirkcaldy's men were advancing swiftly. Desperately, Bothwell turned to face the attacking troops. Fists clenched, choked with fury, he had the mad impulse to charge into their ranks single-handedly. Better to die like that than bear witness to the inevitable slaughter.

A voice behind him shrieked, "No!"

He turned and saw Mary. Her terror told him she had guessed his intent. Drained, he said flatly, "Lindsay never came. I waited, but he never came."

She stroked his face. "I know, love. It was another of their tricks to play for time."

"Aye, and look how well they've succeeded. Had they the stomach to fight now, our troops wouldn't have a prayer. They are too few. Our only chance is another parley, to make what terms we can."

Bothwell sent a herald to the rebel camp. None of the lords could show his face; Kirkcaldy came to represent them. He pledged their loyalty to Mary if she would leave Bothwell and return to Edinburgh with them. For Bothwell, Kirkcaldy could guarantee him free and unhindered passage wherever he wished to go.

Mary listened in silence, then told Kirkcaldy to leave them, promising he would have her answer shortly. She turned to Bothwell. "I shall accept their terms."

Her determination chilled him. He seized her roughly. "No,

you will not. I would sooner go with them myself—in fetters, if need be—than see you deliver yourself into their hands."

"I agreed to your duel with Lindsay, because you said there was no other way. Now it is you who must agree, because *this* is our only chance."

"We have another outgate. Return to Dunbar; let me stay here with my Borderers. The others may have lost heart, but my troopers and I will hold the field and fight."

"To what end? You will all be killed—slaughtered like animals."

"Is that why you've chosen to go with them—to save my life? Forget it—I'll not seek protection from you."

"No, I cannot bear such needless bloodshed on my conscience—not if I can prevent it."

She lied; he knew she lied.

"Listen to me," she pleaded. "I shall only pretend to part from you, until I have won them to obedience. Give me a week—less perhaps—then I will come to you. Is a week too much to ask in exchange for so many lives?"

She was thinking of her triumph after Rizzio's murder.

"Aye," he said, "you cowed them then, because I gave you an army at your back. That was your bludgeon then; what have you to keep them in line now?"

She drew herself up proudly. "I am their Queen; they will obey me."

He laughed harshly. "The divine right of kings, eh? You don't know the extent of their treachery; they would dare anything. Go with them and God alone knows what they will do with you. Their purpose is the same as in your mother's time—to depose you and proclaim a regency. They need only your son, and he is in their custody already."

"They have given their word that no harm will come to me. Kirkcaldy swore that in God's name."

"Aye, and I have heard them use God's name before, then

turn and do otherwise. Despite their fair words, they are on a plain course of treason and will not be deterred from it."

He glanced at the road again, hoping even now for a miracle. A movement on the horizon could still mean Huntly and reinforcements. Desperately, he sought the means to change her mind.

She said, "Do you think I want it this way? To part with you for even one hour is more than I can bear. You have fought for Scotland countless times; let me do it this once."

Everything she said made good sense; if anyone could win them over, she could. Yet, something warned him against it. He would sooner carry her away by force than let her go to the rebels.

"No," he said, "I'll not agree to it. Once they have you, they'll never let you return to me."

"A month ago you promised never to force your will on me again."

His own guilt had made him promise that, because he had insisted that she wed him in the Protestant faith. She had risked too much for him—if this brief separation would end the rebellion, he had no right to stop her. Still he made one last try.

"Will you not reconsider and return to Dunbar?"

She shook her head. "Please do this for me."

In an instant he could lift her up, carry her to his horse, and ride away with her. He looked at Kirkcaldy's troops, now only a few yards from them, and saw murder in their eyes—and he knew how impossible that plan would be. Before he had gone a foot with her Kirkcaldy's men would kill them both. He could not risk her life.

All at once the days since his escape from Borthwick took hold of him. His body screamed for rest; the sun baked down on him; he felt grilled in the armor that cut into his joints. Exhausted, worn, his strength ebbed away.

Heartsick, he said, "What would I not do for you?"

They had no privacy; their farewell must be made in full view of both armies, yet neither of them cared. He drew her close and held her, cursing his armor because he could not feel her. Now he knew the full torment in his fear of losing her and it ripped him apart. Her tears wet his face and slid down his cheeks.

He kissed her a dozen times, feeling the heart go out of him. Kirkcaldy had warned them to be brief; he could not vouch for his men if the royal army remained on the field. But they could not part; they clung together desperately.

He asked, "Has it all been worth it? Have you any regrets?"

"Only that I put you off when we could have had more time together."

"You will keep faith?"

She nodded. "Unto death—and beyond."

A restlessness rose from the enemy camp, and Bothwell remembered Kirkcaldy's warning. He put her from him and turned to go. She looked so pale and drawn; the agonies of the day lay on her face. How could he part from her?

He drew her close again. "Write to me, let me know how you are—come to me as soon as you can."

She nodded, her words choked back by a fresh flood of tears.

In all the turmoil, he had forgotten the child she carried—his child. "Care for my son," he whispered. "If I never see him, tell him about me. Tell him the truth so he will remember; there will be too many to tell him lies about me."

Overcome with weeping, she could only nod.

Kirkcaldy came up to them. "We must go, madam," he said.

One more kiss. They had said only a week; he felt a sharp stab of fear—so much could happen in a week. But they could remain no longer; if he went at all, it must be now, at once. He put her from him, stepped back, then turned quickly away.

Mounting his black charger, Bothwell headed east for Dunbar, followed by a dozen friends. He rode up the hillside, drew rein, and paused for one backward glance. For the first time he knew the bitterness of defeat—defeat for a battle never fought.

It was finally dusk; the unrelenting sun had finally surrendered. Daylight faded as it had begun, in shades of burnished gold. Had it been only this morning that he had watched the dawn from their window at Seton, or a lifetime ago?

CHAPTER XXII

1

Dunbar rose in great, broken lines against the sky draped in the velvet of night. A strange numbness had taken hold of Bothwell; he neither saw nor felt; voices spoke to him, but he was unable to grasp the words. His armor grew heavier, yet he was unaware of it. Even Mary seemed remote, unreal, almost as though their lives had never touched.

Wearily, he dismounted and went into the Great Hall on leaden feet. It smelled of the sea and rotting fish. Dalgleish brought him a tankard of ale; ignoring it, he brushed past to the stairway and climbed to his chambers with tremendous effort. Ormiston followed and ordered Paris to light candles.

The room flared to brightness, then steadied to a soft glow. Some garments lay crumpled on the bed; they were the breeches and doublet Mary had worn on her escape from Borthwick—and their painful parting stabbed at him afresh. Clumsily, he fumbled with the hooks on his armor.

Ormiston said, "Here, let me help you." To Paris he added, "Snap to it, lend a hand."

Together, they undid the hooks; the breastplate and back came apart, then the chain-mail sleeves. His boots were eased from his aching, blistered feet, then his shirt, now gray and wet, clinging to him in creases. Mary's gold crucifix fell to the floor.

Ormiston, a staunch Protestant, picked it up gingerly. He held it out to Paris. "Yours?" he asked.

Bothwell snatched it away. "It is the Queen's," he said, "my lady's favor to wear into battle."

"And Your Grace carries it—an object of idolatry?" Ormiston asked in amazement.

"Ignorance and fear will hurt you more than this harmless trinket," Bothwell said, placing the crucifix on the night table.

Paris brought him a basin of water for washing; it cooled him for only an instant; the heat had settled too deeply in his body. Tired—too tired to even sit—he crossed to the bed and sank down on it. Mary's scent still lingered on the pillows, and he ached for the feel of her beside him.

He tossed restlessly all night, his sleep a series of tormented dreams. Mary's face drifted in and out, tear-streaked, distorted by anguish. Cannon blasts, thick mists, streaming blood, and mangled bodies mixed in one hideous scene. And there was always Mary.

She called to him—always so very close—yet always just beyond his reach. She called his name; it was such a sharp cry, full of pain, that he woke at the sound. He sat up and looked about wildly; then, slowly, he realized it had been a dream. He lay back and fell into another fitful sleep with more troubled dreams.

Toward evening he heard the splash of rain, and a cooling breeze drifted in through the open casement. Below, a rough sea slapped against the reefs. *One day*, he thought, *one day would have made such a difference.* Without that accursed heat his army might have stood and fought. He could have beaten the rebels if there had been a battle, and Mary would be here with him now.

There were so many ifs; if Huntly and the others had come, if his troops had been well trained, if Balfour had turned the castle guns on the rebels. So many ifs that his head split to think of them. But there was still some hope in one of those ifs.

If Huntly were still in the castle, then he likely held it in Mary's name. The town would be hers and the rebels' cause lost.

Surely that had been Huntly's reason for not meeting him at Carberry Hill. For fear of losing the castle, Huntly had stayed in town to keep it loyal for Mary. That may have been the smartest move; by now Mary likely had the rebels on their knees asking her pardon. He slept again, this time more peacefully.

Bothwell had slept more than eighteen hours; his body had taken the rest it sorely needed. Refreshed and somewhat encouraged, he got out of bed thinking he might have word from Mary by morning. His mind was already busy with plans; she might ask him to join her immediately, and he wanted to ride into town with an impressive show of force. He would summon his Borderers by sending a call to arms across the territories that were his. The vision cheered him; he saw himself leading them into town by the thousands, strong and ready, armed to the teeth.

He felt suddenly hungry and called for Paris. The deserted corridor came to life. Heavy boots clattered on the stone stairs, and Dalgleish came toward him.

"Where are my clothes?" Bothwell snapped. "Am I to parade about without a stitch to cover me?"

Dalgleish grinned happily.

"What are you grinning at?"

"Your Grace seems his old self again. Last night we thought—"

"That I had been beaten? It will take a deal more to lay James Hepburn low."

Ormiston came in. "No need to ask how you are from the sound of your bellowing," he said. "It like to shook the timbers from the roof."

"Aye, it appears I've roused everyone but Paris. Where is that lazy lout?"

"Where else, but in the kitchen where he has both food and wenches?"

They laughed. Alone they ignored the formalities of overlord and vassal. Ormiston, many years Bothwell's senior, had known him since a lad in the Earl of Patrick's time.

Ormiston's expression changed to concern. "You gave us all a fright last night," he said.

Angry with himself for having displayed even a moment's weakness, Bothwell said, "Am I a horse, never to need rest?"

"I confess, it seemed to go deeper than that."

"How so? What fool meaning did you read into it?"

"We thought you had despaired at yesterday's outcome. God knows, no one could blame you—to lose a crown that you had within your grasp."

Bothwell shook his head sadly. "You too? Will no one believe it was for love alone that I wed her? It's the woman I love—not her crown."

"I thought—"

"Aye, so think they all. Precisely the reason our army deserted. They were not willing to die to make James Hepburn king." Then he asked, "Thinking that, you were still willing to fight?"

Ormiston nodded. "So were all the Borderers. And why not? Scotland could do worse with others I could name."

That pleased Bothwell more than he cared to admit.

2

Bothwell spent the afternoon and most of the evening writing messages and dispatching men to issue his call to arms. He was so sure of hearing from Mary by morning that he had a lookout posted at the gatehouse tower. Artillery and munitions were his next concern; he cursed his luck for losing the great brass cannons at Carberry Hill.

By the following afternoon, he gave up hope of hearing from Mary that day; the next would surely bring word from her. But again he was disappointed, and when at the end of the third day he still had nothing, a feeling of uneasiness gripped him. By evening he was frantic with worry.

His cousin Willie had ridden in that day with thirty retainers; Thomas Hepburn, the Parson of Oldhamstocks, had been at his side since the abduction, and Patrick and Adam Hepburn had joined him, with more friends and relatives said to be on the way. However, despite the encouragement of their support, his uneasiness would not leave him.

He had been restless all day; that extra sense he always trusted so warned him that something was very wrong. Only the most dire circumstances could explain Mary's silence. He had been mistaken; Huntly had not subdued the rebels, nor had they disbanded. And though he tried to push it aside, the same sickening thought persisted—Mary had come to harm. He had not heard from her because she could not write.

Desperate with worry, he thought to ride to Edinburgh—he had to know. Whatever he learned, it would be better than to leave it to his imagination. Now he understood the greater terror of those who waited behind while the battle raged.

But he realized it would be foolhardy for him to go; if his suspicions were correct, he would be of more use here, where he could raise troops in Mary's defense. He was too well known to slip in and out of town without being recognized. Someone else would have to go, and Paris was his first choice.

Paris made an excellent spy; he had a way of ferreting things out. He could gain entry into the most unlikely places, then slip out again, without anyone even knowing he had been there. Paris left that night, and Bothwell watched him ride off, wishing himself in his place. Patience had never been his virtue, and this would be his worst trial.

The sleepless night crawled by. Bothwell walked along the beach and watched the endless procession of foam-tipped waves. In his chambers, he watched the night from the window seat; he followed the moon's path through silver-tipped clouds, willing the stars to fade—but they remained in stubborn brilliance.

The night finally faded, and faint streaks of light showed in the sky. The stars had gone and the moon was now a ghostly circle. Far out at sea the light was stronger; he watched intently, waiting for it to fan out into dawn. At last, the sun rose as a huge flaming ball on the horizon and he went to the gatehouse tower to continue his vigil.

He recognized his sorrel mare in the distance and mounted a horse to gallop off to meet Paris on the road. Paris paled at the sight of him, drew rein sharply, and the sorrel reared up, whinnying. Bothwell swung around and grabbed the reins from Paris to steady the mare. Careful breeding had produced a spirited but highly nervous nature in the sorrel; she reacted to the slightest upset. Bothwell favored her over his other mounts for her sleek beauty and demonlike speed. Even now, distraught with worry over Mary, he acted instinctively.

He cuffed Paris on the shoulder, nearly tossing him out of the saddle. "Mind how you handle her," he rasped. Then he was contrite, for he saw Paris' tired, begrimed face, the back of his sweat-soaked jerkin, and knew that he had ridden hard. He said more gently, "You've made good time. What news have you? Good, I hope."

Avoiding his glance, Paris said, "No, Your Grace, none of it is good."

With a sinking feeling, he asked, "Did you see the Queen? Is she well?"

"No, to the first. For the second, that you may judge for yourself."

Pressure throbbed against Bothwell's temples like a seawall collapsed with water rushing in. He listened to Paris' story, each word falling on his ear with a sickening thud.

Contrary to their promises, the rebels had taken Mary to Edinburgh a prisoner. Their troops had reviled her, and in town she had been greeted by a stoning mob who shouted, "Burn the whore—kill her . . . "

A small muscle pulsed in Bothwell's cheek, his eyes had narrowed to slits, his expression revealed unbearable pain, and his fingers clamped the reins tightly, showing his knuckles white. A quiet, deadly rage built up inside of him—more deadly because it was quiet. It was a rage built on a hardness that would never soften with time or circumstance.

They had brought Mary, nearly fainting and weeping uncontrollably, to the provost's house and cast her in a room overlooking the High Street. Townsfolk had gathered under her window, shouting vile insults and curses—chanting, "Murderess, Jezebel, and Bothwell's slut."

They had reached Dunbar, and Paris followed Bothwell to his apartments, where he resumed his story.

Mary had tried to write a letter to Bothwell that night, but it had been intercepted. The following day the rebels had pressed her with their demands to abandon Bothwell. She refused and wept bitterly because they had "separated her from a husband with whom she thought to live and die with all the contentment in the world." She told them, "I will leave my kingdom and dignity and live as a simple demoiselle with my husband." She pleaded for them to set her adrift on a ship with Bothwell, "for the winds to carry them where they will."

She had risked her kingdom for Bothwell; now she was willing to give it up entirely to be reunited with him. How often had she told him that—and he had always answered her with anger. At Carberry Hill he had chided her for trusting in the divine right of kings, yet he too had trusted in it. He had thought she was inviolable, that no one, other than God, could pull her from her throne. What fools they had been to believe in that; it was a world corrupted and gone mad, and such things counted for nothing. In his mind, Bothwell knelt to her in humility and loved her more than ever.

Later, Paris told him, the people had softened and took pity on Mary. They swore to rescue her, and the Blue Blanket was waved in her name. But Morton and his allies prevented it by sending a few hundred hackbuteers out to disperse the crowd.

That night Mary was taken to Holyrood, then secreted out after midnight and sent to the castle of Lochleven with Lindsay and young Ruthven. Then the rebels subscribed themselves to a bond in which they banded together to dissolve her marriage with Bothwell and to punish him for the late King's murder. So much for their promise to let Bothwell go free and unhindered, for they knew that as long as he lived he would seek the means to free Mary.

3

That same night, Bothwell sailed from Dunbar, leaving it in the care of Patrick Whitelaw, who was a trusted follower. He made first for Linlithgow, where he gained the support of Lord Claud Hamilton. He took to the west coast then, for a talk with Fleming, tactfully bypassing the burning question of why he never came to Carberry Hill. He left with Fleming's pledge of loyalty and then contacted Huntly in the north and won his support as well.

In less than a week Bothwell had the names of fifty important houses backing him—at last they saw the issue clearly. He was not fighting to make himself King, but to save Mary. This would give him an army even greater than the one he had rallied after the Rizzio conspiracy; ten, fifteen thousand men at his command. If they would not release Mary willingly, then he would storm Lochleven. He would smash them all, destroy every one who had ever troubled her reign, crush forever those who had plagued him since his succession.

Loyalists flocked to Hamilton; soon they would have enough men assembled to march. But the rebels were desperate; they gave warning that if any hostile forces attempted to march on Lochleven, it would cost Mary her life. They had chosen well in Lochleven, for it was James Stuart's boyhood home and it had a reputation for being impregnable; those strong walls and the lake surrounding it made it impenetrable. The Bastard's mother was Mary's jailor there and would not be won over to her cause.

Bothwell called the lords together for another conference—he wasn't willing to risk Mary's safety. He had decided to wait before taking any overt action; meanwhile, he would return to Dunbar to alert his Borderers.

Within the week Bothwell was back at Dunbar, but three of his men, who followed him in another ship, were apprehended at sea and taken to Edinburgh. He could imagine the fates awaiting Will and John Blackadder and James Edmonston, for they shared the dubious honor of being named murderers in the placards. And before the night was out, he learned of still more trouble.

Dalgleish, whom he had sent to Edinburgh for his clothes and the silver casket that contained his letters, deeds, and charters, had been captured. Bothwell thought immediately of the letters and sonnets that Mary had written to him. He had kept them in the casket, and each one testified to their love affair before and after Darnley's death.

What foul luck to have them fall into enemy hands! With that evidence at their disposal, the rebels could claim that Mary had been Bothwell's accomplice in the murder. The casket also contained the letters Mary had written him prior to her abduction, which proved that she had connived in her own kidnapping.

Why had he kept those letters? What had possessed him to hold on to them? Sentiment? The sonnets perhaps; she had composed them as an expression of her love. But the letters; why had he kept *them*? The silver casket had once belonged to Mary's first husband, Francis. She had given it to Bothwell as a gift, and he had carelessly tossed the letters and sonnets in with other papers he had transferred to the casket.

More of Bothwell's men fell into enemy hands—Will Powrie and John Spens, Captain Cullen—and they were also after Ormiston, but he fled to the wilds of Teviotdale, escaping capture just in time. Little by little his enemies were closing in on him. He decided to pay a visit to the Borders while he still could.

Surely his friends would join him; he rode to Haddington, Kelso, Melrose, Jedburgh, and Hawick, stopping at small villages between, and his following increased. The Kerrs of Ferniehirst, Langton, and others answered his summons; a night spent with Ormiston, who had all of Teviotdale with him, and the next morning Bothwell started back for Dunbar.

More bad news greeted him there; aware of his progress, and fearing the consequences, the rebels issued a proclamation giving Bothwell three weeks' notice to answer their charges—the murder of Darnley, Mary's kidnapping, and his subsequently forcing her to marry. For support, they brought Knox out of seclusion to administer his severe exhortations against Mary by threatening "the great plague of God to the whole country, if she were spared from her condign punishment."

Now their pretext for revolt was official. A reward of one thousand crowns was offered for the capture of Bothwell, "who thought to persuade and entice simple and ignorant men to assist him." Men of all degrees were forbidden "to supply him with their houses, to support him with men, armor, horse, ships, boats or other furnishings by sea and land." Anyone disregarding this warning would be considered "plain partakers with him in the horrible murder." The first to come under this heading was Bothwell's captain in charge of Dunbar, who was summoned to surrender the castle where the "murderer had taken refuge."

Bothwell knew that if he should decide to answer those charges before a jury, there would be only one verdict. More, he knew that once they had him, he would not live long enough to answer any charges. The evidence he could give would ruin them all; their only hope lay in a dead prisoner, not in a live defendant. Within five days of the date fixed for trial, he was declared an outlaw and rebel.

Now Bothwell's cause seemed totally ruined; no one wanted to be associated with an outlaw who had a price on his head—especially if it would cost them and their families life and land. When Seton and Fleming, the last of the Loyalists, withdrew, Bothwell decided to leave Dunbar. On June 30 he sailed up the east coast and headed north to Huntly's stronghold.

"With your great force of Highlanders," Bothwell told Huntly, "we could storm Lochleven and free the Queen."

Bothwell had arrived at Strathbogie very late the night before. The welcome he had from his former brother-in-law had not been unfriendly, which he took as a sign of encouragement. The late hour had prevented him from discussing his plans, but first thing in the morning, Bothwell began to urge Huntly's support—this was his last hope in Scotland.

Immediately, Bothwell had detected a great change in Huntly. He had heard that Huntly had suffered a stroke of some kind; now, from his shrunken listlessness and vague speech, the rumor seemed true. Huntly seemed older; his eyes in particular were very strange; they seemed like pale, darting balls that had great difficulty focusing themselves.

For the last hour Bothwell had been trying to interest Huntly in his plans. They had touched briefly on Huntly's unexplained failure to show up at Carberry Hill. Vaguely, Huntly told of himself and the Archbishop of Hamilton entering the castle because the rebels had the greater strength on their side. He gave no further reason, only that Balfour had by then already made some agreement with the rebels.

Then in a moment of greater clarity, Huntly said, "Balfour kept a foot in both camps; he dealt with the rebels in great secrecy—that way he held himself safe from repercussions should you be the victor. The rebels were vacillating, for they had expected full support from the townsfolk. But when that support was not forthcoming, they spoke of disbanding—and well they might have, had it not been for Balfour. He saved the day for them by sending word to you that an immediate march on Edinburgh would decide victory in your favor. Had you but waited at Dunbar two days more . . . " He paused, his eyes turned blank, and he became a ghost of his former self again.

Bothwell felt a sickening sensation in the pit of his stomach as the impact of what Huntly told him penetrated. His suspicion of having been duped by Balfour was confirmed. The difference of two days would have changed everything. The rebels would have disbanded, and Mary would be safely with him now. Mutely, he cried: *Oh, God, two days . . .*

Now, as he urged Huntly to rally the Highlanders, he saw a glimmer of interest. "If we could take Lochleven by surprise," Huntly said, "before they can harm the Queen."

"Aye, a few of us could swim ashore by night, overtake the guards, and gain access to the tower where she is imprisoned." The thought fired Bothwell's imagination; to have Mary back with him, to feel her in his arms. . . . It was just three weeks since they had parted, a separation that was to have lasted only a few days.

Huntly asked, "Do you really think it will work? There is so much risk involved. Doubtless, they keep her heavily guarded."

"We risk more by allowing her to stay there. In order to smash the rebels, she must be freed, for as long as they hold her, they hold a sword over our heads. Aside from that, her life is in constant danger; there is talk of bringing her to trial for Darnley's murder—and well you know the justice she will have from them. They want to be rid of her, so they can crown the Prince and establish a regency. Should they succeed, rest assured the Bastard will be made regent."

Huntly shook his head. "Even they would not dare that—the people would not stand for it."

Bothwell snorted. "The people! What have they to say about it? Have you seen the proclamation drafted against me? Every word in it a blatant lie—yet who among the people questions them? They use my so-called crimes as the pretext for their revolt, and no one has confronted them with the truth. *They* tried me for the murder and found me innocent, *they* hold the Queen prisoner, and lastly, the Prince is in *their* custody and certainly in no danger from me. So much for the people who will swallow all such falsehoods without a murmur."

"Still, I cannot believe they would dare take the Queen's life."

"Perhaps you have forgotten that come December, she will reach her twenty-fifth birthday—when she can revoke all lands, grants, and titles given during her minority. I doubt she would exercise that right, but the possibility cannot have escaped the rebels' notice, since they are the ones who usurped most during that period and would therefore have the most to lose. They also know that she will never willingly part from me, and that I alone can put a clamp on their greed."

"These points are well taken. I cannot justly argue with

them. But what of the other lords you have won to your cause
—will they be with us at Lochleven?"

This was the moment he had been dreading, but he would
not lie. Bluntly, he said, "They have withdrawn their support.
There is some squeamishness on their part to associate themselves with an outlaw." He attempted to lighten the moment
with some humor. "Though I take it as an insult that a mere
thousand crowns is deemed adequate reward for my capture."

Huntly appeared to miss the jest entirely. "That would seem
to alter matters somewhat," he said. "I would be alone with
you. Should our plan abort, the rebels' vengeance would fall
solely upon me."

"Aye. But should it not, the Queen's gratitude would be
solely yours. Her generosity is well known; you would enjoy the
highest favor bestowed upon a subject."

"I must consider this very carefully. Let me think on it a
night. I will give you my answer tomorrow."

There he left it, and there Bothwell was left to stew for the
rest of that day. Bothwell had never been much for prayer; now
he employed every one he knew. He had banked on Huntly's
support, for without it he had no present hope of rescuing
Mary. If Huntly refused, he would be forced to seek outside
help.

At his last meeting at Hamilton, the lords had suggested he
go to Denmark and France for help. They were of the opinion
that he could win the support of Frederick and Charles, which
would restore Mary to her throne. Bothwell had been reluctant
to take their advice, since he felt strongly that her rescue should
not be relegated to outsiders, but to Scotsmen.

"Surely it has not slipped Your Grace's notice that my husband is not himself—so much so that I will confess to a deep
concern for him."

Bothwell studied the woman who hovered over Huntly. A

tall, severe, dark-haired woman with intense, burning black eyes. She had that strange Highland eeriness about her and was reputed to possess second sight—that special gift attributed to so many in the north. She was said to rule Strathbogie with a rigid hand, which he had seen for himself, for the servants quaked in their boots when she spoke to them. Huntly too seemed entirely under his wife's thumb; when she had raised an objection for his health, he had turned to give her a grateful look.

Bothwell realized that if he could convince her, then Huntly was as good as won. He said, "In times of desperation we must place the interests of the Realm above our own, my lady."

"Should my husband partake in this hazardous enterprise and lose, he would also lose everything he has regained these past two years."

"Aye, my lady, regained indeed—and all by the Queen's generosity."

"And all that was rightfully his, lost five years ago—for which he may also thank the Queen. His father and brother murdered, the family ruined, lands, titles, and possessions robbed, and himself imprisoned. What gratitude shall he show for that, Your Grace?"

"We have all suffered reverses. Imprisonment, exile, privation, destitution—I've known them all intimately myself. Yet on my return to favor I bore the Queen no grudge, knowing she might have prevented such unjust treatment from my enemies."

"We are not all as fortunate as Your Grace. Not all men may assuage their bitterness in royal beds."

A man would pay with his life for that remark, yet he forced himself to keep a cool head—he needed Huntly and couldn't risk alienating him. He glanced at Huntly; surely he would silence her. A woman so outspoken in the presence of men—it was unheard of. No man he knew would tolerate such behavior. Few would have allowed her to speak as freely as she had thus far—even before that unfortunate remark. But Huntly appeared not to mind; he even nodded his approval and took courage from her.

"Aye," he said, "what thanks do I owe the Queen when she and her brother were responsible for my ruination in the first place? What help did *you* give me when I came begging for your Borderers? You refused to become involved in anything that smacked of rebellion. Had we banded together then, we might have smashed the Bastard and put an end to all future trouble." Pounding the arm of his chair, he shouted, "But no, you chose to cling to your anachronistic notions of loyalty, chivalry, and honor, when such things have been dead a century and more."

"So, an old sore has opened and festers," Bothwell murmured.

"That is where you are mistaken—it never closed. Aye, you were never good at hating, which in part accounts for your troubles now, but my Highland blood equips me better for it. There is aught but time to think in prison—thoughts that cannot be washed away with a few gifts and a pledge of friendship that comes too late. Where was the Queen's gentle nature and faultless generosity at Corrichie? Where were you—my good friend—when I needed your help? Aye, what good does your love of honor do you now, when there is not a man in Scotland willing to lift a finger to help you or her?"

Suddenly Huntly covered his face with his hands and sobbed. "I wish to God I were dead, for I can see that neither of you will ever fare well again—and I cannot live with that on my conscience."

Amazed, Bothwell stared at him. That Huntly bore such hatred all this time and had managed to keep it so well concealed seemed incredible. He rarely experienced pity, a thing he reserved for the very weak, yet he felt it deeply now for this man who professed himself an enemy. Pity for the poison that had been brewing in Huntly's veins all these years, pity for the guilt he now felt in refusing his help.

It was useless to argue further. Bothwell glanced at Huntly sitting there sobbing and broken, and he saw him as a man already dead.

4

"Well, nephew, you have come a long way since leaving here. The Hepburns have always aimed high, but none climbed to your heights."

Bothwell laughed. "I have you to thank for that, uncle. I've never forgotten the advice you gave me as a lad. 'Take what you want and keep it in your grasp; to the devil with the cost,' you used to tell me."

The Bishop cackled delightedly. "So I did, so I did—and good advice it was too. But it's not what I would tell everyone, only those I know could follow it."

He leaned back and beamed proudly at Bothwell. A lifetime of debauchery had taken its toll on the once handsome face; in his seventieth year, the Bishop looked eighty. Heavy lines creased his face, wrinkled pouches fell under his eyes in layers, his fine, straight nose had become slightly bulbous and discolored with purplish veins, and his once sensual mouth had grown thin, though it still held evidence of self-indulgence. It was a face that bespoke all of his past excesses.

Although it had been years since Bothwell had seen his great-uncle, the fondness they shared for each other had not lessened. Over the years, they had maintained a regular correspondence, and now resolved that he must seek help from abroad in order to free Mary, Bothwell had been taken with a sudden desire to see his uncle and Spynie again.

He had never been a sentimentalist, but he wanted to go back to the place he associated with the happiest time of his boyhood. On his arrival, the Bishop had ordered one of the lavishly furnished state apartments made ready for him, but

Bothwell had refused and insisted on having his old chambers again.

Back in those chambers, he had found everything the same. The matched twin chests were still there and the huge wardrobe in which he used to hide from his groom. The familiar oversized bed was still there too, though he recalled maroon hangings, whereas now it was curtained in green velvet with silver fringe. Even the chip in the fireplace wall remained. He had a sensation here of time stood still, and for some unexplainable reason he took pleasure in that.

Now the Bishop's alert scrutiny caught the flicker of worry that crossed Bothwell's eyes. He asked, "How do you mean to deliver the Queen out of her captors' hands?"

"By convincing the Danish King to lend his support. From there I will sail to France with the same purpose in mind."

"Aye, you've a chance at success, for there is one strong point in your favor. I wager that every monarch sits his throne a little uneasy now for what happened to Queen Mary, knowing it may happen to him."

"I've thought of that. Despite the political advantages, even Elizabeth is disturbed by it and has issued a strong complaint to the rebels for taking such treasonous action."

"Do you think it will have an effect on them?"

"Not likely, for the advantage of this cannot long escape her. There is always the danger of an uprising among the English Catholics, and they would naturally look to Mary for strength— whereas, the rebels are all Protestant and in sympathy with England. With this in mind, I am well assured that any scruples Elizabeth may have now will doubtlessly fade in the interests of what is best for her kingdom."

The Bishop nodded. "Aye, we tend to forget all the underlying causes of Scotland's troubles: the Bastard's undying ambition to rule and the nobles' readiness to support him in the name of religion. Rome embroiled in the struggle to maintain the old faith here, England on the opposing side, fearing a Catholic power as its near neighbor, with the added threat of Spanish intervention. Frankly, I marvel that you still hope to extricate her from this with such strong forces against you."

"I *must* hope," Bothwell said fiercely. "Life is nothing without her—she is my universe—I cannot tell them apart." He had never spoken this way to any man; now that he had, he was somewhat abashed at his frankness. Embarrassed, he glanced at the Bishop, expecting to see those cynical blue eyes turn hard with amusement—instead he saw compassion and understanding.

"It is a strange yet incontestable truth," the Bishop said, "that men like you either never love at all or fall so deeply in love with one woman that no other can take her place. God grant her freedom to return to you, for there can be no middle ground for you ever again."

Awed, Bothwell wondered how this dissolute old man could have such deep understanding of love. Even those closest to him found it difficult to believe that he really loved Mary, yet his uncle, a man to whom love was merely a moment's pleasure, not only believed him but understood.

"She will have her freedom if I must move heaven and earth to accomplish it. I've already thought of an alternate plan, should the Danish King refuse to help. Being Admiral of Scotland, I could establish my own empire on the sea. I could hire ships for a start, enough for a small fleet, and man them with sailors from my dukedom. It would be a challenge to all men with a spark of adventurousness in their souls."

That night Bothwell wrote to Mary, hoping to smuggle a letter in to her.

From Spynie Palace
My dearest, Though we must be apart for a time, never lose faith and believe that it will not be for long. Remember,

*neither time nor distance can separate us—we are too close.
My thoughts are with you always. I hold you close in my
heart. I leave for Denmark soon, thence to France where I
hope to win support for our cause. Be of good heart, for I
am certain to succeed.*

Yours, as ever,
James D.

Care for my son.

"I have the weather to thank for that stroke of luck,"
Bothwell told the Bishop a few days later. "Imagine my delight
in finding a ship in Cromarty Firth, bound for St. Andrews,
packed with goods and foodstuffs for the Bastard."

The Bishop chuckled. "More, I would like to imagine his
fury when he learns you have not only commandeered the ship,
but its goods as well, since he paid for them in advance."

"Aye, the loss will stand him a few hundred pounds at least,
but more, it's another vessel added to my fleet. That, with the
one I've sent down to Eyemouth for stores and munitions,
makes six I have now."

Patrick, the eldest of the Bishop's illegitimate sons, sat with
them, listening to what they said. "Apparently the crimes
already listed against you are not enough, cousin," he said.
"Now you add piracy to them."

Bothwell grinned. "Your concern is touching, cousin."

"Rest assured, any concern on my part is purely for the
welfare of my aging father. Perhaps you have not heard, but in
your absence, my father's tenants were given notice to refuse
him rents as punishment for sheltering an outlaw in his house.
Does it not trouble your conscience to have an old man
deprived of his living because of you?"

Bothwell stifled the impulse to laugh. He knew the Bishop's
coffers swelled to overflowing; if the old man lived another

seventy years without collecting another groat, he'd still have enough to keep himself in luxury.

The Bishop's voice rose in anger. "Need I remind you that I am master here? Who goes and who stays rests solely with me—he is of my blood, and worth ten of you any day." He turned to Bothwell. "You are welcome to remain here for as long as you wish, nephew."

Patrick sprang to his feet. "I fear age has unhinged your reason. This will be our ruination for certain. My brothers and I will not allow it; we will not stay and see everything brought down on our heads."

"Then go—and good riddance—see how far you get without my support," the Bishop shouted. "What means have you without me? God knows you three have been like millstones about my neck—you make me ashamed to claim you as offspring."

Muttering, Patrick walked out.

"Perhaps I should go," Bothwell said. "I've no wish to cause trouble."

"Nonsense. This was your home once, and it pleases me that you should make it so again. In any case, I'll not be intimidated by those cowardly sons of mine who place greater value on a few groats than the life of a kinsman. They count my wealth and the days I have left, so they may inherit what it took me a lifetime to accumulate. But they'll not have it so soon; they'll wait a while before tasting of my fruits." Then, frowning, he said, "Nevertheless, keep an eye to them; hungry men make dangerous enemies."

Bothwell acquired two more ships that week. One, the *Pelican*, was a large two-masted vessel, equipped with guns and chartered from its owner, Geert Hemelingk, a Bremen merchant. For that transaction, Bothwell agreed to pay fifty crowns a month, or sixteen hundred crowns if it were lost at sea. The second he chartered for the same terms from a Hamburg man.

Eight vessels were still a very small fleet, but he had also acquired a complement of three hundred men, and for that he was satisfied.

Bothwell's messenger had been able to smuggle his letter in to Mary and he had brought one back from her. Through bribery, the messenger had given Bothwell's letter to Mary's physician, and he had news of her life at Lochleven—tragic and heartbreaking news.

In mid-July, Mary had miscarried. She was ill and seriously weakened by it, and her physician had voiced concern for her condition.

Bothwell's first thought was: *Thank God she has Arnault with her.* Then a stab of pain gripped him—they had been twin sons. She would have given him twin sons! His first legitimate heirs, conceived in so much love. He had felt such pride when Mary told him that she was with child. Now, without having even known them, he mourned the death of his sons—death before they had even lived.

He recalled the last line of his letter: *Care for my son.* How that cruel reminder must have stung her. She had shared in his joy and pride and had told him once, "I bore Harry's child out of duty; I bear yours for love." He could take no consolation in their loss; even if she gave him others it would never be the same, for with his dead sons, the joy, the pride, and the dream were gone.

There was more, and the shock of hearing it was almost as great as the loss of his sons. Threatened with violence, and her letters and sonnets to Bothwell being made public, Mary had abdicated. She had put her name to three documents; in the first she agreed to lay aside the burden of the Crown, in the second she consented to the coronation of her son, and lastly, she approved James' appointment as Regent.

James had finally won his lifelong ambition; he would finally rule Scotland. They had used Bothwell and his marriage to Mary as an excuse for rebellion, but it was really James' ambition they had forwarded. He had sparked this sedition from his safe retreat on the Continent.

There was also news of Bothwell's men; more had been captured, his cousin John Hepburn and Bolton among them. So many had already been captured—Will and John Blackadder, James Edmonston, Will Powrie, Dalgleish—how many more would it take to satisfy his enemies?

Bothwell had heard of Will Blackadder's trial before a packed Lennox jury; his defense had been futile, and in the end he suffered a hideous death. Will's arms and legs had been broken, and after the gallows had finally ended his suffering, his limbs had been fixed on the gates of Stirling, Glasgow, Perth, and Dundee. Of the others he had heard nothing yet, but he knew they would fare no better.

5

Alone in his chambers, Bothwell sat down to read Mary's letter. From her uneven writing, he pictured her hand weak and trembling on the page:

Dear Heart, Thank God you are safe and among friends. Having word of you cheers me greatly. Forgive this scrap of paper, none other is available to me. I am watched constantly, no one but my tiring women are permitted near me. Though they never cease in their demands that I relinquish you, I will never forget or abandon you—you are too deeply rooted in my heart. The bearer will tell you all, for I dare not write more, lest I be discovered. Forgive me, and love me always. I kiss your hands, and pray that God will reunite us soon.

Yours eternally,
Marie, R.

The ink on her signature was blurred, as though a splash of tears had caused it to run. *Forgive me*, she asked; he had always been so adamant on her right to rule; no wonder she asked his forgiveness. He could imagine her thoughts while signing the abdication papers. Her mere mention of doing just that had always brought his threat of leaving her; did she fear that he would abandon her now?

But who could blame her for giving in? If he were with her now, he would tell her that it didn't matter—crowned, or stripped of all worldly goods, he would always love her.

His chambers were suddenly close; he had to think, but his brain felt weighted down, dulled by the things he had just heard. The cool night air would clear his head, then he could decide what to do next.

Outside, he walked toward the gardens. He judged it to be past midnight, and in the sharp quiet he heard the rushing waters flowing into the River Lossie. Something swished past him in the high grass—a rabbit, he thought. He knew every inch of these grounds, even in the dark. In the four years he had spent here as a lad, he had explored every nook and crevice until he could find them blindfolded.

Loneliness crept into him. He longed for Mary, to hear her voice, to touch her. . . . Without her he felt incomplete. The sound of her voice, tinged with a French accent, filled his ears. Her laughter seemed to travel across on the breeze. He turned suddenly, thinking he had heard her call his name—and just in time.

He saw three men rush toward him from behind a row of fruit trees. Instinctively, his hand flew to his dagger. He looked around quickly; the high curtain wall was at his back, the garden was on his left, and a steep downward slope that led to the stables on his right. He stepped back and threw his weight against the wall, ready for the attack.

An instant later he was face to face with them. A glint of steel told him they were armed. Slowly, they closed in on him, but he was too fast. He took the one closest to him, locking his foot with the assailant's; then, throwing him off balance, he crashed him into the stone wall. He heard a deep groan and saw the body fall in a heap.

He turned to the others as they rushed at him. Ramming his booted foot into the groin of one, he knocked him breathless for a moment, as the hilt of his dagger crashed into the other's jaw. They staggered backward, but neither fell.

A fist caught Bothwell hard on the mouth; he felt a trickle of blood run down his chin. Another fist crashed into his chest. Savagely he drew his arm back and lunged his fist into one of their faces; he heard the crack of bone, a dull thud, and a limp body fell at his feet.

The fight was evenly matched now; his opponent was closer to his own size and strength. They exchanged a few blows without much effect. Then he felt himself dragged to the ground with the man's full weight on him and a dagger dangerously close to his throat. Managing to free his left arm, Bothwell held the dagger off only inches away from its mark. More weight pressed on him; his arm was beginning to give way. In a desperate effort, he arched his back and tried to throw his attacker off. They grappled and rolled, and Bothwell was pinned under again.

The pressure on his chest increased; every breath was agony. He could feel the dagger's hairline blade nearing his throat in earnest now. His assailant, having the advantage, was ready for the kill. Once more, Bothwell arched his back, mustering all his strength, and thrust himself upwards. At last the advantage was his, and without hesitation he plunged his own dagger into the man's chest. He felt the warm sticky blood on his fingers. The body under him stiffened convulsively, then fell back limp.

Getting to his feet, Bothwell forced the air back into his lungs and went back to the palace to rouse some of his men. They returned to the fight scene with torches; the dead man was Adam Hepburn, one of the Bishop's sons; the other two were Patrick and John. Despite the Bishop's warning, Bothwell hadn't expected this treachery from his own kinsmen. He looked down at the three men, but he felt no anger—only disgust for their cowardly assault.

The next morning, the Bishop called Patrick and John to his study and insisted that Bothwell be present to hear what he said to them. By then the entire plot had been uncovered; an English spy, kept prisoner at Spynie, had been drawn into it to save his life.

Urged by the three brothers, he had written the English envoy, Throckmorton, informing him of Bothwell's stay there. Then he asked if Throckmorton wanted Bothwell killed or arrested. But Throckmorton hedged, saying that since Bothwell had fourteen of his own men living at the palace, he would never be taken alive. In the end the matter was referred to Lethington, who with Huntly's approval encouraged them to do their worst.

Lethington's willingness to have him murdered didn't surprise Bothwell; he had attempted that before. But Huntly's part really shocked him; a man whom he had called friend had proved himself in the end an enemy.

Patrick and John faced their father, looking much the worse for the beating Bothwell had given them the previous night. Bothwell had only a small cut on his mouth, though his ribs were badly bruised from the pummeling Adam had given him.

Glaring, the Bishop said, "You have brought shame upon my house. Are you so hungry that you conspire with Englishmen and rebels against your own kinsman? Was it the reward?" He spat, "Blood money no decent man would touch."

"One of your own sons lies dead because of this man," Patrick said, "yet you continue to shelter him."

"It was his life or Adam's, and well you know which I hold of more worth. More's the pity he did not send both of you to hell with your brother. What use are you, that sons of mine should dishonor me so?"

"We will avenge our brother," John said. He turned to Bothwell. "Take care, murderer, lest you find a dagger in your heart like the one you plunged into Adam."

The Bishop half-rose in fury. "Silence," he shouted. "Take yourselves out of my sight, lest you find yourselves with a deeper cut—such as removing your names from my will."

"I think you are a little overhard on them, uncle," Bothwell said, after they had gone.

The Bishop threw his hands up in exasperation. "These men attempted to take your life—at best, they would have delivered you to your enemies—and you accuse me of being harsh."

"I have contempt for them, but not hatred. I can even understand their motives: the loss of your rents, the future consequences you may suffer for harboring me. These are no small considerations when added to a reward of one thousand crowns for my capture." He grew thoughtful and said, "I've always had enemies, some left me by my father, others acquired on my own. They never troubled me before—I was content to go my way and let them go theirs. Now I wonder why my enemies are so many."

"It's not difficult to understand. You have always been at cross purposes with these men; while your sole aim has been to support the Crown, theirs was to usurp it. They tried to win you to their side, but you refused; therefore you are detestable to them—as all honest men are to thieves. The devil cannot exist in harmony with goodness."

Bothwell laughed. "You make me out a saint."

"You a saint! God, no. You are merely a man who places the welfare of his country above his own."

"With so many traitors there have been few enough men willing to fight for the good of Scotland."

"And there you have the answer to the riddle that is you. You love the Queen and you love Scotland, but you cannot tell which you love more."

There was an amazing truth in that; Mary too had seen it. He nodded. "I don't know where one begins and the other ends. In the past, Mary spoke of relinquishing her Crown to those who coveted it—perhaps I should not have opposed her so violently . . ."

"Don't reproach yourself for your principles; you could not have done differently. A man without convictions and the ability to uphold them is nothing in the eyes of God and other men."

"What good are they in the end? My enemies have none, and look how they prosper. They saw, as I did in my youth, Scotland torn and rent by the English butchers who invaded us. I could never forget, but they could, and more, they dealt with those same butchers to the dishonor of Scotland. Now *I* am proclaimed traitor, while they hold themselves as saviors of the Realm. Where is the justice in that?"

"If they escape punishment now, there is a higher justice they must eventually face. Their punishment will come in the next life."

"You quote Romish propaganda. It will not matter when we are all dead! I want them punished now, while I am still alive to see it."

"You blaspheme God to speak so. The Queen would agree; her life's premise is embroidered on her winding sheet, *'In my end is my beginning.'* I marvel that you can care for each other so deeply and have such divergent faiths."

"I envy you both your beliefs; doubtless they give you great comfort. For myself, I cannot accept such blind faith. We live in an age of treachery and faithlessness, and that too is difficult for me to accept—my very nature rebels against it."

"You would change men to suit your ideals, but you might as soon try to turn back the tides. It is you who must change in order to exist in the world as it is—or else you will surely perish."

"Compromise, is that it? Someone else said that to me years ago." He laughed bitterly. "God knows I've tried even that. Three months ago they all professed themselves my friends and willingly endorsed my marriage to the Queen. One month later they banded together against me, and every man who called himself my friend became my sworn enemy." He snapped his fingers scornfully. "That for your compromise."

"That, in part, accounts for your present troubles. One does not make friends of past enemies—one destroys them."

A servant came to tell the Bishop the undertakers were here, and at the mention of Adam's name Bothwell realized that aside from the battlefield, Adam was the only man he had ever killed. He said, "If they had waited a few days, Adam might still be alive. I have decided to leave for the Orkneys the end of this week."

"So soon? You have been here scarce two weeks."

"It is already August. The sooner I raise men and enlist King Frederick's help, the sooner I may free the Queen."

The Bishop made the few miles' journey with Bothwell to Lossiemouth, where his ships lay anchored. On the *Pelican's* deck, the Bishop turned and placed his hands on Bothwell's shoulders. "I fear we shall never meet again in this life," he said.

"What nonsense is this? I shall pass this way again soon, and we will take a cup of wine together."

"No. I am an old man. I can feel death's icy breath upon me."

"You've years to live yet, and let the wenches still beware."

This brought a smile to the wrinkled old face. "Would it were so, but I fear my wenching days are long since gone." Then, frowning, he said, "Take care, nephew; the arms of your enemies will reach far to destroy you. I pray God they never succeed."

"Will you bless this voyage, uncle?"

"Aye, it is a simple prayer, used by fishermen." He held out the huge gold crucifix that hung from his neck and raised it heavenward. "O Lord," he chanted, "Thy sea is so great and these ships so small, protect them and the men they carry and bring them safely to shore." There were tears in his eyes when he looked again at Bothwell. He seemed unable to tear himself away.

Bothwell said gently, "The tide will not wait, uncle."

Embracing Bothwell again, the Bishop murmured, "God go with you."

Bothwell stood at the railing and watched the old man's slow steps down the gangplank. With great effort he mounted his horse, waved a last farewell, and turned for Spynie.

Bothwell gave the signal to pull in the cables, and the ships slowly slid out of harbor. He stayed at the rail to watch the shore disappear, and deep inside he felt a dull ache that brought to mind his sadness in leaving Spynie fifteen years ago. He had thought then: *All my life I will be forced to ride away from the things I love best.* He felt a chill and wondered if that had been a warning of things to come.

CHAPTER XXIII

1

The weather held good, and Bothwell's little fleet ran before the wind all the way. They touched South Walls on the second day and he rowed ashore, but his enemies had sent a herald before him to warn the inhabitants against supporting him. But these islanders were of a different breed; changes in government held no sway here, and the patent to Bothwell's dukedom brought a hearty welcome. It was the same at every island he visited; they gave the benefices due him gladly for the maintenance of his crew.

From there Bothwell sailed to Kirkwall, hoping to establish naval bases at the castles of Noltland and Kirkwall, but anticipating trouble, he approached Scapa Flow with caution. Balfour's brother had been governor there for a year and held the castles, and Bothwell's reservations were confirmed when the castle guns opened fire on his fleet. The bombardment continued all day, even though his ships were well out of range.

Bothwell decided to wait, hoping Balfour would weaken; he wanted those bases desperately and the munitions stored in them. Once, he put out a few small boats, but cannon opened fire on them. After two days of waiting he was finally forced to withdraw. His crew of four hundred men were not enough to launch an attack on the castle, and he set sail for the Shetland Isles.

Autumnal storms began early in these waters, and mid-August was none too soon for them. With bad weather ahead and the tricky currents to navigate, they were four days at sea before anchoring in Bressay Sound. Unsure of his reception there, Bothwell went ashore with one hundred fighting men, but his precautions proved unnecessary, for he found the bailiff here was a kinsman on his mother's side.

One look at Oliver Sinclair revealed the strong family resemblance of his mother's Highland kin. Sinclair had their dark eyes and hair, their strong, well-defined features, and their tall, sturdy build. He was delighted with Bothwell's unexpected visit, since strangers, outside of a few trading ships that stopped here, were a rarity this far north. He insisted that Bothwell lodge with him, and that he think of his house as his own. Glad to be on land again, Bothwell accepted.

Sinclair protested vigorously when he heard of Bothwell's intention to travel to Denmark in a few days. "Storms are already raging in the north; come September they grow more fierce."

"My business with the Danish King will not wait," Bothwell said. "The sooner I enlist his help, the sooner I can rescue the Queen."

"What good will you do her if you perish at sea?"

Bothwell shrugged. "Then I may sit out the storms here."

Sinclair's house was comfortable if not pretentious. Here, where the weather could wreak havoc, the houses were built low and sturdy on a style combined with a Norse and Scottish flavor. The nights were strange and unbelievable with sunlight lasting until midnight, when the sky retained its flaming tints of sunset until dawn. In winter, Sinclair said, daylight lasted less than six hours.

From his bedchamber window, which overlooked the Sound, Bothwell could see colonies of seabirds gathering amid families of seals that romped along the shore. His ships, bobbing on the water, framed by the green, indented shoreline, looked golden in the sun, dwarfing the smaller fishing boats putting out to sea. Beyond, red, blue, and white sails dotted the horizon with fishing boats at work.

"There is a merchant at Tingwall who may have some ships to charter," Sinclair told Bothwell as they sat at dinner. "I have business there next week; we could go together."

Bothwell speared another slice of fish and brought it to his plate. He had been at Bressay Sound a week now and was thinking of adding more ships to his fleet. He nodded. "Aye, if this merchant agrees to terms."

"Olaf Warburg is a reasonable man; he'll ask only what is fair."

"With more ships I can take on another hundred men—if there are any willing to join me."

"Rest assured, you will have no difficulty there. Scarcely a man on this island will pass up the chance for adventure at sea."

Bothwell smiled. "They'll have adventure aplenty—of one sort or another—if my recent fortunes are any indication of the future."

He saw that something behind him had caught Sinclair's attention. Jumping to his feet, Sinclair pointed to the window. "Look! Do my eyes deceive me, or are your ships leaving the Sound?"

Bothwell dashed to the window and saw his ships sailing out of harbor on a northward course up the channel. He ran out toward shore as the last one touched near the Coss of Noss. Then he saw the reason for their sudden departure as it came full view into Bressay Sound.

A flotilla of four heavily armed ships was in hot pursuit of them. He recognized their lead ship; it was the *Unicorn* out of Dundee, undoubtedly sent in hope of taking him by surprise. They had succeeded in part, for although his ships had got away, most of his fighting men and captains were still ashore with him. Should his ships be forced to engage their pursuers, their odds for survival were small, for they carried only sailors.

Bothwell made some quick plans to join his fleet; a dash overland to the north was his best course. Gathering all the men he could find took time, and he started to make his escape as one of the enemy ships landed. Unfortunately, he caught sight of the first man ashore and turned back. He knew that moment's hesitation could cost him his life, but blind hatred controlled him now. He counted the risk as nothing, for the man he saw was Kirkcaldy of Grange.

Kirkcaldy, the man who had given his pledge at Carberry Hill that Mary would have safe conduct back to Edinburgh. The bitter taste of rage blocked all sensible thoughts from Bothwell's mind; only the flow of Kirkcaldy's blood would cool the burning fury that coursed through him. In that instant he would have turned on Kirkcaldy like a wild beast and would gladly have done the gory work of scattering his parts from one end of the island to the other.

Captain Grant tugged at his arm. "Come away, Your Grace, or we will surely be captured."

Bothwell shook him off, unable to hear for the pounding in his brain. He was blinded to everything but Kirkcaldy.

"Come away, Your Grace. Come away now, or it will be too late," Grant pleaded.

At last his mind cleared and reason returned; he saw the futility in what he would do. Even if he had the satisfaction of killing Kirkcaldy, the others would take him. Captured, aye, but never brought back to Scotland alive. He knew too much for his enemies' good; alive he was a threat to them, dead they had no need to fear him. He would have to let Kirkcaldy go for now, but he vowed that he would see a day of reckoning for that traitor.

2

From the northernmost tip of the island, a boat took Bothwell and his men across Yell Sound. They crossed Yell Island on foot and rendezvoused with their ships at Unst. There, Bothwell heard the reason for Kirkcaldy's disembarking at Bressay. Pursued by the enemy ships, Bothwell's fleet had dashed north; all were making good progress except the *Crane*, the slowest of his vessels. Kirkcaldy, assisted by the Bishop of Orkney, was on the *Unicorn* and following her, lessening the gap between themselves and the *Crane*.

But luck was with the *Crane*, for she was a lighter ship and her captain knew the waters well. He led a path over a sunken rock and passed easily with only a grated keel, but the *Unicorn* struck the rock hard and sank with Kirkcaldy and the Bishop scrambling for shore. The rest of the enemy ships followed to pick up survivors and equipment.

The success of their narrow escape gave the men a false sense of security; they thought the encounter was over and themselves safe. But Bothwell knew better; his enemies had not come this far to turn back now. He thought of his detachments left behind at Bressay; they were of vital importance to him.

If they were to rejoin him, he had to send a ship back for them. He chose the *Andrew*, a vessel that carried his plate, jewels, armor, and personal belongings. The *Andrew*'s captain had instructions to follow the west coast down to Scalloway, there to pick up the men, then to proceed to Denmark by an agreed route where he would meet Bothwell. Watching the *Andrew* sail away, Bothwell thought: *Whatever the outcome now, at least my enemies will never get their hands on my valuables.*

Sometime late in the afternoon, Bothwell sighted the enemy ships coming his way fast. He had been waiting for them off

Unst the last hour and a half. He let them get close, then engaged them in a running fight out to sea. Kirkcaldy and the Bishop were conspicuously absent; only the Laird of Tullibardine was in command now.

Bothwell's ships were taking the worst of it as both sides exchanged heavy cannon fire. Badly hit, the *Crane* was losing ground rapidly, and one of Tullibardine's ships was closing in on it. Bothwell's one hope lay in the *Pelican*, from whose deck he issued commands. She was the largest of his fleet, built to take more punishment and to carry the strongest arms. Most of the hits made on his side came from the *Pelican*, for the others merely struggled along as best they could.

The *Crane* fell to Tullibardine, and its men and cannon were lost. Even that bad sailor was a loss Bothwell could ill afford. Yet, seriously doubting the outcome now, Bothwell continued the desperate fight that was already in its third hour. The final stroke came when the mainmast of the *Pelican* was shot away by a cannon blast. It looked really hopeless now, defeat seemed imminent—still Bothwell fought on.

Then, as if by a miracle of Providence, a southwesterly gale blew up and carried Bothwell's two remaining ships out to the North Sea. But Tullibardine was not yet discouraged; he was still after them. Despite their battered ships, Bothwell's captains were expert seamen and managed to extricate themselves from their danger.

Tullibardine kept with them for sixty miles, but he was finally forced to turn back. The remainder of Bothwell's fleet now was two badly crippled vessels and a crew reduced to one hundred and forty men.

They floundered about in the gale all that night with little hope of coming out alive. To have made one miraculous escape after another these last three months, only to perish at sea on nature's whim, seemed the final irony. It appeared that every desperate move Bothwell had made since Carberry Hill had deliberately led him here. All the struggling had been for naught—and yet, even that seemed better than to give his enemies the satisfaction of taking him.

Bothwell reached into his pouch and drew out Mary's gold crucifix. It felt cold to the touch, then slowly warmed in his hand. His fist closed around it until the edges cut into his palm—this was the closest touch he had with her now. Before she gave it to him, the crucifix had never left the hollow of her throat.

All the next day, the battle-scarred vessels ran before the wind that carried them farther out to sea. Bothwell stood on deck, disheveled by the hard battle he had fought, drenched by the gale, wearied and hopeless. Their steering devices were gone, but working, they would have been of no use, for these waters were totally unknown to any of his men. Land could be just beyond the horizon, or a thousand miles away, for all they knew.

Before nightfall, Bothwell allowed his men their tiny rations of water and food from the precious little provisions they had left. Then as daylight began to fade, some of the crew sighted another vessel off starboard bow. It looked at first like a ghostly outline in the graying mists of dusk, but as they neared it, Bothwell saw it was a Hanseatic vessel that flew the flag of Rostock.

He hailed the captain and shouted across, "Where are you bound?"

"We are for Karmöy," a voice answered.

Land, Bothwell thought, *the chance to recondition and revictualize.* "These waters are unknown to us," he shouted. "Will you act as a guide to take us there?"

"Aye, gladly."

The Rostock ship stayed with them through the night, keeping them on course. At dawn they slid into Karm Sound, where perched over craggy cliffs lay great snow-capped peaks against the distant sky. The Rostock master lent Bothwell a small boat to carry his cables ashore. Hopeful again, Bothwell climbed down the side into the boat, followed by some of his crew.

Sunlight streaked the hilly Norwegian coast in varying shades of bluish gold. On shore, houses with pointed roofs crouched together with a certain urgency, as though if one fell, the rest would tumble with it. Fishing boats crowded the harbor that began to fill with curious people who had come to look at the strange ships.

Bothwell's prime concern was fresh food and water. He had only a little money; the rest was on the ship he had sent back to Scalloway. He glanced down at the sapphire ring he wore; it was worth a fortune, but he wondered who among these peasants could afford such a bauble.

Yet he felt optimistic. August was nearly over; had he stayed in Shetland, he would have been forced to wait until the end of September before leaving. He had already been given a taste of the autumnal storms on the North Sea and had no wish to endure them again. Now he was even closer to Denmark and the help he sought.

Once his ships had been repaired and had taken on provisions, he could follow the coast of Norway until he reached Danish shores. He stepped out of the small boat onto the rocky shore. Several pairs of curious eyes watched him; towheaded children fell into step behind him, laughing and pointing to his tattered boatswain's garments, which he had borrowed from one of his crew. He turned, gave them a fierce scowl, and they ran away shrieking in delicious horror.

He was back on the *Pelican* with his scant purchases only a few minutes when another ship came into harbor. From its cut and the flag it flew, he recognized it as a Danish warship. Since Norway was a dependency of Denmark, his ships were officially in Danish waters; this demanded that he pay certain honors to the newcomer.

"Strike topsails," he ordered.

The Red Lion of Scotland was lowered in salute and his crew lined up at attention on the port side as the warship, called the *Bear*, slid into harbor. Receiving the salute and returning it, the Danish captain ran down his flag and the Red Lion fluttered high above the *Pelican*'s broken mainmast.

The *Bear* lowered a small boat and the captain rowed across to board Bothwell's ship. Preferring to keep his identity secret, Bothwell sent Captain Grant to welcome him. Pride kept Bothwell from coming forward to announce himself; one look at his shabby clothes would certainly bring snickers of doubt from the Danish sailors. That, and the unusual circumstances of his hasty departure from Scotland, made him want to keep well out of things.

Bearing in mind the war between Sweden and Denmark, Bothwell told Grant to say they were Scottish gentlemen about to join the Danish army.

The *Bear*'s captain came aboard and introduced himself as Christiern Aalborg. He was a tall man, about Bothwell's size, broad-shouldered and very capable-looking. His reddish-gold beard framed a face that bespoke a life at sea—tanned and leathery, with finely etched lines around his blue eyes. Bothwell guessed his age as about forty, possibly less, for weather added creases that might not otherwise be there.

"Who are you, and where are you bound?" Aalborg asked.

Grant gave the answers Bothwell had told him to.

"I shall have to see your ship's papers," Aalborg said.

"We have none," Grant said uncomfortably. "Present conditions in Scotland forced us to embark without passport and letters of marque."

"A most unusual circumstance, I fear," Aalborg murmured, letting his glance travel slowly over the ship's battered hulk.

"The Queen of Scotland is kept a close prisoner by rebels," Grant told him. "Fearing reprisals from them for supporting the Royalist side, we left hurriedly, without waiting for the necessary papers."

Again Aalborg's glance swept the deck. "It appears you have been recently engaged in battle."

"Aye, but not with men—nature was our opponent. We had the misfortune to meet with a gale at sea, and had it not been for the Rostock merchant ship, we might all have perished."

Aalborg nodded thoughtfully. It was impossible to tell what he thought. "I will return to my ship to consider this," he said. "Rest assured we will work it out somehow. In the meantime, I must ask that neither you nor your crew attempt to go ashore."

"Do you think he accepts my story?" Grant asked Bothwell after Aalborg had gone.

"He's wary of us—in his position I would be too. But he has no cause to mistrust us."

"What if he will not let us pass?"

"Then we are in for it. True, we outnumber him, for I judge his crew as no more than sixty—we could fight it out, but our ships are scarcely in condition to outrun him."

"Aye, with two of our cannons wrecked, our stores low, there seems little hope."

"We've come this far on luck; it may carry us further. He has no legitimate cause to keep us; we've committed no crimes against his Realm. Why should he detain us?"

The afternoon passed slowly. Some of the *Bear*'s crew rowed ashore. Heavy winds skirted the rocky coast and funneled into the Sound, causing the anchored vessels to list queerly. By early evening, the *Bear*'s crew returned. The shipbuilder who had promised to come aboard the *Pelican* never arrived.

At dusk Aalborg returned to speak with Grant. "I am prepared to offer you provisions," he said. "Naturally, I haven't enough on my ship to provide all that you need, but if you will send some men to carry supplies and some ashore for the rest you will have all you require."

Grant glanced at Bothwell, who nodded his agreement.

"My hearty thanks for your generous offer," Grant said, extending his hand, and they shook on it.

"I will need twenty-four of your men to accompany me," Aalborg said; "the same number ashore should suffice."

Grant selected the men to go with Aalborg from the *Pelican*; the rest he took from their other vessel. As he passed, Bothwell whispered, "To be safe, ask for his promise in writing that your men may return when they wish."

Aalborg hesitated at first; then, smiling, he agreed. It took only a few minutes to complete the transaction. Finished, Aalborg set his seal and signature to a promise that every man who accompanied him could return to his own ship at will. He further promised that after taking on provisions, the Scottish ships could proceed at will.

Satisfied, Grant dispersed the crew. Bothwell stood by congratulating himself on their good luck; not only had he got out of this difficulty but Aalborg was providing him the things he needed. Aye, he thought, this was a good omen; his other plans should meet with equal success.

Aalborg remained on the *Pelican* and watched the men row to his ship. When he saw the last of them climb aboard he turned to Grant. "And now, captain," he said slyly, "it is with regret that I must inform you that you are all my prisoners."

Outraged, Bothwell came forward. "You would go back on your word?" he demanded. "We have your promise, signed and sealed by your hand."

The Dane shrugged. "A necessary expedience with which I was forced to comply. But it is of no account now."

Rage suppressed what pride or vanity Bothwell had for keeping his identity a secret. Aalborg had deliberately lied to

Grant; he had given his word, by mouth and in writing, that they would be free to go. Now, scarcely half an hour later, he broke his word with a mere shrug. *An expediency*—more, an act of treachery!

Bothwell pushed Grant aside roughly. "What grounds have you for detaining us?" he asked.

"That you are pirates, all of you, who would plunder His Majesty's ships, given the chance." Then, thinking apparently that he stooped to haver with a mere crewman, Aalborg asked, "Who are you to question me?"

"I am the Duke of Orkney, husband and consort to the Queen of Scotland. I have urgent business with the King of Denmark."

Frankly incredulous, Aalborg's glance swept over Bothwell. It was not difficult to guess his thoughts, nor could he be blamed for doubting the statement he had just heard. A duke, husband and consort to a queen, in old, torn, and patched boatswain's clothes? A pirate, yes, but never that.

Aalborg said, "I am taking you and your ships to Bergen; there you may have the opportunity to dispute your claims with His Honor, Erik Rosenkrantz, Viceroy of Norway. He will decide the matter of your identify and your failure to present the proper credentials."

Exasperated, though his voice was still highly confident, Bothwell said, "I am the Supreme Governor of all Scotland; that is all the credentials I need. Now, for the last time, I demand that you let my men return to their ships and give us free passage from these waters."

Aalborg shook his head slowly. "I cannot do that. We leave on the morning tide for Bergen."

Bothwell finally gave up; he was already planning a way to escape. Perhaps he could slip over the side during the night and swim for shore. With luck, he could bribe some of the islanders to help him. He thought of his sapphire ring again; these poor inhabitants might be persuaded at the sight of such a jewel.

However, as though reading his thoughts, Aalborg said, "In case you contemplate going ashore during the night, let me warn you, the people have been alerted. They believe you to be priates and will take up arms against you."

Now Bothwell knew why the shipbuilder hadn't come; the Bear's crew had rowed ashore earlier to enlist the peasants' help.

All that night Bothwell paced the deck, railing against the fates, his trusting nature, and the treachery of men. Earlier he had been so hopeful; the end of Mary's imprisonment had seemed so near, their reunion, their future, had almost seemed assured. But in the space of an afternoon everything had been dashed to the ground.

He was weary beyond endurance—three days without rest and scarcely enough food to sustain him since that day he had left Sinclair's table at Bressay. He felt ready to drop with fatigue, yet anger, frustration, and a stubborn will to survive kept him on his feet—and thinking.

Now he had to deal with someone named Rosenkrantz; somehow that name struck a familiar chord. Where had he heard it before—even his brain seemed unable to function at this point. He probed his memory; he had been in Bergen with Anna Throndsen seven years ago. Suddenly he knew—Rosenkrantz was Anna's cousin.

She had boasted of having a very influential relative in Bergen, and had suggested they visit him, but Bothwell had refused. Now he cursed his obstinacy; how much better if he could claim a past friendship with this viceroy.

He hadn't thought of Anna in almost a year. They had quarreled violently the last time they were together; by then he had been too deeply in love with Mary to care about other women—though he continued to support Anna. She had made her usual complaints of neglect and had threatened to return to Denmark—he had been a shade too eager in agreeing.

Wild with rage, she had flown at him like a hellion, claws bared, lips drawn back from her teeth, and a murderous look in her eyes. To quiet her, he had been forced to strike her—he could still recall the hatred in her eyes when she swore revenge. A few weeks later, she had applied for a passport, and Mary had signed the papers with his blessing.

A gray, misty, chilling dawn broke over the sea. Torches that had flared through the night from the *Bear* were extinguished. Boots clanking on wooden decks echoed strangely in the Sound. The screech of hoisting sails grated on Bothwell's frayed nerves; soon the tide would carry him out to Bergen and God knows what.

Captain Grant came up from the cabin. "I've saved some dried fish for your breakfast, Your Grace," he said.

A wave of nausea that comes only from the combined effects of deep hunger, extreme weariness, and despair swept over Bothwell. He shook his head, bent over the side, and vomited into the water.

3

On the 2nd of September, the *Pelican* and the *Salamander* sailed into Bergen. Above the busy waterfront, rising in tiers on the mountain slopes, sat houses in a kaleidoscope of blues, reds, greens, and whites. At the water's edge a great stone tower looked out on sea to regulate the traffic of the town's only access to the outside world.

Bergen had undergone few changes in the seven years since Bothwell's last visit. The Hanseatic merchants' narrow wooden houses that lined the waterfront were still there, and from

memory he knew the vile stench of the cod-liver oil lamps that
lighted their dark dwellings.

Rosenkrantz was informed of Bothwell's arrival immediately. The question of his freedom demanded higher authority
than that of a mere sea captain, and a board of investigation,
consisting of twenty-four prominent town officials, had been
appointed to hear the evidence and vote on it.

Two days later Bothwell condescendingly appeared aboard
the *Bear* to meet with these men. They were seated at a long
table on deck, each dressed in black with sable-lined sleeves and
collars. He eyed these stolid men scornfully; they looked as
though they might all have been carved by the same sculptor.
Each man had blue eyes, a long nose, and a light beard, and
despite the hats that covered their heads, he knew that
underneath lay fair hair.

The Justice addressed him. "Before proceeding, will you tell
this commission who you are."

It was a needless formality; some Scottish merchants residing
in Bergen had already identified him to everyone's satisfaction.
"I am the Duke of Orkney," he said wearily, "husband of the
Queen of Scotland."

The commission nodded in unison.

"What business have you in these waters, Your Grace?"

"Before Captain Aalborg took it upon himself to interfere, I
was on my way to see the King of Denmark. After that, it is my
intention to go to France."

"We find it strange that Your Grace travels without passport
or ship's papers."

Bothwell rose and looked down the length of the table at
them. Towering over them, still in his boatswain's clothes, he
asked disdainfully, "Who can give me credentials? Being myself
the Supreme Ruler of the land, from whom can I receive
authority?"

The commission seemed confounded by this self-assured answer. They began to confer among themselves. Some of them pointed to the *Pelican* anchored nearby. Bothwell wondered what they found so odd about the ship. He waited with growing impatience until they finished.

At last, the Justice said, "The larger of Your Grace's ships is out of Bremen, is it not?"

"Aye."

"Then perhaps Your Grace will explain how you came by it."

"How does anyone come by a ship he does not own? By contracting for it legally. I have such a contract with the owner, Geert Hemelingk, who agreed to let me charter it for fifty crowns a month."

The commission conferred again.

Bothwell said, "If you doubt my word, I will be ready to answer in court any complaints against me. In the meantime, I demand that you permit me to land so that I may seek lodgings."

He was sick to death of living on the *Pelican*; his feet hadn't touched land for a week, except for the hour he had spent ashore at Karmöy. More than anything now, he wanted a bath, some clean clothes, and the feel of a soft bed under him. He listened to still more of their infernal whispering, then he saw them nod their heads in agreement.

The Justice said, "Your Grace and the members of your crew may land whenever you like."

"Then you will be good enough to order a boat to take me ashore now."

"Certainly, Your Grace. Have you any gold, jewels, or clothes that you wish brought from your ship?"

"There is nothing aboard my ship that I care to have. As for clothes, the ones I have on now are all that I own."

Bothwell found lodgings for himself and his men and purchased a few small necessities to improve his disreputable appearance. He was free to go wherever he wished—but where in that small town could he find diversion? When he walked about, there were always those curious and suspicious stares from the natives. The little money he had was dwindling quickly, but he expected to be in Bergen only a short time before that became too much of a problem.

A few days following Bothwell's appearance before the commission, Rosenkrantz invited him to supper at his castle. His Norwegian host proved generous and anxious to please; a sumptuous meal of fish, meats, and fowl had been prepared in the Great Hall. Tapestries of Viking conquests decorated the walls hung with ancient pieces of armor, and there were rich pieces of gilt-edged furniture everywhere, more elegant than anything ever seen in the royal Scottish palaces.

After supper they played a game of chess, but Bothwell's thoughts were too much at odds and he proved a poor opponent, allowing his host an easy victory. Later, seated before the fire in Rosenkrantz's study, he felt more relaxed. He studied the Norwegian as they spoke and decided they might have been friends under different circumstances.

They shared some things in common, for both were of noble birth and there was a freemasonry between them. They spoke of the responsibilities of fiefdoms, their vassals, and the maintenance of their lands. He was especially fascinated by Rosenkrantz's delicate hands in contrast to his gross body; they commanded notice for their flourishing gestures as he spoke. For the moment they lay serenely clasped over his mountainous stomach.

"Of Your Grace's two ships," Rosenkrantz said, "the small one is of some interest to me."

"The *Salamander*?"

Rosenkrantz nodded. "I marvel that it came through a storm of such violence as the one you described to me."

Bothwell shrugged. "Luck and seamanship, I suppose. Though I must confess we all thought ourselves headed for the deep."

"Good seamanship implies good captains. To survive, the *Salamander* would have had to have one of the best."

"Aye, Wodt is competent enough, though I wager Captain Grant could outship him."

"This man you call Wodt, is he one of your Scottish captains?"

"No, he came with the ship when I chartered it from a Hamburg man. Why do you ask?"

The delicate hands gestured widely aside. "No reason, no reason in particular. Merely idle curiosity."

But hardly a week had passed when Bothwell learned the reason for Rosenkrantz's interest in Wodt. Without warning, Wodt was accused of piracy and ordered into court to answer the charge.

Bothwell confronted him first. "Are these charges true?" he demanded.

"Every man who takes to sea is accused of piracy at one time or another," Wodt said evasively. "Your Grace's enemies call you a pirate."

Bothwell grabbed Wodt by the collar. "Answer me, damn you, or I'll choke it from you. These Hanseatic merchants claim you looted one of their ships some months ago. Did you?"

Apparently Wodt thought better of lying to him. "Aye," he said, "my men and I stopped one of their trading ships and relieved them of their goods."

"Then, unknowingly, I contracted for a pirate ship and crew."

"No, it was another ship—and other men who were with me then."

Bothwell released him with such force that Wodt staggered back against the wall. "If I thought it would do any good, I'd kill you here and now," Bothwell muttered. "The last thing I need is to have my name further compromised by scum like you." He glanced at him contemptuously. "Get out of my sight and make certain you are in court on the appointed day, for if you are not, I'll hunt you down myself and hang you."

Wodt's hearing was set for the following week. Some Hamburg merchants living in Bergen gave evidence against him, and since Wodt could neither deny the charges nor produce evidence to the contrary, he was judged guilty and taken to prison. This, of course, aroused more suspicion on Bothwell's acquisition of the *Pelican*.

To put the court at ease, Bothwell stood and addressed them. "I am content to allow both of my ships to remain in your harbor until you are satisfied they were contracted for legally," he told them.

The jury nodded their assent; what could be more fair?

The judge said, "Since all parties are satisfied, we may adjourn."

A sudden commotion came from the back of the courtroom. In a shrill voice a woman said, "There is still another matter of justice to be aired before this court."

Everyone turned to see a woman and several people entering. She cut a startling figure in comparison to the fair Scandinavians about her. She looked more like a gypsy with her dark hair encircled in a gold chain; huge gold earrings jangled from her lobes, and countless strings of colored beads flew about her neck as she hurried forward.

Bothwell stared in disbelief; this coincidence was unbelievable. He would have welcomed the devil's presence sooner than Anna Throndsen. She was obviously here to press suit in court, and oddly, he felt certain that it was against him. But what possible grounds did she have?

The judge seemed to wondering along those lines too, for he said, "What business have you before this court?"

She whirled about and pointed to Bothwell. "I wish to enter a claim against the Duke of Orkney for money I lent him seven years ago, by reason of certain false promises he made me—which to this day he has neither repaid nor honored."

So this is how the vindictive bitch meant to have her revenge! That was money he had repaid a hundredfold by supporting and maintaining her throughout her stay in Scotland; he had given her a house of her own with servants and new furniture to outfit it—most of which she had taken back to Norway. What of that gold chain that adorned her forehead, those earrings she wore, and the huge pearl ring that covered nearly all of one finger? Those baubles alone more than repaid the debt. But these were facts he would not lower himself to reveal before an alien court—her accusations had humiliated him enough.

The judge asked, "Of those promises, could you be more specific?"

That look of triumph Bothwell knew so well came into Anna's eyes. She said, "Seven years ago he seduced me, a young and innocent maiden then, with the false promise of marriage. I left my family, friends, and home to journey with him to a foreign land. Yet, once he had me at his mercy, he would not hold me as his lawful wife, which he had promised to do with hand, mouth, and letters. That he has three wives already, myself being one, another whom he put away by divorce, and last the Queen of Scotland, bears proof against him that the promise of marriage has no weight with him."

Her long speech concluded, Bothwell found himself scarcely able to keep his seat. Only by the greatest effort did he refrain from answering her. In his mind he reviewed the actual truth:

first, that it was Anna who tricked him into taking her to Flanders by fabricating a tale of being with child. Maiden, indeed, he thought scornfully, she had lain with others before him and countless more since. As for his promise to marry her, that had been withdrawn before they had left Denmark.

"Precisely what does my lady seek of this court?" the judge asked.

"That the money I lent the Duke of Orkney be returned to me."

Bothwell thought: *If that's all it will take to silence the wench, then let her have it.* He rose and rewarded Anna with a contemptuous glare. "I am prepared to give Mistress Throndsen an annuity of one hundred crowns a year from Scotland," he said. "And if that does not seem sufficient, she may also have the smaller of my two ships with anchor, ropes, and tackle."

The judge nodded thoughtfully. "In the eyes of this court, the Duke of Orkney's settlement seems fair and generous."

Anna accepted the terms and flounced out with her entourage close at her heels. Bothwell watched her go, hoping never to set eyes on her again. He had only one small piece of satisfaction; since he was outlawed in Scotland and could under the circumstances possess no property, Anna would not see one penny of the annuity—he knew the rebels would never honor it.

4

Convinced that with the end of his court hearing, his troubles were over, Bothwell applied to Rosenkrantz for his passport. He had already expressed a wish to go to Holland or France, or even back to Scotland, but his words had gone unheeded.

Now he said, "If I could have a yacht to take me along the coast of Denmark, I could thereby reach my destination."

Rosenkrantz shook his head sadly. "That would take Your

Grace to the Swedish frontiers," he said. "I fear an enemy's passport would stand you in little stead there and might easily become a hindrance. However, since Denmark was Your Grace's intended destination, I strongly urge that you sail with the *Bear* up the Skagerrak to Copenhagen."

That was the least palatable alternative, for Bothwell somehow felt that traveling on a Danish warship would suggest that he was going to Copenhagen more a prisoner than a visitor. He declined the offer and returned to his inn, hoping that Rosenkrantz would still change his mind.

September was drawing to a close, and Bothwell was still in Bergen. Although he was not officially a prisoner, neither was he free to leave. The old desperation of being penned in returned, and he was nearly frantic with worry for Mary. The last news he had out of Scotland had been at the end of July; the Prince had been coronated, and James, on his return from the Continent, had been made Regent.

The rebels no longer needed Mary, and he wondered what they would do with her. There had been rumors of bringing her to trial for adultery and complicity in Darnley's murder. If she were found guilty, he knew the penalty would be death by burning. Certainly, he had no illusions that she would have a fair trial.

Ready to risk any mad venture, Bothwell decided to force Rosenkrantz out of this stalemate. It occurred to him that his identity might still be in some doubt; he had sufficient proof of that in his patent to his dukedom, which was on the *Pelican*. There was also Mary's letter from Lochleven proving that he was her husband—there were two other documents in Scots, but he preferred to keep them hidden, for one was the rebels' proclamation against him, the other a copy of Kirkcaldy's and Tullibardine's commission to hunt him down.

These papers were in a letter case which he had concealed in the ship's ballast, and unfortunately, some of Aalborg's men were posted on watch there so he could not get them without Rosenkrantz's permission. No whit disturbed, however, he applied to the Viceroy for them, who in turn ordered Aalborg to get them.

But Aalborg did not bring the portfolio to Bothwell; he brought it to Rosenkrantz instead, who opened it and read the contents. Now everything was out in the open; despite the confirmation of his titles and position, it was now clear that Bothwell had left Scotland under suspicious circumstances. Confronted with this, Bothwell chose not to explain, but rather to save the truth for King Frederick.

Rosenkrantz said, "With this additional knowledge, I must insist that Your Grace journey to Copenhagen on the *Bear*. You may take only four of your men; the rest may stay here or return to Scotland according to their wishes. If Your Grace has any complaints to make against anyone, you may seek an answer in a Danish court."

Bothwell shrugged. "I have no complaints; Captain Aalborg merely did his duty—had I been in his place I would have done the same. As for others, with the exception of you, my lord Rosenkrantz, I have been regarded with such suspicion as might be afforded the worst criminal. Let these men beware, lest they someday fall under my jurisdiction, then I shall repay them for every humiliation and indignity to which I have been subjected."

Rosenkrantz set the day of departure for the thirtieth of September. In the meantime he invited Bothwell and his men to lodge at his castle, an invitation that Bothwell could not refuse, for it was more an unspoken order. He suspected that Rosenkrantz thought it more prudent to keep a watchful eye on him.

On the twenty-eighth, Rosenkrantz gave an enormous banquet for him and forty of his men. The food was rich, delectable, and plentiful, all in the manner of Scandinavian tradition; beer, ale, brandywine, claret, and Madeira flowed, jesters, musicians, dancers, and troubadours performed, and after the last course was served, four great bearlike men took the center floor for an exhibition of the most brutal wrestling Bothwell had ever seen. Later their considerate host even provided wenches.

But nothing could lift Bothwell from his overwhelming depression; seated next to Rosenkrantz, he ate sparingly but drank heavily, though even the brandywine, which usually lifted his spirits, failed to lighten his mood. If anything, it gave him a dull headache and plunged him deeper into gloom. The music grated in his ears; the smell of food, added to the wrestlers' sweat-glistening bodies, their grunting and rolling about on the floor, sickened him.

The banquet continued all night, and Bothwell wanted desperately to be off somewhere in the quiet dark. He was brought to mind of a place several miles from Hermitage, where he used to go to be alone. It was a moor, different from the others for its haunted quality. The only colors there were dulled purple and browned withered heather and bracken.

He could recall standing there on a bright summer day, when the sun sparkled brilliantly on the Cheviots, but no sun touched that moor, and the sky above had hung heavy and low with a strange cloudy pearlescence. He had found true solitude there, for he could be alone with only the earth, sky, and God. Though others might call that moor godforsaken, there was neither church nor minister, nor any prayer he knew, that could bring him closer to God.

He left the table abruptly and went out on the terrace adjoining the Great Hall. A full moon and an endless array of stars glimmered overhead in the balmy night. A night hawk soared up in the cloudless sky, circled the castle ramparts, then flew off. Bothwell watched its flight until it disappeared from sight, envying it for its unrestrained freedom.

EPILOGUE

From the moment that Bothwell set foot on Danish soil he became a living dead man. The doors to the dungeon that would hold him five years later clanked shut on the man to whom freedom meant more than all else. King Frederick of Denmark had in Bothwell a valuable prisoner, one whom he hoped to release to the highest bidder.

Despite Bothwell's desperate attempts for an impartial hearing, his efforts were thwarted by France and Scotland. Both nations were too deeply implicated in the Kirk o' Field plot to risk having the evidence Bothwell could give made public. Queen Elizabeth wanted Bothwell dead, for she knew that as long as he lived he would expend every effort to reinstate Mary on her throne.

But Frederick refused all demands for extradition or execution; he was not entirely convinced that the charges against Bothwell were true. Bothwell was brought to Copenhagen Castle and kept under heavy guard, but his reputation for daring recklessness made Frederick uneasy. The strong Fortress of Malmö lay just across the Sound from Copenhagen, heavily garrisoned with soldiers—that would keep his unwilling prisoner more securely.

Bothwell entered Malmö in January of 1568 and began what was termed "an honorable imprisonment." His apartments were spacious and elegantly furnished to befit his rank. His treatment was not unkind; he had limited exercise, visitors, and an allowance for his wardrobe, provided by Frederick.

The days and months passed slowly for Bothwell in this island fortress whose sole access was a heavily guarded moat. Despite his ingenuity and inventiveness, escape was impossible. Then in May of 1568 he had news of Mary's escape from Lochleven and he dared to hope for his release.

Mary's loyal nobles had amassed an army to meet James Stewart and his allies at Langside. But the one leader who could have led her army to victory was a captive in Denmark. The battle was over in less than an hour; three hundred of the Royalist Army lay dead; twice their number had been wounded. Mary escaped capture and fled to England for safety, only to become Elizabeth's prisoner.

Throughout the years, Mary and Bothwell corresponded regularly. She wrote him of the Duke of Norfolk's plan to raise the English Catholics in her name. Bothwell's hopes soared again, then fell to despairing. Elizabeth had learned of the plot; Norfolk was beheaded and the plan collapsed.

Early in 1570 James Stuart was assassinated and the Earl of Lennox succeeded him in the Regency. Fresh demands came from Scotland for Bothwell's execution. Frederick still refused, but he did agree to impose more restrictions on Bothwell. He no longer allowed Bothwell to take exercise in the courtyard or to receive visitors. Mary interceded with Frederick for Bothwell's good treatment, "for," she wrote, "it is my wish that my husband shall never fare worse than myself."

Less than a year later, Lennox was dead, murdered by some of Mary's adherents, and Lord Mar stepped up to the Regency. Within the year Mar, too, died mysteriously—poison was said to be the means that sped him to the grave. One after the other, Bothwell's enemies were passing from the scene—even Lethington and Kirkcaldy of Grange were dead, executed for their turnabout loyalty by holding Edinburgh Castle for three years in Mary's name. Knox, too, was gone, leaving the world on the same day that the Earl of Morton was sworn into the Regency.

But these events were of scant interest to Bothwell, for he was beyond caring. Confinement had taken its toll; a fretting restlessness ate at him, perpetual boredom, unendurable loneliness, his past glories, and the vacuous future that loomed ahead robbed him of his reason.

In the summer of 1573 Bothwell was moved from Malmö to Dragsholm Castle, a hideous prison for those whom the world had forgotten. Reports came out of Denmark that Bothwell had become violently insane. His dungeon below the ground was a stark stone chamber, windowless and cold, with only a wooden post driven into the center of the earthen floor and a pile of dirty straw for his bed.

Here Bothwell paced away the last five years of his life in raging madness, wearing a path the shape of a half-moon into the floor beneath the post to which he was chained. Finally, merciful death claimed him.

Free at last, his spirit, held fast to a body chained for so many years, soared and fled. And somewhere on a crest of the Cheviot Hills, nearly seven hundred miles away, a lonely shepherd saw the ghostly shadow of a rider on horse dashing across a desolate moor. He heard the thud of hoofs, the chink of metal on leather, exultant laughter, as they disappeared into the mist.

AUTHOR'S NOTE

Of the Kirk o' Field plot, this did originate in Paris with the Pope's legate, Bishop Laureo—and it is certain that Rome directed it. The Pope was dissatisfied with Mary's leniency toward her Protestant nobles. He wanted a Catholic revival in Scotland and demanded the execution of the six top men who opposed it. By refusing to comply, Mary lost her value to Rome.

I have gone to Major General R. H. Mahon for his excellent reconstruction of that mystery in his *Tragedy of Kirk o' Field*. No one else has dealt more thoroughly with the subject, or delved so completely into the rationale of the plot. His conclusions are logical and go far to explain much of the mystery surrounding that episode.

Speaking of the explosion that night, General Mahon says, "Bothwell proposed that Mary should remain at Holyrood. . . . He would return to Kirk o' Field simulating her return, if the expected result occurred, he craved her warrant to take Darnley in ward. . . . It is improbable that he ever saw Darnley's body. . . . *The deed was not his doing.* . . ."

Of the letters quoted, most of them are authentic, taken from the famous Silver Casket. The letter Mary wrote to Bothwell from Glasgow proves her love affair with him, and that they intended Craigmillar Castle, not Kirk o' Field, as Darnley's place of convalescence.

The letter dealing with Mary's abduction proves that she and Bothwell did plan it together. It is also interesting because of the almost exact wording found in her later instructions to the

Bishop of Dunblane when he took her excuses for her hasty marriage to Bothwell to the French Court. Mary's defenders have sought to prove her innocence by branding the Casket Letters a forgery, but the abduction letter cannot be explained away so easily.

The time between Mary's defeat at Carberry Hill, Dunblane's arrival at the French Court, and the discovery of the casket was too short for the rebels to compare the papers. Therefore, forgery must be ruled out in this case, as must the chance coincidence that someone wishing to incriminate Mary would have shared her thoughts and used nearly her exact words.

Among other abuses, Bothwell is charged with cowardice for his conduct at Carberry Hill. There were countless witnesses present who gave testimony that he was anxious to fight the duel with Lindsay. The French ambassador, Du Croc, certainly not partial to Bothwell, wrote to his king afterward: "I am bound to acknowledge that the Duke [Bothwell] seemed to me a great general, speaking with undaunted confidence and leading his army bravely and skillfully. For some time I took pleasure in watching him and judged that he would have the best of the battle if his men remained faithful. I admired him when he saw his enemies so resolute; he could not count on half of his men and yet was not dismayed. . . ."

Incredibly, historians have ignored the fact that all the charges against Mary and especially Bothwell were both contradictory and false. Whereas the rebels claimed they wished to free Mary from Bothwell's captivity, they also claimed they held her prisoner because she would not relinquish him. Whereas they charged Bothwell with kidnapping her and keeping her prisoner at Dunbar Castle, they also charged Mary with conniving in her own abduction. For this they brought an act of forfeiture and attainder against Bothwell in December of

1567. This contradiction may be explained without too much difficulty.

In order to divide Bothwell's vast holdings and titles among themselves, the rebels had to legalize his forfeiture—the charge of laying violent hands on his queen provided them with the means. But they were also obliged to prove Mary's wantonness, which according to them rendered her unfit to rule. Thus, they accused her of consenting to her own abduction.

Not once in Mary's nineteen years of imprisonment did she ever speak ill of Bothwell. There were times when repudiating him might have helped her cause—she might even have gained her freedom. Instead, she interceded with Frederick for Bothwell's good treatment. As a major participant in the events that brought about her downfall, Mary would certainly know the truth. In a statement made by Mary, after her escape from Lochleven, she referred to those same men who charged Bothwell with his so-called crimes as the true murderers, traitors, and tyrants.

After ten years of imprisonment in Denmark, the last five of which he spent violently insane at Dragsholm, Bothwell died alone in his wretched state, nine years before Mary was beheaded by Queen Elizabeth. Undoubtedly, he bore no resemblance to the man he had been. According to accounts coming out of Denmark at that time, he was "swollen, overgrown with hair and filth"; he must have looked like a great beast felled by the hunter. This simple record under the date of April 14, 1578, marked his passing: "Died the Scottish Earl Bothwell in his protracted imprisonment in Dragsholm."

His final resting place is in the chapel of a peaceful little red and white church in Faarevejle, Denmark. The church, which stood on a promontory of the now dried-up Lammerfjord, is only a few miles from Dragsholm, where the road between is slightly reminiscent of his Border country in Scotland. There the land rises in gentle slopes and stretches out to the sound that looks across to Jutland.

Every summer more than 20,000 people come to view Bothwell's skeletal remains in a glass-enclosed coffin. Though Mary and Bothwell have been dead nearly four hundred years now, the furor of their story rages on. It may be hoped that Bothwell has found in death the peace he never knew in life.

BIBLIOGRAPHY

Anderson, Robert Gordon, *The City and the Cathedral.*

Anthony, Katherine, *Queen Elizabeth.*

Armstrong, R. B., *The History of Liddlesdale.*

Bax, Clifford, *Letters and Poems of Mary Stuart.*

Bell, H. G., *Life of Mary Queen of Scots.*

Benger, E. O., *Memoirs of Mary Stuart.*

Borland, R., *Border Raids and Reivers.*

Brown, P. Hume, *Scotland in the Time of Queen Mary.*

Buchanan, George, *The Tyrannous Reign of Mary Stuart.*

Byrne, M. St. Clare, *Elizabethan Life in Town and Country.*

Caird, A. M., *Mary Stuart, Her Guilt or Innocence.*

   Calendar of State Papers Relating to the Borders.

Chalmers, George, *Life of Mary Queen of Scots* (vols. 1, 2).

Club, Bannatyne, *Les Affaires de Conte de Boduel.*

Cowan, S., *Mary Queen of Scots.*

      Mary Queen of Scots and the Casket Letters.

Dakers, Andrew, *Tragic Queen.*

Danish Archives.

Davis, W. Stearns, *The Elizabethan Days.*

De Lamartine, A. M., *Mary Queen of Scots.*

Diggle, Henry, II, *A Vindication of Mary Stuart.*

Dumas, A. D., *Mary Queen of Scots.*

Ellis, R. S., *Latter Years of James Hepburn.*

Finley, Ian, *The Lothians.*

Fleming, David Hay, *Mary Queen of Scots.*

Francis, Grant R., *Mary of Scotland.*

Goodrich, F. B., *Mary Queen of Scots.*

Gore-Brown, Robert, *Lord Bothwell and Mary Queen of Scots.*

Gorman, Herbert, *The Scottish Queen.*

Hackett, Francis, *Henry VIII.*

Harvey, George Rountree, *Book of Scotland.*

Henderson, T. F., *Mary Queen of Scots.*

Hepburn, E., *Genealogies of the Hepburns.*
Hillson, Herman, *Discovering the Lowlands.*
Hosack, J., *Mary Queen of Scots and Her Accusers.*
Hume, H., *Love Affairs of Mary Stuart.*
Jamieson, James H., *East Lothian Biographies.*
Jenkins, Elizabeth, *Elizabeth the Great.*
Keith, Robert, *History of Church and State in Scotland.*
Kurlbaum, M. S., *Mary Queen of Scots.*
Lang, Theo, *The Queens of Scotland.*
Lebanoff, A., *Lettres de Marie Stuart.*
       Recueil des Letters de Marie Stuart.
Lindsay, Colin, *Mary Queen of Scots and Her Marriage to Bothwell.*
Long, G. M. V., *Mary Queen of Scots, Daughter of Debate.*
MacCunn, F. A., *Mary Stuart.*
MacGregor, Beddes, *The Thundering Scot.*
McGuckin, Mildred, *Mary Stuart.*
Mackenzie, A. M., *Kingdom of Scotland.*
McMichael, Archibald, *The Border and East Lothians.*
Mahon, R. H., *The Tragedy of Kirk o' Field.*
Meikle, Henry W., *Scotland.*
Mignet, F. A., *History of Mary Stuart.*
Millar, A. H., *Mary Queen of Scots.*
Mitchel, C. A., *The Spurious Marriage Contract.*
Morrison, N. Brysson, *Mary Queen of Scots.*
Odom, William, *Mary Stuart.*
Petit, J. A., *History of Mary Stuart.*
Peyster, J. W. de, *Vindication of James Hepburn.*
Pitcairn, R., *Criminal Trials in Scotland.*
Rait, R. S., *Mary Queen of Scots, Her Life and Reign.*
Raumer, F. L. G. von, *Queen Elizabeth and Mary Queen of Scots.*
       Register of the Privy Council in Scotland.
Roeder, Ralph, *Catherine De Medici and the Lost Revolution.*
Schiern, Frederick, *James Hepburn, Earl of Bothwell.*
       Scots Peerage.
Shelly, H. C., *Tragedy of Mary Stuart.*
Sidillot, René, *An Outline of French History.*
Skae, H. T., *Mary Queen of Scots.*

Skelton, Sir John, *Mary Stuart.*

Stevenson, J. (Claud Nau), *History of Mary Queen of Scots.*

Stewart, A. F. (ed.), *Memoirs of Sir James Melville.*

Strickland, Agnes, *Life of Mary Queen of Scots* (vols. 1, 2).

Thomson, George Malcolm, *The Crime of Mary Stuart.*

Thorndyke, Lynn, *University Records and Life in the Middle Ages.*

Tuelet, *Letters of Mary Stuart.*

Tytler, William, *Mary Stuart.*

Whitaker, John, *Mary Queen of Scots Vindicated.*

Zweig, Stefan, *Mary Queen of Scotland and the Isles.*